Four and a Half Billion People

Catherine Pomeroy

NBBP

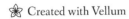 Created with Vellum

Dedicated with unquantifiable love to my wonderful, wayward children.

Acknowledgments

Many thanks to editor Marilyn Pomeroy for her work and the generosity of her time, to Theresa Halvorsen and S. Faxon for their energy and belief in this project, to Chris and Annette, and always to my beloved TVH for his love, support and donuts. Finally, my mother grew up in a farmhouse in Jackson County, Ohio, so I must give a nod to this special place where a little bit of our hearts will always live.

FOUR
AND A HALF
BILLION
PEOPLE

***

"Neither the Fourteenth Amendment nor the Bill of Rights is for adults alone."

-Justice Fortas, writing for the majority, *Application of Gault,* Supreme Court of the United States, May 15, 1967

A Letter from James

February 22, 1978

Dear Columbus Crashing Crankers Bicycle Club,

Warmest greetings! James Jenkins here again. Just in case you might have misplaced my prior letters, let me remind you that I am seventeen years old and a senior at Jackson High School. I write to you faithfully and check our mailbox for your answers every day. Sure hope I'm using the right address.

Anyway, how excited you must be that the great bicycle tour is only a few months away!

I have so many questions. Today, my thoughts are on wind. I read in the Farmers' Almanac about prevailing westerly winds in the continental United States. Since the route for the great two-hundred-mile tour runs north to south, I'm wondering how crosswinds affect the ride. Is a crosswind different than a headwind? Do the bikers adjust the angle of their draft lines? Do trees along the road act as a buffer? Do the gusts blow differently on flat terrain than in hills? As far as drag, you must have to factor in the speed of the gusts along with the width of the tire, the depth of the tread, the weight of the bicycle, the size of the rider, friction on the asphalt, and so many other factors I'm probably not even thinking of. Temperature maybe? I'm working on an equation for all this. When it's complete, my equation will be orange and green. It will smell like spearmint.

Where I live, in Jackson County, we have a hilly landscape, with some valleys and salt springs and coal beds. The wind plays tricks on my ears. Erwin Hollow Road, which has some long gradual hills, is a sound mirage where the cars sound like they're right behind you even when they're a few miles back. It's very mysterious. When the wind speaks, it doesn't tell the truth. It lies, it cheats. It doesn't follow the rules. And instead of carrying coal from the next town over like the train passing by my house, it's arrived all the way from the Pacific Ocean, carrying heat, sand, silt, water, spores, dandelion seeds. Maybe even a secret whispered upward into a whiff and a draft. It smells of spices, hurricanes, volcanic ash, pollution and the spray from whale holes, and I see colors of tan and mauve. It feels like the number eleven, everything plus something more. So... yah. That's wind. Do you guys put your bikes on rollers in the winter so you can stay in shape?

I promise to write again very soon, maybe next time with some questions about gear ratios. Please write back ANY TIME, and or even better, give me a call, I'll write my phone number under my return address on the envelope!

Sincerely yours,

James Jenkins

(proud owner of a red Schwinn 3-speed Sting-Ray chopper bicycle)

P.S.—just don't call on a Wednesday, we can't hear the phone ring when my brother's band is practicing. It's really annoying.

Chapter 1

Jorie

I HEARD THEM—AMPLIFIED guitars, crashing cymbals, pitchy teenage vocal cords shouting out lyrics—before I'd even rounded the corner from the alley, bags from Henry's filling my arms, purse dangling from my shoulder. Of course, Wednesday. Band practice day. "Oh Lord, not again..." I muttered under my breath. Maybe it was time to have a little talk with Will and his fourteen-year-old compadres about turning down the volume. That's certainly what most parents would do. Yes, I told myself, *definitely* what any responsible parent would do. I snuck sheepish glances at the houses I passed, kind of proud, kind of amused and kind of mortified all at the same time.

Latchkey kids. That's what my boys were called. Divorce was practically in style for the rich and famous, rock stars, Mick and Bianca, people you read about in the tabloid gossip magazines. But Jackson wasn't Hollywood. Here, there was always that feeling, unspoken, that we, the Jenkins family, had something to prove. And being the loudest house on the block sure didn't help.

Anyway, walking didn't bother me. Walking to and from work. Walking to and from the grocery. Walking gave me time to think. My stride matched the beat of the band. I was almost bouncing along, practically floating and, with each step, I chanted to myself, *in control, in control. Everything in control.* I didn't buy anything too heavy today. Grocery shopping was all about price and weight. Could we afford that cut of meat? Could I lug it home? Buying the large can of Hawaiian Punch wasn't worth destroying my back; easier to carry lightweight powdered Tang or lemonade and mix it up in a plastic pitcher. Today's tips—over ten dollars in change, even after buying groceries—jingled in the quilted coin purse in my bag. My self-congratulatory mantra played in my head like a song, reminding myself how far we'd come and everything I'd done to raise these boys. *Good job, Jorie,* I told myself. Might as well say it I allowed, there was no one else to cheer me on.

Bringing that drum set home from the resale shop was one of the best things I've done, I told myself for the hundredth time. *Proud* mom. *Successful* sole provider.

Well, maybe the whole neighborhood wouldn't agree. But so far, no one'd complained.

"Hello Mrs. Grenadine," I called, grinning slightly to myself as I passed the neighbor's house. Her laundry was air-drying, clothes-pinned to the line by her side door. The boys had finished up Bachman-Turner Overdrive and moved on to Alice Cooper, strains of "Eighteen" blasting for the entire block to hear. To me, their music was modern and exciting, a world away from trains, dirty coal, rickety antiques, or rusty Appalachian poverty. Echoes from Will's drums bounced off aluminum garbage cans lining the alley. Mrs. Grenadine's cat, ears twitching from the auditory assault, winced in displeasure on the gravel drive. Mrs. Grenadine quickly let her front curtain fall shut, pretending she hadn't been watching me pass.

"Hey, Jorie," drawled Lana, my other neighbor, puffing on an afternoon cigarette with her feet propped on the railing of her front porch. She tapped her bare toes to the beat. Lana's my buddy, closer to my age. "Those kids sure sound good."

2

"Someday we'll be saying we knew 'em when," I called over my shoulder.

I turned down the stone walkway into our yard and climbed the steps to the front porch, the wide wooden planks, James' red Schwinn Sting-Ray leaning against the black wrought-iron gate, rusty porch glider with plastic floral cushions. The tiny yard wasn't much, but the bushes were neatly trimmed and the flower bed weeded. Faded black shutters set off the white trim. The roofline rose to a peak, scalloped carvings in the vinyl siding and gauzy white curtains hung in our front window. A slight film of black dust from the railroad coated everything.

Our house, which was a fine little paid-off place on High Street, quivered and shook eight or nine times each day even when there wasn't a teenage rock band practicing in the front room. When it happened, the floors rumbled like they were humming some ancient, secret song. The single-pane windows knocked and banged in their wooden frames. Antique teacups rattled in the hutch and even scooted a few fractions from their original position. The chandelier swayed over the kitchen table in an alarming imaginary breeze. In fact, the whole place was usually in constant movement, and more times than not, my brain rattled right along with it.

Tectonic plates shifting under our feet? Fault line cutting through rolling foothills, limestone, coalbed? Nope, nothing that dramatic. Locomotives—passing so many times, so close, we never even registered the piercing whistle, the percussive clacking, the black smoke poisoning our lungs. The Coalton-Gallipolis short line cut through town, right on the other side of High Street. But it wasn't noise, not to us anyway. James and Will and I always slept right through the noise from the train. Coal, iron and rail kept the town of Jackson humming. It was the pulse of southern Ohio running just as natural in our blood as the red blood cells bringing oxygen and the white blood cells whisking away infection.

"Hey there, sounds real good," I called brightly from the hallway, on my way to the kitchen, though they probably couldn't hear me.

Four gangly teenage boys in blue jeans were crammed into the front room, what Granny used to call "the parlor." Like always, they'd pushed the recliner up against the wall to plug in their amps and make room for the synthesizer. Our old weathered spinet piano bordered one of the walls. Will's drum set, his pride and joy, occupied the entire northern corner of the room.

Will drummed energetically mid-song, his lips moving silently as he counted the beat, *one*, two, three, four, *one*, two, three, four. We were at our best when we were counting. I didn't think he'd even seen me, but he nodded and tipped his stick to an imaginary hat in salutation at my entrance. His friends had their backs turned to the hallway, deaf to anything over their booming amps.

I stuck my head into the second bedroom. Empty. James must not be home yet. Strange he was gone, yet his bike was on the porch; usually he was off somewhere on the Sting-Ray. A quiver of foreboding, a bad gut feeling, passed like a shadow, but I shrugged it off. James was seventeen years old, after all. Almost grown.

Depositing my bags on the avocado-green countertop, I started to unpack. Will having friends over lifted my spirits, made me proud he had this group of buddies, made me proud they'd accepted him. It seemed so normal. James didn't ever have friends over to the house. But of course, it's wrong to compare your children. Everyone knew that. I set the Teflon skillet on the stovetop to brown the ground beef.

The house shook as Will's foot pedal rhythmically struck the bass drum. Boom, boom, boom. I swayed a little, danced, and snapped my fingers as I set the eggs in the fridge. Boom, boom, boom. Now my rhythm was off. The house shook with a different vibration, and I glanced around the room, disoriented. Could be the bass line from a Jimi Hendrix song, the train passing through from Portsmouth, an earthquake, or... of course, the phone was ringing.

I grabbed the bright yellow receiver off the wall and tucked it between my shoulder and neck, continuing to unpack groceries, allowing the coiled cord tethering me to the base to wrap around my waist. "Hello?"

4

Louder this time. "Hello!"

Someone was talking, but I couldn't make anything out.

"Hold on!" I twirled to unravel the cord, set the phone on the kitchen table and ran to the parlor, my arms waving. "Boys! I've got a phone call and I can't hear a thing." The kids finally saw me and set their guitars down, with dazed looks, like they were coming out of a spell. "Sorry, Mrs. Jenkins," said one of them. Will set his sticks on the snare and shook out his hair.

I grabbed the phone again.

"Sorry about that—couldn't hear. Who'd y'all say is calling now?"

"Mom, it's me—"

"Oh, James! Sorry hon, Will's practicing with the boys—"

"Mom. Listen to me."

"Will you be home for supper? I'm making Hamburger Helper."

"Mom!"

I stopped. Something in his voice sent a shiver down my spine. The bad gut feeling returned like a punch to my stomach. It was very strange indeed for James to be calling home in the late afternoon, for his bicycle to sit abandoned on the porch. "James. What's wrong? Where are you?"

He choked out a sob.

"What?!" I pressed, my hands going clammy, fingers clamped around the phone like a vise.

"An accident..." he blubbered, gasping for breath. The words started spilling out, "*terrible* accident, Mom, glass exploding, hundreds of pieces, maybe even a thousand, it was ice cold, and shiny, very sharp, smelled like fish, not a good smell at all, a sickening smell, sickening." He shuddered out more cries.

"James! Where are you?"

"It was red. Ice cold, shiny. But red, too. They got me in the Jackson County Jail."

"An accident... what kind of accident?" My mind raced. "Are you okay? Are you hurt?"

"I got arrested. It's bad! Can you come down here?"

"James! I don't understand what you're saying! What does that mean, it was cold and shiny and smelled like fish? What do you mean that it was *red*?" I was screaming the words.

My legs collapsed beneath me, no longer functioning. I plunked down into the kitchen chair like a rag doll, ears ringing, not able to construct a thought. The uncooked pink ground beef sat in the skillet, mocking me like some kind of grotesque, still life painting. Our loud house on High Street had gone completely quiet, now unnaturally still. All the air had left my lungs, but I managed a strangled whisper, *"James, did you just say you are in jail?"*

I looked up to find Will hovering in the kitchen doorway, watching me, listening.

Our eyes met.

Will's friends, his bandmates, stood behind him in the hallway, exchanging shocked glances as they overheard the whole thing, at least having the good decency to look embarrassed on our behalf.

In control, in control.

Nothing in control.

* * *

Most folks in Jackson County traced back to Welsh ancestors, if you counted three or four generations back, so much so that Jackson was also known as "Little Wales." Welsh men and women settled here in the rolling foothills to work the mines, which was kind of funny, since mining was exactly what they did back in Wales. Go with what you know, I guess. Not only did they mine the earth, but they farmed it, working the land of the Ohio River Valley where the Hopewellians had built their earthen mounds two thousand years earlier. The Welsh drank tea. They fought for the Union in the Civil War. They brought their songs, their Celtic traditions, their churches, and their language—strange, long words with not enough vowels that read like gobbledygook to me, even though these were my people.

Daddy mined coal too, working for the Wellston Coal and Iron

Company. It smacked of unfairness that he was taken so soon. Cancer snuck up and snatched Mama too, only a few months after it stole Daddy. Even Granny had lived longer than my parents, certainly not the ordinary course of events when the past generation outlived the next, especially for those from hardy Welsh stock. Every day their absence hurt. We lived amongst many of their belongings, things too dear to part with—Granny's cast-iron skillet, Mama's set of Encyclopedia Britannica, Daddy's tool chest. Sometimes I wondered if things might have been easier, all those years ago, if I could have turned to my parents, if the boys could have benefited from the wisdom of their grandparents.

Anyway, daydreaming over what might have been was a fruitless endeavor.

When Daddy and Mama passed, I inherited the house. I'd moved out when I married Garth, of course, but that didn't work out, a fact well known to every busybody in this small town. I moved back in with the boys eleven years ago, back to the familiar furniture, the familiar smells. *Home*, I had declared as we unlocked the front door and lugged in our boxes and suitcases to unpack. James and Will were toddlers at the time, running to pick out their bedrooms, gleeful to run Hot Wheels tracks down the center hallway.

And from then on, it'd been just the three of us. Things were tight, but with no mortgage to worry over, we weren't cash poor. I got no help from Garth and didn't waste any thought over him. When the boys were little and would get in a squabble and come crying to me, each blaming the other, I'd sit them down and hush their tears with one question, "How many people are there in the whole world?"

"Mom," they'd whine, teary-eyed and fighting over some toy, wanting to tell on each other for this or that.

"Never mind that. *Tell me.* How many people altogether in the whole, wide world?"

They understood counting to one hundred, so we'd start with that. *Count one hundred, ten times over. That's one thousand. Now one thousand, a hundred times. That gets you to one hundred thousand. Now do that ten times. That's a million.*

How many people in the town of Jackson? *The townies, we're called.*

How many people in Jackson County? *The country kids, they're called.*

How many in Ohio? *Eighty-eight counties in Ohio...*

How many millions in a billion?

Once we'd settled on a number, my next question: "And *exactly* how many people, out of *all* those billions and billions of people, can you call your brother?"

"One," they'd concede, mumbling and shifting their feet. Usually there'd be some jealous half-hearted shove to re-establish whatever brother-to-brother pecking order they'd fought out that day.

"What was that? I didn't hear you!"

"One!"

They'd finally collapse into squeals and giggles, abandoning their fight, and I'd encircle them in my arms and swing them round and round the kitchen. "You only have *one* brother in the whole world," I would tell them, over and over. "Don't forget. You gotta be kind to your brother."

"And only one mom," they liked to point out, such earnest little kids, crowding closer, still young enough back then for hugging.

My motto was simple—keep it gentle. The world could be a scary, cold place. If a person couldn't find unconditional love from their own mother, then from whom? Sure, I got lonely sometimes, but the last thing I needed was the complications a man would bring. If there was a way to slow time and keep them little, it sure would be something worth figuring out. But of course, they just kept growing. In the blink of an eye, it was 1978, I had two teenagers on my hands, and we could say there were four billion people in the world for sure, maybe even four and a half.

We had balance, the three of us, like an isosceles triangle. These two boys, brothers, alike and yet so different—two sides of equal length, rose to the top. Me, the mother—well, I was the third side, the base, holding the whole thing up. I tried to balance them on my shoulders, so they could see far into the distance. This I knew for sure —if I were to fall down, the whole thing would collapse.

So, I didn't.

* * *

I walked quickly, keeping a brisk pace and my head down, hoping to avoid any neighbors or beauty salon customers. What on earth could have happened? How could my son, *my seventeen-year-old son*, be in the county jail? Various theories churned in my mind. Fistfight after school? A problem with a teacher? James never got in trouble, never even had to stay after school for detention, I reminded myself, trying to stay hopeful. He had talked about an accident, though not much of that was making sense. Red? Smelled like fish? I tried to think, tried to prepare myself, but my brain kept circling.

I'd had the thought to bring money. Thank goodness I'd taped cash to the underside of the sugar canister in the kitchen; my secret emergency fund. Wasn't there usually some kind of payment involved to spring someone out of jail? And if this didn't constitute an emergency, what did? My heart pounded. I walked as fast as I could without breaking into an all-out run.

Sweating and out of breath, I climbed the steps to the courthouse, but the front doors were locked for the evening. I circled around to the side entrance. I knocked, and the sheriff waved me in.

Sheriff Jason Robb stood behind the counter, writing in an open file spread atop a metal file cabinet.

"Evening, Jorie." He let me inside, frowning. He was two grades ahead of me in high school and in my opinion, always been a bully. I cut his wife Shelly's hair every month, and she's a mousy and nervous little woman, but I always try to be kind to her. Shelly stayed home; she was a housewife, a strange word since a woman couldn't marry brick and mortar and vinyl siding. Last time I'd cut her hair, I'd noticed fingerprint bruising on her arm. "Are you doing alright, Shelly?" I'd asked. She insisted that she was. "Let me make you a cup of herbal tea so you can just relax while I fix you up pretty." She'd given me a grateful nod. "Thank you Jorie, you're sure a nice lady." I'd nodded and hadn't said another word.

Jason grew up to become the county sheriff. I grew up 'justa hairdresser', despite acing every math class I ever took. I knew the rules. He could address me by first name, but I must address him by title. I felt the weight of his judgment and recoiled from the power this man had over my family. He could afford to appear unrushed, conversational. It wasn't his son sitting in lockup.

I swallowed my panic and tried to speak evenly, with that calm, sing-song twang, no particular hurry, the way we all spoke, even when something urgent was happening. The kind of talk where it was understood: *I'm one of us. I grew up here.* "Evening Sheriff. What happened?" Please.

He closed a folder and refiled it in the cabinet, swinging the drawer shut. "Well, Jorie, we picked up your boy, James. He and the McKowan brothers and some gal decided they were going to go joyriding or drag-racing or something in that old truck."

Those darn McKowan boys! No common sense in that family. Why was James hanging around with that kind, anyway?

"They put that old truck into a ditch or something?"

"Jorie, sit down. It's serious." He gestured toward a folding metal chair and took a seat at his own desk.

My eyes swept the room in a moment of panic. I didn't want to sit. I didn't want to hear what he was going to tell me. But like an actress playing a part in a play, I was swept along, as if it was all preordained somehow. I sat and set my purse on the floor, crossed my legs, then uncrossed them.

"Okay." He looked at me carefully, speaking slowly, as if to a child. "James was driving. They were speeding down 93, where it turns to go into town. You know the speed limit drops there at that turn. As they came toward the light, Ernie Cragen was in the cross-walk, crossing the street from the gas station."

"Ernie Cragen, in the crosswalk..." I parroted. I felt the color draining from my face.

"They hit him."

"Oh, my God. They *hit* him? Ernie Cragen? Is he all right? Were the boys hurt?"

Sheriff Robb's face tightened into serious lines, and he shook his head. "Jorie. Ernie was dead on arrival when they got him over to the hospital. Wasn't anything the docs could do to save him. Your son, James, killed him."

I stared, unable to comprehend. "*What?* When?" My voice sounded tinny, too high.

"Just about two hours ago."

"Killed him," I repeated slowly. The words tasted bitter on my tongue and coiled tightly around my chest, so incomprehensible they might as well be spoken in a foreign language.

The ambulance must have gone right down Main Street when I was walking home from the grocery. I hadn't even heard the sirens over the sound of Will's band. Tears welled in my eyes. I'd known Ernie since grade school days. His kids went to school with my kids. He was a kind, mild-mannered, easy-going kind of fellow, one half of a golden couple, married to his high school sweetheart. *And* his wife, oh my God—Candy Cragen—was nothing less than the mayor of Jackson herself.

I swallowed hard. How could Ernie Cragen be dead?

"Oh my God, poor Ernie, their poor family." I shook my head back and forth, imagining the horrific scene unfolding. Candy must have been summoned to the hospital, must have been sat down into a folding metal chair, must have been informed her husband was gone... just as I had been informed my son was driving the truck that killed him.

"Is James hurt? Is he here? Is he okay?"

"Your boy had a hit to his head on the steering wheel, just a bump, nothing serious, and the McKowan kids weren't hurt either."

Just a bump? To his head? I couldn't keep up with the pace of the information being provided to me. Suddenly, inexplicably, I was angry.

"Well, if he hit his head, why isn't he at the hospital?"

"He got checked out before they brought him over here."

"And no one called me? I'm his mother; he's just a boy! How does he get checked out at the hospital without anyone calling me! And how do you know my James was driving the truck?" I went on. "It's not even possible. James doesn't know *how* to drive. He doesn't have a license. And it's not even our truck. It belongs to the McKowans. Why would they be letting James drive their truck?"

"There were eyewitnesses, Jorie. I don't know why they were letting James drive it."

I wiped my eyes, shaking. "Well, it was an accident, then. A horrible, horrible accident. James would never intentionally hurt anyone. He was so upset on the phone... I want to bring him home. Why do you have him in jail?"

The sheriff looked at me and blinked, non-committal. "Well, now, it's an ongoing investigation at this point, so I really can't share too many of the details with you, Jorie, but he's going to be charged with vehicular manslaughter. You might want to hire a lawyer for him. Or, I suppose you could go with the public defender, if he doesn't just decide to plead out."

Now it was my turn to stare and blink. This was all a huge, colossal misunderstanding.

"Plead *out*? It was an accident. He's just a kid!"

"Yes, ma'am, but he's seventeen and likely to get bound over to the adult court, so he'll be our guest here for the night."

"Wait. I brought some cash." I fumbled into my purse, sniffling and swiping the back of my hand across my cheek in a sloppy attempt to wipe away my tears. "I don't know how these things work, how much bail costs... it's not much," I conceded awkwardly as I pulled out my sixty-three dollars, leaning to spread the bills out on the edge of his desk.

"Jorie, sixty-three dollars isn't enough to meet bail. You can call the bondsman in the morning and work all that out."

"I need to see him. I need to talk to him."

"You sure you want to do that tonight? I'm sorry, Jorie, but he seems kind of out of it, talking crazy, not making a whole lotta sense."

This was what I'd been fearing. Lately, there'd been times where James *had* been talking crazy, rambling some nonsensical narration about colors, numbers, sounds. Going on and on about every little detail of his bike riding, sometimes pacing and raising his voice. Will and I usually just gave him space and retreated to our rooms. Will usually had homework to do anyway, and I could bury myself in a good book to finish. Keep it gentle.

It was scary when he got in these moods, but it only happened now and then. That wasn't the real James. Why hadn't he been out looking for a job like we talked about? I thought we had an agreement. He was going to finish out high school and get a job. We had a plan. Or so I had thought.

I swallowed. "On the phone, James mentioned the smell of fish, something ice cold?"

The Sheriff supplied the response that I'd already known before asking the question. "There was nothing about that crash that had anything to do with fish or being ice cold. Like I told ya, Jorie, your boy's not making much sense tonight."

I steeled my shoulders and raised my chin. "I want to see my son. Now."

Sheriff Robb shook his head but grabbed a large key ring and led me through two locked doors into the hallway with several holding cells. One was empty. In another sat Leroy Perkins, the town drunk. "Well now, hey there, Jorie," Leroy drawled in a surprised, pleasant, and pathetic sort of way, but I ignored him as I proceeded to the third cell, my eyes on James. Our eyes met and I read his horror, his grief, his fear, his confusion, his panic.

"All right, just a minute then," Sheriff Robb said, unlocking the holding cell to allow me to enter.

In an instant, James was in my arms, sobbing.

"Mom!"

"I'm here."

Not too old for hugging. I held him as tight as I could.

Chapter 2

Jorie

"I owe you big time for giving me a ride, Lana."

She took one hand off the steering wheel to wave me off. "Don't be silly, Jorie, of course I'm gonna give you a ride."

We were cruising north in Lana's Chevelle, past Chillicothe, toward Circleville, the last small town you passed through before you could spot the skyline of downtown Columbus. The winding hills of Jackson County gave way to flat, two-lane Route 23. Venturing from the hills always left me feeling exposed, unsettled. They loomed over us like silent sentries and just when it seemed you'd be safely encircled by them forever, you rounded a bend and suddenly the world was ironed flat.

I clutched the page of the phone book I had torn out, the full-page ad under "A" for "Attorneys", with the photo of the man with the friendly, self-assured smile, handsome in his suit and tie. The full body shot revealed a fit young professional, and my eyes were drawn to the flash of kindness in his eyes, as well as his polished, impeccable dress shoes. A man who wore shoes like that, expensive and polished to that kind of shine, would have attention-to-detail, take-charge confidence. A man who could afford a full-page ad in the phone book would be successful, well-respected in the community. He posed casually, mahogany desk and bookshelves with volumes of legal journals in the background. Scholarly. Competent. "Benjamin Atwater, Attorney-at-Law," read large letters across the bottom of the photo, "Bankruptcy, Divorce, Criminal, Personal Injury."

The ad instructed me to "Call for Free Consultation." So I had, immediately. It wasn't a difficult decision. The public defender was Randy Carver, who used to look over my shoulder in eighth grade and copy when we had pop quizzes and was always whispering over across the aisle: "Hey Jorie, how do you spell niece?" "Hey Jorie, how do you spell unequivocal?" "Hey Jorie, how do you spell ambassador?" So, Randy ended up going to law school, and I ended up cutting hair. No doubt he'd learned a few things along the way over the years, but it didn't inspire confidence, and as far as I was concerned, asking him to defend James was out of the question.

A secretary had answered the office phone with a cheery and perfunctory, "Office of Attorney Atwater, how may I help you?" Professional! Impressive! She'd taken down our information and then consulted the schedule of Attorney Benjamin Atwater. "Let's see, now, he's in court all day Monday and Tuesday, deposition Wednesday morning, but can we work you in for Wednesday afternoon? Will that work for you, Mrs. Jenkins?"

Busy! A successful practice! Yes, Wednesday would work for me. I had wanted to get in sooner, with James still in lockup, but there was nothing to be done. We needed to wait for the best.

"Good-looking fellow," Lana said, nodding down toward the photo.

"Look at those shoes," I pointed to the photo.

"Jorie, you didn't choose him just because he has nice shoes, did you?"

"Of course not," I said, ruffled, turning the photo over and setting it on the dashboard.

"He looks expensive too," Lana went on.

"That's my worry," I agreed, "but I need the best for James, so it doesn't matter. Thank God for Granny's glassware."

"You're lucky she left you that collection," she said. Yesterday Lana had also given me a ride, past the Hocking Hills, to the antique store in Logan, where I had sold a few of the Fenton pieces. I'd yielded $300.00, hopefully enough to cover the retainer fee and give Lana some gasoline money. I wanted James out, desperately, but was scared that if I spent it on his bond, I wouldn't have enough left for his legal defense. Plus, quite frankly, the mood in town was ugly, angry. The mayor's husband was dead. Hit by an irresponsible joy-riding teenager driving too fast. The funeral was going to be on Friday, and the accident, the widowed mayor, the grieving children, was all anyone was talking about. For now, James was better off in jail.

"The sheriff tell you anything else?" Lana asked.

"Just that it's an ongoing investigation. He's pretty tightlipped about the whole thing."

"It'll be fine, Jorie. James is a good kid." Lana's lived next door all my life, except for those years with Garth. We used to walk to school together, complaining about our mothers and ogling the boys. She knew my kids as well as anyone, so coming from her, it was as true as anyone could hope for. She gave me a sideways glance. "You hear anything from Garth?"

I scowled. "Course not." I fixed my gaze out the window. Farm stands, used car dealerships and a massive junkyard lined the road nearing Circleville proper. Then came the endless pumpkin patches. Just as Jackson was known for its September Apple Festival, Circleville was known for its October Pumpkin Festival. Families came from Kentucky, from Indiana, everywhere, for a look at the humongous prize-winning pumpkins. Hay mazes, apple cider, antique tractors, and a demolition derby made for a real festival atmosphere. But the rest of the year, the thing most noticeable about Circleville was the stink from the paper mill. Kind of made you want to speed up and drive through fast. Assuming you had a car, that is.

17

"Damn!" Lana shook her head and put her arm over her nose. "How does anyone live next to that disgusting thing?"

"Maybe they're so used to it, they can't smell it anymore," I mused. It was a rhetorical question, one we debated every time we ventured up this way. Lana just shook her head, burying her nose into the crook of her elbow.

We pulled up to a simple one-story brick building sharing a parking lot with a McDonald's. The inside had worn carpeting, fake plants, and Reader's Digest in the waiting area. Deflated, it occurred to me that maybe I was making a mistake. None of this looked much different than what I could find in Jackson. But before I knew it, the man himself was stepping out of his office and shaking my hand. The phone book photo was no exaggeration: tall, full head of wavy hair, searing blue eyes, white movie-star smile. What was he doing practicing law near a paper mill in small-town Appalachian foothills?

"You must be Mrs. Jenkins." His voice was warm. "Ben Atwater. So glad to meet you." He sounded like he really meant it.

"Call me Jorie." I said, blushing and mortified to realize it. "And this is my friend Lana." I ducked, pushing Lana forward.

"Hi there." Lana nodded, offering her hand.

"Call me Ben." He flashed a smile.

Lana and I simultaneously glanced down to check out his shoes before pulling our eyes back up to sea level, sharing a quick, knowing look.

"Come on in and have a seat. Lori is making coffee," he said.

Lana and I each took a seat while the attorney settled at his desk and grabbed a pen and fresh legal pad. "Let's talk about your son's case. I understand this is a high-profile situation, what with the victim being the mayor's husband?"

I frowned at his use of the word 'victim.' *Crimes* had victims. I cleared my throat. "Yes, the person who was hit, the *accident* victim, Ernie Cragen, *is*, I mean *was*, the mayor's husband. His wife, Candy Cragen, is the Mayor of Jackson, and they have two kids." I wrung my hands. "It's probably the worst thing that's ever happened in our town. Ernie was such a decent fellow. It's all everyone is talking about, and everyone knows everyone. But it was just a tragic *accident*. That's why I wanted to hire a lawyer from out of town to represent my son..."

"Sure, smart," he nodded, eyelashes fluttering across eyes such a remarkable shade of blue that any word fell short to properly describe them. Cerulean? Aquamarine? "Tell me about your boy."

I took a deep breath, telling myself to focus. "Well, I have two boys, James and Will. My James is seventeen and my Will, he's fourteen. They're good boys, *wonderful* boys, and it's just the three of us. Their dad's not around, we're divorced. So, the three of us watch out for each other. I take care of them. I work hard. They're *good* boys, and James has never been in any kind of trouble before." I took a breath, aware I was blushing again. How embarrassing to have a son in jail, to be accused, to try to explain my family to this good-looking young lawyer who seemed larger than life.

I pushed on. "It's James, though, who had this awful accident."

"Right." He nodded. "I looked into James' charges, the police report. He was driving without a license. Was it your vehicle?"

"A friend's truck."

"With permission of the friend?"

"Yes, I'm sure. They were all together."

"Other teenagers?" he asked.

"Well, yes, some fellows from school he hangs out with, older teenagers... I suppose it's their parents that actually own the truck."

"So, we aren't clear on whether the owner of the truck gave permission or knew James didn't have a license," he said, writing on his pad. A conclusion, not a question.

He looked over his file for a moment. "Witnesses report the truck was speeding... has he had any driver's education at school, or practice driving?"

"No, he didn't take that class at school. We don't have a car, so it didn't seem necessary."

"Okay." He paused, writing again on his pad. "Never practiced driving with an adult, with you, or with his dad?"

"No, I told you, Mr. Atwater, I mean Ben, his dad is gone; he's not in the picture. And he took the car with him."

"Jorie," Lana said softly, squeezing my hand. "It's all right now."

"I'm sorry," I said, closing my eyes for a moment. This was our lawyer. He was just trying to help.

He watched me a moment before setting his legal pad down and rising from his chair to perch on the side of his desk. "This is tough, I know," he said softly. "You don't need to apologize for anything. People don't come see me on their best day. They come on their worst day. Every client who sits in that chair is sweating it out over some crisis. If you decide to hire me, I promise I'll work hard and do everything I can to help your boy. I don't abide by lazy lawyering, and I promise you, I'm no lazy lawyer. But Mrs. Jenkins, I'm going to explain two very important things. One is attorney-client privilege. This is a safe place; we discuss, we strategize, and sometimes I play devil's advocate with my questions—not because I'm trying to give you a hard time, but because I'm testing how those questions are going to be answered when the prosecutor asks them. Do you understand?"

I nodded, silent. Attorney Ben Atwater was as good as the ad promised. James needed this man. "What's the second thing?"

"You and your son have to tell me everything. *Everything*. No holding back on details or information, even if you think it might hurt your case. Got it, Mrs. Jenkins?"

"Got it, Mr. Atwater."

"Good." He smiled and appeared genuinely keen to tackle the challenge I'd laid at his feet. "Do you want to proceed?"

"You are right about it being our worst day," I said. "A man is dead, a decent family man, and my son, just a boy, had a terrible accident. But it was just that, an accident. He has his whole life ahead of him. It's not just a crisis. It's a nightmare."

"You love your children and you're a fighter," Ben said. "I like that. We'll make a good team. What do you say, Mrs. Jenkins?"

"Call me Jorie."

"Call me Ben."

"We have a deal," I said.

Chapter 3

Jorie

"I DON'T EVEN WANT to show my face. Everyone's talking." Will sat, firmly planted in his kitchen chair, balking as I tried to hand him his brown paper lunch bag.

"Don't pay attention to other people's talk," I told him. "It's just gossip. You can't just quit going to school."

He looked at me incredulously. "How come I gotta go to school when you called off sick yesterday?"

My sons always had a way of calling out adult hypocrisy. I pulled out a kitchen chair to join him. "Hey now. We've got to keep up our lives, our normalcy, and you can't be missing school. I took off so I could talk to that lawyer for James. But today, I'm going into work, and I'm holding my head high, because I'm proud of my family, and I know deep in my heart James might have made an awful mistake, but he never meant to hurt anyone." I tried to keep my hand from shaking as I set down my coffee cup. Will watched me. I sighed and loosened my forced bravado. "Why? What are they all saying at school?"

He looked down and spoke slowly, with deliberation. "They're saying that James is crazy. A crazy, raving lunatic, who crashed his truck into Mr. Cragen."

"James is not crazy," I told him sharply.

The little television in our kitchen, squeezed onto the counter with rabbit ears antenna shooting up, played the morning news show. Familiar words drew our attention away from our conversation, and we turned to watch. The newscaster, with bright pink lipstick and curling iron curls immobilized with copious amounts of hairspray, gushed enthusiastically, "Over three thousand cyclists from all over the world are expected to descend upon southern Ohio the first weekend in May for the great Tour of the Scioto River Valley, also known as TOSRV. Local businesses are gearing up for the influx of customers, extra police will be handling road closures, and Girl Scout Troop 684 is getting in on the fun with a lemonade stand, strategically stationed right along the route of the great bicycle tour." Footage of Girl Scouts organizing boxes of lemons, sugar, and paper cups flitted across the screen.

TOSRV. For the past month, James had been talking and talking about this darn TOSRV, this bicycle tour. He'd made sure I understood it was not just a century, but a *double* century. "They ride one hundred miles in one day, Mom, all the way from Columbus to Portsmouth. And then the next day, they ride one hundred miles again. Back from the Ohio River to where they started in Columbus."

I didn't know where this obsession had come from. He would go on and on. "How many hours do you think it takes them to ride one hundred miles on a bicycle? What do you think they do if they get a cramp in their leg?" Will and I had patiently listened as James endlessly expounded on the subject of the bicycle tour, day after day, until we had finally just started tuning him out. "Ummm hmmm," I'd distractedly answer, as he held court on the tools needed to change a tire or the best food to eat for optimal long-distance energy.

"TOSRV has grown to become the largest organized bicycle tour in the country," the newscaster said and turned to her colleague. "Aren't we lucky to have it here in Ohio?" The other anchor picked up the banter and soon they segued on to sports. We turned from the television.

"Has your brother been going on about that big bicycle tour at school? Is that why the kids think he's crazy?"

Will ducked his head. "I guess they just see whatever James is into," he responded cryptically.

"And what *is* James into?"

"I dunno, Mom." He paused. "I think James just wants to go fast. Whether it's on a bike or in a car."

I blinked. Could it be that simple? Teenage love affair with speed?

He grabbed his lunch bag, resigned. "I better go, I don't want to be late."

"Now there's a good decision. Hold your head high."

"What should I say when they talk?"

"You don't have to say a thing. We're gonna stick together; that's just what we're going to do."

* * *

After Will left for school, I pulled out my address book so I could make my difficult phone calls. First, the high school. "Yes, Mrs. Jenkins," the secretary responded in a cheery voice after I said my name. She knew darn well I was phoning to excuse James from school; undoubtedly every person in the school, if not the entire town, knew what was going on. But she wasn't going to make it easy for me.

"James Jenkins won't be in to school today," I said, evenly.

"Should we expect him tomorrow?"

"I'll phone in the morning," I responded calmly, adding, "Goodbye now," and hanging up quickly.

Then, my call to Eva's to let my boss, Beverly, know I'd be in late. "Oh Jorie, I'm so sorry," she clucked, sympathetic. "Take the time you need. Joanne is covering for you, no problem."

I had not been entirely truthful with Will about going into work today. This morning I would not be cutting hair. This morning I would be at James' arraignment hearing. Sudsing up the breakfast dishes in the sink, I worried over what the hearing would be like. Ben Atwater said these were normally quick hearings, just to hear the charges and take the plea of the accused. James, of course, would be pleading not guilty. But for James, there would be the additional question of whether he would be tried as an adult. As a juvenile, tried for delinquency, the worst he could face was confinement to the youth reformatory until age twenty-one. He could get it expunged and go on with his life. But in the adult system, James would be a convicted felon. And worse—the thought that had my hands shaking so badly that my coffee cup slipped and thudded into the sink—he could end up in adult prison, serving hard time.

My heart pounded in syncopated rhythm with the rumble of the floorboards as the train passed.

My mind flashed a picture of James as a toddler, pedaling up and down the front walk on his red Flexible Flyer tricycle. He stood more than six feet tall now and used a razor to shave the adolescent stubble on his face, but inside he was still a boy, a boy with a big heart, a radiant smile, an offbeat humor. But also a boy with mood swings, obsessions. I thought of the tricycle again. Is that when this obsession with bicycle riding started? And what about this wanting to go fast, like Will said?

I poked my head into James' bedroom, unnervingly still. How well did I really know my own child? I ventured a step in, studying posters on the wall, books, and clothing on the floor, wishing they could offer some silent clue. Envelopes and stamps lay on his desk for his letter-writing to the bicycle club. I pulled open his top desk drawer, not surprised to see page after page of notebook and graph paper filled with endless numbers and equations, James' slide rule and pencils grouped in the corner. For a moment I considered opening more drawers, poking around, but there was no time for that. Snooping was wrong, everyone knew that, plus, a little part of me, deep down, was frightened of what I might find.

I dressed carefully, a floral dress, my mother's pearls, low heels. A little bit of makeup, a little bit of arranging from heat of the curling iron. Ben Atwater had advised dressing conservatively and the importance of projecting an image of respect for the judicial process and sorrow for the Cragen family. What would the Judge think when she looked at our family? Would she understand the goodness in my child's heart?

My *child*. My *son*. Keep it gentle. I grabbed the phone and called the school back.

"It's Mrs. Jenkins," I said firmly, pushing on without waiting for the attendance secretary's response. "James is going to need all his assignments. His books, his homework. Everything. So he can keep up. Until he's back in school," I added.

"Oh! Well—" the receptionist started.

"I'll be by in twenty minutes to pick everything up."

Chapter 4

Jorie

THE TOWN of Jackson was the county seat of Jackson County. As such, all the important government buildings lined Main Street, with various official-looking seals and engraved Latin phrases no one could read, but must offer up some ancient wisdom about justice. The courthouse sat back from the street to allow space for the front lawn and the iron bell. In my entire life, I'd never heard that bell rung. I climbed the front steps, no railing to hang onto, columns flanking the front entrance. Why were entrances to courthouses designed to be so uninviting? Climbing these steps left me feeling unworthy.

Maybe I should have asked Lana to come with me. Maybe Garth should be here to support his son. I guess that would depend on me knowing exactly where he was. I pictured him joy-riding somewhere exotic, maybe Mexico, Highway 66, or the California coastline, our car flying down the road, him without a care in the world. In my imagination, our old Dodge Dart was transformed into a red convertible, and Garth wore trendy sports goggles, ascot flying in the wind as he motored through scenic mountain turns, blue ocean reflecting rugged cliffs. And there was probably some gorgeous woman in the passenger seat.

Angry over the injustice of abandoning one's family, I pulled open the heavy door to the halls of justice. *Easy, Jorie*, I told myself. *You're* the one who decided to leave, *you* chose single parenthood, and you're so better off. Who cared what Garth was doing?

I'd brought James' polished dress shoes, pleated pants, button-down shirt, and tie. Ben Atwater hovered by the entrance, waiting for me. "Good," he called over his shoulder as he quickly plucked the bag from my arms and headed to the holding cell, all business. "See ya in there, Jorie," he added.

I found my seat in the front row, on the defense side, so I'd be right behind James. Familiar faces surrounded me, but I fixed my gaze ahead, ignoring their stares. The air was tense, low murmurs of muted conversation. Phrases floated up through the marble columns.

"Boys wrecked that truck."

"Heard they were speeding. Bet ya alcohol was involved."

"What I want to know is, where were the parents? Where was the supervision?"

"You ever hear all the racket coming from that house when her younger kid's banging on those drums?"

"How ya think Candy and the kids are holding up?"

I tried to tune out the talk, concentrate on breathing in and out, but the voices rose. There was a stir of excitement to my right. Out of the corner of my eye, I saw news cameras swiveling to catch the object of everyone's attention. Heels clicked loudly on the polished floors. Unable to help myself, I turned my head.

Candy Cragen was entering the courtroom, her two children, a girl and a boy, trailing behind. "Hello Mayor," murmured a few spectators to her. "So sorry for your loss."

She nodded stoically, her eyes puffy from crying, though her makeup was perfect. The news cameras filmed her, following close behind, and then suddenly she looked right at me. The crowd gasped. This was undeniably high drama for sleepy little Jackson; the grieving widow staring down the mother of her husband's killer. Mortified, I glanced down into my lap. I wanted so badly to tell her I was sorry, that I was so sorry. God, I wished I could say some words of comfort to the children too. Their loss felt like all our loss. And poor Ernie Cragen sure didn't deserve for his last act on this earth to be something as simple as crossing the street. But this wasn't the time or place to say my piece. Being pitted against them, seated on opposite sides of the room, felt so wrong. James might be eccentric, might go on and on about colors and smells, but of this I was certain: he would never intentionally harm another living being.

Keep it gentle.

"All rise," called the bailiff. "The Court of Common Pleas of Jackson County is in session, the Honorable Betty Jean Fraser presiding."

We rose to our feet and Judge Fraser entered. She settled at her bench and adjusted her black robes before instructing everyone to be seated. A court reporter assumed her post near the podium, and then James entered, escorted by a deputy. We achieved a small moment of eye contact, and I smiled and nodded, trying to send telepathic messages of love and support. James looked pale and somber, handsome but uncomfortable in his dress clothes. I knew he was frightened.

The judge read off the names of the prosecutor, defense counsel Ben Atwater and the defendant: James Jenkins. The prosecutor read off the charges.

"The Grand Jury returned an indictment very quickly in this matter. Do you understand the charges against you?" Judge Fraser addressed James directly, peering down upon him over the tops of her glasses.

"Yes Ma'am," James answered.

I allowed the air to exit my lungs in a quiet exhale of relief. Thank goodness James was himself today, the true version of James, not the rambling, making-no-sense version of James. He was doing good, and I was proud of my son's courage, although I doubted he truly did understand the charges against him.

"And how do you plead?"

James looked to Ben, who nodded encouragement, and James responded as they had planned, "I plead not guilty."

"Very well then. Any preliminary matters we need to address?"

"Yes, your honor." Ben Atwater jumped to his feet, his voice confident. I felt the spectators twittering behind me. Our movie star defense attorney commanded the courtroom, like a celebrity in our small-town midst. My breath quickened with a flutter of hope. "Two matters from the defense," Ben said. "The very important matter of whether this boy is being charged as an adult or as a minor and our motion for change of venue."

Judge Fraser raised an eyebrow. "Attorney Atwater, I realize you don't typically practice in Jackson County, so there are a few things you should know. We may not be fancy like the big city forums you may be accustomed to up north, but I conduct my courtroom with decorum. With tradition. With respect for the rule of law. So, I'll let you know only once, Mr. Atwater, that the prosecutor speaks first in my courtroom."

She turned to the prosecutor, not interested in any response from Ben. My shoulders sagged. Maybe I'd made a mistake hiring him.

"Thank you, Your Honor," began the prosecutor, rising to his feet. "The State respectfully moves the Court for bindover to the adult system. We will be filing a formal motion requesting the same."

"Mr. Dean, you are looking to prosecute this youth as an adult, and not as a delinquent minor?" the judge asked.

"Correct, Judge. Our motion will be filed by tomorrow. The State further requests that Your Honor establish a reasonable timetable for discovery and set the matter for trial on a date convenient to the Court's docket."

"Yes, very well," she nodded. "We'll go off record and retire to chambers with our calendars to pick dates. And I'll remind counsel I tolerate no tardiness and do not entertain motions for continuances," she added, speaking in the general direction of the defense table.

Panic churned in my stomach. Picking a trial date? Things were moving too fast.

"Now. Any preliminary matters from the defense?"

I clenched my hands, hoping Ben didn't do anything to further irritate the judge. He swung to his feet and gave a slight bow toward the judge, gesturing toward the lectern. "Your Honor, may I approach?" Judge Fraser nodded to go ahead, and Ben went to stand at the lectern.

"May it please the Court," he began. "My client, James Jenkins, is a seventeen-year-old high school student. He's lived all his life in Jackson. He has almost perfect attendance at Jackson High School and has never been in trouble with the law. Now, I've met with his mother, Jorie Jenkins, a hardworking beautician, and I've met with James. I can tell you that the Jenkins family wishes to extend their deepest sympathy to the Cragen family. No crime or act of delinquency was committed; rather, what transpired was an accident that resulted in a tragic, unintended loss. James is a minor. He's still amenable to rehabilitation through the juvenile system and shouldn't be subject to a life of confinement for youthful folly. We will be submitting a brief in opposition to bindover, and we request a full hearing to give James the chance to be tried as a juvenile, because he is just that. A juvenile. And given the widow's prominence as town mayor, we respectfully request a change in venue. Now, Your Honor, we are in no way questioning the impartiality of the Court, or the magnitude of this Court's command of legal jurisprudence. But you see, we have news media in the courtroom today. We have a packed galley. We have Mrs. Cragen, the mayor of this fine town. People are already forming opinions based upon emotion and assumption. Should this matter go to trial, there's simply no way an impartial jury can be seated from Jackson County."

Damn. The man *was* good. My churning nausea calmed a bit.

But Judge Fraser appeared unfazed. "I'm glad to hear you are not questioning this Court's impartiality or command of legal jurisprudence, Mr. Atwater. The Court understands the high-profile nature of this case. Your client will receive a fair trial in my courtroom. There will be no change of venue."

31

My heart plummeted. They were talking about the case, not the person; my person, my James, who was still a child. It felt like we were losing already, and my son was slipping away from me.

"I'll be expecting the timely submission of motions from both sides, prior to our bindover hearing. Anything else?"

A charged moment of silence followed, and I felt Ben weighing the benefit of picking his battles and maintaining some reserve of goodwill with the judge.

Do something, I silently willed again in Ben's direction. But he just started writing on his legal pad. I dug my nails into my palms. This whole thing needed to slow down, the judge needed to understand. I had to make her see.

My eyes fell on the navy-blue backpack on the bench beside me. Before thinking anything out, I was on my feet, raising my hand like a student waiting to be called on in class. "Judge Fraser? I'm sorry, but I have something, a question, if you don't mind."

Her mouth hung open in surprise, and Ben had swung around. "Jorie!" he whispered sharply.

But I pressed on. I held up the backpack for all to see. The news camera swung to point toward me. "Your honor, I'm Mrs. Jenkins, James' mom. I have James' school assignments here." I opened the zipper and pulled out his geometry textbook. "Geometry is one of his favorite subjects. Actually, both my boys do pretty well in math. Believe it or not, we like talking about numbers at home, and sometimes I give them little problems to solve, like if Tide Detergent costs $5.39, but it's on sale for 20% off, how much are you going to pay?" The judge looked at me in astonishment, but I kept going. "The teacher moves pretty fast in that class, so if you don't keep up your assignments, it doesn't take long to get behind." Next, I pulled out a paperback copy of To Kill a Mockingbird. "Now here's an American classic. They're reading this in English class, and then James is going to need to write a paper about the book. Here's his bookmark. Only on chapter three. He's going to fall behind in English too without his books. And then there's history." I held up the history textbook.

"Every productive citizen needs to know American history. See, there's a reading assignment for that class too. The American Revolution, Civil War, World War I, then they'll be on to the roaring twenties, The Great Depression, then the whole unit on World War II."

"Mrs. Jenkins," said Judge Fraser. It was hard to tell if I was reading impatience, weariness, or the tiniest twinge of sympathy in her voice.

I didn't care. They could lock me up too.

"Judge Fraser, please, I'm begging you. Let my boy keep up with his homework."

"There's a process, Mrs. Jenkins," she began.

"He's not going to school while he's sitting over in the adult jail, is he Judge Fraser?"

She looked at me evenly. "No, he's not. He's not in school right now." She paused a second, then turned to her bailiff. "Please collect the homework assignments from Mrs. Jenkins and give them to the defendant. Mrs. Jenkins, you will be permitted to drop off school assignments every day at four o'clock."

"Thank you." I breathed, feeling for the second time this week like my legs might give out from under me.

"Court is adjourned."

People stood, gathering their things, and I scrambled to make eye contact with James again, but he looked past me, smiling shyly and giving a little wave. Who was he waving to? I turned to scan the crowd and spotted a young girl with long dark hair in the back of the courtroom, her eyes fixated on James as if she was trying to tell him something. She put her hand on her heart and stood on tiptoe to wave back, watching him until he was out of sight.

Well now.

Chapter 5

James

THIRTEEN STEPS from the wall with the cot with the thin mattress to the wall with the metal desk. Eight steps from the wall with the toilet to the wall with the gate and the bars. I counted my steps one hundred times yesterday to be sure. Of course, it changed depending on whether you took big or small steps. So, it really wasn't accurate.

Walking and counting kept me busy, but now I had my school books, so there was no reason not to sit at this metal desk and dig in. Funny, all the reading, essay questions, geometry, and algebra was easier in this place, with nothing on the walls or floors and no clutter to look at. Emptiness was also perfect for writing my letters to the Columbus Crashing Crankers bike club, and I felt I'd composed several very good ones. Quiet was space. When sounds, vibrations, smells, and movements got smaller, it made space for my ideas and colors to get bigger. No one to talk to, except when they brought the food around or when Mr. Perkins in the cell down the hall started chattering. His talk made me nervous, so I decided to just quit answering him. He sounded disappointed that every question he tossed my way was met with silence. "Not much of a conversationalist, are you, boy?"

No, I am not. Not much of a conversationalist at all, Mister.

Mom and Will seemed so far away. They hovered in the corner of my mind, along with pictures of home, somehow all fuzzy images colored orange. Orange for warmth. Orange for smells of Mom's cooking. Orange for voices from the television. Will's drum set. Humidity and sweat. Orange was cozy, but sometimes it was suffocating. Just too much going on. Here, everything was gray. I liked the gray. Cool, calm, quiet. One thing at a time.

The numbers calmed me, and when I got too nervous, I started going through my multiplication tables. Memorizing those in grade school was fantastic. We had flash cards, and the teacher timed us, faster and faster, until we could produce the answer as easy as batting an eyelash. I really liked timing myself.

Mostly this cell was very orderly, but my eyes kept returning to a loose screw in the bed frame. I could fix that if I had some tools here, I thought, picturing Grandpa's tool chest in our garage. I was good at mechanical things, like adjusting my cadence and shifting my bicycle gears, so I was always spinning smoothly. I learned all about shifting strategy from my bicycling magazines. There's a whole science to it.

The only thing I didn't like in here was not feeling the vibration from the train.

The stillness was really bothering me the day my lawyer came to see me.

He started asking me questions about the crash, trying to write things down on his yellow legal pad (yellow was a very hopeful color, futuristic I think, like landing on Mars), but then he stopped writing and looked at me very directly. "James. Are you listening? Why are you rocking back and forth?" he had asked.

"Our house shakes," I explained. "All the time. I miss that. There's no rumbling in here."

He looked confused. "Okay, James." He put the legal pad away, closed his briefcase and stood up. "We'll talk again soon, son. You take care now."

I'm not your son. Why does everyone call me son?

It was a relief when he left, and I could sink back into the cool, quiet, gray. I had been listening to every word he said, but the crash was not something I wanted to talk or think about. The awful thud, the front bumper smacking Caroline Cragen's father, then Caroline Cragen's father flying up in the air, actually landing on the front windshield, at the same time my head cracked against it, and my head moved forward along with Caroline Cragen's father moving backward caused the glass to shatter all around us, and then time just stopped. And just before it happened, our eyes met. His eyes were brown, brown like a squirrel burying brown nuts in the brown earth, brown like someone about to die. No time to jump, no time to brake. An object in motion tends to stay in motion. We learned that in earth science in ninth grade, which was a precursor to physics, which the kids who wanted to go to college took their senior year. Guess I wasn't going to college. Mom wanted me to get a job. That's how things went around here.

The color of the crash was something I could not even fathom. Too many colors all at once: red, glitter, and neon, fireworks. The smell of fish. Ice cold. There wasn't enough space in my head for this.

Before Mom left, she and Dad used to fight. I'd pull the pillow over my ears, but I could still hear. Mom doesn't think Will and I remember, but I do.

Anyway, we never talked about it. But I still remember.

Besides counting steps, the main thing I wanted to do was think about Sarah Jane. Remembering talking to Sarah Jane, holding her hand, pulling her close for a kiss, made everything all right. She was there in the courtroom for me. The color of Sarah Jane was blue, a really beautiful, soft, cornflower blue: calm gray, infused with hot, sexy pink.

And that was just right for me.

Chapter 6

Will

THE HANDS of the clock must be broken, stuck on 2:27 for about three hours now. I kept one eye on the frozen minute hand and one eye on the back of Caroline's head, two rows in front of me. Miss Ritchie droned on in front of the classroom. She called on Sandy Michaels, having her come up to solve yesterday's homework on the board. Tense muscles relaxed, and the class gave a collective sigh of relief, feeling sorry for Sandy, but better her than us. She rose glumly and picked up the chalk, shifting from foot to foot as she surveyed the chalkboard. Sandy was cute in her blue jeans and earth shoes, but she was not pretty. Certainly not pretty like Caroline.

"Think how to start the problem, Sandy," Miss Ritchie prompted. "What value is X? Which side of the equation are you going to solve first?"

"Ummm, okay." Sandy responded, chalk poised in front of the board, but not starting to write anything. She stole a quick glance at the clock, which I saw still read 2:27.

Why was Caroline in school today? She was out all last week and of course on Friday, the day of her dad's funeral. Some of the girls were also excused that day so they could be there for their friend. I'd seen the hearse going down Main Street out the window from homeroom, followed by a line of cars with purple flags and headlights on. It stretched for several blocks. Seemed like most of the town must have been there. Mom had insisted I go to school that day, just like she had this morning.

Caroline was sweet, she's always talked to me, always said my name when we passed in the hall. *"Hi there Will." "Mornin' Willie."* She certainly didn't have to talk to me; she was pretty, popular, already on the varsity cheerleading squad, even as a freshman. I would've forgiven her for not making eye contact. That she could be that generous with her smile just made her that much more wonderful.

But now everything was awkward, to say the least. I'd purposely dawdled, head down, burrowing for some phantom notebook in the bottom of my locker this morning when she passed. Saving her from deciding how to handle the morning greeting was the only gift I had to offer. Honestly, I wished I could just disappear.

"Will, please go up and help Sandy out," Miss Ritchie asked.

I joined Sandy at the chalkboard, and she handed me the chalk with a grateful glance. "I don't know what she's looking for," she whispered with a shrug.

"Okay, hmmm." I paused, but I'd already solved it in my head. All that was happening now was for show, a demonstration of solidarity with my classmates leveled clueless by algebra.

I looked over to Miss Ritchie, who looked exasperated by my pretend hesitation. "Go on, solve it, Will."

I wrote out the steps and the solution quickly and felt murmurs behind me, part grudging admiration, part hostility. Sometimes it's better not to stick out too much.

"That's correct, Will," Miss Ritchie said with a nod. "You may both take your seats."

I studied the floor on the way back to my seat, terrified to look at Caroline.

Brian Miller whispered low from the back row, but loud enough for the back three rows to hear. *"Your brother's a murderer."*

Gasps from the other kids, heads turned to seek my reaction. I clenched my fists. Caroline shifted in her seat and turned her head just a bit to the left, but not all the way around to look back. It didn't matter. I knew she heard. I sunk further into my seat, miserable. I wanted to say something to Caroline, tell her I was sorry about what James did, but the clock miraculously read 2:45, and the bell was ringing. I sprung to my feet and flew out the door.

I made a beeline for my locker, stuffing three books, my spiral notebooks, and my homework into my backpack. The guys were down the hall, over by Rick's locker. I couldn't wait for practice; I'd been listening to Zeppelin and working out some of the solo sections from Moby Dick.

"Did you hear that asshole Brian Miller in Miss Ritchie's class?" I said as I walked up.

Rick ducked his head into his locker. "Just dumb," he mumbled.

Brad looked away, and Andy studied his feet.

"You guys ready to head over?" I asked.

They glanced at each other. "Maybe not today," said Andy.

"I got my days mixed up?" I looked from face to face. No one answered. Andy looked at his feet again. We'd practiced every Wednesday after school since September in my mom's parlor. My drum set was there, and we had two amps in the corner. None of the other guys' parents would put up with the noise, but Mom'd been cool about the guys coming over.

"Brad?" I asked.

"I got to help my dad clean out our garage today."

"Why's everyone acting so strange?" I looked to Rick. He sighed and at least had the guts to look me in the eye. "Will, we got to cool it with band practice for a while. You know, with everything going on right now. With your brother."

Now it was my turn to look at my feet.

"Our parents don't want us going over to your—" Andy started, his voice soft, but I didn't need to listen to any more of this.

"Yep, got it," I snapped, cutting him off. I heard Rick call my name, but I was halfway down the hall and out the door in a second, running toward home. I ran past the bowling alley, past the grocery. Past the post office. Past Eva's Place where Mom works. Down the alley and then up the front walk. I fumbled for the key in my pocket, and then I was inside, lungs heaving, as I paused to look at my drum set, our amps stowed in the corner. We had the idea for the band a year ago. We've all known each other since kindergarten.

Jerks.

The house was empty, so quiet.

James' room sat empty.

Deflated, I poured a glass of water and tried to think.

What do you do when a bunch of guys turn their backs on you, when they've been over to your house a million times, gone to the movies, traded baseball cards, told ghost stories by flashlight on all those Boy Scout camp-outs? Especially Rick. So much for best friends.

I set the water glass down and let the screen door slam after me on my way to the front porch. I grabbed James' red Sting-Ray, the stupid bike he's so obsessed with, just like that crazy bicycle tour. Pushing it onto the grass by the tree, I took a running start, swinging my leg over the banana saddle. In an instant, I was off. Pushing my feet hard on the pedals felt good. Up and down, my anger pushing my legs to push the pedals, faster and faster.

It'd been a long time since I'd snuck off with my brother's bike for a ride. I cut across the lawn onto the sidewalk, then hard cut right onto the street. *Ride on the sidewalk*, Mom would say if she saw me. But I wanted speed, wanted to get far away. The wind was warm through my hair and rippled my shirt as I flew down High Street, crossed Main Street and buzzed past a shocked Buddy Williams with his mail bag as he walked his postal route. The Powler's dog barked as

I whizzed past their house in a blur of velocity. Sweat beaded on my forehead and under my arms, but I kept pushing, faster, faster. The hell with the guys. The hell with people's talk at school. The hell with James for crashing the McKowan's truck. My legs were powerful, and I was lean and light. My arms, muscular from drumming, commanded the handlebars.

An incline began as I neared Grove Hill, but I refused to be slowed. I stood on the pedals and rocked the bike right, left, as I climbed the hill hard, conquering it in no time. I was unstoppable. The further I rode, the faster I went, the better I felt. No wonder James liked this so much. Guess I'd never really thought about it before.

I pulled up to the intersection with Route 93 and screeched to a stop as the traffic light turned to red. Heaving for breath, balancing one foot on the curb, I blinked and tried to get my bearings as I waited at the light. My heart pounded in my chest, and now sweat stung my eyes. Everything seemed different from the bike.

Oh shit. I was at the intersection where James hit Mr. Cragen. How did I end up here?

Spent, I didn't feel like riding anymore. I swung my leg over the seat and walked the bike carefully across 93, looking both ways, thinking about a speeding pickup truck and a man flying through the air, blunt force trauma destroying internal organs. Did the truck shred his liver? Puncture his lungs? Fracture his skull?

By the gas station, I let James' bike fall against the brick wall and bent over, light-headed, my breath heaving. My head hung low, and a rush of nausea pushed my lunch up. I vomited by the garbage can at the back side of the store. Afterwards, I looked to see if someone saw, but there was no one around.

I sank down against the wall and wiped my mouth. I needed to wash the taste of vomit out, needed to cool down. Pushing slowly to my feet, I circled round to enter the store, nodding to the woman at the counter. Coolers in the back held the colas, fruit drinks. Ah yes.

Orange Crush. Grabbing one of those, passing down the candy aisle, I slid a chocolate bar into my pocket, not even thinking about it. The lady didn't see a thing. I paid for my drink and returned to the wall by the garbage can, plunking down to enjoy my cold drink and crunchy chocolate bar, which tasted outta sight.

What would happen to James?

What would happen to me?

Jackson High was small, and everyone knew everyone. Heck, everyone knew everyone in the whole town, though it occurred to me I'd never seen the woman working the counter inside the little gas station store. But that was unusual. I knew all the kids, knew their parents, my mom cut their moms' hair, everybody talked. There just plain wasn't anywhere to hide here.

Come to think of it, there really wasn't anywhere to ride a bike either. I wondered where James had gone when he took off on the Sting-Ray. Up to the McKowan place, I guessed. Not sure why he was hanging out with those guys. Maybe since Sarah Jane's family lived in their trailer up that way. Yes, that must be it. It was hilly toward that part of town. Maybe James found some trails to ride in the hills. I liked that idea, cutting through trails and brush on the bike seemed kind of badass, like a cowboy or something.

What if James went to prison? I'd be the kid with the older brother in prison. Nobody would see anything else when they looked at me.

I got up, shaking myself off. Worrying about myself was selfish. *Do something to help your brother*, Mom would say. But I hadn't a clue what to do. I pulled the bike back toward the road and mounted, slower this time and headed toward home. Mom would be home soon. She'd be asking why the band wasn't practicing. Maybe I could make something up, so she didn't have to know the guys turned their backs on me. Mom didn't need anything more to worry about right now.

Cresting Grove Hill, enjoying the coast down the other side, a pile of broken glass near the sewer grate caught my eye too late to avoid. A loud pop, like an air gun. The bike quivered and wobbled, front sinking low to the rim.

Flat tire.

I had nothing figured out, nothing at all. Nothing except that math problem on the chalkboard.

I walked the bike the rest of the way home.

Chapter 7

Jorie

"JORIE, you can't just blurt things out like that at a hearing. You're not a party to the case, you're just there to watch and be a support to James. We've got to present a united front. You've got to trust me. You've got to let me do the talking in court." Ben Atwater had rapped on my side door late this afternoon, and now he was pacing back and forth in the parlor, going on and on, gesturing with his hands.

I sat on the couch, nodding and trying to show Ben I was listening and understood.

"Well, it worked, didn't it?" I said, when I could sneak a word in.

"We're a team, remember? We didn't talk about anything like that ahead of time. I had no idea what you were doing or going to say. The last thing we need are any surprises in court. Plus, I was about to request the judge to close the hearing to the public, to the press, and then you pulled that stunt holding up his backpack, playing right to the cameras in the courtroom."

Ben seemed kind of angry. I reminded myself that James needed him, *we* needed him, desperately. Plus, I was paying a lot for the legal bills.

"I'm sorry," I conceded. "It wasn't planned. It just kind of happened. Guess my mom-instinct kicked into high gear and all that was out of my mouth before I knew it. Do you think I made the judge mad? Is she going to hold this mom's craziness against my boy?"

Ben threw up his hands, shrugged, and softened. "Actually, you're right. It did work. You humanized him. You reminded the judge he's just a school kid, which was exactly what we were trying to do."

I flashed an impish smile and caught a twinkle in his eye as he grinned back, shaking his head.

"Have a seat." I indicated the couch. The man was going to wear a trench in my floors with all his pacing. "How about a cup of coffee?"

He sat and rubbed his forehead, thinking.

"Or maybe something stronger?" I ventured. I wasn't much of a drinker, but there was a bottle of Wild Turkey in the back of the cupboard, leftover from New Years when Lana, who hadn't had a date either, had come over for a toast at midnight. Ben sat up and looked at me, a question in his eyes. "And no, if you're thinking, am I a drinker, the answer is no. I don't run around with men, I don't drink, I don't smoke. Cigarettes or anything else," I added defensively.

"I wasn't thinking that, Jorie," he said.

"You're thinking something."

"Actually, I was wondering about your name. It's unusual. I've never met a Jorie before. Short for something?"

"Marjorie." I looked down, startled at the question and surprised to feel awkward. "It's a mouthful; I'm not crazy about it. Jorie's easier."

He smiled. "Try Benjamin. *Also,* a mouthful. But I think Marjorie is a very nice name. Marjorie Jenkins."

There was almost a sweetness in his voice. How bewildering to be having a conversation with a man, in my home, to hear him speak my name. Shyness overcame me. I was completely unable to think of any response.

"Let's have that shot." He jumped to his feet. I nodded and pulled two shot glasses out of Granny's hutch. Ben followed me down the hall to the kitchen and leaned against the counter as I pulled the bottle down from the back corner of a top shelf and carefully poured each glass. The amber liquid trembled, threatening to spill over the rim as the train passed. Wait a moment, I gestured to Ben with one finger.

Once the train had rumbled on, we raised our glasses and held them awkwardly toward each other, searching to name what we were drinking to. His eyes held mine, for a second too long maybe, and something fluttered inside me, something not felt in a long time. "To James," I said, firmly.

"To James," he agreed.

We downed our whiskey.

The sting and the burn made me shake out my hair. "Whoo, now there's a punch."

"They don't call it Wild Turkey for nothing," he said.

Awkward silence followed, heavy with whatever Ben wasn't just coming out and saying. "How often does that train go by?" he asked, setting his empty glass on the counter as he wandered back into the parlor, pausing to look at the china in Granny's cabinet.

"Ah, you know, I don't even hear it anymore; I've lived here all my life."

"Your parents' house?"

"Yep. I grew up here. Daddy mined coal up in Richmond Dale. It was me, Mama, Daddy, and then we had Granny in the third bedroom with us until she went to the nursing home."

Ben ran his hands over the keys of the old piano. "Do you play?"

I smiled and shook my head, picturing my mother and Granny gathered around the spinet, one of them at the keyboard, singing folk songs from the homeland with sweet soprano voices. "Not really, I just plunk around on it sometimes with some old family songs."

"Sounds kind of nice. A musical family," he said, looking at Will's drum set. "What kind of old songs?"

"Oh, old songs from Wales. Little melodies about fair maidens, soldiers, spinning yarn from wool, rocky cliffs. Stuff like that."

He smiled and turned his attention back to the china cabinet, peering more closely through the beveled glass at the antique plates, colored glass vases, china teapots. "Have you ever had any of this appraised? Some of it might be pretty valuable."

I laughed. "One of those pieces paid your retainer. Guess you could say that's my bank account, sitting right here in the front room."

Ben straightened. "Don't pawn any more of these. This is your family history, right here."

"I'll do whatever I need to do for my kids," I said. "Those are just things."

He nodded, his gaze distant, lost in thought. "So you've lived here all your life? With your parents and now with your children?"

So now we were dancing around the inevitable "where's their father" question.

I smoothed my hair, feeling him watching. Might as well get it over with. "I was married. Moved out when I got married, had the boys. We lived over in Oak Hill." I jerked my head, gesturing west. "Things didn't work out. My parents were gone by then, but they'd left me this house, so it made it easier for me to leave 'cause I had an easy place to return to."

"How old were the boys when you left?"

"James was five and Will was two. Pretty little."

"That must have been tough, Jorie," said Ben. "Your ex up-to-date with his child support?"

"Ha!" I spit out, a few decibels too loud. "Now there's a good one."

He looked at me curiously. "He's behind with his payments? He owes arrearages?"

I shrugged my shoulders and fluttered my hands in the air, shaking my head. The rush of the alcohol had my face burning, no doubt flooded with color.

"*Nothing?*" Ben pressed, incredulous. "But it's the law. He has to pay. How's he not supporting his kids?"

I looked down. At the hearing, when our separation agreement was finalized, which lasted a whole eight minutes tops, I had agreed to support being set at zero. Garth had been working, but was planning on leaving town. I had no clue if he had a new job lined up and, frankly, I didn't want to know—where he was going, what he had planned, who he was planning on living with. I just wanted it over with.

"Guess we didn't really get into all that, at the time," I said, fixing my eyes on a spot on the ceiling. "I knew I could just move into this place and not have to pay any rent or mortgage, and I had my cosmetology license by then. But all that's water under the bridge. James, Willie and I—we do just fine."

"Well, sure, I can see that you take care of everything they need, I wasn't suggesting you don't." He gave a quick sweeping hand gesture meant to compliment our little house on High Street. "Your home is very nice. But a man shouldn't be able to walk away from supporting his own sons. Didn't your attorney fight for any alimony or child support in your divorce settlement?"

I gave a nervous laugh. "You're looking at her."

"Ah, you represented yourself." He smacked his hand to his forehead, and we both laughed. "Now I understand your little speech in court today."

"Oh Lord," I said, shaking my head.

"You missed your calling, Jorie. You should've gone to law school."

"Naw, you wouldn't say that if you could see me wield my scissors at the beauty salon." I chuckled and gestured toward the couch, relieved to shift away from the subject of my ex. Explaining my family, defending my ability to manage everything, bothered me. And what would Ben think if I told him I'd also agreed to allow Garth to keep the only car? I wanted to draw my boys close and keep our little circle intact, keep it gentle forever, like an impenetrable fortress. For the hundredth time, I silently cursed that James stood accused for a mistake. How many teenage boys do I see speeding through town every day, gunning their engines at stop lights, trying to impress their girlfriends? The image of the girl with the long, dark hair in the back of the courtroom flashed through my mind.

I thought Ben would want to leave, but he reached for his brief-case by the screen door and pulled out a file and legal pad. His face grew serious as he settled onto the settee. "There's something else we need to discuss. Do you remember when you retained me, and I went over the rules? The most important one was that you have to tell me everything. I can't help my client if you don't tell me everything."

I smoothed my hands over my jeans. "Of course, Ben. What do you need to know?"

"Jorie." He paused a moment, his forehead wrinkling his face into a frown. "How long has your son been having delusional thoughts and hallucinations?"

My jaw hung open, and my mouth went dry. The room spun sickeningly, and I swallowed hard.

From the porch there were steps and a thud as the bike landed against the side of the house, and Will burst in, his shirt soaked in sweat. "I got a flat tire!" he announced. "Had to walk it home all the way from the Quick Mart."

* * *

I jumped up, and Will stopped short as he spotted Ben. "Ben, this is my younger son, Will. Will, this is Mr. Atwater, your brother's attorney."

"Oh, hi." Will stiffened a bit as he looked over the briefcase, the polished leather shoes.

"Hi Will," said Ben, standing. "I've heard nothing but good things. You need any help fixing that flat on your bike?"

"Well, it's not my bike." Will looked sheepish, looking back and forth from me to Ben. "I was just borrowing it. James can't use it where he's at right now."

"Guess that's a fact," Ben agreed.

"James is the real bicycle rider in the family," I offered. "It's been his latest craze, talks about it all the time. He's got that Schwinn Sting-Ray he likes to ride all over town. Subscribes to some bicycling magazines, too."

"Ah, I see. He didn't tell me about that when I met with him the other day. Sounds like a good hobby. And a good way to get around town," said Ben. "Where does James like to ride?"

Will and I looked at each other. Neither of us really knew the answer. For as much as James went on about gear ratios and cog size and two-hundred-mile bicycle tours, he didn't really talk much about where he took off to. Funny, it hadn't occurred to us to ask. "I think he just cruises around town," I said.

"You got some pretty hilly areas in these parts," said Ben. "He must be in good shape if he's riding up and down those grades. Especially on a Sting-Ray. How many speeds?"

"Three speeds," Will said. "I know he wants a ten-speed. But he's just got the three-speed."

This hung in the air a moment. Had I known James wanted a ten-speed? Maybe I'd heard him mention it, but it hadn't really registered. Here I was telling everyone how I could take care of everything just fine on my own, but now I could picture what Ben must see: no car, only one bike for two teenagers, a kid obsessed with bicycle touring who didn't even have a ten-speed. Clearly, this family was strapped in the transportation department. No wonder James couldn't resist the chance to try driving a friend's truck.

"Well, let me give you a hand changing that tire then," Ben said. "Is there a pump?"

Will gave me an embarrassed glance; he hadn't a clue how to fix the flat, and we both knew it.

I nodded brightly. "Now there's a very kind offer, Ben. Thank you so much. There's an old bicycle pump in the back of the garage.

I'm sure James has everything you need out there to fix it right up." I motioned Will toward the porch. "Go on now and wheel that thing around to the side and show Mr. Atwater where the pump is."

"Call me Ben," I heard Ben telling my son, as Will pushed the bike around to the garage.

It wasn't often my boys had a man around to show them anything. Sure, I could cut hair and talk numbers and percentages, but I wasn't mechanically inclined. There's no one to show them how to pour gasoline into the lawn mower and prime it before starting it (Okay, well, I did show them that), how to change the oil in one's car (not necessary, no car), or the names of the constellations if you look at the summer night sky once it gets really dark (Okay, come to think of it, I showed them that too.) But fixing a bicycle tire? This was a decidedly manly mechanical lesson. Ben helping Will was kind of thrilling and terrifying at the same time. I wrung my hands a few moments, torn between curiosity and wanting to leave them alone to talk about whatever men talked about.

I tidied the already tidy kitchen, distracting myself. But curiosity won. In the garage, I found them huddled in the corner, going through the drawers of Dad's old tool chest, filled with mysterious nuts, bolts, and unnamed implements of every variety. Their heads were bowed together in concentration.

"Is this it?" Will held up what looked like some kind of wrench. "Is this one?"

Ben straightened a bit to peer at what Will held, but quickly hunched back over to resume his search. "No. That's a wrench. We're looking for a tire iron." They continued pawing and sifting through the tool chest.

"Look at this!" Will held up a long rusty metal stake.

"That's a rail spike," Ben told him. "Someone must've pulled that right off the train track."

"Huh," said Will, turning it around in his hands. "Would that make the train crash?"

"I certainly hope not," Ben responded. "But it's never a good idea

51

to start pulling things apart from the tracks, that's for sure now," he added, easygoing and conspiring as they shared the bond of a common project.

"You guys finding everything you need?" I chimed in.

"Well, naw, interesting collection of tools, but not the things we're going to need," Ben said. "You got a pump, but we're going to need a new inner tube. Plus some tire irons to take the tire off the rim. Thought maybe we'd find some, but if it's okay with you, I'll run Will up to the hardware store and we'll grab what we need. Let's see, looks like this bike is going to take a twenty-inch tube. And you got Schrader valves on the tire."

Ben was talking like some of James' daily rants, the same mysterious language of bicycle mechanics I knew nothing about.

"You sure you have time to do that? We don't want to impose. That tire doesn't have to get fixed today," I shared a glance with Will, who looked excited. A ride to Kings Hardware Store in a car? Not something we did. Ever.

"No trouble at all," Ben replied. "Easy to take care of."

I looked at my wristwatch. Half-past five. "How about I fix supper while you fellows run your errand?"

Now it was Ben's turn to flush a bit. "I don't want to impose on *you*."

"It's not an imposition; we'd be happy to have you join us for supper." My voice felt more sing-song than normal. I saw Will watching me closely. "Y'all go on now, and I'll get supper started." I gave Will an encouraging nod, smiling brightly at Ben. They made their way to Ben's car. Before heading to the kitchen, I stopped in the bathroom and perused my face. Couldn't hurt to fix the makeup a bit, put on fresh lipstick. I spent a few moments brushing a little powder and blush on my cheeks, providing some cover for my freckles, then mascara on my lashes. I brushed out my light brown-not-quite-blond hair and tried composing the loose strands in some orderly fashion around my face. What kind of hairdresser are you? I asked, before giving up.

Although I made my living helping other women look their best, the mechanics of chasing beauty felt elusive to me and kind of boring. I didn't fuss long over myself in the mornings, didn't give much thought to what others must see when they look at me. When I looked at myself, I saw a small-town, simple, plain mom not trying to be anything flashy or anything I'm not. Silly, I thought as I set the hairbrush down. A fruitless *and* a fool's endeavor.

I got to work on meatloaf, mashed potatoes, peas, and carrots. Perhaps I'd whip up some quick biscuits too with the dried mix out of the box. Since we had company and all. The potatoes boiled in the water as I heated up the stove, mixed egg and breadcrumbs and started forming the meatloaf in my roasting pan. I added salt, pepper, and some steak sauce for a little kick.

Once all that was under control, I dug place mats out of the cabinet and set the table for three. Pausing for a moment over the seating, I decided to set the third setting at the fourth chair, the one that normally remained empty, rather than the spot where James sat. He'd be back home in no time, no time at all, I told myself.

Soon, car doors slammed, and I stepped outside, watching Ben and Will back at it in the garage; prying the tire off the rim, lining the new inner tube up with the valve, putting the wheel back on, the chrome fender, then pumping it full of air. Mrs. Grenadine's curtains had fluttered when they'd arrived back. The whole damn street likely knew there's a strange man at my house, helping my boy fix his bicycle.

"Wash your hands," I told Will when they'd finished and came back in through the kitchen door.

"I better do that too," Ben said. "Got some oil on that chain, which should help that bike ride a lot smoother." He'd rolled up the sleeves of his button-down shirt and sweat glistened on his forehead.

"That was nice of you, helping him with that. Hope you didn't get grease on your nice work clothes. How much do I owe you?"

He held up his hands and shook his head. "Not a thing."

"No, that's not right. Just tell me and let me settle up."

"Well, they were having a special today at the hardware store, actually all the bike tools were on sale, and they were practically giving them away. Isn't that right, Will?" Ben gave a wink to Will, who responded with a grin and gave the thumbs up sign. "Besides," added Ben, "your cooking smells delicious, so you can pay with an extra helping of mashed potatoes and biscuits on my plate, if you really feel like you need to settle a debt."

Our kitchen felt smaller and a bit shabbier with Ben filling the fourth chair at the dinette. The gleaming white of his perfectly aligned teeth seemed to project a spotlight onto tiny piles of crumbs under the toaster, fingerprint marks on the handle of the refrigerator, scratches on the woodwork. The tenor of a man's voice, which he raised to be heard over the passing train, added a new reverberation to the echoes bouncing off the hardwood floors.

Ben certainly seemed to enjoy my cooking. He complimented everything, accepted second helpings. I couldn't help but feel proud, blushing at his comments, flipping my hair self-consciously. I wondered what Ben's dinner plans would have been without my invitation. I didn't recall seeing any personal photos in his office, no framed wedding photo on the credenza, no wife and kids smiling next to a family dog.

Will seemed to be enjoying the attention, sitting up straighter and talking animatedly when Ben brought up the drum set and asked him about his band. Ben smoothly avoided cliched what's-your-favorite-subject-in-school questions, instead drawing Will out by asking how he learned to roll his sticks on the snare, what he thought about progressive album rock, and was disco really dead?

"What's the name of the band?" Ben queried.

Will cocked his head, enjoying the suspense before happily delivering, "Manzana."

Ben looked confused.

"It's Spanish for apple. Apples are big in Jackson. Home of the Apple Festival," said Will.

"Right...." Ben snapped his fingers. "Makes sense. That's a great name for a band. Exotic and local at the same time—I like it."

"Will's been playing with those boys for almost a year now, and they sound better and better all the time," I said. "We found that old drum set at the Goodwill store, and he's really taken to it. So, Will has his drum set and his band, and James has his bicycle riding."

"Two very nice young men," Ben said with a nod.

"Ya, we're nice young men when James isn't talking about which smell goes with which color," Will giggled, rolling up his napkin into a ball and tossing it playfully toward the center of the table. "Or writing all those letters to that bike club that never writes back. And last year James got obsessed with the frequency of cell vibration, like on the molecular level, he thought he could actually *feel* the cells vibrating, and it was all he talked about for two weeks. Remember that, Mom?"

"Will," I said sharply.

He gave me a look. "Sorry, Mom."

"Why don't you clear the table and take out the garbage?" I told him. "Then I'm sure you have some homework to get after." Keep it gentle.

"Yes Ma'am."

Ben watched quietly for a moment, then jumped up. "I'll take care of these dishes. Just point me toward your dish soap."

"It's all right," I said. "We'll just stack them in the sink for now."

Will pulled the plastic closed on the top of the garbage bag and slung it over his back as he headed out to deposit it in the garbage can in the alley.

"Jorie," Ben whispered urgently, once Will was out of the room. "Talking about smells and colors? Feeling molecular cell vibration? We need to talk about James."

"I know, I know, it's terrible I haven't bonded him out, I'm a terrible parent, I lay awake at night so guilty that he's over in that jail cell instead of sleeping in his own bed... I'm so ashamed... but we can't afford it, can't afford the bail."

"Jorie, that's not what I'm referring to, and you know it."

I busied myself setting leftovers in the fridge, not meeting his eye.

"I would like to request the Court to have him undergo a psychological evaluation."

"Ben, it's getting late. You probably have a good two hours to drive back up to Circleville." I set the dishcloth on the counter, running my eyes distractedly out the window, across our backyard. "Thank you for helping Will fix the tire."

He put his hand on my arm, rejecting my pretense at formality. "Whatever's going on with James can't be pretended away. You hired me to help him. I can't defend him unless we address this."

My fear, my worst fear, was that my boys would have some kind of strife or suffering that I couldn't fix. I couldn't protect them from everything, but it'd all been so good so far, so safe, so predictable. Like a math problem. Every time you went to solve it, you got the same answer. The right answer. No equivocation. But whatever had snuck up on us with James and his ramblings, his obsessions, just didn't add up and couldn't be solved. And I didn't know what to do.

I turned my head to the floor, not meeting Ben's eye.

Taking a deep breath, I nodded, once.

Chapter 8

Jorie

THE NEXT MORNING was busy at Eva's, permanent waves, cuts, blow dries, manicures. Beverly maneuvered between our stations with the broom, sweeping up hair from the floor, greeting all the customers personally, asking if anyone wanted coffee. She checked them out when they were done, making change from the cash register at the front desk and writing the next appointment time on a little reminder card.

Everyone knew everyone, and Eva's Beauty Salon was Gossip Central. These days everyone wanted that layered look, though some ladies went for the permanent waves, with lots of hairspray, of course. Big black chairs for the customers lined up in a row before a long mirror that spanned the entire wall. My hairdressing station, with my scissors, combs, brushes, and curling iron, was toward the back. My cosmetology license hung on the wall. My tip jar sat near the mirror. I'd taped a photo of James and Will to the mirror, a picture of them clowning around when they were little. It made me smile and was an easy conversation starter with the customers: *My, how your boys have grown since that one was taken!*

My nine o'clock was Rhonda Browning. She hadn't changed her hairstyle in about thirty years now. Usually we chatted about our children. Hers were all grown up now, and she was crazy for grand-children, but hadn't gotten her wish yet. I always felt kind of bad for her daughters and daughters-in-law; seemed like she must pester them a lot. Usually I heard her out, kept things going with the occasional question or "umm-humm" while she unloaded the same spiel I heard every month. When that ran its course, she'd throw out, "Well, your boys are too young to worry about all that yet," and then politely inquire how my children were doing, and I'd tell some innocuous little story. She wasn't really interested in James and Will, but since I was her sounding board for every little detail in her family, she felt she had to ask.

Today she was strangely quiet, and I had to work harder to keep the conversation going. "Are you having everyone to your house for Sunday dinner this week, Rhonda? Going to make that good ham and bean supper after church?"

Her answers were polite, but short. Her eyes nervously darted to the photo of my boys on the mirror.

Of course, she'd likely been watching the news, reading the paper. There'd been plenty of sideways glances from the other chairs as well. Everyone knew. That didn't mean I had to talk about my private business with my customers. I had a right to work my job. I stubbornly kept up with the small talk. "Did you see they're having a 50% off sale next week at the Big Bear? I hear they're fixing to reno-vate the lounge over at the bowling alley."

Mercifully, her hour was finally up, but my ten o'clock didn't show.

"Let me run that broom," I told Beverly, trying to keep busy. After that, I rinsed out the perm solution for Sylvia's ten o'clock, so she could finish the manicure for her next customer.

But my eleven o'clock appointment didn't show either.

Beverly watched me, face creased in a worried frown. "Sorry. I don't know what's going on," I whispered to her.

She clucked her tongue, shaking her head. "Small town, small-minded folks. Already made their minds up about what they don't even know."

I sighed. Most of my customers were long-term clients, ladies I'd known for years. Did they all of a sudden just no longer need their hair done? It hurt to be stood up, not even given the courtesy of a phone call. And humiliating having it happen in front of my boss and coworkers.

"Jorie, you don't have anyone else scheduled till early afternoon. Why don't you take your lunch break early? Maybe walk around, get yourself some fresh air, clear your head," she prompted.

I reluctantly organized my brushes and combs, fussing over the tools and straightening my area. I looked into the mirror and adjusted my own locks, fixed my lipstick. Slinging my bag over my shoulder, I slipped out the back door into the midday sun. I checked my watch; several hours to kill. I could walk home and then walk back to work, but I had another thought. Several blocks away, down Main Street, was the Jackson Florist. The front window was filled with budding paperwhites and amaryllis, bouquets bursting with color, green plants, balloons and greeting cards. I stood outside a moment, looking in the window, considering my options.

The door sounded a cheerful chime as I entered. Ilene Baker was at the counter. "Morning, Jorie. Can I help you with something?"

"Morning, Ilene. Yes, actually. Do you have time to put together a floral arrangement while I wait?"

She nodded, glasses perched on her nose. "What kind of arrangement are you looking for?"

"Something beautiful, tasteful."

"Birthday? Get Well Soon? Wedding? Funeral?" The last word hung in the air.

"Sympathy," I said. "A sympathy arrangement."

She nodded solemnly and got to work, soon assembling a wicker basket with graceful lilies, greenery, yellow rose, white alyssum. "What do you think?" I agreed it was perfect, paid and left. She looked troubled but didn't say anything, and I noticed she hadn't asked who I was mourning for.

Ernie Cragen was always kind, the type of person who'd go out of his way to help anyone. I never quite understood how he'd ended up with someone like Candy, so pushy, so loud, so self-promoting. When she'd run for mayor, she had her photo up on billboards littering the hillsides going into town and by the diner. She leafleted all of our front doors with her picture, and she was constantly on the local radio station being interviewed about this or that. Guess all that marketing was how she was so easily elected. I didn't fault her for it. Takes a lot of courage for a woman to put herself into a contest for a leadership position. But now she'd won, she was just about intolerable, charging around in four-inch heels and power suits, too many bracelets clanking on her wrists. Still, their kids were decent. And they'd suffered a horrible loss. I had no right to offer sympathy, but I had to try.

City Hall was down by the courthouse, next to the statue of Governor James A. Rhodes. He hailed from the Appalachian region of Ohio, Jackson County as a matter of fact, so was a big celebrity in these parts, despite that Kent State thing.

The mayor's office was right off the center hallway, behind glass doors. "Is Mayor Cragen available?" I asked the receptionist. She gaped a moment at me, at the floral arrangement.

"Why hello, Mrs. Jenkins, ummm, let me see if she's available." This was Mabel Green's daughter, a nice enough girl, married last year and expecting her first baby. Her hand hovered by the phone a second, but she seemed to think better of it and jumped up to poke her head into Candy's office. I heard hushed voices as my arrival was announced and the gravity of this unannounced visit parsed and debated. Perhaps she just wouldn't see me. I wouldn't blame her. It'd be simple to say she was in a meeting, on a phone call, or just couldn't be disturbed. I could leave the flowers here at the front desk and be on my way, at least able to tell myself that I tried.

But Candy Cragen was a go-getter. Fearless, she didn't procrastinate, and she didn't shy away from confrontation. So it was really not surprising when Mabel Green's daughter returned, eyes large, and beckoned me toward the mayor's office.

I gathered myself up, steeling my resolve to say what needed to be said. I knew Candy's daughter Caroline knew my boys from high school. I knew Candy's mother stayed at the Hickory Hill nursing home, where my granny lived until she passed, and I thought perhaps I could mention this as some common ground, some social nicety I could use as a conversation starter before I tackled the hard stuff.

But when I saw Candy's face, everything crumbled. Her eyes were puffy and red, and it was obvious that in the few weeks since the accident, she had lost weight. Sure, she was obnoxious, egotistic, brash. But she was also smart, brave, passionate. And she was grieving her husband, the love of her life, the father of her children. A new adjective was now affixed to her persona, a word nobody chooses: widow.

To the mortification of both of us, I burst into tears. Then, blubbering, "Oh my God, Candy, I'm so, so sorry. James didn't mean to hit him. Never in a million years would he hurt another soul. I'm thinking about you every day, just sick about it, thinking about you, about Ernie, about your kids. Ernie was such a good man. My God, I don't know what to say. Please, please know we are just so, so sorry, and I don't blame you one bit if you never want to look at my face again. We are just sick about it, and I wish I could fix it. I wish that so bad. It's just a nightmare. I'm sick about it, and there's nothing I can say, but I wanted to come here and try—" I gasped for air. Nothing was coming out the way I'd planned. Rather than comforting her, I was a spectacle.

She swallowed, watching me, her face progressing through exponential emotions that I could not decipher.

Unable to bear it, I clumsily thrust the floral arrangement into her arms and fled. Mabel Green's daughter clutched her pregnant belly, aghast and stood back to allow me to pass.

"I'm sorry, I'm sorry, I'm sorry," I muttered as I rushed past in retreat.

I'd never felt so alone.

Chapter 9

Will

On Friday after school, I set out again on James' bike. It rode easier with the tires inflated to the right pressure and the chain lubricated. Ben had helped get the banana seat adjusted to my height, making it easier to pump the pedals and navigate around the turns. My legs even felt stronger, too.

Each ride, no matter which direction I set out, seemed to circle around for a pit stop at the gas station on Route 93. I'd gotten into the habit of filling my pockets with candy from the Quick Mart. The woman at the counter never said a word. I always bought a soda pop, so it didn't look like I was just coming in to shoplift. She rang me out, and I was on my way.

I thought back to Ben's question, where does James like to ride?

With a few hours to kill before dinner, I slowed my pace to a more exploratory ramble and headed out of town a bit, keeping the bike on the gravel off to the side of the road whenever a stray car passed by. Tiny houses on the outskirts of town gave way to the nursery that sold gravel, headstones, bird feeders, mulch. A corn crib sat dilapidated on someone's acreage. Trailers perched up the sides of the hills. The tracks ran parallel on my right, and I waved back to the conductor on the afternoon train. For a moment it almost appeared we were moving at the same speed, like a mirage, but soon, I was over-taken, chugs and whistles evaporating into the stillness of the afternoon.

A bit further, there were more trailers. The kids out here took the bus into town. The country kids, we called them. The townies, they called us.

The McKowans' trailer was out this way, and I passed it cautiously, angry to see the black pickup truck sitting there, front hood dented and windshield all smashed up. They didn't even bother getting it fixed. The McKowan boys were older, why had James been hanging with them? I was riding on the same route James drove that busted truck down right before he hit Mr. Cragen at the gas station. How did James even know how to work the gas pedal, the brake pedal, hit the clutch and shift gears while swinging that big steering wheel? Mom didn't have a car for us to practice on. Guess I'd thought James and I were in the same boat, but somehow he must have learned these things. And he'd learnt them by riding this bike out this way, toward Wellston.

I shivered a bit and kept going.

About half a mile down the road, a dirt trail intersected. I pulled to a stop, looking to see where it veered away from the road and then up into the hills, before disappearing into brush. Must be the moun-tain biking hills Ben had talked about.

The dirt path seemed to call my name. Someone must have cut it for four-wheelers; it was about that wide. Once I'd passed alongside a cornfield and crossed the railroad tracks, I was in the woods, climbing into the hills. Gnats buzzed in the afternoon heat and I swatted a fly from my forehead. There was a small stream, not deep, more like a creek really. I pedaled right through, not sinking into mud, stagnant water splashing my leg. Then it was up again, more climbing. The trail switchbacked up the hill.

This was pretty cool, I thought. I must be deep into the woods, far from civilization. But then, there were voices. Up ahead in a clearing, I saw a dirt driveway to my right cutting through the trees and snaking its way to a trailer home. Stone steps led to the door and folding lawn chairs in front encircled a fire pit. A dog slept in a few slivers of sunshine, tied to a clothesline. I stopped the bike and got off, pushing the wishbone kickstand to the ground, craning to see.

"Damn girl, what you gone and gotten into now?" a man yelled.

The sound of a smack, hand on flesh, struck like a lightning bolt in the afternoon heat.

I flinched as if hit myself. A blurry memory of huddling under covers with my big brother flashed through my mind. We were counting. James was teaching me how to count. To protect me from that sound, and everything that went with it.

"Pa!" a girl's voice shrieked. "Leave me alone!"

The dog barked and I startled, sinking back behind the brush, scrambling to pull the bike from sight.

The front door burst open and Sarah Jane Billings bolted from the trailer, her dark hair flying behind her. Sarah Jane's a senior, like James, and I'd seen them talking in the hallway at school, so I knew they hung out together. She ran right toward my trail and it was too late to duck. She didn't seem surprised at all to see me clutching my brother's bike, hiding in the brush, watching her house.

I stared, embarrassed to have witnessed whatever'd just happened. She probably thought I was spying on her, if she even knew who I was. "Umm, hi, I was just riding by," I started, feeling like I needed to explain myself, even more embarrassed to hear how dumb I sounded.

She clutched her arms around her chest and heaved for breath.

I gawked. "Are you okay?"

Tears trickled down her face. "Yah." She glanced back toward the trailer, then looked at me. "You're Will, right? James talks about you."

"Are you my brother's girlfriend?" I blurted out.

She put her arm to her cheek and wiped away her tears, sniffing. I saw a bruise rising on her cheek. "James really likes you," she said. "And your mom."

I jumped back on the bike and shifted back and forth a moment, aware of the sticky sweat under my arms. I glanced at the trailer, nervous and then back down the trail. "I gotta get going," I told her.

"You guys are lucky. You have a really good family," she said.

I turned my bike around, ready to take off. I looked at her face again, at the angry red blotch rising on her cheek.

"Umm, Sarah Jane, if you ever need it, I'm pretty sure my mom would help."

I felt her watching me as I flew down the descent, back toward the road.

Chapter 10

James

SHERIFF ROBB GAVE me a LOOK as he walked Mom down the hallway to my holding cell, but I didn't need him to let me know I was going to have to answer some questions. Mom carried my homework papers and assignments, her purse swinging from her arm, wearing her sensible working shoes with the foam insoles designed for standing all day, very buoyant secret weapons. They might even make her a little taller. The Sheriff wandered off after letting her in the cell and locking the door behind her. The lines on Mom's face scrunched into a question mark.

Today Sarah Jane came to visit after her last seventh period class. She got out earlier on Fridays 'cause eighth period was just a study hall. They let the seniors do that. Plus, she was eighteen now. She could sign herself out without her pa's permission. Sheriff Robb had grumbled something about making an exception in allowing visitors to come right into my cell, since I was a minor, and something about how I should be "damn grateful to him for allowing it." He still made Sarah Jane, even Mom, open up their purse and turn their pockets inside-out like they'd be bringing in a nail file baked into a cake. I hadn't thought about Mom bringing over the assignments, and usually Sarah Jane visits after Mom's already left. But today she was here not even one minute ago. They must have crossed paths in the lobby.

I wasn't sure if Mom knew who she was. In my head, I saw color charts. If Sarah's cornflower blue met up with Mom's springtime green, it would make—purple?

I thought about the ring Sarah Jane wore that changed colors based on her mood. Dark, swirly colors, sometimes deep crimson, sometimes forest green, sometimes mushy brown. Did it work based on body heat?

"James, honey, who was that girl I just saw in the lobby?"

So much for keeping things to myself. "Just a friend from school. She just stopped by to see how I was doing."

"Well," Mom said, her eyes darting around the small cell, as if looking for clues. "I didn't realize your school friends are allowed to visit you here. Do they allow minors to come visit at the jail?"

"I dunno. They let minors stay locked up in here, don't they? But," I added hastily, seeing how Mom winced when I pointed out the obvious. "She's actually already turned eighteen. So she's allowed to come in."

"She..." Mom said, fishing for a name.

"Sarah Jane," I told her.

"Ah, okay. Sarah Jane. Pretty name. Does she live in Jackson?"

I ducked my head toward the wall to hide my eye roll. Why did it matter if she was a townie or one of the country kids that got bussed in? And who were we to get snobby about that when we didn't even have a car?

"She goes to Jackson High School, so ya, guess she lives around here."

Mom shrugged and nodded at my non-answer. She sat on the side of the cot and started pulling notebooks out of the backpack. I was relieved she was letting it go, and we could change the subject. The room had started to buzz and turn dark purple, anxiety churning in my stomach, the color of the bruise on Sarah Jane's face. I wanted to go slug her dad myself, let him know how it feels. I'd started pacing angrily when I'd seen her face. "If I was outta here, I could protect you," I'd said. But Sarah Jane had been calm, damnit, she was used to it. She'd stopped my pacing with a long hug. "You're protecting me already," she'd told me. Her hug had calmed my breathing, and I'd picked up her hand and turned it over in the light, watching her mood ring swirl through a mosaic of possibilities before settling to sky blue. She was right, of course. We had to stick with the plan. "Shhh..," I'd whispered into her hair. Sheriff Robb or Leroy Perkins were probably listening to every word we said. Mr. Perkins'd been out for three days but went on a bender and got himself thrown back in the slammer, right down the hall again in the next cell. I wonder if he'd carved his name on the wall in there.

"Did they have a lot of homework for me today?" I asked Mom, eyeing the folders as the room cooled to a quiet gray and white.

Mom smoothed her hands over her corduroys. "I think you're in good shape. The school says you're keeping up with everything really well. But there's something else we need to talk about. I don't know if Ben got a hold of you yet, but Ben thinks the judge is going to grant a bindover hearing."

"Ben told me he expected she would, though she was kind of mean at the hearing. That's good news, right Mom?"

"Oh sure, James, it's really good news, great news. We don't want them to prosecute you like an adult when you're only seventeen years old," Mom replied, working to sound encouraging. "It's just, well, the thing is, Ben thinks it's going to help us prepare for that hearing if you have an evaluation first."

"An evaluation? Like what?"

"Just a checkup, to see how you're doing, you know." She looked at me kind of helplessly. "To see how you're thinking."

The cool gray started to bubble. "What kind of evaluation?"

She finally came out with it: "James, he's recommending you have a psychological evaluation. There's someone Ben works with up near Columbus, an expert who can meet with you, meet with the whole family really, interview all of us, maybe run a few tests, then testify at the hearing. Ben thinks it will help."

What level of heat would generate from my body if I were wearing one of those mood rings? Would it change depending on whether I was out on the bike or sitting in a gray prison cell?

"So everyone thinks I meant to plow down Mr. Cragen? They think I meant to kill him?"

"No, no," Mom said. "Nobody thinks that at all. Nobody who knows anything about you would think that. But the judge doesn't know you, she doesn't know our family, so it will help at the hearing if she... understands how you think."

Her words made the colors start to swirl. The equations made sense before, but this new number, this new variable, changed everything. I didn't like when the numbers didn't add up. It was dangerous. "Is the expert trying to solve something?" I stared at my Algebra II textbook rather than look at Mom's cool green. "How is he going to grade my answers? Is it some kind of percentage, Mom?" Tears ran down my cheeks, out of nowhere; I was crying just like a goddamn baby.

"No, of course not." Mom put her arm around my shoulder and smoothed my hair.

"How's he going to quantify what I think?" I sniffled through my choked-back sobs.

"Blow your nose, James." Mom pulled off some tissue from the toilet paper roll and waited for me.

From down the hallway, Mr. Perkins let out a long whistle, followed by low mumbled commentary to himself.

Mom lowered her voice to a whisper. "Now, of course he can't quantify how you think, son. He's not a mathematician, and he's not there to solve an equation. He's just going to *describe* how you think. And what he observes. About you, about all of us, I guess. At least that's what I think."

"Then the judge has to plug in all the integers to solve it?" I pressed.

"Well sure, she's going to listen to all the evidence, then make a decision. But it's not like math. It's not an exact thing. I don't think you should think about it with numbers," she added with a nod.

Mom sounded so reassuring, but when numbers and equations couldn't predict an outcome, I get really, really nervous. I rocked back and forth a moment, like the rumble of the train. I sure missed Mom's cooking. Funny, but out of nowhere, it hit me that I really missed Will too.

Mom gave my shoulder a squeeze. "Don't you worry. We have a good lawyer and we're going to trust his advice. All you have to do is talk to the psychologist and tell the truth. It's always a good thing to tell the truth, right?"

"Right," I mumbled.

"So we'll let you know when you're going to meet with the psychologist, and when we get a court date for that bindover hearing. Come to think of it, the psychologist is a lady, not a man. And if Ben stops by, you cooperate with him, do you understand?" Mom asked. "This is important, James." I nodded. "And in the meantime," she went on. "You stay focused on your homework. Good grades are your ticket to bigger and better things. This is just a rough patch, but things are going to get better. You keep your head up, now. Okay?"

"Okay."

"And don't get distracted by friends coming here to visit," Mom added. "A jailhouse is no place for school friends to visit." She paused as if trying to decide whether to say something else, but seemed to decide against it.

I pictured Will's snare rolling while his foot tapped the big bass drum, sound vibrations rippling in the air from the Tom-Toms, rattling the china teapots in the cabinet. "How's Will?" I asked Mom. "How's the band sounding?"

"Oh, you know, come to think of it, he hasn't had the boys over for a few weeks now. Don't think I've heard him practicing his drums, either." She ran her hands through her hair, worried over this a moment, then perked up. "What he *has* been doing is riding your bicycle."

"The Sting-Ray?"

"Yes, sure is, he's heading out on longer and longer rides. Had a flat tire the other day but got that all taken care of. He really seems to be taking to riding that bike."

I gave Mom a curious look. Did he lower the seat so the bike fit him? How did he know how to fix the flat? Were his "longer and longer" rides taking him out Route 93, into the hills away from town? I closed my eyes. I could hear the crash of my little brother's cymbals. I could feel the roll of his sticks on the snare, flowing smooth and white like a bubbling downhill mountain stream. But I couldn't figure out which color described the feeling of him riding my red three-speed Schwinn Sting-Ray chopper bicycle.

Chapter 11

Jorie

GARDEN GLOVES and clippers in hand, I piddled about in the backyard, cutting back the rose bushes and pulling a few weeds. Will had run the lawnmower earlier, then disappeared on the communal family bicycle, destination unknown. Well, unknown to me, at least. The screen door fell shut next door, and Lana appeared with a basket of laundry to hang on her line. "Hey, Jorie," she called as she started to pin sheets to the line to dry in the sun. "You've been busy lately, girl." She had her shorts on and sunglasses perched on her head, hair tied off her face in a bandana, like a hippie.

"Just trying to keep my head above water, you know," I said, joining her over by her brick patio and fold-up lawn chairs.

"I see you've had company a few nights this week," she said with a wink. "That handsome attorney coming over for supper?"

I sprawled into her chaise lounge. "Naw! It's not like that. We're just strategizing to get ready for the bindover hearing. Folks gotta eat while they're working, don't they?"

She laughed, leaning over to grab a pillowcase out of her laundry basket, pausing to snatch one of the clothespins from her teeth. "If you say so."

"Well, I say so," I insisted. "It's all business, all work."

"Now Jorie, who could blame you if it wasn't all work? Like I said, he's a handsome fellow. You're single, you're available, you're a *catch*. You do everything for those boys. Nothing wrong with doing something for yourself."

Usually we joked and gossiped over every dating possibility in Jackson, which typically added up to not much of anything, but today I couldn't be more serious. "Yes, there is everything wrong with that," I said emphatically. "My boy is in jail. Ben said we have to get James evaluated by a specialist up in Columbus, a psychologist. She's going to interview me and Will, too. When she finishes her report and testifies, everyone's going to hear about James, about me, Will, our family, how I'm raising them, everything I've done wrong, all the mistakes I've made... the whole town will be soaking up every word, crawling up our butts with a microscope. I can't be painting the picture of some philandering single mom, out on the party scene. That psychologist, every character witness that testifies about us, has to see that we are law-abiding, normal, go-to-church-stay-out-of-trouble people." I threw up my hands.

"You know I'm just teasing, ya," said Lana.

"The last thing I've got time for is a man in my life. If I want romance, I'll sit down with a tub of ice cream and watch a soap opera."

"Amen to that," she murmured, laboring to arrange a damp pair of jeans on the clothesline before sinking into the chaise next to mine and putting her feet up.

"Whole street is probably already gossiping that I'm carrying on with Ben. If you've noticed he's stopping over, then all the other neighbors must've noticed, too."

"Well, of course," Lana agreed, lighting a cigarette. "No secrets in a small town."

I thought of the girl with the long dark hair I saw in the courtroom, then passed in the lobby at the jail. Sarah Jane was the name

James had said. "Maybe there are some secrets after all," I told Lana. "I think James might have himself a girlfriend."

"Really?" Lana looked surprised. "A girlfriend? Even with his funny moods and crazy talk?"

I was stricken, and my stomach somersaulted. Lana caught herself when she saw the look on my face. "I mean, no, I didn't mean anything, Jor. I didn't mean to say 'crazy talk.' It's just, well, you were saying how he got so obsessed over that bicycle tour they keep talking about on the news and talking about numbers all the time, so just wasn't thinking about our little James getting all grown up and starting to have girlfriends."

My sideways smirk let her know her conversation save was a lame effort, but she was forgiven. If your best friend couldn't tell it to you straight, no one could. And Lana's right, it *was* surprising. The mysterious bike rides, the joy-riding in the McKowan's truck, this girl— guess I didn't really know my son that well after all.

"Wanna get some baby oil on your legs, get working on that sun tan?" Lana passed over the bottle. "Tan legs for the church-going, boring, beautician-mom," she declared with a grin.

"Sure," I agreed.

"And whatever your boy is going through is probably just puppy love," Lana said. "I wouldn't worry too much about it."

"Might seem like that to us, but remember when we were that age? High school kids? Every crush meant the world, every feeling multiplied times a hundred. We lived and died over every glance in the hallway, who sat next to who at the football games, whether the phone was going to ring..."

Lana looked thoughtful. "I remember time just seemed to pass more slowly. And when those crushes hit, they didn't feel like puppy love."

"Romeo and Juliet were teenagers," I finished Lana's thought.

"Well, I don't miss that pain, but first love, now that made you feel alive. Like you and Garth," she said.

"Oh Christ, Garth," I said. I shook my head. "Your memory is off.

Garth and Jorie were never any kind of Romeo and Juliet. Good riddance to bad rubbish."

"You don't ever wonder where he went off to?" Lana had her sunglasses down over her eyes now, but I sensed the curious sideways look.

"No. Best thing that came out of that whole enterprise was two people, the only two people out of four billion I can call my sons. But," I added, "Ben has been asking lots of questions too about Garth, if I know how to find him, why he's not paying child support, why he doesn't ever visit the boys, whether he knows James got into trouble. Heck, I don't know what to tell him."

"You can't explain someone else's decisions," said Lana.

"I'm worried, though," I admitted. "We're different. We're no apple pie-TV family. That judge is going to see a loser-mom, 'justa hairdresser', no husband, kids with no father, no stepfather. Shit, I don't even have a car."

"*Hey*." Lana sat up straight and pushed her sunglasses up so she could look into my eyes. "No, they're not going to see that. They're going to see a really smart woman, with a head for math and crunching numbers, living in a paid-off nice little house in town, polishing her granny's glassware, trimming her rose bushes, cutting the hair of the women of this town, dishing out advice while keeping all their business confidential, and knocking herself out taking care of those two boys. You're a good mom, Jorie."

"Sometimes I think if I just had a car to teach him how to drive, he wouldn't have gotten himself into this mess." I said. "Shoot, I don't even have a bicycle for each kid. Two boys gotta share one bicycle."

"Let me think about that one," Lana said, after a moment. "I don't know how to help you get ready for that hearing, but maybe I can help find you a ten-speed. They've outgrown that Sting-Ray."

Lana really was a damn good friend.

Chapter 12

Will

I WAS EXCITED to get out of school early to see Columbus, my first big city, but didn't really understand why the psychologist for James' trial had to talk to me, too.

My knees pressed against the back of the front seat of Ben's Mustang. Mom sat up front next to Ben.

"Don't be nervous, Will," said Mom, reading my thoughts. "Dr. Davis is just going to interview you."

Ben looked in the rearview mirror and caught my eye. "Oh yah, this will be a cakewalk Will—no big deal, just a short interview," he told me. "She doesn't need to do any psychological testing on him like she did on James," he added, directing the last comment to Mom.

I tried to look out the window instead of at the back of Mom and Ben's heads. Mom looked pretty, more colorful somehow, and they were chatting away up there like best buddies.

"Here's where I went to elementary school," Ben said as we got into Circleville. He slowed and showed us a one-story school building with a row of windows and monkey bars on the playground. "I grew up just a few streets away, so it was an easy walk."

"How nice," said Mom. "You must have been a good student to

get into college and then law school. You can be anything you want, Will," she called back to me, "if you study hard enough."

I hated when grownups used that line.

"I'll drive us by my office building," Ben offered, "so you can see where I practice law, Will."

"Oh, good idea," said Mom.

"Right this way," he pointed, after turning off onto a side road. "This building, right here."

The brick building had a sign over the front door with Ben's name on it and underneath his name, Attorney at Law. He waited for my reaction. "Cool," I declared, trying to sound bored and unimpressed. But honestly, it was kind of cool. Ben had his own business. He went to Court and represented people, collected evidence, put on trials. And he knew things, like how to fix a flat tire on a bicycle.

Mom gave a small laugh at my response and flipped her hair. "Cool," Ben echoed quietly, just to her, and they smiled like it was the punchline to some kind of private joke.

I pivoted away from them and pressed my face against the window, noticing for the first time the tall buildings initially so far away on the horizon had swelled larger until they were right in front of us. Just like that, we were in the city. The streets were four lanes across, with a lane just for the buses. People in suits carrying briefcases hurried through the crosswalks, and a cop directed traffic by a roundabout near a big white domed building.

"Capital building," Ben said, waving to the left. "And the Ohio Supreme Court." He pulled into a parking garage connected to a tall office building. The sign in front said "Psychology, Ohio State University."

We took the elevator to the Eleventh Floor, higher than any building I'd been in, in my life. I paused by the window in the waiting room to check out the view of the city, but in no time, they were calling me in.

Why did I have to go in first, without Mom?

"Hello Will, I'm Dr. Davis," said the psychologist. "Very nice to meet you." She pushed her glasses up on her nose.

Was she really a doctor? She wasn't wearing a white coat. Was she going to hypnotize me or something? Was she going to probe the inner workings of my mind and find out everything that was wrong with me?

"Please have a seat," she said, pointing to one of two chairs in front of her desk, while she settled at her desk and opened a folder. "We're just going to have a little chat so I can get to know you better. My job is to meet you and everyone in your family and learn more about you. Does that sound okay with you, Will?"

"I guess so." I sunk into the black leather chair and drummed a few rhythms on my thigh.

Her eyes flew to my hands, and she cocked your head. "Your mother mentioned you're a drummer, and you play in a band with some school friends."

"You already met with Mom?" I asked. This was news to me. Had Mom and Ben driven up here before, for that appointment? They must have gone while I was in school. I frowned at the thought of them riding together up to Columbus, just the two of them. "We're not doing this for me," I told her. "I'm just here for my brother. To help James."

"Yes, Will, I've met James and had a chat with him, too. And you are correct, the purpose of my evaluation is to offer information to the Court for James' hearing, to help the Judge better understand James and your whole family. So you should know that whatever we discuss here today is not confidential; it will be reported to the Court in my written report and when I testify. But this is not all about James," she added. "It's about you too. I want to get to know you."

"There's nothing important about me," I said. "I go to Jackson High, I'm a freshman. Don't know what else you need to know."

"Well," she said, tilting back in her chair, "why don't we start with your drumming? How does it make you feel to play the drums with your friends?"

"How does it make me feel?"

"Yes. How does it make you feel?"

What kind of dumb question was that? I sighed. "Well, you know, it's fun, we have a good time. I mean, had a good time. Their parents won't let them come over to my house anymore." Why had I let that slip out? I really didn't want her telling Mom the guys weren't coming over anymore.

Dr. Davis looked interested. "And how does that make you feel, your friends distancing themselves from you?"

"I dunno," I said.

She waited.

The room was quiet.

I was going to have to answer. "Bad, I guess."

"When you feel bad, what makes you feel better?"

I thought about this for a moment. Really, not too much ever made me feel bad, at least until James got himself arrested for hitting Mr. Cragen, and everyone started treating the Jenkins family like we had the plague. But, I admitted, that wasn't really true. There was more. A long time ago, when I was little, things happened that made me feel bad. Counting with James had made it better. I cleared my throat, careful this time to think through my answer. No way I was going to tell this lady about the numbers and all that. My thoughts turned to the red Sting-Ray.

"Riding my brother's bike makes me feel better," I said. I snuck a celebratory crack of my air cymbal with my air drumstick.

She seemed very interested in this and wrote a small note on her notepad. "Ah, you like bicycling too! You and your brother have that in common. Do you like riding together?"

I shook my head. "We don't ride together. There's only one bicycle. James is really into it; he talks about biking all the time and he writes all these letters to some bike club. I didn't start going for rides until after he got locked up in jail. It's not really my thing."

"Oh, so this is a new pastime for you," she said. "And it makes you feel better."

I nodded.

"So, can you tell me about any activities that your family likes to do together?"

That was an easy one. "Math," I told her. "We throw out problems to each other, story problems, questions about numbers. Like, Mom will talk about surface area while she's cooking."

"Smart family." She smiled and nodded. "And how does your mother discipline you and James if you get into trouble?"

"We don't. She doesn't."

She studied me for a moment. "It must be lonely without your friends coming over for band practice."

Why were we back to that subject? "I guess."

"What do you think would happen if you told your friends that you miss them?"

I shrugged.

"Have you talked to your mother about this?"

"Huh? No!" I sat up straight in the chair. That wasn't going to happen. "Mom has enough to worry about right now with James. She doesn't need to know about my problems. You're not going to tell her, are you? Please don't tell her."

"You worry about Mom and want to protect her," Dr. Davis said. "Do you think withholding information is the best way to protect her?"

I slumped back in my chair and crossed my arms.

She paused to write another note in her notebook.

"Are there things that you think everyone in your family knows about, but you just don't ever talk about?"

Geez, I thought, where do we start? There was James with his crazy talk. There was the fact we didn't even have a car. There was my shoplifting the other day. There was... I shook my head. This conversation was not going there. But Dr. Davis was way ahead of me.

"Your father?" She asked. "Do you and James and your mother ever talk about your father?"

My stomach tightened. What had Mom and James said? Why was she asking all of these stupid questions?

"Will, do you remember your father?" she asked softly.

The clock on the wall ticked, and I glanced toward the plants on the windowsill, then at the titles on the bookshelves behind her desk. Some of the books were really thick.

"Your parents are divorced. Do you remember your parents ever arguing? Fighting? How did that make you feel?"

I resumed drumming on my thigh, wishing hard I was somewhere else.

She waited.

"I don't remember anything," I finally said. "And drumming is my thing. Biking is James' thing. Shouldn't this appointment be over by now, I can't answer all these questions. Can't you just get my brother out of trouble so he can come home? I don't understand what more you need to know."

She made another note in her notepad, then looked up at me.

"Will, there aren't any rules about your brother's path or your own. Please understand, I'm just trying to get a picture of who you are."

I let out a breath and studied the floor. The carpeting had a swirling black and gray pattern. How could I explain to Dr. Davis who I was, when I couldn't even explain that to myself? I silently started to count, then realized she was still watching me.

"Okay, I think we are through here," she said with a friendly smile. "It's okay to not have all the answers, Will, especially when you're fourteen years old. I'd say that's pretty normal. Thank you so much for talking to me today."

She stood and walked me to the waiting room, back to Mom and Ben. "Will did just fine, Mrs. Jenkins. Thank you for allowing me the opportunity to talk to him. You take care, Will."

Mom beamed as if I'd passed some kind of test.

I returned to my spot by the window. The blocks stretched below; you could even see rooftops on the shorter buildings. One had a courtyard and garden right on the roof, but some buildings were even taller than where I stood on the Eleventh Floor. Dr. Davis had said I was normal. Was James normal? And had I said the right things, had I helped my brother?

"Ready to head home, Will?" Mom waited by the elevator.

I turned quickly to follow, more than ready.

Chapter 13

Jorie

KEEPING my eyes on the spot on the wall and my face composed was harder than I'd expected. I'd thought about bringing something to do with my hands, like knitting or something, but figured that might be a little overblown on top of the floral dress. And I didn't want the judge to think I wasn't listening. A few feet in front of me, James sat at the defense table next to Ben, a legal pad in front of him. From my vantage point, James had some long division going. That was probably best. Working those numbers calmed him better than anything.

Ben had explained over dinner last week what would happen at the bindover hearing. The judge would find whether there was probable cause James had committed what he was accused of. Then, she would decide amenability, could James benefit from rehabilitation through the juvenile system, or did the interests of justice and public safety demand he be tried as an adult?

The prosecutor called Sheriff Robb first to the stand.

"Now whose truck was the defendant driving?" the prosecutor asked.

"Gus McKowan owns the pickup truck; his two boys were in the truck along with the defendant James Jenkins," the Sheriff testified.

"Have you had prior dealings with the McKowan brothers?"

"Yes, they live up out of town, in the hills. Had some arrests last year, I believe, over in Meigs County involving some of that Sinsemilla marijuana."

The crowd stirred and twittered, as knowing glances and hushed whispers were exchanged. I picked up a few of the comments:

Trailer trash.

Why was a townie hanging out with that kind?

Judge Fraser gave a sharp look toward the galley, stern enough there was no need to admonish the spectators to stay quiet. I pondered how she maintained such perfect posture underneath the weight of that huge chip on her shoulder she carried toward my son.

"Anyone else in the truck?" the prosecutor asked.

"Sarah Jane Billings was a passenger."

This time, the crowd collectively held their breath, allowing that last tidbit to hang in the air and percolate. I'd spotted the girl in the back row of the courtroom. I didn't dare turn around, but I wondered if she'd brought anything to do with her hands or if she was also scrambling to maintain her poker face.

"Did you look into the speed of the vehicle before the, uh, impact?" The prosecutor gave an apologetic glance in the mayor's direction, seated directly front and center.

Sheriff Robb shifted in his seat and nodded. "Yes, we had an engineer take a look and do some accident reconstruction. Them kids must've been doing at least seventy, maybe eighty miles an hour when they came around that turn from 93 into town, just reckless joy-riding with no thought at all to human safety and the rule of law."

"Objection," called Ben. "We don't need to hear the sheriff's theories about joy-riding and my client's state of mind. And, Your Honor, this is a bindover hearing. We're not here for the State to present its case in chief. We're here to decide if James Jenkins is to be tried as a minor or an adult. I object to this whole line of questioning about the mechanics of the accident or what happened on that day."

Good Ben, good, I thought, hopefully.

"I have to agree," said Judge Fraser. "Prosecutor, refocus."

"Well, sure," he agreed. "So let's talk about the defendant's state of mind, since his attorney brought it up. Sheriff, what have you observed about James Jenkins, both prior to his arrest, and while he's been a guest of the Jackson County Jail?"

The sheriff shifted a moment and glanced briefly in my direction before answering. "The boy's odd. Rides around town on his bicycle, big tall boy on a Sting-Ray. Seems to be mumbling to himself. And in his cell, he counts aloud and paces, over and over."

"He counts?"

"Yessir," said Sheriff Robb, "just starts counting from one while he's walking, then he writes down numbers and talks to himself. That's what he does." He looked thoughtfully at James, judgment written all over his face.

My hands clenched in my lap, and my eyes narrowed.

"And how old is the defendant?"

"Seventeen years old. Senior at the high school. Old enough to know right from wrong," Sheriff Robb added.

"Objection!" Ben cried, throwing up his hands.

Judge Fraser sighed. "Sheriff, please just answer the question before you."

"Okay, right, he goes to school," said the prosecutor, checking his notes. "We'll be hearing from the principal momentarily. Do you know if he has a job?"

"I don't believe so," said Sheriff Robb. "Like I said, I've often observed him on his bicycle when I was out on patrol, so seems he uses most of his free time that way. I don't know about any part-time job. I think his mom works to support the family. The father ran off."

James' hand paused over his writing, and I detected a slight tremor as he clutched his pencil. *Keep dividing James*, I silently screamed. Tune out this ignoramus, this bully with a badge.

"Did he cooperate with you when you investigated the car crash?"

"Yes, he was cooperative," the sheriff agreed.

"What did he say?"

"He really just confessed to the whole thing. Said he was behind the wheel and just couldn't stop in time."

Oh Lord. I didn't know James had confessed. I looked at Ben's back, wondering if this information was a surprise to him as well. This damn cop had tricked James, probably talked to him without even letting him know he had a right to have an attorney present, and James, trusting and naïve, brought up to respect authority, no idea what was going on, did what he thought was expected of him. Wasn't the sheriff at least required to contact me first, as the parent, before questioning my boy? My poker face was crumbling. I shifted my weight on the bench and tried to take deep breaths.

"Nothing further," said the prosecutor, returning to his seat.

Ben jumped up quickly for cross-examination. "Those were his words? He said he was behind the wheel?"

"Yep, he sure did say it exactly that way."

"Did you think it odd he would volunteer that he was behind the wheel, without you even asking him who was driving the truck? And that he would start out by saying he was behind the wheel?"

The sheriff frowned. "A confession's a confession. Didn't really read anything into the way he said it. And like I testified before, the boy's kind of odd."

Ben looked at his notes. "Yes, that's what you said before. But I'm wondering what that judgment is based upon. How many times before the date of the accident did you talk to James Jenkins?"

"Well, like I said, I always saw him out riding around on his Sting-Ray bicycle, talking to himself. But I didn't have a conversation with him."

"So that's never," said Ben. "You never had any reason to stop him, right?"

"Well, right..."

"No prior arrests, correct?"

"Correct."

"James Jenkins has never been arrested before for anything and has no record of any prior delinquent or unruly behavior." Ben paused and looked to Sheriff Robb. "Isn't that correct?"

"That's correct," Sheriff Robb agreed. "Boy's not been in trouble before."

I sat a bit taller in my seat.

"Right," said Ben. "The *boy's* not been in trouble before. And isn't it true that the boy spends quite a bit of time in his cell doing his homework?"

"Now I don't have time to check on him every minute, I have work to do," answered Sheriff Robb. "I can't really say how he's spending his time."

"So you can't really say if he's doing his schoolwork or spending his time pacing and counting, then can you?" Ben pressed.

"Well, I suppose not," the sheriff conceded. "Can't watch him every minute."

"A minor is locked up in an adult jail, in the same cell block as adult prisoners, but sure, you can't watch them every minute, can you?" Ben said.

"Was there a question in there?" the prosecutor called out.

"Counselor..." the judge started, looking irritated.

"I'll withdraw that last statement," said Ben. He shifted a moment and checked his notes. "So, just to recap, James Jenkins has never been in trouble before, he goes to school, does his homework and likes to ride his bicycle. Sounds like a hardened criminal, doesn't he?"

"Objection," called the prosecutor. "Argumentative."

"Mr. Atwater," said the judge with exasperation. "Sustained. You've made your point. Move on."

"Yes, Your Honor, thank you," said Ben. He cleared his throat. "Sheriff, at what point did you read my client his Miranda rights, and at what point did he waive his right to counsel before you started questioning him about the accident?"

"I didn't, Mr. Atwater. I didn't have a chance. The minute I arrived on the scene, I checked Ernie Cragen's vitals and radioed for an ambulance. Ernie was on the ground, broken glass everywhere. Unconscious. Blood on the pavement. I was focused on getting him some medical attention and trying to determine if I needed to start CPR before the ambulance arrived. Questioning the kids in the truck wasn't my immediate priority. But James ran up, all upset, and he wanted to make sure I knew he was behind the wheel, and he was sorry he couldn't stop in time. That was the first thing he said. No Miranda warning was given because no questioning had started. The information was volunteered."

The room hung in silence, even James had stopped his long division and stared at Sheriff Robb. Ben hovered a moment, then sat. "Nothing further," he said.

Candy Cragen turned and looked at me, sorrow in her eyes.

Chapter 14

James

Principal Wilkins testified next. Ben did a good job with Sheriff Robb, I thought, but Ben looked at me funny when he sat back down. He'd tried to talk to me a few days ago about what I told Sheriff Robb the day of the accident; guess he read it in the accident report. "James, why would you run up and say all that?" Ben had asked. He looked really frustrated when I hadn't answered him.

"Check out the grade I got on my pre-calculus exam," I'd said, pushing my A-plus under his nose, with the little gold star sticker Miss Ritchie had stuck to the paper, next to where she wrote *Very Good, James!* Miss Ritchie sure was a sweet teacher, and she really knew math.

"James, can we talk about your confession?" Ben had asked. "We really need to go over your statement in this police report."

"I hit him, but I didn't mean anything. I just want them to try me as a kid," I'd said. "I'm not eighteen yet." Ben had let it go and agreed to just work on our arguments for the bindover hearing.

Principal Wilkins walked up to the witness box, and I turned to catch Sarah Jane's eye. Seeing her here made me feel better.

After Principal Wilkins was sworn in, the prosecutor wasted no time asking him about how strange I am. Hearing him testify about me talking to myself by my locker, arguing with the gym teacher, how apparently, I bore everyone by talking all the time about the great bicycle tour, made the room go crimson red. Everyone was looking at me. Mom was looking at me. Caroline Cragen's mother, Mrs. Mayor, right there in the front row was looking at me. Their eyes bore into my back, like bullets, lethal and jet-black.

Back in third grade, our elementary school principal came and talked to the class, and I still remembered her teaching us the difference between "principle" and "principal," which sounded almost the same when you said them, but "principle" means an idea. "Princi*pal*, she had emphasized, "is the head of the school, and you can remember how to spell it 'cause the word "pal" is at the end. Just like your pal or buddy, I'm here to help you. So all you boys and girls remember that your princi*pal* is your pal." Well, anyway, she was the princi*pal* back in elementary school.

I'm pretty sure Princi*pal* Wilkins was not my pal.

They must all think I'm crazy. I didn't care. I went back to my long division, concentrating on getting it exactly correct.

It just didn't matter. I knew what I was doing.

Chapter 15

Jorie

I'm THE MOTHER, so everything was my fault. My son's pain was my pain. It hurt in my heart, in my gut, and tears stung the corner of my eyes as I listened to the school principal testify. We'd worked so hard at home to keep it light, keep it gentle, when James got in those moods or started going on and on about numbers or angles or his bicycling. Will and I had mastered tiptoeing around anything that might set James off, listening to him rant, not questioning. It was a little dance, a balancing act, *our* little dance. And we just didn't talk about it. How foolish I'd been to think it was just something we were seeing at home, and that no one at the school would see any of it.

Principal Wilkins sat on the stand, describing a strange young man with some odd behaviors, but had he ever really talked to my boy, talked to me, for that matter? I watched James working his division and wondered what he was thinking. I ached to gather him in my arms, to hug him and promise that everything was going to be all right. None of his funny ways justified putting him in an adult prison for an accident. I considered writing a note to Ben, share my ideas, but before I knew it, the prosecutor had finished with his questions and Ben was on his feet for the cross-examination.

"Now Principal Wilkins, has James ever gotten into any physical altercations with the staff at school? Ever become aggressive with a teacher, a secretary, the janitor?"

"Oh no," Principal Wilkins readily answered. "Nothing like that. Not at all."

"How about with other students? Any fistfights?"

"No, don't believe I've ever heard of James Jenkins getting into a fight with the other kids."

Ben nodded and picked up a stack of papers. "No fights, no suspensions, not even one detention where he had to stay after school for getting into trouble, right?"

Principal Wilkins said, "Don't believe so."

"Don't believe so, or don't know so? May I approach your honor?" Ben asked. "I've marked this as Defense Exhibit One. Mr. Wilkins, will you please take a look and identify what I've just handed you?"

"Assuming the prosecutor got to look at what you're presenting the witness, Mr. Atwater?" Judge Fraser peered over her glasses.

"I reviewed it, no objection at this time," the prosecutor said.

"All right, go ahead," the judge directed.

Ben handed Mr. Wilkins the paperwork; he shuffled through the packet a few moments and then nodded. "This is our student record for James Jenkins, a twelfth grader at Jackson High School."

"Can you take a look and tell me how many times James has ever been suspended, or gotten an after-school detention, or a warning, or any disciplinary action of any kind?"

"He hasn't."

"Never?" Ben pressed.

"Never," the principal agreed.

"Have you ever had occasion to telephone his mother, Mrs. Jenkins, to talk to her about her son's behavior?"

"Naw," said Mr. Wilkins. "Her boys don't get in trouble at school. Neither one of her kids. Hasn't been a need for any parent conferences about behavior."

"Has anyone at the school ever called Mrs. Jenkins to discuss anything concerning that you all were noticing about James?"

"Objection," interceded the prosecutor. "Not unless he somehow has personal knowledge about every phone call every school employee makes."

"I'll rephrase," said Ben. "Have you ever personally called Mrs. Jenkins to discuss James, or asked your secretary to set up a meeting?"

"I have not."

"Okay," said Ben, seeming to gather momentum. "Let's talk about attendance. I'll direct you to page six of Defense Exhibit One." He leaned over the witness box as Principal Wilkins shuffled through the paperwork. "Right there," Ben pointed. "Would you please read for the Court how many absences or tardies James Jenkins has had this school year?"

"No tardies. Fourteen days of absence."

"Now, those absences didn't start until March 8, the day after the accident, when James was put in the county jail. Isn't that right?" Ben asked.

"That's correct," said the principal.

"And have those fourteen days of missed school been excused or unexcused absences?"

Principal Wilkins blinked. "Well, his mother calls the attendance secretary every day to call him off, so in that sense, I suppose excused. Our policy allows for excused absences for illness, of course, doctor or dentist appointments, bereavement leave, or family vacations in limited circumstances. The policy doesn't really cover, um..." he searched for the correct word. "Incarceration." He looked over at James.

"So you can verify from what I'm showing you, Defense Exhibit Two, Student Policy and Procedure Handbook, that the attendance policy does not allow for excused absences due to the incarceration of the student, correct?" Ben spoke rapidly now, building.

"Correct, I don't need to read it. That wouldn't be listed as a reason."

Ben stopped and looked at Mr. Wilkins pointedly. "*Why* is it not listed? Could it be that imprisonment of a school child is a very rare event?"

Mr. Wilkins nodded. "Right, it is a very rare event, and if we get a serious juvenile delinquency matter, typically such a child might be placed in the detention of the State of Ohio, in one of their youth facilities like the one up by Chillicothe, and the youth would be provided educational services in that facility."

"As opposed to being locked up in the same hallway with adult offenders in the adult county jail," Ben said.

"Objection," said the prosecutor.

"Sustained," said the judge.

"Withdrawn," said Ben.

Ben shifted, looked to James seated next to him and put his hand on James' shoulder, protectively. James looked up from his math, sandy hair combed to the side, his adolescent stubble shaved neatly from his smooth, young face. Ben and James together looked toward the witness. "Has this young man been keeping up with his assignments, Principal Wilkins, over these last fourteen days, when he's been unable to attend Jackson High School?"

"Yes, his mother picks up his assignments every day and drops off the completed work."

"And would you please now tell us how James Jenkins is performing academically, even under such trying circumstances where he cannot be present in the classroom?"

I leaned forward in my seat, heart clutching in my throat. I'd tried not to be too nosy going through the books and assignments I'd ferried back and forth, but the other day on his precalculus work I'd caught sight of the gold star and A-plus. *Please, please,* I silently begged. Let his other work, not just the math work, be just as good.

"Academically, he does very well. In fact, his grades are up even higher over the past few weeks."

There was a murmur of surprise from the courtroom, whispers and exclamations over the interesting revelation of a teenager getting better grades in the county jail than when he was attending the brick and mortar school in person every day.

But Ben wasn't done yet. "He does very well. What does that mean? *How* well does James Jenkins perform academically?"

Principal Wilkins paused and gazed at James, a mixture of curiosity and admiration. "He's going to be the valedictorian of his class."

Small gasps erupted from the crowd.

"At least if you go just by grade point average," Principal Wilkins scrambled to add. "We're going to have to figure out what to do about letting him walk at the ceremony where the kids receive their diplomas... cap and gown, all that... usually the valedictorian gives a speech at commencement. Never had to figure out this type of situation before." Principal Wilkins reddened and looked flustered. The courtroom was full of excited chatter, no one even bothering to keep their voices down.

"Order," Judge Fraser admonished the gallery.

Ben waved the school Policy and Procedure handbook high over his head with both arms and flapped the booklet theatrically. "Not spelled out in here either, is it, Mr. Wilkins? Whether you let an incarcerated minor give his valedictorian commencement speech?"

"Order!" Judge Fraser cried.

James turned in his seat, and I watched, thinking he was looking again for that Sarah Jane, but no, it was *me* James sought out with his eyes. And despite everything going on around us, everything he had to lose, we had our little mother-son moment. He flashed a humble smile, and I beamed back, proud, so very proud of my son. Top of his class.

Valedictorian!

Keep it gentle.

Chapter 16

Will

SCHOOL WAS NEVER FUN, not since James' arrest, but today was the worst. I'd seen the headline on the front page of the newspaper this morning, before Mom quickly set a dish rag over it at breakfast to try to cover it up. "Controversy over Local Valedictorian Pick," it had read, noting all the parents were "in an uproar" over allowing the boy "accused of mowing down the mayor's husband" to garnish this "top academic accolade." When Mom was in the bathroom finishing getting ready, I dug it out and quickly read the rest. Some of our teachers were quoted. They thought "good moral character and behavior" should be "just as important as academic performance." So now I knew exactly what those teachers thought of James and of me too, I guess.

Mom had sounded so excited, so proud of James finishing top of his class, when she and Ben had talked about the hearing last night, while I was in my room doing homework. "Hard work, doing well in school—it's all going to pay off—that judge is going to see what a good boy he is," she'd kept saying.

Ben had sounded more cautious. "A positive step for sure, Jorie, and things went very well for us today. But the hearing's not done yet. Let's just take it day by day."

But Mom hadn't been listening to him. "We probably don't even need that psychologist to testify after all, do we, now that the judge knows James is going to be his high school valedictorian? Oh my," she'd paused. "Valedictorian! My parents, Granny, they'd all be so proud. If only they were still here to see it."

"Jorie..." I heard Ben trying to break in.

"*And*," Mom had gone on. "Never got in trouble a day at school! How many other kids can they say that about? Heck, I cut Shirley Dawson's hair, and she's always talking about her son getting caught smoking cigarettes, getting caught cheating on some exam, staying after school."

I'd heard their footsteps pacing in our kitchen, and was pretty sure I'd heard Ben pouring a shot of whisky, too. "Bindover hearing continues all day tomorrow," he'd muttered. "More witnesses to testify, thing ain't over yet. You can't go assuming anything..."

"Who else needs to testify?" Mom had asked. "We did so well today."

"Jorie, the prosecutor gets to call witnesses too, you know. And we've got the psychologist. We need that testimony after the court heard the sheriff and the principal testify about the odd behaviors they've observed. We can't start cutting corners now."

And today, at school, despite Mom's bright talk from last night, a feeling of dread chewed in my stomach. I didn't talk to anyone and kept my head down, especially whenever I felt the eyes of a teacher on me. I worried over what was happening at the courthouse and counted the minutes until the bell sounded.

Mom wasn't letting me go to the court hearings, but when I biked out of town, up into the hills, I could usually find Sarah Jane on the trail near her trailer, and she would tell me everything that happened in court.

From what I could see, it was just Sarah Jane and her father living up there. They had the dog, a fire pit, and a charcoal grill. Like us, no car. She walked down the trail in the mornings to catch the bus to school. I wasn't sure if her dad worked, where he worked, how he got to work, or how they got to town, unless maybe they caught a ride with the McKowan's, who lived further down the hill, closer to the road. I was careful to avoid running into her father, especially after that day I'd heard him yelling and saw Sarah Jane crying with the bruised face. If I caught a glimpse of him, I accelerated and stood, pumping the pedals hard until I'd passed their clearing. My thighs burned during these climbs and the muscles were getting harder, larger. Even my triceps seemed bigger, and my arms felt stronger from muscling the bike through the woods.

If I climbed past their trailer, I could go way up the hill, really high, above the tracks and the creek bed. But for the dense brush, there's probably a view where you could see all the way back to town. Eventually I discovered where the trail just ends, giving way to thick forest. No way to get the bike through that part. That day, I turned and flew back down, wind blowing my hair, crouching to absorb the bumps, my eyes on the ground, giving me a split second to react to what came next.

Today, on my freefall descent, I caught a blur of color on the trail up ahead and braked hard, screeching to where Sarah Jane stood partially hidden behind a thick tree trunk.

"Hey," I said, brushing sweat off my face and catching my breath as the bike halted a few feet from her. I swung my leg over the banana seat and set the kickstand.

"Hey," she said. We moved to sit on a downed tree. "Court was good yesterday," said Sarah Jane quietly, keeping one eye toward her trailer. "James is going to finish at the top of our class. Everyone was really surprised."

"Well, they're not happy about it. I saw the paper this morning. Mom tried to hide it from me, but I read it anyway. They don't think a kid in jail should be valedictorian."

99

"But he earned it," Sarah Jane said. "That's so unfair. What's wrong with people, anyway?"

I fiddled with a knot in the bark of the rotting wood, rubbing it with my palm. Bitterness soured my stomach. Everything used to be so normal, Mom walking to her beauty salon, cooking supper, the guys coming over for band practice, going for frozen custard at the Shake Shoppe, hoping for a smile or hello from Caroline Cragen in the hallway at school. Even with James' weirdness, things were mostly normal. Now everyone at school, everyone in the whole town, had an opinion about us. My drum set sat quiet, and I didn't feel like touching it. The guys weren't allowed to hang out with me. Mom's worried and upset, and Ben was over all the time, which I kind of liked and kind of didn't. It was kind of cool at first, but he's just an intruder. Mom acts weird around him. Her voice sounds different, even when they talk about serious stuff about James and the trial. She laughs too much. Why laugh at something that's not even funny?

"Ya, he earned being the valedictorian, but all people see now is that he's in jail, so it doesn't matter," I said.

Sarah Jane put her head in her hands. "I'm sorry. James shouldn't be in there. He doesn't deserve this."

"It's not your fault."

She looked at the ground.

"I heard Mom and Ben talking last night; that psychologist is still going to testify."

"Yes," Sarah Jane replied slowly, "I know. James was pretty upset after meeting with her. I guess she asked a lot of questions about your dad." She looked over at me directly. "She was asking James where he is, why he thinks he doesn't visit you guys. And she was asking James what he remembers from when your dad lived with you."

Now it was my turn to look at the ground. I'd been pretty little when we'd moved out. Fuzzy images sometimes floated to the surface of my memory. Angry voices. Doors slamming. Mom sitting on the bathroom floor in her nightgown, crying. "Pull the covers up over your ears," James would say as we hid together, always protecting me

100

when I'd run to jump in bed with him. "Don't listen to the noises, just think about colors," James would tell me. "Or numbers. Numbers are even better." Then he'd start counting, and sometimes we'd count together, whispering in the dark. Usually by the time we got up over fifty things were quieter, and once we got up over one hundred, we could just drift off to sleep.

Did that stuff even happen? Or was it all something I'd dreamed? I didn't want to think about it, or talk about it, with anyone.

"I don't really remember anything about my dad. I was too little."

She watched me carefully, but seemed to accept this. "So, is that what you told the psychologist?"

"Yep."

"I think James remembers a little more than you; he was older when you guys and your mom moved out. He's told me a bit about what he—"

I cut her off. "Dad took the car. That's really the main thing. So we have to walk everywhere. My mom has to carry all the groceries home. Even in the winter. Once she slipped on the ice and sprained her elbow and busted up her knee. Once I had to walk with her to the doctor when I had strep throat. I had a fever." I realized I was shaking with anger, not even sure where it was all coming from. "Mom has to bum rides from our neighbor. We're the only family I know who doesn't even have a car," I finished, only realizing my mistake as I looked at Sarah Jane's thoughtful face.

"I mean the only family living in town with no car," I hastily added. Of course, we're not the only family I knew without a car.

"Most of the townies have cars," she agreed kindly. "It is hard taking the bus and bumming rides."

In that moment, it hit me that Sarah Jane was a grownup. She was eighteen, after all, and listened to my fourteen-year-old rant without making me feel like a stupid kid. I saw why James liked her. I wondered if this was what it must feel like to have a big sister to talk to.

"What's the hardest part for you, Sarah Jane, living up here in the hills, without a car?" I ventured.

She gazed up through the trees, sun flickering through the canopy of budding springtime greenery and violet blooms of the redbud. A blue jay swooped over to the next tree and clucked disapprovingly. She glanced back over to the trailer.

"Not being able to escape," she whispered.

Chapter 17

James

THIS MORNING I picked over the lumpy porridge, which I usually kind of liked. My collared shirt, tie, and dress pants hung neatly on the hanger in my cell. Mom took everything home last night after yesterday's hearing, washed it, and brought it back before nine o'clock, so we'd be ready for court again today. The light from the hallway flickered eerie fluorescent, which felt silvery and smelled like smoke burning off an electrical fire. No morning sunshine in here. Day and night were starting to blend together.

I set the bowl of porridge on the desk, unable to eat anymore.

Looking at my clothes from home kind of hurt, made me miss home. The cool gray of the cell was getting less and less calming. Way too still in here. I missed flying around town on my bike. I missed the feel of the wind. So weird that Sarah Jane said Will was riding all the time now. Bicycling magazines Mom brought from home lay next to my textbooks, and I couldn't help but think about how the great bicycle tour was only a month away. In the back of my mind there had been fantasies about somehow getting along the route to watch them go by, to cheer at the draft lines pacing within centimeters of each other's wheels, blocking wind to create a collective machine of speed. Even crazier was the secret daydream that, somehow, I might ride it, too. To ride two hundred miles in two days! I was pretty sure I'd be the first person in town to ever do anything like that.

What a joke. First of all, I didn't have the right kind of bike. Second, even if I did, how would I even get up to Columbus to the start of the ride? Third, I was in jail. I wasn't going anywhere. The whole thing would happen without me, while I sat in this too-quiet, too-still, too-small space, by myself, missing everything.

I shoved the books onto the floor and jumped up to kick over my metal chair.

From down the hall, Mr. Perkins grumbled to "shut-the-hell-up."

"Sorry," I called.

Clouds in my mind churned black, making my hands shake. "One, two, three," I whispered as I started pacing. As the numbers climbed, the danger passed. Numbers could do this. The black faded back to cool gray. I needed to get dressed, get ready. Today, that psychologist was going to testify. I had to be ready.

Fifteen minutes went by, and I was dressed and calm when Sheriff Robb came down the hall to unlock the cell.

"Ready for your court hearing, James?" he said, his voice loud and echoing down the hallway, as if he was giving me something by making conversation.

I nodded, but said nothing. He liked to swagger in that uniform, liked to make people around him cower.

He shrugged. "Come on, then." We walked in silence upstairs to the courtroom, and I found my seat next to Ben.

"James, how are you doing this morning?" Ben greeted me.

"Okay, I guess." I glanced over to where the prosecutor shuffled papers and made a few notes.

"Now remember we talked about how today might be difficult, how it might be hard to listen to Dr. Davis talk about the evaluation, right?" said Ben. "You don't have to do anything today. No one is going to call on you to speak at today's hearing. And there's no reason to turn around to look at the people seated behind you. If you hear something upsetting, just keep your face calm and file it away in your head to go over later. If you have a question, write it on the legal pad for me to read. Other than that, just calm listening, face forward, is all you do today. Got it, James?"

"Got it, Ben," I agreed.

He slid an extra legal pad in front of me with a pen. The parallel blue lines on the yellow paper were orderly, somehow making me think of vanilla and that clean smell. Once when Mom was baking, we'd joked about the vanilla extract as she put a teaspoon in the cookie batter. How can something smell so wonderful but taste so bitter, I'd wondered. Kinda like the feel of the rough sandpaper tongue of a kitten. The image of a soft fluffy kitten hung baby blue, which then made me think of Sarah Jane. I hoped she'd be in the courtroom, even though she shouldn't be missing school to come to these hearings. It occurred to me I hadn't asked her if she was doing her assignments anyway, the way Mom was bringing my books so I could keep up. It's important that we both graduate, I knew that, but even more important for Sarah Jane to graduate. She had to find herself a way down the hill from that trailer. Maybe with her high school diploma, she could get a job in town.

I twitched, aching to turn to scan the benches to see if she was back there, but Ben was stern beside me and cleared his throat pointedly as he watched me fidget out of the corner of his eye. And then the bailiff entered and called on everyone to rise for the judge.

Judge Fraser was all business, quickly telling everyone to be seated. "And we are ready now for the next witness," she said. "I understand Dr. Davis is listed on the pretrial statement for both the prosecution and the defense?"

"Both sides are calling this witness, Your Honor," said the prosecutor.

"Who wishes to question first?" asked the judge.

Ben jumped in. "Mr. Dean can question first, your Honor. We'll cross examine after the State has finished their questions."

They all seemed satisfied with this. I thought about how strategy plays into the game of the trial. Like a chess game. Ben was smart to let the other side make their move first, I thought.

* * *

Dr. Davis had been pretty friendly and nice when I'd met with her. Her office was filled with books, black and white photographs, and interesting things to fumble around with your hands: a Rubik's cube, an hourglass filled with neon green sand, stuffed animals. She'd let me start the metronome on her shelf ticking, and I sped it up, then slowed it down until we had just the right tempo. Click, click, click. The switch of the click and the space between the clicks was just right, and it kept the beat for the whole time she interviewed me. Before the interview though, there was a written questionnaire, kind of like a test, I guess. The questions were more like statements: "Sometimes when I'm really angry, I can't remember later what I said or did." Then you had to check a box: Always, Most of the time, Occasionally, Rarely, Never.

"I wish I was in the military," was another question. Then again, you had to check: Agree, Disagree.

"Meeting new people makes me nervous." Check box: Always, Most of the time, Occasionally, Rarely, Never.

I had sat with my pencil and went through the questions quickly, just telling the truth like Mom always said. Whoever wrote up this test sure was curious about the workings of the mind. Seemed like some of them were just looking for different ways to ask the same question, over and over again. Was there a science to it? I searched for a pattern, an equation, but came up with nothing.

It wasn't hard. At least, until I got to this question: "I have a secret I'll never tell." Check box: True, False.

My pencil hovered, and I froze. Didn't everyone have secrets? Which secrets were they referring to? Old secrets? New secrets? My own secrets or ones kept for someone else? If I checked True, even if I didn't tell what the secret was, I'd be letting on there was a secret. Which seemed like a betrayal to the whole concept of keeping a secret. And if I checked False, I'd be fibbing, which I knew was wrong. This was some kind of trick question. These psychologists were sneaky, after all. With shaking hands, I checked "False," and started off my interview with Dr. Davis feeling rattled and off center. Like weighted balls tilting a fulcrum too far left. Was she going to ask me about secrets?

She didn't. She asked me to talk about my family, to start with drawing a picture of us. I drew Mom, Will, myself. I put our white house with the black shutters in the background with my red Sting-Ray on the porch. Very cleverly, I smudged the colored pencil lines to show the house in motion, shaking from the train. She asked about the earliest memory I could recall from when I was really little. We talked about the counting, about math. Then I told her all about the great bicycle tour, TOSRV. She asked about friends, and I told her some stories about the letters I was writing to the bicycle club people in Columbus. The address was listed in the back of one of my bicycling magazines. Well, a post office box is really all it was.

* * *

Dr. Davis raised her right hand and the judge swore her in.

"Good morning. Please state and spell your name for the record," the prosecutor said.

"Dr. Gwendolyn Davis, D-A-V-I-S," she replied with a smart nod, folding her hands in front of her. Dr. Davis looked very professional in her suit with a white blouse, tied at the collar, and heels. Glasses perched on her nose and a gold watch sparkled from her wrist. I felt proud of her, somehow. She'd spent a lot of time with me, with Mom, with Will, even. She listened carefully, really listened, saw me with her ears, listened with her eyes. Somehow, I trusted her.

Prosecutor Dean asked her questions about the dates she interviewed me, how many times she met with me, her interview with

Mom and Will, the test she administered. I learned the test was called the MMPI, which stood for the Minnesota Multi-Phasic Personality Inventory. And I learned the test is designed to weed out false responses, deceptiveness.

"Results were mostly valid," Dr. Davis said. "It's expected that people will always try to present themselves in a more favorable light and deny having what they may perceive as character flaws. Really, these are not flaws, but are common human traits, things we all do."

"Can you give us an example?" asked the prosecutor.

"Such as having the test-taker rate as True or False the statement 'I never lie.' Of course, we all lie. It's human nature to lie. You've heard the phrase 'little white lies.' These are innocuous little fibs we all dabble in to present ourselves in a more favorable light. Or, we presume to decide what others need to know or don't need to know, parse and dole out information accordingly. Lies of omission. We tell ourselves these decisions are necessary to protect those we love, but really, the act of withholding information is purposeful, premeditated, condescending, even. It denies your loved one their own self-determination, or gives them a false reality. A decision is only as good as the information it's based upon."

Judge Fraser nodded her head thoughtfully as she looked down at her notes. Her job was to decide things. This struck me as a heavy, heavy thing, and smelled of licorice. Licorice, black and tangy, hints of smoky currant and wood. *Stay focused,* I told myself. *Keep listening.*

"So it's expected that people will answer that they never lie?" asked Prosecutor Dean.

"Actually, it's expected that about half will answer that they do lie, at least if they are being honest. If they deny ever lying, the results do become more suspect. But if they deny ever lying, other questions built into the test will double check that to measure validity. Like I said, it's not uncommon to try to present oneself more favorably, but repeatedly denying basic human traits will lead to more questionable results."

"And how did James Jenkins answer the questions designed to measure validity?"

"As I said earlier, his results were mostly valid," she said and paused, cocking her head.

"*Mostly* valid?" asked the prosecutor, "Please explain."

Dr. Davis nodded. "James actually took the test very honestly, extremely honestly, I would say. He denied that he never lies. His answers suggested a very concrete, literal, transparent thought process."

"Very concrete..." Prosecutor Dean checked something off on his legal pad. I pictured a concrete wall like the retaining wall on the side of the high school, behind the baseball field. Sometimes I rode my bike past there. It was gray, of course, which most concrete would be. I pictured myself, concrete, holding all that earth in place. I sat up taller in my seat, feeling strong and mighty.

"So, he's kind of thick, hah."

"Objection," interjected Ben. "Mischaracterization of the witness's testimony. She said he was concrete, not that he was thick. Whatever 'thick' means," Ben added, scowling toward the prosecutor.

"Sustained," said the judge.

"I'll rephrase," said the prosecutor. "Does that mean he has intellectual delays? Or that he's slow to process things?"

"Why no, not at all." Dr. Davis looked startled and blinked. "In fact, his IQ score was very, very high. James is a highly intelligent young man. But it seems he can miss social cues; he's a logical thinker, and he does best when he discerns patterns in his environment and in those around him. Illogical behaviors, emotional reactions, nuances..." She seemed to search for the right words, "throw off his worldview. Injustice, in particular, upsets him quite a bit," she added.

"So, emotional nuances are difficult for him?" asked the prosecutor.

"Yes," she nodded. "James gravitates to math, equations, predictability."

"Four teenagers in the cab of a pickup truck, three boys and a girl, all between the ages of seventeen and twenty years old, talking, maybe a couple of people talking at once, maybe playing the radio loudly, trying to impress each other, trying to be cool." The prosecutor had his hands up, index finger to index finger, thumb to thumb, making a viewfinder. "Maybe the girl is even someone James has a crush on. Such a scene could be perceived as chaotic, right?"

"Yes, could be."

The prosecutor went on. "And that would present an emotionally charged social situation for James, would it not?"

"It likely would," Dr. Davis agreed. "James might feel challenged to navigate that type of social situation."

"And for a young man who likes a predictable environment, driving a truck without a license, without ever having had any driver's education training, no rudimentary knowledge of the rules of the road, traffic rules we all follow and expect other drivers to follow, all the while with other teenagers and the girl you're trying to impress crowded in the truck with you, might cause such a young man to panic a bit, right?"

"Objection, leading the witness," said Ben. "And it calls for speculation."

I pictured Judge Fraser in a black-and-white striped umpire outfit, hovering over the catcher behind home plate. *Ball! Strike! You're out!*

"Overruled. You can answer the question, doctor," said Judge Fraser.

"It might cause him to panic," Dr. Davis agreed.

"Maybe cause him to drive too fast?" Prosecutor Dean seemed to swell, his brown hair pluming into a mane, his hands morphing into huge paws, until he looked like a lioness ready to pounce on a doomed wildebeest.

"Your Honor, the prosecutor is asking the witness to speculate," Ben called out.

"Yes, agreed. We will not have speculation. You can answer the question, but only if you know the answer," directed the judge. "If you don't know, you don't know."

Dr. Davis looked at me, almost apologetically. "Well, I *do* know. I know because he told me. James *told* me he was speeding."

The hunter made the kill. But I met Dr. Davis' eyes, sending her warm messages of forgiveness. She didn't need to feel bad about repeating what I had told her about speeding. She was being honest, exactly as she should be.

Ben stood up. "Your Honor, once again, the State is veering into the events surrounding the accident. May I remind the Court that this is a bindover hearing, to determine if this young boy is to be tried as a juvenile or an adult."

"I can assure you there's no need to remind the Court of the purpose of today's hearing," the judge sighed, seeming irritated with both attorneys. "Move on, prosecutor."

The prosecutor nodded. "Of course, Your Honor. Thank you." He shuffled his notes a moment. "Let's talk about some of the behaviors the Court has heard about with James. Riding his bicycle around town, mumbling to himself. Pacing and counting in his jail cell. Talking to himself at school. Talking excessively about some bicycle tour." He pulled his reading glasses off as he looked up from his notes. "Did you evaluate these behaviors, Dr. Davis?"

"Yes, I did. James does tend to exhibit some compulsive behaviors, which can be a way to exert some control over one's environment, a relief from anxiety, a way to establish order, predictability."

"And riding around on his bike by himself?"

"Even if he's obsessing about this hobby a bit, I see the cycling as a positive in James' life," said Dr. Davis. "Sometimes adolescents don't have the emotional maturity to keep up with their level of brain functioning and they tend to overthink things. The bicycling—any exercise, really—is a healthy outlet. I *would* like to see him do it on a more social basis, however. But apparently, he has reached out to some cycling clubs in the Columbus area," she added. "It could just be that there isn't a community in this area of bicycling enthusiasts for James to link in to."

"Is mumbling to oneself considered *normal?*" asked the prosecutor.

I felt Ben flinch next to me, itching to object again. But Dr. Davis smoothly skated right over the ice. "I don't believe *normal* is a term of art," she gently countered. "Or even something we should all strive for. Geniuses, artists, musical prodigies, for example, can exhibit behaviors that others might not consider normal. So I guess I don't understand the question."

"Well, you're not saying James Jenkins is a child prodigy, are you?"

"No, I'm not saying that. He's highly intelligent, and he's particularly gifted in math."

"But his behaviors are compulsive. Do they demonstrate someone trying to create order out of chaos, say, perhaps, a chaotic home environment?" asked the prosecutor.

"From my collateral interviews with the family members, it appears that the home environment is not chaotic. In fact, James' mother inspires his love of numbers and math, and seems to have mentored both of her sons in their familiarity and command of equations, geometry, algebra."

"Well then what, in your opinion, spurs the compulsive behaviors?"

Dr. Davis put her hands on the edge of the railing and sat up tall, gathering herself into the moment. "Trauma."

"Trauma?" asked the prosecutor.

"Trauma from early childhood, in my opinion," responded Dr. Davis.

Prosecutor Dean didn't seem to like this answer. He pivoted like an acrobat on a high wire at the circus. I pictured a black top hat on his head and a baton in his hand. "A seventeen-year-old young man, a *smart* young man, so smart in fact that he's under consideration to be valedictorian of his senior class, has the intellectual wherewithal to make decisions about his conduct, correct?" said the prosecutor quickly.

"He has the intellect, yes," agreed Dr. Davis. She looked a little deflated that she hadn't had a chance to talk more about trauma.

"Does he know the difference between right and wrong?" asked the prosecutor.

"He does."

"Is he able to reason out likely outcomes from his actions?"

"Yes, he has the intellect and judgment to do that," Dr. Davis said.

"Geometry, math, physics..." Prosecutor Dean went on, "and a good command of bicycling, bicycle racing, bicycle touring. Would a highly intelligent young man who is gifted, even obsessive about these subjects, understand the physics of speed, stopping distance, force upon impact..."

A crime of velocity, I thought. I'm on trial for a crime of velocity. This felt very red, bright candy apple red. I was a superhero with a red cape, nimble and stealthy. But Caroline Cragen's father, lying on the ground, was also bleeding red. My hands started shaking. I couldn't handle this red, damnit. Red was very, very bad. Sharp. Smelled like fish.

Prime numbers, I told myself. They're all so unique, each one of them special. I started writing them on my legal pad: 2, 3, 5, 7, 11, 13...

Ben was objecting again, but the prosecutor withdrew the question and said he had no further questions. I wasn't sure if the testimony went well for me or not. A break would be nice. I really wanted to turn around and look for Mom, look for Sarah Jane, but the hearing kept going.

It was Ben's turn now to ask Dr. Davis questions. Ben stood up, buttoning the top button of his jacket. "So, Dr. Davis, you mentioned James has a compulsive quest for order in his environment, equations that add up. He's a concrete thinker. Would you agree this means James is not creative, not inclined to make up stories and lie?"

Dr. Davis looked thoughtful. "James is very honest, I believe. But I would not agree that he is not creative. My impression is that James has a condition known as synesthesia."

Ben looked interested, and actually, the judge looked pretty interested, too.

"What is synesthesia?" asked Ben, after he'd had Dr. Davis spell s-y-n-e-s-t-h-e-s-i-a, to make sure the court reporter had it down correctly.

"Confusion between the five senses: sight, sound, taste, touch, smell. Persons with synesthesia may see numbers as colors, may attribute smells to feelings, may feel they are hearing words they are reading."

Five?!? I stopped writing my prime numbers, shocked. Sight, sound, taste, touch, smell? This didn't sound right to me. What about gravity? I worked against it climbing hills on my bike. The drag when the wind came right at me, holding me back? The feeling that I knew what my hands were doing, what my feet were doing, where they were, even if I closed my eyes, which you probably shouldn't do when you're riding a bike. The feel of the speed the bike was moving, the feel of the motion of my feet circling to turn the pedals? And what about balance? Leaning into turns, staying upright on two wheels. And the feel of whatever it was inside me, that force inside, the invisible inertia pushing against all that to make the bike go? There were so many more senses than five. Did other people only have five? I scoffed, not even realizing that I'd started muttering "five, five, five," until Ben shot me a sharp warning look to be quiet.

"Is synesthesia a mental illness?" asked Ben.

"No, it's a product of imagination, a heightened or perhaps confused sensory response. Just the brain blending senses and assigning unique qualities to feelings, people, objects."

"How does synesthesia manifest with James?" asked Ben.

"He assigns colors to people. He associates colors with feelings, for example, orange with the warmth of home, cooking smells. He is highly aware of sensory images and feelings in his environment. Like the vibration of the train that passes by his house. Ideas can have sounds for James. He *feels* numbers. He *sees* sounds, *hears* smells. At least in his mind."

The courtroom had gone really, really quiet. I didn't have to turn around to know that it was chalk white back there.

"Is this a form of psychosis?" Ben asked.

"Putting labels on children is not an approach I subscribe to," said Dr. Davis. "James is not out of touch with reality, but he takes cues from his environment and spins beyond what all of us might be aware of. At times, he goes into free-form associations that might lead to unexpected places."

Ben seemed unsure of these answers. I didn't think he could tell if these answers helped our side or not.

"So... highly imaginative?" he struggled.

"Yes," Dr. Davis nodded. "Highly intelligent, honest, concrete. And yet imaginative."

"Almost sounds like a contradiction?" said Ben. He wiped sweat from his brow.

"James is certainly a very interesting young man, an enigma of sorts. There's more than meets the eye with him."

Enigma. Now that was an interesting word. I turned this over in my head a moment, getting the feel for it. In ninth grade biology class, we looked at amoebas under the microscope. One cell that can divide all on its own. Asexual reproduction, the teacher said. Is an enigma like an amoeba? I pondered this a moment, then screeched to a chilling halt. Was Dr. Davis hinting about the secrets question? Is *that* what she meant when she said enigma? I swallowed down my panic. Back to the prime numbers.

Ben shifted, and I felt him trying to think out the next question. "You said emotional nuances, social situations might be confusing to James. Does that mean he lacks people skills, empathy?"

"Well, actually, despite his love of order and predictability, and the precision of numerical equations, I found James has a very high degree of empathy. James is highly loyal to the ones that he loves. His family. Or maybe others who are close to him. James wants to protect the ones that he loves from harm, and he feels their pain, their fear, very vividly, and very sympathetically."

Ben perked up, understanding now where he wanted to go with his questioning. "Empathy. A sign of emotional maturity, responsibility. Yes?"

"Yes."

"So the mumbling, the counting, the obsession with the bicycling... it's just eccentric, right? James is picturing emotions, feeling others' pain, wanting to protect them. Are these admirable traits?"

"Certainly, empathy and wanting to protect others from harm are admirable traits."

"Where do you think those traits in James came from?"

"Mr. Atwater, I'll tell you the same thing I told the prosecutor. It's trauma. It comes from trauma."

Ben seemed unsure again. He didn't really want to ask the next question, but I knew he felt like he had to.

"What kind of trauma?"

Dr. Davis looked very serious. "From his early childhood. James has memories of his parents fighting. Before his mother moved out and divorced his father, James was exposed to arguments."

I paused, writing the prime numbers and just held very, very still.

"Verbal arguments?" asked Ben.

I held my breath, hoarding it for my own lungs, refusing to release it into the room. *My* air. I will not share.

"Verbal... and physical. James recalls his father hitting his mother. James was very young, but was highly distressed he couldn't protect his mother and little brother. Chaos, violence in his environment, that was set off seemingly arbitrarily. There was no predictability. James retreated into numbers as a way to self-soothe, and this affinity was reinforced by his mother's early lessons in math."

Ben glanced back at my mother. I could feel how nervous he was. Had I been wrong to tell Dr. Davis about this?

Ben asked, "Could James be remembering all that wrong?"

"Well, he could be, he was very young. But I verified that domestic violence did take place between his parents."

"How did you verify James' memories?"

"I interviewed his mother. She glossed over some of it. She's a survivor, and she displayed strength in removing herself and her young sons from that situation. And I verified the memories with James' father. After you were able to locate the father, Mr. Atwater, and put me in touch with him, Mr. Garth Jenkins came to my office to meet. I interviewed him. He minimized; he didn't take responsibility for his actions. But he acknowledged the violence happened."

I braced for impact as the screech of the train's brakes pierced and screamed, a long, blood-curdling scream, shattering the stagnant afternoon, while the bell at the crossing rang frantically, helplessly, ding, ding, ding, over and over, but it was too late, too late to stop, too late for any warning, we were past the point, past where brakes work. The smack of a hand on skin, a cruel crack, the dark purple of Sarah Jane's black eye, the thud as Caroline Cragen's father hit the windshield of the McKowan's truck. The rubbery, watery melting of my kneecaps, unable to support me any longer.

I was falling, falling.

I have a secret I'll never tell.

True.

Chapter 18

Jorie

As soon as the judge called recess, I gave Ben a quick sharp look with a jerk of my head toward the hallway. He nodded grimly, signaling me to wait one minute until the sheriff had led James out of the courtroom. Ben patted James tentatively on the shoulder, and I saw him whisper a few words in his ear, but James seemed a million miles away. I knew there was no talking to James right now. He'd retreated into his own world, probably sunk into his numbers and equations. Probably for the best right now.

I paced in the hallway, my head exploding.

"Marjorie..." said Ben when he joined me in the hallway.

Ben glanced toward the spectators spilling out of the main courtroom doors. He grabbed my hand and pulled me into a conference room.

"You, you, *contacted* my ex-husband?" I sputtered.

Ben closed the door. "Jorie. Sit down. Breathe."

He motioned toward the conference table and pulled out a chair, but I refused, glowering, hands on my hips. My heart pounded in my ears.

Ben shrugged, but spoke seriously. "Yes, I contacted Garth. I had to. Dr. Davis needed to talk to all the family members to make a complete evaluation. She needed to interview both parents. I had my paralegal do a little skip-tracing, and we tracked him down."

"Without my permission?" My hands shook and my voice seethed.

"You hired me to defend your son. To save his life. To save him from years in prison. Your son is charged with vehicular homicide and could be tried as an adult. I don't have to tell you what's at stake here."

"You had no right." I sank into the chair, tears clouding in my eyes. "You should have asked me first. You don't know how this is going to affect me, affect my boys. Our safety." I wiped my eyes, then whispered fiercely: "I left him for good reason, you know."

"I'm sorry, Jorie." Ben put his hand on my arm, and did truly seem sorry. "But no, I *don't* know, because you didn't tell me. When you hired me, I asked you to be honest with me. So I can do my job. To help your son."

I looked away.

"You told me you left him when the boys were young, that you represented yourself in the divorce, that you waived child support payments. But Jorie," He stopped a moment, then his voice was gentler. "You didn't tell me about any violence in the marriage."

Ben pitied me, I could feel it, and it just made me angrier. "Because none of that matters," I hissed. "It happened *years* ago. I did what I had to do to get us out, and I'm proud of how I've raised my boys. We moved on, and we don't look back. And just when everything was good, you went and stirred the pot, brought it all back."

"It never really went away. You might think you've moved on, and your kids don't remember, but Dr. Davis thinks it hasn't been dealt with. You're in denial."

"So what?" I crossed my arms.

"So it might explain why James is having some mental issues, some strange behaviors," Ben said. "Denying the past is not helping James, Jorie."

"Bunch of psychology mumbo-jumbo."

"Well, you're right," he nodded, "psychology is not my field. I can't tell you what's mumbo-jumbo and what isn't. But law *is* my field." He cleared his throat. "You need to know that I pulled up your divorce case and re-opened it with a petition for child support."

My jaw dropped open, and for a second, I almost just wanted to hit Benjamin Atwater, attorney-at-law; land a whammy square into his perfectly chiseled jawline. How could I ever have felt attraction for this man? Why hadn't I just gone with the public defender?

"So, you found him? Your paralegal tracked him down, you say?" My voice shook.

"He's living in McArthur. He's working, he has income. So, he should be paying child support. Jorie, I was just trying to help you, to help James and Will." Ben was on his knees now, grasping my hands, searching my face. He read the fear in my eyes. "But this morning, in the courtroom, was the first time I heard about the past violence."

"McArthur, McArthur... it's just the next county... really not far at all from Jackson," I muttered aloud, thinking. "And he has a car."

"Okay, right, I understand. Filing for the back support might trigger him. I understand you're afraid."

"You don't understand anything."

"Jorie, please. Let me fix this. I'll file for a restraining order. I'll get it drafted and filed this afternoon."

It's not like we'd ever been hard to find. But Garth never had any reason to before. I'd let him go, given him a pass, waived collection of any debt. It was an uneasy truce, but one that allowed us to live peaceably. And I'd had no idea he was just in the next county. James was upset, I knew, but James was in his cell. James was safe. *Will*, I thought frantically. Will should be getting out of school about now, walking home, to my parents' old house, where I grew up, where Garth used to come over to pick me up to go bowling, see a movie. Everyone knew I lived with my boys in my parents' house on High Street. No secrets in a small town.

"I have to go!" I burst from the conference room and flew down the courthouse steps, past the statue of Governor James A. Rhodes, who gave the order that killed those kids at Kent State. The protesters, they were just young people, just kids, and the National Guard, they were just kids too. So much hatred and killing, pain and injury, murder and regret, speeding trucks, children without fathers, dark purple bruises. And dammit, the only problem with leaving Garth was leaving behind our only car. So, I walked. I walked everywhere. Everyone in Jackson knew Jorie Jenkins walks everywhere.

Except now, I ran.

Chapter 19

Will

CAROLINE GOT CALLED out of math class today, about halfway through. One of the secretaries from the office walked in and interrupted, handing Miss Ritchie a note. Miss Ritchie had read the note quickly, her face scrunching into a serious frown. "Caroline, close your books and gather up your things and go with Mrs. Winters," she'd instructed. We all watched, wondering what was going on. I thought about the courthouse and wondered how things were going for James. Caroline's mom was probably there, my mom too. I fidgeted with worry, certain something bad was happening; I felt it in my gut. Something bad enough for Caroline Cragen to be pulled out of school early.

Sarah Jane wasn't in school today, so she must be at court too. If I could find her later on the trail, she would tell me what's going on. Sarah Jane talks to me like a grownup. She'll tell me the truth.

In thirteen minutes, the bell sounded, and I was out of my chair, books thrown into my locker, out the door and onto the bike without a word to anyone.

This time, instead of stopping at home first, I decided to ride past the courthouse. Dodging around cars parked in the metered spaces along Main Street, I slowed to study the courthouse carefully as I passed, but the empty windows yawned dark and silent, telling me nothing. Well, nothing I could tell from the outside, anyway. I thought about James being in there, maybe in his jail cell, and wondered what he was doing right now. It'd been four weeks since I've seen my brother. I've gotten to know the feel of his red Schwinn chopper Sting-Ray, the slopes of his favorite trails, the spot in the woods where his girlfriend lived. But there's so much I wanted to ask.

I didn't feel like going home. The bike steered itself to the Quick Mart by Route 93. As usual, I filled my pockets with candy bars, bags of mixed nuts, beef jerky, then paid for one can of soda, and as usual, the lady rang me up without a word. There were mirrors in the corners near the ceilings, set up so the clerk at the cash register had a clear view down all the aisles. There's no way she hadn't seen me shoplifting.

"Just one," I announced loudly as I plunked my can of pop on the counter, brashly looking her in the eye, almost egging her to challenge me.

"Just one," she agreed simply, ringing up the sale. She was the type of person who seemed to blend into the background, who you'd have a hard time describing later if someone asked you to. I tried to concentrate and look more closely. Medium build. Thick curly dark hair. I had no idea how old she was. "Bettina," said the name tag on her shirt. Okay, her name was Bettina.

"I'm Will."

She nodded again, but didn't respond. *My brother was the one who hit that man right outside your store*, I wanted to add. *He's the one in the papers going to be valedictorian, except he's in jail. His name is James. In fact, it's his bike I'm riding.* Foolish. I shrugged and walked out, climbing back on the Sting-Ray with my pockets bulging. I paused at the road, the intersection where my brother killed Caroline's father, thinking about which way to turn. That feeling in my gut, a dark, gnawing pull. Going home didn't feel right. Heading out toward Sarah Jane's trailer also didn't feel right. She wouldn't be home yet.

James was in jail. Caroline's dad was gone. Mom was worried all the time. The guys in the band wouldn't play with me anymore. Everybody at school had made their mind up about us, the Jenkins. But all that was true yesterday, too, I told myself, trying to be logical. Nothing had changed, so why did today feel different? Why was something not right about today? I circled back toward town, then west of town, toward Mason Way Park. If you pulled into the park by car, which of course I'd never do since we didn't have a car, you'd see a playground, picnic pavilion, restrooms. Further in were the baseball fields. On a bike, you could explore the trails running parallel to the railroad tracks and then cutting deep into the forest and down by Salt Lick Creek. Lately I'd been alternating my rides over by Sarah Jane's trailer with this ride and now knew every twist and turn by heart: where to start pumping to climb the steep inclines, how to cut a sharp right to avoid puddles of mud that sat at the bottom, closer to the river, where to duck my head to avoid taking a low-hanging branch to the face, and which spot to hit the tree roots at a perpendicular angle so my wheel didn't lock up and bring me down.

The wastewater treatment plant bordered the park to the north, and to the west was the old folks' home, where Great Granny used to live after her dementia got so bad she couldn't stay with my grandparents anymore. I wasn't sure how many acres made up the park, but it didn't matter. Once you're deep into the heavily wooded part, it felt a million miles away. Here, I didn't have to worry about accidentally running into Sara Jane's pa or the McKowans, if they were outside of their trailers. Sometimes I just pushed through the brush, using the Schwinn like a kind of machete to cut my own path, branches and thorns scratching up my arms. I guessed hunters shot deer here in the fall, but I'd never seen another person.

Until today. I'd just crested the top of the turn before the trail cuts down by the river when I saw her. She stood about fifty feet below me, by the river, turning in each direction, wringing her hands.

Talking to herself. I was so surprised to see another person I almost ran right into a tree. I squeezed my brakes and screeched to a halt, getting off the bike for a closer look.

"Hey," I called down the hill, but she didn't seem to hear. I hung the top bar of the Sting-Ray on my shoulder and teetered down the cliff. Twigs snapped as I approached, and she turned at the sound.

She looked as surprised to see me as I was to see her. Her eyes were swollen from crying and cheeks reddened with streaks of dirt. She wore a thin dress but no sweater or coat. Leaves and twigs stuck in her hair. Her hands were dirty and mud-streaked, as though she'd had them in the river.

When I stepped forward, she stepped backwards. I stopped, not wanting her to back into the river. "Uhh, hello there. My name's Will. Do you need some help?"

The old lady stared at me blankly, and I saw she wore no shoes and her feet were cut up and black with dirt. She shivered as a gust of wind hit us. I took off my hoodie and held it to her as I continued my approach, trying to put together a friendly smile. "Would you like to put on a jacket, Ma'am, to help you warm up?"

She allowed it. "It's cold out here," she said. I gently put my arms around her shoulder and led her away from the water. There was a rock with a flat, smooth top.

"Let's sit down for a minute, okay? My name is Will," I tried again, but she seemed to be somewhere far away.

"Are you hungry?" Sliding off my backpack, I pulled out the stolen bounty from the Quick Mart. Her eyes flickered as I opened the peanut butter crackers and offered the open bag. She reached out for one and took a hearty crunch.

"Oh, isn't that nice," she murmured.

She ate all the crackers, and then I pulled the soda from my backpack and popped it open so she could drink. When I unwrapped a candy bar, the sight of the chocolate brought a smile to her face. I tried again, "My name is Will... what's your name, miss?"

She stopped chewing the chocolate for a moment and looked at me, stricken. "What's my name?" She shook her head. "I don't know. I can't remember. Do you know what my name is?"

"Ummm, no I don't, sorry... do you live somewhere around here?"

She hung her head and sighed, and my eyes followed down to her bare, muddy feet.

"You can call me Grandma," she said, perking up a bit, like she may have remembered something.

I had to do something. I tried to make my voice sound reassuring, like I knew what was doing. "Okay, Grandma, don't worry. I'm Will and I'm going to help you. I'm going to take you home."

"Take me home, yes, take me home," she agreed, back into the chocolate. "Such a nice young man," she commented to herself.

I looked around, trying to think. We must be about three miles from the road going through the center of the park. If I yelled, no one would hear, and it'd probably just scare her. I had to get help, but no way could I leave this confused old lady by herself, especially by the river. My eyes went to the cliff I'd just come down, from the trail. It seemed too steep for this fragile woman to climb. How had she gotten down here? Had she wandered away from the old folks' home near the park?

She was stranded, barefoot, and cold. *Use math,* I thought. Slopes, angles, numbers.

I looked down the creek, pebbles, and rocks along the side. If I could walk her along the creek for a way, we might be able to find a gentler slope where I could pull her up. I put my foot alongside hers, comparing the size of our feet. Pulling off my shoes and socks, I moved to sit directly in front of her, in her line of vision, just the way Mom always said she saw her mom take care of Great Granny when she had her dementia. "Grandma, I think your feet must be cold," I said carefully, slowly. I held up my shoes and socks. "If I put some socks and shoes on your feet, I think you will feel much better."

I carefully showed her each sock and shoe. She let her legs go limp, watching me silently. I tightened the laces and tied the shoes tightly so they'd better fit. "How does that feel? Do you think you can stand up and take a little walk with me, if we hold hands?"

She looked doubtful now. "I'm tired of walking."

I looked around again, getting a little desperate. There was no choice, we must move. "If you will hold my hand and go for a walk with me, we can eat some more candy, some more chocolate. And soon we'll be home for supper."

She stood. "Just a short walk."

I nodded and held my index finger up to her. *Wait.* She nodded and watched me pull the backpack onto my back, grab the Sting-Ray and hang the top tube of the frame on my right shoulder, and then hold my left hand out to her. We started slowly along the bank. I limped as the sharp rocks cut into my bare feet. The river rocks seemed a bit less jagged, so finally I just kept my feet in the icy creek while I guided her next to me on the dry bank. We proceeded slowly, but at least she was cooperating, and we were moving. "Very good," I said. "Let's keep walking, this is very good."

Presently we came across a wider part of the creek, and it seemed we had progressed up in elevation a bit, where the cliff up to the trail was not so steep. I stopped and looked over the terrain. There's no way the old woman who couldn't remember her name could climb this slope. I looked at my bike, my backpack, searching for an idea. I took off my backpack, unzipped it and pulled out the contents.

"Oooh," she said, looking at the rest of the stolen candy and chips.

"Yes, we're going to eat that in just a minute, after you sit down here, on this." I patted the empty backpack that lay on the damp grass. She hovered in confusion, looking at the backpack.

"Like a sled," I said. "Did you ever go sledding, in the snow? I'm going to pull you like a sled ride." I helped her sit on the backpack, trying to center her best I could, wishing the pack was wider. The straps flayed out to the sides, and I grabbed the top of each one. "Sled ride, then we'll get you home."

I started to pull. She was heavier than I thought. My feet had long gone numb from the cold creek water, but that wouldn't last; I had to hurry. I tugged and strained, inch by inch, pausing every few moments to get a better grip on the handles, trying to dig my bare heels into the ground so we wouldn't slide back down to the base. Finally, we were up.

I heaved myself to the ground next to her, catching my breath. I held my index finger up to her again. *Wait.* She nodded. I climbed back down to retrieve the bike and the contents of my backpack and then returned and unwrapped a Mounds bar. Once she'd finished it, I helped her to her feet, and we were again walking, putting more distance between ourselves and the drop off to the river. When we reached a downed tree, I sat her down on the log. I had to ride now, to find help. Once more I held up my index finger, *wait*, but this time she looked really scared and shook her head, seeming to understand that I was about to leave her alone.

"I'm gonna come along with you, young man," she said, standing up.

"No, I'm sorry, Ma'am, Grandma, but it's too far to walk from here. I'm going to ride my bicycle and bring back help, to bring you home. But you have to stay here, right here in this spot, and wait until I get back."

"No, don't leave me. Don't leave me in the woods."

Feeling awful and wishing there was another way, I begged, "*Please.* You must wait here. I *promise* I'll come back. Wait right here on this log. It's really important. Okay? Do you understand?"

"Ah..." she looked around a bit fearfully, "... okay." She sat back on the log.

"Sometimes, when I'm frightened, I count. My big brother taught that to me when I was little," I started, and she joined in, "One, two, three..."

I opened a last piece of chocolate, pressed it into her hand, then turned to speed away on my bike, without saying bye. I glanced back at my shoes on her feet. The afternoon had worn on and the light would soon be fading. I rode faster than I ever had, my bare feet, no longer numb from the ice creek, painfully pressed into the sharp indentations in the pedals.

Through the forest, over by the baseball fields, empty today of all days, past the wastewater treatment plant, I looked over to the holding pond sitting low between the plant and the nursing home. There was activity over there—an ambulance, police vehicles. I saw a news crew van from the station over in Charleston. Many people, a chain of people, in fact, were holding hands and walking slowly through the water. A human chain. For some reason, I thought of Hands Across America, millions of people across the United States holding hands, lined from coast to coast.

I steered off the trail, through the grass, toward the group. Sheriff Robb was there. I rode up, breathless, dropping to slide off the bike and leave it on the ground. "I know where she is!" I yelled. He was deep in conversation with another officer, looking over a map. He looked up at me, his gaze wandering down to my bare feet. "James Jenkins' brother..." he muttered to the other officer, turning away.

I wildly scanned the scene. Over by the television news van stood Mayor Cragen in her high heels and business suit, giving an interview, microphone in her face. She was crying and yelling into the camera about the negligence of the nursing home in allowing her mother to wander off, not even sure how long she'd been gone. I blinked a moment, registering that this was Caroline's mother, and the old lady in the woods must be Caroline's grandmother. "She has dementia, she's confused..." the mayor was saying.

I ran smack into their space, getting in front of the camera. "I found her, I found your mother. She's down by Salt Lick Creek in Mason Way Park, I pulled her up from the creek, I gave her my shoes, I gave her some food and some soda pop—I left her there just twenty minutes ago and came for help—I can lead you back to where she is!"

Mayor Cragen looked at me in surprise, and the reporter paused, unsure.

"She's wearing a flowered green and lavender dress. She was barefoot, but I gave her my socks and shoes," I went on.

Mayor Cragen looked in astonishment at my bare feet. "She does have a green and lavender dress!" She nodded her head excitedly, snapping into action. Yelling and pointing orders at the others, the police began to listen and people swarmed in activity. The television crew kept filming, and everyone's attention was on me. A four-wheeler was produced. Sheriff Robb and the rest of them followed me as I cycled back, slower this time.

"Do you know the way?" one of them called out, but I just raised my arm and waved at them to hurry. If there was anything I understood in this town, anything I understood about anything at all, it was the angles and slopes of these trails.

Chapter 20

Jorie

The house was terrifyingly silent, no James, no Will, no chatter between two brothers, no turntable spinning records, no sticks banging the drums, no teenage boys with shaggy hair and amplified guitars in the parlor. Not even a rumble from an afternoon train. I heaved for breath, not caring about the spectacle I'd made running through the streets of Jackson.

"Will!" I screamed, poking my head out the backdoor toward the alley. Nothing.

Had Garth already been here? Was I too late?

In the kitchen, I grabbed the phone off the wall to call the school. School let out over an hour ago, and no, Will Jenkins was not held after for any reason, I'm told. "No, no unknown adult male was seen picking Will up. Perhaps Will went over to a friend's house after school?" the secretary suggested helpfully.

Yes, of course, the boys in the band. Manzana. "I will check," I agreed, trying to hide the panic in my voice.

Andy's mom, Karen Overfield, sounded surprised to hear from me. "Oh Jorie, the boys haven't gotten together for band practice for some time now, didn't you know?"

"Guess I hadn't realized they weren't getting together anymore," I faltered.

"Well, of course, what with everything y'all got going on with your family right now," she offered awkwardly, her voice trailing off.

I'd been so focused on James that it hadn't even sunk in that Will was no longer having any friends over. His sticks lay across the top of his snare drum, abandoned, now with a faint coat of dust. Seemed Will lost interest in drumming about the same time he took up riding his brother's bike. I ran to the front and poked my head out onto the front porch, seeing what I'd missed the first time; the red Schwinn was gone. For once, I was grateful. Collapsing onto the couch, head in my hands, the tears finally came. If he was out on the bike, maybe Garth hadn't gotten to him.

It'd been eleven years since I'd laid eyes on my boys' father, eleven good years. We didn't want for anything, I told myself: roof over our heads, food on our table, clothes on our backs. A steady stream of customers at Eva's, my regulars. Will, so talented, his own drum set. How many other families in this town got their fourteen-year-old a drum set? James, so smart, so good with numbers, the head of his class! All those kids with a mother and a father, but it's my son, *my* son, who was going to be the valedictorian. And *I'm* the one who got it all figured out. Who got up the guts and left. The biggest thing I did in my life, and I didn't do it for myself, I did it for my sons, *I left*. When one leaves, one doesn't want to look back.

Or be found.

But we were fragile, I admitted to myself. Dark memories of the fights, the yelling, how shocked I was when he hit me the first time. Lord knows I'd tried. "Give me another chance," Garth had pleaded. So I did. Over and over. And then, when I saw how those same numbers were going to keep adding up the same way, to the same outcome, every single time, I changed the equation. I left.

The rectangle was no more. Four became three. Our fragile triangle.

James, talking to himself, mood swings, counting and pacing.

Mixing up his sense of smell with his sense of hearing, seeing colors instead of feeling emotions, associating colors with people. Obsessing about a bicycle tour he'd never ride, on a Sting-Ray bike he's outgrown, because he was in *jail*, for God's sake, for *killing* a man, for God's sake.

Will, off for hours on his own, on his brother's bike, not even telling me that his friends' parents wouldn't let them come over to our house anymore. Smart with numbers, just like his brother, but how soon until he too started obsessing about equations and counting? The psychologist's testimony rang in my head: retreating into the world of equations as a way to cope.

And me, bumming rides from my neighbor. Customers canceling, no-showing for their appointments at the salon. My son in a jail cell, on trial, in the newspaper. Walking, always walking.

Everything used to feel so safe, our lives here in my childhood home, secure lineage to our Welsh ancestors, Granny's glassware in the hutch, everything my parents left us through Daddy's life of work mining coal, knowing everyone in town—the people I grew up with, went to school with, whose hair I cut. We were *townies*, not country kids. We might not have a car, but we belonged, I'd always assumed. How blind I'd been. I was an imposter. A divorcee, a failed mother. The whole town was talking about us.

And now, on top of everything else, we had to worry about Garth.

From the front window I saw the police car coming down High Street, and I knew, I just knew, it was the worst news. Something terrible had happened. Garth had gotten to Will, my Will, my baby... I put my hand over my mouth to swallow my scream, clutched my stomach, dizzy with fear. It was the sheriff. The car slowed and stopped in front of our house as I knew it would. The door opened and out stepped Will.

Flying out the front door, he was in my arms in a second. "You're all right!" I cried, clutching him.

"Mom, I'm fine," he drew back, shaking out his hair, looking around at Sheriff Robb, at Lana, who stood on her front porch, watching. Curtains fluttered in the neighbors' windows. I'd embarrassed him. Too old for hugging.

"Well, what's going on?" I demanded, pulling back.

Sheriff Robb got out of the cruiser and lifted the Sting-Ray from the trunk, joining us on the sidewalk. "Jorie, Will found Mayor Cragen's mother. She'd wandered away from the nursing home. We were getting ready to dredge the holding pond. But she'd wandered into Mason Way Park, no coat, no shoes or socks on, and your boy here found her and gave her food, gave her the shoes off his own feet. Pulled her up away from the river. Rode his bike barefoot to get help. Led us right to her."

I stared at Will, speechless.

"You should be very proud of your boy," added Sheriff Robb, his eyes on the ground, like he hadn't wanted to say it.

I swallowed. "Oh, I am, I am proud," I said. "Of both my boys."

* * *

Hours later, we were still trying to settle ourselves. I'd set up a bath with Epsom salts and insisted Will soak, then helped him put some ointment on his cut feet and wrapped them with gauze bandages. "You did a wonderful thing today," I said. "Stay off your feet now, for a while. You can stay home and rest tomorrow if you like."

I'd ordered pizza for dinner, a treat, Will's favorite.

He'd told me the entire story, how he found the mayor's mother in the park, how he pulled her up the hill with his backpack, away from the creek, so he could ride for help.

"That was smart, the way you figured that out," I said. "And I can't believe you rode the bike barefoot, how that must've hurt..."

"It hurt," he said, looking at his feet. "But it was worth it—to rescue someone, to protect someone—I never knew what that felt like before. Saving her, having all the deputies and ambulance guys listening to me, following me. It made me feel like a hero."

"You *are* a hero," I said.

Will was tired, but proud of himself, glowing even. He's growing up, I thought.

"I wish James was here," he said.

"Me too." Tears slid down my face as emotions from everything that happened today erupted to the surface.

"Did things go okay in court today, Mom?" A shadow of worry crossed his face.

I wanted to warn him about the possibility his father may show up, but just couldn't bring myself. *Keep it gentle.* I swept the tears away and smiled. "Sure, hon. It was a long day of testimony, but your brother did just fine. It's going to be fine."

Finally, he was in bed, and I started to think about just locking up the house and staying up all night, to watch, to guard against Garth. But I didn't have to.

A knock on the side door, and Lana was over. "I saw Will on the news," she muttered as she set her cigarette case and lighter on the kitchen counter, "and some footage of that court testimony 'bout James. Thought I better stop over and check on you."

Another quiet knock a few minutes later, and Ben was over.

Ben wordlessly presented the restraining order and allowed me a moment to read it over before explaining that he had already filed it with our local law enforcement, and the court process server would be delivering it directly to Garth.

Lana raised her eyebrows, giving me a questioning look.

"Garth has... resurfaced," I explained to Lana in a hushed voice. "Or been found, I suppose." I scanned the paperwork setting forth the restraining order, searching for magic words, powerful words that could protect us. "So he'll get served with this tonight?"

"Probably," said Ben. "I'm going to stay right here on your parlor couch tonight. You and Will are going to be safe, Jorie."

I swallowed. "Ben, I'm sorry I went after you over at the courthouse..."

"No need for any apology, Jorie. I should have talked to you before filing for the child support. That was my fault. I wanted to surprise you, wanted to do something for you."

I pulled the reheated pizza out of the oven and set out paper plates for Ben and Lana. We sat around the kitchen table, keeping our voices low while Will slept.

"Well, you did surprise me, that's for sure," I said. "I'm just kind of at a loss. After hearing that psychologist testify, hearing all that information about James. Learning my ex is only one county away. Finishing the day with Will becoming the new town hero." I threw my hands up. "I can't even process all this."

"It was hard testimony to hear, I'm sure," Ben said softly. "Those memories must be difficult."

I studied my fingernails. "It was a long time ago; I don't think about any of that anymore." Which wasn't true, of course. The life I'd fought to give my sons was fueled by the kind of determination a person only got from fear, from suffering. It took so much energy to keep it all going. Those memories, that fear, that determination were there every day.

Lana cleared her throat, shaking her head. "They showed some of that psychologist testifying about the violence on the news. You never mentioned it. Was he like that in high school, when y'all were dating?"

"No. He was charming when we were dating. It changed after we got married, after we moved to Oak Hill." I gingerly allowed my mind to sift through that period in my life. "I mean, at first, I guess things were good," I spoke slowly. "We were happy when the boys were born. But then it was almost like Garth got jealous of the time I was spending taking care of them. And his temper, his anger... just came out of nowhere, like nothing I'd ever seen."

Lana cursed softly. "I feel so bad we fell out of touch. I'm sorry I wasn't there for you, Jorie."

"That's not on you, Lana," I said. "Garth didn't like me keeping up with friends, or with my own family, even. Getting my hair license was a battle. He was jealous of everything, everyone, accused me of cheating on him all the time."

"Hells-bells, Jorie, I would have come and got you, picked you and the boys up. Just one phone call."

"You don't understand. I wouldn't have called, not you, not my parents when they were alive. Because I was too ashamed about what was going on." I ran my hand over my arms. "Wouldn't have even worn a short sleeve top like this one. Used makeup to cover the bruises."

Saying the words aloud was embarrassing and liberating at the same time. I'd never told anyone before, not even my own mother. Putting words to these memories felt like painting a landscape in a strange land from another time, staged with actors reading their scripts. Except it wasn't a movie, it wasn't make believe. It was real. It was our story. It was me, Garth, James, and Will.

"What an ass, that Garth," Lana said angrily. "What was it that finally gave you the courage to leave?"

I clenched and unclenched my fists.

Ben watched me, those beautiful blue eyes on mine.

After a moment, I spoke. "James was five. Will was little, two, almost three. I was holding Will. Garth threw a plate at me. I ducked in time. It crashed on the wall right over Will's head. Within a few inches, well, probably about eight centimeters, if you want to measure it with the metric system, which is all based upon ten. The metric system makes much more sense than the English system, which is why scientists use it. Anyway, that time, I'd been able to duck Will's head down faster than the plate was flying through the air. But in all probability, we wouldn't be so lucky the next time. I had to get out, or the boys were going to get hurt."

Lana and Ben stared at me, mouths agape. "Why isn't anyone eating any of this pizza?" I said. "Eat. Don't make it go to waste."

Lana turned to Ben, demanding, "Do you think Jorie and the boys are at risk? What all did you find out about Garth?"

"Well, we know he doesn't have any remorse. When Dr. Davis

interviewed him, he was pretty open about controlling Jorie, hitting Jorie, pretty much thinking he was in the right because Jorie was his wife. Dr. Davis asked for an example of when it would be okay for a husband to hit his wife. His answer was dinner not on the table when the man gets home from work. This guy doesn't get it, that's for sure." Ben went on. "And what we found out about him is that he has a job, he lives in McArthur."

"By himself?" I asked warily.

"No," Ben answered slowly. "Not by himself. He's remarried." Ben paused a moment. "And he has other kids, Jorie. He has kids with his new wife."

This sent the room reeling a bit. James and Will had siblings. Four and a half billion people in the world, but exactly only one brother in the whole world, we'd always said. Except it wasn't true. They had siblings. Maybe a sister, maybe another brother. It all felt like too much. At least right now, I didn't want to know.

"We found a domestic violence conviction from three years ago. His pattern hasn't stopped. He just has a new set of victims, I'm afraid," said Ben.

"Oh," I cried, head in my hands. I couldn't bear the thought of other children getting hurt. Of another woman getting hurt. How could just one person generate so much pain to so many others? And how, in the world, was I going to keep my boys safe? The newspapers covered each day of the trial, the valedictorian with synesthesia who killed the mayor's husband. And tonight, fourteen-year-old Will on the evening news, the boy on the bicycle rescuing the mayor's mother. Two brothers from the same family have both killed and rescued members of the same family, the most prominent family in town. We're a soap opera. Our family was under a microscope, every detail broadcast far and wide. Nowhere to hide.

"I don't know what to do," I said.

"We've got the restraining order. And I'm here tonight. On your couch," Ben added, blushing.

"And I'll stay in your room, I can sleep in that rocking chair," said

Lana. "You're strong, Jorie, and you're not alone. You, James, and Will are going to be all right." She stood and started gathering up the paper plates for the garbage. "We don't have to figure everything out tonight. You're exhausted. I'm going to step outside and smoke a cigarette, then I suggest we all turn in."

There was a rap on the kitchen side door, and Lana startled, screamed and jumped so hard that her cigarettes went flying out of the case, all over the kitchen floor. Ben and I scrambled to our feet, staring at the door. He braced, motioning Lana and I to stand back, frozen as he poised for battle. My eyes wildly scanned the kitchen for a weapon. I grabbed the fire extinguisher and passed it to Ben. He nodded and cautiously moved to the door, peering through the curtains. Ben relaxed and set the fire extinguisher down. He opened the door.

The girl with the long dark hair was at my door.

Chapter 21

Jorie

"I'm sorry to bother you so late," she said, her hair tousled and her lip bleeding. "I didn't know where else to go."

I recalled the last time I'd seen her, she'd had a black eye. I didn't know this girl's story or what was going on in her life, but the look of fear was unquestionable, and something I instinctively recognized. Someone was hurting her.

"Sarah Jane." I took her hand and pulled her into the kitchen. "It's okay. You did the right thing coming. You're safe now."

Ben and Lana stood back as I ushered Sarah Jane to the bathroom and sat her down on the side of the tub. I wet a washcloth and dabbed at her cut lip. She shook, her hands jumping so much she had to sit on them, but I allowed it. "We'll get some ice on that to keep the swelling down," I said. I looked over her arms, neck, elbows, shoulders. "Where else does it hurt?"

"I'm okay," she whispered.

"Who did this to you?" I asked. She didn't respond, but I had my suspicions. The talk around town was that Rosemary Billings had left Sarah Jane's father, Roy, for the same reason I'd left Garth, except for one huge difference; while I'd taken my children along with me,

Sarah Jane's mother had left her behind. Unprotected. What kind of mother did that?

"Your father? He hit you on your face. And where else?"

"Just on my cheek," she said, looking to the floor.

"Open hand or fist?"

She studied her own hand, turned it palm up and then to the side. "Pa just backhanded me. I've gotten it worse. But he was so angry, I had to get out of there."

"What about your teeth, any loose teeth?"

She ran her tongue over her teeth and gums and put a hand to her cheek, wincing with pain. "I don't think any teeth are loose."

Ben stood in the open bathroom doorway, his face tight and grim. "We should call the Sheriff," he said. "This needs to be reported."

"No!" Sarah Jane and I both startled as we shouted in unison. We looked at each other in surprise. I lowered and calmed my voice. "I think we can handle this without getting Sheriff Robb involved."

"But if her father hit her, that's an assault, Jorie. The man should be arrested and charged. She has obvious injuries." Ben grabbed my hand and gently pulled me into the hallway, lowering his voice to a whisper. "And maybe we should take her to the emergency room so she can get checked out. You know, a blow to the head can be a serious injury. It can cause a brain bleed."

I frowned and peered at Sarah Jane, perched on the edge of the bathtub.

She stood, holding the washcloth to her lip and having overheard us, said, "I don't want to go to the hospital. I don't want the Sheriff called. Please. Like I said, he just back-handed me. I just don't want to go back to the trailer. If you call the Sheriff, they'll make me go back."

"Would she?" I said to Ben, "have to go back there?"

"You're eighteen years old, right?" Ben asked Sarah Jane. "You're an adult. The Sheriff can't force you to return to your father's home. But, as an adult, she also can refuse medical treatment," he told me. "We can't take her for medical treatment against her consent."

"Really, I'm okay," Sarah Jane insisted.

I sighed and shook my head. "Give us a little time," I told Ben. I realized he was still holding my hand and squeezed his fingers before pulling away. "Would you please get some ice or a bag of frozen peas from my freezer?"

"Already got it!" Lana called out, reaching over Ben's shoulder to hand us a bag of crushed ice.

"Thanks Lana." I took the ice and stepped back into the bathroom, softly closing the door.

Sarah Jane accepted the bag of ice and held it to her face, sheepish.

"I'm glad you and James are friends," I told her. "Seems you both can use a good friend in this town."

"Thank you," she whispered.

I took a breath and brushed a strand of hair away from her face, exposing where the past black eye had now progressed to faded purple and yellow. "When your Pa has hit you before, who did you go to for help? Did you call the Sheriff on those occasions?"

She looked at me evenly. "There's no help there, from the Sheriff," she said.

I cocked my head, meeting her gaze. Interesting that of all the kids to befriend at Jackson High, this poor soul was the one James had gravitated to.

I stood to wring the washcloth at the sink. "It's late. We'll talk more in the morning. For now, I'm going to put you in James' room, and you try to get some sleep."

When we emerged from the bathroom, Ben and Lana hovered in the kitchen, and Ben caught my eye. "Jorie, we got a situation here." He gestured out the window. Under the streetlight was the McKowan's truck—the truck that hit Ernie Cragen, that they hadn't even bothered to fix—in our driveway. The front fender was smashed in, the front hood warped and mangled.

"Huh?" I spun to Sarah Jane. "You drove that over here?"

Sarah Jane hung her head. "Sometimes when things are really

bad with Pa, I run down the trail to their place," she whispered. "They always leave the keys in the truck."

"Do they know you drove off in their truck?"

"It's happened before and they haven't minded," Sarah Jane said.

"Do you even have a driver's license?" I pressed, incredulous.

Sarah Jane kept her eyes to the floor and didn't answer.

Okay, she was desperate, she was hurt. I got it. Fleeing an enraged abuser was something I understood. But driving into town in *that* truck, taking the same route James took when they hit Ernie in the crosswalk—what in God's name had the girl been thinking?

"I can't have that truck in my driveway when the sun comes up. I can't have my neighbors seeing that truck in this driveway."

"No, of course not," said Ben quickly. "We're going to get that truck back where it belongs tonight. I'll drive it back over to the McKowan's and put it back in their yard. Lana, do you mind following me in your car so we can get back?"

"Of course," she agreed.

Once again, I was relying on friends with cars.

"Sorry for keeping everyone up so late," I mumbled.

I watched through the side door as Ben started up the truck and backed it out, Lana following in her Chevelle. As I watched their tail lights recede, I ran my hands over the fire extinguisher, my ridiculous weapon to fight back in case Garth was the next one rapping at the side door. Would he knock? No, of course not. He'd just bust in. And then what? I'd defend myself and two teenagers with a pressurized stream of fire-retardant chemicals?

Ben and Lana will be back in half an hour, I told myself. With Sarah Jane watching, I turned on the lights in James' room, set out fresh linens and a clean towel. The poor girl was here with only the clothes on her back, not even a toothbrush. She lay down and settled, exhausted, her dark hair splayed over the flannel pillow on James' bed. I pulled the door shut.

In my parlor, I laid out blankets and an extra pillow for Ben on the couch. I stretched the blanket over myself and burrowed down, waiting for them to return. Streetlights shone through the windows, lighting the room and casting elongated shadows from Will's high-hat cymbal. Granny's tea cups started to gently rattle, and soon the rumble of the train rocked the floorboards; familiar, comforting, rocking. My clenched jaw relaxed as I succumbed to the rhythm of our shaking house. I was still scared, but somehow, having it all out in the open made me feel less alone. And I wasn't the only one. Just one county over was a family—an unseen woman, her children. They were victims. Sarah Jane, just eighteen years old, was a victim. James and Will were victims. They must remember, on some level, even though they were so young. But it wasn't my story any longer. I'd chosen another life. I left. And Sarah Jane, as reckless as gunning that cursed truck over here without a driver's license was, had also mustered some courage to leave, to knock on my door. Somehow, her coming here for help made me proud. I could be strong. Just like Will, with Granny Cragen, I could be a protector of others.

The headlights from Lana's car turned into her driveway next door, car doors closed, and in a moment she and Ben walked back up to my door.

My good friends were here.

* * *

Three days went by, and Garth didn't come.

On Friday, amongst bills and junk mail and the grocery store flier advertising a discount on pork chops, was a notice from the Ohio Child Support Enforcement Agency. I pulled it from the other mail and opened it by my bedroom dresser. Carefully, I tore along the perforated lines and spread the creases flat. The number by the dollar sign made me catch my breath. Garth's working, all right, and the State had garnished his wages. Back support plus a current monthly payment. How had Ben ever managed to get back support when I'd waived it? I didn't understand the mechanics of it, but here it was, more than I'd dreamed possible.

This check, Garth's money, felt like an invasion. To cash it was to let him back into our lives. If I accepted it, I wasn't supporting my boys all on my own anymore. Taking this was conceding defeat. And, perhaps, antagonizing more violence.

For now, this went into my sock drawer, tucked underneath folded t-shirts—right next to the hidden rubber-banded stack of James' letters to that bike club I'd retrieved from the post office, all returned back to us. *No Such Address. Return to Sender.* I sighed. Just one more piece of information to add to the long collection of things I kept to myself.

Chapter 22

James

"Your bed has the softest flannel sheets," Sarah Jane whispered into my ear, and I pulled her close to me as we perched on the edge of my cot. "But it's really weird being at your house without you," she added with a sigh.

Having her here has pulled me from my deep, deep dive into numbers. The long division wasn't enough. My calculus book sat on the metal desk. Starting at the beginning, I'd gone through every proof, solved every one, cover to cover. Page after notebook page was filled with equations. I'd used a number two pencil, sharpened to a point, never once had I rubbed the paper with the eraser. Never once had I thought about anything that was said the other day in court. The proofs were majestic, violet, high in the stratosphere, perfect works of art. They smelled like lavender.

I ran my hands through Sarah Jane's long, dark hair. It ran all the way to her butt, like a river flowing down her back, rocking like a heavy metal band. I heard the booming beat in my head and took a moment to count the time signature. "Say, what day is it, anyway?"

"Friday, James. It's Friday. I got to your house three days ago."

"Home is orange," I told her. "The bed's soft, like the smell of the

146

woods after it rains. And everything rumbles. Do you like it when all the stuff in the china cabinet starts rattling?"

"I feel so safe there," she murmured into my shoulder.

I pictured her cornflower blue melding with the orange. What color did that make? I liked the idea of her sleeping in my room. Her lip was still a little swollen, but this was the very last time. No bruises, no cuts, no injuries on Sarah Jane, ever again.

"You did the right thing going to Mom. I'm proud of you for going over there."

"I don't know," said Sarah Jane. "You should have seen your mom's face when she saw the truck in her driveway. Maybe it wasn't the smartest idea."

"You got out, you had to run."

"But look what happened last time we used that truck to run away," she pointed out, still whispering against my shoulder.

Chapter 23

Will

On Monday, I returned to school, and Sarah Jane walked with me. Only about four weeks left before summer break. Last night, at dinner, Mom told us both that we had to go to school each day and get our grades up as high as we could. That despite everything going on right now, we had to concentrate.

I glanced over to Sarah Jane. She held her books to her chest with both hands, head forward but glancing curiously at the houses we passed.

"What did you think of Mom's little speech last night?"

"I didn't mind it. Your mom's really smart. She talked to me after dinner too. I'm allowed to stay with you guys only if I go to school every day and finish high school. No more skipping out on class for the court hearings. And she said every evening we're going to have the television off, and we're going to sit at the kitchen table until all our assignments are done."

"Geez," I grumbled. "She never made me do *that* before."

"Sorry Will, I think the whole thing was directed more to me."

"Mom's usually not that strict with James and me," I said.

"I don't mind it," said Sarah Jane. "I never had rules before.

Nobody's ever bothered to check whether I do my homework or not. And I'm grateful she took me in. She said since I'm eighteen it could be my decision to stay with you guys, and she didn't need to go to my pa for permission. But she said that for the next month, my job is to go to school every day, do every single assignment. Do everything I need to make sure I get my diploma. That's my end of the deal, so I can stay with you guys."

We paused at the stop sign and looked both ways before crossing High Street. In the distance, I heard the engine of the school bus rumbling down Main Street.

"It's strange walking instead of taking the bus," Sarah Jane said. "You get to school, in what, ten minutes? My ride was taking forty minutes or more, all the stops to pick up the other country kids."

"It's even faster when I ride the bike," I said.

"Sometimes I just walk the tracks instead of taking the bus," she said.

"Doesn't that take forever?" I asked. "That would be a pretty long walk from town out to your place, following the tracks."

"Bus in the morning, train tracks in the afternoon. I was never in any particular hurry to get home." Sarah Jane ran her hands through her hair. "People are going to be looking at me. They're going to notice I walked with you instead of riding the bus." She brushed her hand over her lips, where Mom had helped apply makeup this morning to cover the bruise by her mouth.

"Hey, don't be nervous," I said. "They're going to be looking at me, too. *I* was just on the news."

She smiled. "The town hero's escorting me to Jackson High School. I'm honored." We laughed and linked arms, and I gave a little disco-strut, feeling good in my bellbottom jeans, a freshman walking a senior to school.

We parted at the door, Sarah Jane heading to her locker in the senior section and me to the hallway with the freshman lockers. Familiar faces brushed by, and I felt curious glances. The stuff with James and the last hearing was in the papers, so the other kids must know my dad used to hit my mom. But my rescue of Granny Cragen was also in the papers, on television too.

"Hey Will, what's up?" said Andy, his face lighting up when he spotted me,

"Hey," I replied, continuing past him to my own locker. He wasn't forgiven for abandoning the band, abandoning me.

He tailed alongside. "Saw you on the news last night, man, that was cool!"

I studied my lock as I twirled the combination and swung open the door, depositing my English books.

"How'd you ride that bike barefoot?" Andy tried again. "Didn't that hurt?"

"Just did what I had to."

"Did you walk in with Sarah Jane Billings this morning?"

For a guy who'd not bothered talking to me for three weeks, he sure was chatty. I wasn't going to make this easy for him. I kept my head buried in my locker, waiting a good minute before responding. "Yup."

"Hey, my mom got on me yesterday after your mom called looking for you, and then after we saw you on the TV. She thinks maybe the band should start getting together again. She said maybe by you saving Granny Cragen, your family paid back what your brother stole from the Cragen family by hitting their dad."

I straightened to look at Andy, but before I could respond, there was Caroline, not a foot behind Andy in the hallway. She must have heard every word.

"Caroline—" I started.

She looked at me, her face searching. "Will..."

The bell rang, the moment was gone, and she pivoted toward the art room. I watched her retreat, her long hair swinging. The pain was raw. But saying her name, and hearing her say mine back, felt really, really good.

Chapter 24

Jorie

With James and Will, there was balance, equilibrium. Control. No need for anyone else. Not lonely. Or so I had thought. And for so long, it was just the three of us in this house. But now, there was a new rhythm to our days.

Ben camping on the living room couch, Sarah Jane cocooning in James' room, Lana popping in all the time over the past several days. It was kind of nice, and we'd struck up new routines. Staggering bathroom times. Sarah Jane setting the table for dinner. Ben washing dishes, Will taking the garbage out. Lots of chatter. After supper, the kids set up at the kitchen table for homework. Will and I helped Sarah Jane with her math. Ben helped both of them with history and proofread Sarah Jane's paper for English Lit. I pointed her toward the dictionary in James' room to check her spelling.

"You've got a dictionary right here in your house." She seemed surprised. "Usually I wait to use the one in the school library, at study hall."

Ben told jokes at supper, told us stories from trials, from famous legal cases. "Eyewitness testimony is the *least* reliable form of evidence," he announced dramatically, slicing the ham and scooping cheese potatoes onto his plate.

Will, especially, was an eager audience for these tales. "Why is that, Ben?"

"People don't pay attention. They don't notice details. And memories are susceptible to subjective interpretation, embellishment."

Will's fork hovered in the air, a bite of food forgotten. "Ben, do some people not *want* to be witnesses, not *want* to see things? Even when those things are right in front of their face?"

Ben looked curious. "Now why would you ask that, Will?"

Will popped his cheese potatoes and green beans in his mouth. "Just wondering."

"Don't talk with your mouth full, Will," I interjected.

Ben gave Will a wink. "You're right, Will. Some folks don't want to get involved, don't want to report what they see, don't want to be subpoenaed to come testify. They might think they're minding their own business. Most of the time, they'd be right. But if you mind your own business too much, then you're not helping your neighbor, your friend. You might not be doing the right thing."

"So you should always speak up? To do the right thing?" Will asked.

"Sure," Ben replied. "Just the way you reported finding Granny Cragen in the woods. You described what she was wearing to lead the authorities to her. You were a very reliable witness."

"Would some people see her and not speak up, not get help?"

"Yah, I suppose some might. Now *that* would make for an unreliable witness."

"Would some people see one thing but say another? Lie about what really happened?"

"Yup, people lie, all the time," said Ben. "For many reasons, people lie. But if you lie when you testify in court, you're committing perjury, which is a crime in and of itself."

"It's always good to tell the truth," I said to Will and Sarah Jane.

Sarah Jane pushed her food around on her plate. "Depends on what's going on. Sometimes it's best to keep your mouth shut."

We all turned and considered her thoughtfully. She put her napkin on her plate. "May I be excused?"

"Of course, dear. Hope you got enough to eat," I said. Sarah Jane was respectful, quiet, a studious observer of our routines, our chatter, our family, the house. She was healing. Normalcy, routine, boredom even, was welcome rest and relief. But I insisted upon school attendance and homework. For those, for Sarah Jane, there was no luxury of time.

Ben kept finding little things around the house to fix. The leaky faucet in the stationary sink by the washing machine dripped no more. Light bulbs in the overhead fixture I hadn't even realized were burnt out have been replaced. He even got up on the roof and adjusted the TV antenna so we didn't get static on Channel Four.

And at night, in bed, Ben's presence a few feet away on my parlor sofa changed the feel of everything. My hand rested on the pillow by my head and I gazed over, imagining what his face would look like resting on that pillow. What his lips would feel like.

But mostly, I missed James.

He'd been in jail for over a month now. Five weeks away from us. Five weeks away from his plaid flannel sheets, from his stereo and albums, from his Levi's bellbottoms with the Dr. Pepper belt buckle, and his Adidas tennis shoes. From his favorite spaghetti and meatballs dinner. Five weeks away from his final semester of high school. Five weeks away from feeling the sun on his skin. Five weeks away from walking down the street, from running down the street, from flying his beloved red Sting-Ray around town. My son, my smart, kind, quirky, wonderful son—was in a cage.

Even with new people and new activities in our rumbly little house on High Street, even as I continued to work, to cook, to nudge Will and Sarah Jane to concentrate on their schoolwork, we were in a holding pattern, waiting.

The judge took everything under advisement. We'd cleared the probable cause hearing, the amenability hearing, as Ben had explained. Now Judge Fraser had to weigh all the evidence, consider James' age, school record, family environment. His mental condition. The seriousness of what he's accused of. Everyone would be called back to the courtroom when she was ready to announce her decision. If James was bound over to the adult system, he'd be tried as an adult, probably with a jury. If James was tried as a juvenile, she'd hear the case, but might exclude the public and the press. And of course, the difference in sentencing, if he's found guilty and sent to prison, made all the difference in the world.

I tried to send little prayers the way of Judge Fraser. *Please let my boy have what's left of his childhood. Please don't let this mistake be the rest of his life.*

And I sent little prayers, silent prayers, to Candy Cragen and her kids. *Be strong.* It's hard to suddenly become a single parent, responsibility for everything falling all on you. Paying the bills, taxes, keeping up the house, the yard. Damn, Candy was running the whole town on top of everything else. She was tough as nails, but I wondered if she also laid awake at night turning things over in her head, worrying. Ridiculously, I wished the two of us could sit down for a cup of coffee and just talk. But what does 'justa hairdresser' say to the town mayor?

On top of waiting for the judge to issue her ruling, I waited for Garth to show up. I carried a copy of the restraining order in my purse. But what could a piece of paper really accomplish? To enforce it, if Garth were to show up, I'd have to call the police. And then I'd have to rely upon a sheriff who lays hands on his own wife.

I'd considered making Will stop with the after-school bike rides, but he seemed to be really blossoming with this new hobby, and with his bandmates boycotting our house, I was glad he had something to fill his time. And thinking back, Garth had never purposefully gone after the boys. The brunt of his anger fell all on me. I didn't think he'd hurt Will, but then again, how well did I really know him anymore? It struck me that I should feel more scared, but telling our story to Ben and Lana had somehow made me stronger, reckless even.

On Monday morning we were still waiting to be called back to court, and I'd made scrambled eggs for Will and Sarah Jane, shooed them off to school and turned down an offer from Ben for a ride to work.

"It'll take me three minutes to drop you off at the salon before I head up to Circleville to my office," he chided. Ben was running his practice from my house as best he could, but still needed to get up to his law books and office at least several times a week.

"It's okay. I'll walk."

"Jorie," Ben started.

I gave him a push toward his car with a smile. "Go! Walking is what I do."

He shook his head and rolled down the window as he pulled out. "Be careful," he called.

I walked past Mrs. Grenadine's house, past the bowling alley, past Henry's. I felt peaceful. Hopeful. Until I saw my old car in the parking lot of Eva's.

* * *

When I saw the Dodge Dart, my legs almost gave out from under me. I halted and took a step back, looking around wildly, before scurrying back across Main Street in a half-walk, half-run retreat. Backtracking for a block, I circled around to approach the store from behind and not be seen from the front windows.

The olive-green car was rust-eaten and faded. Raggedy-edged holes gaped through the metal, and brownish stains marred the wheels. The black bench seat, once gleaming inky black, was now dull and ripped on the passenger side. Slanted crookedly in the parking spot, it looked like someone had pulled in fast, right up to the front of Eva's, not even bothering to aim it between the yellow lines.

Damn old car. In an instant, I was transported through time. Garth had bought it for me early in our marriage, when things were still good. He'd made such a show at the dealer about it, made sure everyone knew he was such a big man, buying a new car for his woman. Back then, it was a shiny showpiece, but it sure hadn't aged well. How was it even still on the road?

I pulled the back door shut quickly behind me.

"Beverly!" I hissed.

She was waiting in the back and grabbed my arm, pulling me toward the coffee machine.

"Is he here? Is Garth here? Is he looking for me? Should I call my lawyer?" I whispered, frantic.

"It's not Garth, Jorie."

"But that's our old car! That's the car he bought for me, the car I had to leave behind when I left him. I'd know it anywhere."

"Jorie, it's not him. It's *her*."

She pushed my shoulder toward the curtain and we leaned together to peek out. At my station was a softly chubby woman with ruddy, wild curls, wearing a horizontal striped brown and maroon baggy sweater layered over bellbottoms, tattered around the bottoms.

"What? Who is she? Why's she in my chair?"

"She was a walk-in appointment about fifteen minutes ago," said Beverly. "I offered her another stylist, but she insisted she wanted you, said she'd wait."

"Who is she?" I said again.

Beverly whispered, "Said her name is Loretta." We both knew who this stranger was and why she was here.

I took a deep breath, tucked my hair behind my ears and pushed the curtain aside to walk onto the floor. If Garth's current wife wanted me to do her hair, well, by God, I'd do her hair.

"Good morning, Loretta, is it? I'm Jorie."

She looked me up and down, silently measuring me up, taking stock of my outfit, my hair, my figure, noticing my jewelry and makeup, the way women do.

"Jorie. Yes, I know, you're Jorie. Know all about you."

"Is that right?" I commented, hating the slight tremble in my voice as I carefully swiveled the chair to swing her toward the mirror.

"We haven't had you in here before as a customer at Eva's, Loretta, now have we? You live in Jackson?"

"You know darn well, Garth and I don't live in Jackson."

"Okay," I sighed, my hands shaking. "You're Garth's wife, I understand. And you're here to talk to me." I glanced to the chair to my right, where Sylvia was giving Mrs. Garrick a permanent wave. "Ummm, Loretta, would you like a haircut? Permanent wave? Manicure?"

"No haircut. You can style it."

"Do you want a shampoo?"

She hesitated. I didn't think she wanted me to touch her, but I sensed she liked the power of sitting in my chair, having me wait on her, shampoo her hair, work in a conditioning rinse. She was the customer. I was the hairdresser. In here, at least, the customer was always right.

"We've got a brand new botanical shampoo-conditioner, just came in the other day, makes your hair so soft. If you're interested."

She looked at me evenly, our eyes meeting in the mirror as we both gazed forward, considering the situation.

"I figured it was high time I came to see you. You know, he used to treat me like a queen, he hated you, everything I did was wonderful. I was better-looking than you. Better cook. Better lover. Smarter. Funnier. You were the stupid loser he left. Said divorcing you was the best decision he ever made."

I swallowed. "You know there's a restraining order. Did he come into town with you?"

"I came alone." Her eyes darted around for a moment. "Garth doesn't know I'm here."

My arms fell to my side, and I took a small step back. "What do you want from me?" I whispered.

She shifted her weight in the chair and glanced around the salon. "I'll take that botanical shampoo."

I nodded silently and gestured toward the sinks. I offered a smock, and she buttoned it under her chin. She followed to the shampoo sink and leaned back over the tub. I tested the water under my hand before beginning to wet her brownish red hair, which felt coarse in my hands. "Let me know if that water's too hot."

She closed her eyes and crossed her arms, succumbing to the shampoo. I worked the soap into her scalp and scrubbed, rinsed, repeated. I carefully aimed the spray around her hairline, taking care not to soak her neck. When all the shampoo had disappeared down the drain, I squeezed a generous portion of conditioning cream into my palm and worked it down her strands. As I worked, her eyes remained closed, and I snuck peeks at the stray hairs on her untamed eyebrows, asymmetrical from a scar running through the left side. Her face was pale, no makeup covering dark circles under her eyes. She'd pushed up the sleeves of her sweater, displaying rolls of fat on her upper arms and those fingerprint bruises I was so familiar with. "We'll leave that on for three minutes, give you a deep conditioning."

"He loved giving me that car, the car you didn't deserve to keep." She spoke with her eyes still closed. "Said I look better driving it than you ever did."

"Is that right? Just one more minute, then we'll rinse that conditioner off."

"Always told me I was a better house cleaner too; you always let the place go, too lazy to be a good wife. Yep," she went on when I didn't respond, "that's just the way I heard it." She twirled the wedding ring on her left finger and positioned her hands so the gold band was on full display.

I checked the minute hand on the clock on the wall. Close enough. "Okay, that's three minutes. Going to rinse you now."

I pursed my lips as we finished up at the sink. Wrapping a towel around her head, I eased her up, gesturing back toward my chair. Once she was settled back in, we warily regarded each other again in the mirror.

"Aren't you jealous?" Loretta said.

"Jealous!" The question was beyond ridiculous. The tension drained from my body. "No." I shook my head. "No, I'm not jealous."

Loretta squinted her eyes suspiciously. "You're not angling to get him back?"

The question almost made me lose my balance. "No," I said emphatically. "Let me assure you, Loretta—I do not want him back."

"Well, when that child support order came through, that's what I figured. Nothing all those years, not a peep from you, then all of a sudden you want child support. What else could it mean, except that you want him?"

"Is that what he thinks, too?" I asked nervously.

"Not sure what he thinks. But I can tell you, I was, I am the queen, and everything I did was wonderful, and everything you did was horrible..." Her voice trailed off, and she squinted her eyes.

"Until he started hitting you," I finished her thought. "Then, when he was hitting you, he was comparing you to me and telling you how fantastic *I* was. How *I* was the better cook, the better house-keeper, the better lover. How *I* looked better driving that car he bought for *me*."

Her mouth hung open.

"I know Garth," I went on. "Dated him in high school, married him, had two children together. I know how he behaved when he got abusive, and I know I had enough of it. Getting out of that situation and saving my boys was the best decision of my life."

Her face reddened, and she bit her lip.

I gently put my hand on her arm. "Let's get you styled up." I sprayed some conditioning spray on her damp hair, grabbed my round brush, and the din from the blow dryer quieted our conversation. She closed her eyes again and seemed to relax a little under the warm air on her head and neck. The rhythm of the work calmed me as well, and I concentrated on each strand, styling her with as much care as a VIP customer. Truth was, I felt sorry for her.

Beverly hovered, checking up on things, and we gave each other a little nod as our eyes met across the salon. Sylvia, I saw, had also been keeping one eye toward my chair. At Eva's, just as at home, there were friends watching out for me.

After the blow dry, I plugged in the curling iron. "We'll let that heat up a moment."

"You're doing a nice job."

"I've got no quarrel with you."

She seemed to have relaxed in the chair. "Things changed between us," she said thoughtfully. "It was so good at the beginning. Then, just out of the blue, he got so angry. Nothing I did was right, good enough. And suddenly, you were perfect. Feel like I've been competing with you for years. You're up, I'm down, I'm up, you're down. So many times, I thought about coming to meet you, so I could take a look at my competition."

"I'm not your competition. I don't waste any thinking on Garth. At all." I marveled at how brave I sounded.

"Well, no doubt you've wondered about me," she said.

"Honestly, I didn't even know until very recently that you even existed."

She seemed taken aback by this. "Well, Jorie, all of a sudden, you and your boys seem to be everywhere. We turn on the television and see your boy on trial for hitting that mayor's husband. See you in the courtroom putting on a speech for the judge. Garth got all excited to see you on the television. And he made sure I heard all about how good you look, after all these years. Then we get the newspaper, and your boy's going to be valedictorian of his high school. Next, the newspaper says your other boy rescued the mayor's mother. And Garth swells up, all proud. That's my boy, he tells me. Now I'm down on the bottom, and you're up on top," she finished.

"So things aren't good for you right now," I said, looking at the bruising on her arms. She bristled and tried to push her sleeves down over the marks. "You know he had a rough childhood," she said defensively.

"Lots of folks had a rough childhood and don't hit their wives."

"And then came that child support order..." she went on.

"Did that set him off?" I asked. "You think he's out to get me now?"

160

"It's strange," Loretta said, shaking her head. "You'd think it would've made him angry. But it's like it had the opposite effect. He likes that you need him. He likes that some of his money is going to you and your boys."

This hit like a jab toward my pride. I certainly *didn't* need him or his money. At least that's what I'd always told myself.

"So now, we got our money going to your kids, away from mine," she said. "Might have to go out and get me a job so we can make ends meet."

She frowned and watched for my reaction.

"Just going to give you a little flip, like Farrah," I said, comb and curling iron in hand. We were quiet for a few minutes while I tugged and twisted her hair, then set it all with hairspray. She closed her eyes as I spritzed around her. As the hairspray dissipated up toward the ceiling, I cleared my throat and spoke quietly. "I'm truly sorry for everything going on with you. But let me tell you, honestly—getting a job might be the very best thing that happens to you. You had a hard time sneaking away to come to Jackson today, didn't you? He watches the odometer on that car, doesn't he? Doesn't let you see your own family, right?" I took a breath and went on. "Your kids, and I don't know if you have girls or boys or how many, but I know they're younger than my youngest, who's fourteen—they're growing up with this. If you're kidding yourself they're not seeing it, we both know they're hearing it. They see the marks on their mom. They're scared. You're scared. Getting out of the house, making your own money, making friends outside of the home, is going to make you stronger. It's going to give you options. Because one day, when you've had enough, you're going to need options."

"It was easy for you," she said. "I hear your parents left you that house. You got yourself a fully furnished, paid-off nice little house in town."

She was right about that. But it hadn't been easy. "I go to work every day to support my children. You can do the same thing. You *should* do the same thing."

I thought for a moment. "I don't have much space. But if you need a safe place to stay, my door is open. To you and your kids."

She stared, speechless.

I glanced toward the parking lot, toward the car that had been a gift given in love. I gathered myself up. Inside, I'd made a decision. "And we both know, Loretta, that Garth didn't leave me; I left him. We both know I had to leave the car behind. I work hard to support my children, but we don't have a car. *Everyone* should support their children, including you. Including Garth. Which is why I'm going to be cashing those child support checks." I turned toward the front of the store. "My next appointment is here. You're all set... you look very nice. Beverly will ring you out up front."

She stood, slipped off the smock and gathered her purse. "Just forget this conversation, I opened my mouth and said too much." She looked in the mirror. "Well anyway, it does look nice," she allowed.

We both gazed a moment, admiring her reflection in the mirror. Just two women, so much and so little in common.

"I'm glad we met," I said. "And if you ever need to.... well. You know where to find me."

"We have girls, Garth and I. Three girls." She patted her new hairdo. "I'll enjoy this for a few hours until I wet it down before he gets home."

I watched as the mother of my sons' half-siblings drove away in my old car and returned to my old life. I was sad for her, but proud of myself and proud of James and Will. And I wasn't afraid anymore.

Chapter 25

Will

AFTER SCHOOL, even though Sarah Jane was now staying with us and I didn't need to find her on the trail to find out what's going on, I decided to take off again on my brother's bike. There was really no news, anyway. We were all just waiting for the judge to make her decision. Ben had explained a little about it to me last night. He said if the judge decided James would be tried as a juvenile, it's called a delinquency. The longest he could be held was up to age twenty-one. And his record could be sealed, so no one knew about his felony. But if the judge decided James was gonna stand trial as an adult, he could get adult penalties, adult prison time. And the felony'd stay on his record forever.

Was it wrong to root for my brother? Whenever I saw Caroline, I felt guilty.

Lately, I felt like myself and James were getting mixed up. I'd been thinking of the Sting-Ray as my bike. After all, the seat's adjusted for my height now. Playing the drums, hanging out with the guys, just didn't seem interesting anymore.

I stopped by the Quick Mart like I always did. Candy and chips tucked into my pockets just tasted better than when Mom bought them for me. If I got caught, I'd go to jail just like James, and there we'd be, The Jenkins Brothers, outlaws. Jailbirds. Bandit-brothers. Since I was only fourteen, I was pretty sure I'd be tried as a juvenile. Would mom hire Ben to defend me too? Would pictures of my arrest, the trial, be in the newspaper like James?

Bettina wasn't at the counter when I walked in; she must be in the back. But when I approached the counter to pay for the one can of pop in my hand, a man I'd not seen before emerged from the backroom.

"Uh, hi, Bettina's not working today?"

His eyes narrowed. "Bettina doesn't work here anymore. Lots of inventory was coming up short. Either she was stealing herself from the store, or she was helping someone else do it."

He started ringing me up. "Just this?"

Sweat beaded on my forehead.

"Huh? Oh, yah, just the pop." I shifted my feet back and forth. "So, did Bettina get into trouble?"

"They let her go," said the man. "Fired her."

My stomach twisted into a sickening knot. The candy bulged in my pocket. I turned sideways and backed out of the store awkwardly after paying for the soda pop. I didn't feel like a cool outlaw-bandit anymore. With everything Mom was dealing with now, she didn't need my stupidity piled on. And my selfishness caused an innocent person to get fired. Why hadn't Bettina ratted me out and fought to keep her job?

This was wrong, I knew it.

Shaking, I climbed back onto the bike, rode straight home, and called Ben.

"Will?" Ben said. "Everything alright?"

"Yes. No. I did something really stupid. I think I need a lawyer."

"Where are you? Is your mom with you, are you guys safe?"

"I'm at the house. I think Mom is still at work. We're safe." I took a big breath. "But I did something really bad and I need your help."

"Okay Will," said Ben. "You did the right thing calling. What's going on?"

"Remember how you were telling me about unreliable witnesses? Well, I know one."

"Who are you talking about?"

"The lady who worked the counter at the Quick Mart."

"Will, you mean the Quick Mart on 93, where the accident happened?" Ben said through the phone, his voice quickening.

"Yes, that one. There's an unreliable witness who used to work there. Until I got her fired."

Chapter 26

James

Ben paced in my cell, and I part listened to what he was saying and part counted his steps. After all, I was the expert in pacing this cell, though Ben's taller, so his stride was a little longer than mine, so the number would add up differently, even though the dimensions were the same. He probably weighed more than me too, and the sound of his feet plodded with a different sound than mine. Then, on top of that, you gotta factor in he was wearing street shoes, and I had on these crazy prison sandals and my tube socks. His footsteps *definitely* sounded different from mine.

Ben asked lots of questions while he paced. His footsteps were all business. I pictured a stapler, heard the crunching sound as the staples punched into the paper.

"... spent several hours at the office going over the paperwork, the police report, the medical records from the hospital," Ben was saying. "One thing I noticed, James, once I received those medical records I subpoenaed, is the injuries of the four people riding in the truck are very curious."

"Umm, curious?" How could injuries be curious?

"Yes, curious. For example, you hit your head, right, and the medical records document you had some bruising to your forehead."

"I hit my head on the steering wheel," I said quickly.

"Right. The steering wheel. No bruising to your chest or abdomen from getting pushed into that steering wheel. Just the one bruise on your forehead."

"Oh, it happened so fast," I said. "My head must have just snapped into the top of the wheel."

"Uh-huh," Ben said. "I'm sure it did. Now the interesting thing, at least what I found very interesting, were the injuries on Sarah Jane Billings."

"Sarah Jane was in the front seat, she went into the dashboard," I said. Crimson red colored the air all around us. Smelled like fish.

"Right. The dashboard." Ben paused a moment. "Is that how it happened, James?"

"It happened just the way I told Sheriff Robb."

Ben pivoted to pace back toward me. There really was not much space in here for pacing. Even less with two people in the cell. The air was starting to feel really crowded. Ben's colors were a jumble, and they threw everything off.

"The way you told Sheriff Robb, the way you confessed you were behind the wheel the very moment he arrived on scene. Before he even had a chance to check on Ernie Cragen, to radio dispatch to send an ambulance, right?"

"Just like you read in the police report," I said, picking a spot in the corner to focus on.

Ben pivoted again and paced toward the hallway. "So yes, the injuries on Sarah Jane were very curious. Now Sarah Jane, she did have some bruising on her chest and abdomen. Would line up right about to the diameter of that steering wheel."

Diameter or circumference? I pondered the circular steering wheel in the truck. Was he figuring in inches or centimeters? Correcting my lawyer wouldn't be polite.

"And that's not all," Ben was saying. "Sarah Jane had other

injuries, too. Bruising on her back. Linear bruising. Bleeding a bit, not even scabbed over yet." Ben stopped pacing and looked right at me. "So those injuries must have just happened. And the marks on her back wouldn't have been caused by impact into the truck dashboard from the crash. At least that's what I think."

I was really good at staying quiet. We waited each other out.

"Then there's the witness statement," said Ben.

"Sheriff Robb was very thorough," I said. "He really knows his job."

Ben rubbed his chin. "The clerk at the Quick Mart. Bettina was her name, I believe. She corroborated the way you told it to Sheriff Robb."

"Well, there you have it," I said, as the crimson red softened to rosy-peach, much easier to breathe now. "She saw everything. She told it just the way she saw it."

Ben fixed a long, serious look at me. He gestured toward the cot. "Mind if I sit?"

"Be my guest."

"James, remember when we first met, and I explained attorney-client privilege, how everything you tell me is confidential? And remember when I explained how important it is for you to tell me *everything*, not hold back on any details?"

"Yessir. You went over the rules, fair and square." I liked rules. Rules told you how to solve a math problem, every time. Rules were predictable and reliable. Very clean.

"Well, I guess I should also tell you that as your attorney, I'm bound to represent your wishes. What you want to see happen with your own case."

This made me sit up a little taller in the chair by the metal desk. I was in charge. My case. My wishes.

Ben went on. "But what I guess I need to explain to you now, is that because you are a minor, and because I do suspect that Judge Fraser *is* going to agree to allow you to be tried as a minor, is that your best interests as a minor are a very important consideration. Very important indeed. Important to me, important to your mom, important to the judge. Important to you. And important to justice."

Justice. I pictured rays of sun piercing through the cotton-ball clouds, angels singing in soprano chorus. A wonderful, pure word.

"And sometimes," Ben said, "what a client wants to do is not in his own best interest. I'm your attorney. I have to represent your wishes. But I'm also an officer of the court." He paused a moment, then spoke very slowly, as if speaking to a child, which I guess he was, because I am a child, legally anyway. I forced myself to listen to what Ben was saying, "Seems to me, James, you might have made some decisions that are not in your own best interest."

The raging red started to boil again, very threatening, just like the sickening red of the crash, the smell of fish, nauseating, like metal scraping on pavement. My breathing quickened to a pant as if I were climbing Grove Hill on the Sting-Ray. I missed my bike. Why, why, was Will riding my bike? Panic, now. Hiding under covers, my arms around Will, angry raised voices from the other room, dishes crashing against the wall, the smack of hand upon skin. The sound of Mom crying. Anger boiled inside me, scalding to the touch. And there, to the side, rose the soft cornflower blue of Sarah Jane, trying to just be, to just be left alone. Not be hit and abused. I could be strong. I couldn't protect Mom; I was too little. But I could protect Sarah Jane.

Ben watched me, waiting for my response.

Counting and numbers were the thing. I planted my feet firmly into the floor, looked my lawyer in the eye, and started: "Three. Nine. Eighty-one. Six Thousand, Five Hundred and Sixty-one. Forty-three Million, Forty-six Thousand, Seven Hundred and Twenty-one..."

"James—" started Ben, but stopped at the sight of Sheriff Robb, standing outside my cell.

"Judge is calling the parties to the courtroom now," said the sheriff. "She's issuing her decision."

Chapter 27

Jorie

PLEASE, *please, please,* I silently willed with each footstep as I pounded the pavement from Eva's, past the bowling alley, past Henry's, down Main Street, to the courthouse. My heart stuck in my throat, making it harder to breathe. The whistle from the afternoon train sounded in the distance. James A. Rhodes stared down from his pedestal, his limestone eyes full of judgment. I looked away.

A crowd was gathering, and people were filing into the court-room. The news cameras were here again. Men and women I'd known all my life nodded and stood aside for me to pass as I made my way toward the front of the gallery. I slid into my seat on the wooden bench just as Judge Fraser entered from her chambers. Shafts of afternoon light from the chandelier reflected a concentric pattern onto the marble floor. James and Ben sat at the defense table.

"All rise," called the bailiff.

"Be seated," said the judge as she took the bench.

"On the matter of bindover," she began. "I will explain my deci-sion-making." She cleared her throat, and the crowd murmured. The prosecutor shifted in his seat. Someone behind me coughed. And then, all was still, all attention on the judge.

"The law requires me to consider multiple factors in determining if a youth will be tried as an adult, including probable cause and amenability. Included in those considerations are age, the mental and physical condition of the youth, prior juvenile record, prior attempts at rehabilitation. I also look at the family environment and the youth's school record." I glanced over at the news camera positioned to capture Judge Fraser and also angled to include a side view of James, waiting and listening.

"There is probable cause to believe that the juvenile James Jenkins committed the alleged act, which would be a felony if committed by an adult. The alleged act resulted in the loss of innocent life." She paused. "I will say that I believe the Jenkins are doing the best they can. James has not had a positive father role model in his life. I understand... that's tough." Judge Fraser was looking right at me now. "And yet, other children also have absent fathers, and they don't drive without a license. They don't speed into an intersection and hit and kill a pedestrian. This was an appallingly reckless, senseless act. And now other children in Jackson are without a father. How will those children cope?"

To my right, Mayor Cragen stifled a muffled sob. I'd never heard her cry before, certainly never any uncontrolled public display of emotion. I sucked in my breath.

"Now, I don't believe this was a premeditated or intended act. And yet, still, this was simply an appallingly reckless event." The judge shook her head sadly.

Judge Fraser went on. "With regard to the mental health of the youth, I'm going to be honest, I'm concerned. Counseling, perhaps some type of psychotropic medication, is in order. Although no link was demonstrated between his mental health and this particular act, the Court is concerned about the odd behaviors, the obsessions, talking to himself. Synesthesia I've not encountered before and admittedly do not know much about. So yes, the Court is concerned. Counter-balancing that was evidence presented, showing that James is a loyal young man demonstrating emotional empathy, some maturity and a desire to protect others. He has no prior delinquent or unruly behaviors. No behavioral problems at school. Obviously, he excels academically. His family environment, despite troubling beginnings, has become one of stability and love, thanks entirely to his mother. Some children exposed to violence become violent later themselves. But not so here. Not with James Jenkins. So yes, the Court does see all of that.

"This seventeen-year-old young man, only six months away from reaching the age of majority, is charged with a very serious alleged crime, which has not yet been proven. Focusing only on bindover, this Court cannot find that James would not be amenable to rehabilitation through the juvenile system. I cannot find the safety of the community would be compromised. I believe James can be rehabilitated."

The heaviness in my heart started very tentatively to lift, just a tiny bit.

Judge Fraser spoke with authority now, all brisk and down to business. "And so. I rule that James will *not* be bound over and tried as an adult. We will retain jurisdiction in the juvenile system and set a hearing on the merits for the alleged juvenile delinquency charge of felony vehicular homicide."

The announcement sent a whoosh of air that seemed to pass right through James, through Ben, through me, through Mayor Cragen. There was excited whispering from those seated behind us. The camera, I saw, had swung to focus on James for his reaction, and then it was focusing on me. Numb and too weak to compose my face, I shook, every part of my body shook. Not shaking from the train. Shaking from within.

Thank you, thank you, thank you, I silently screamed, clenching and unclenching my fists.

James looked to Ben, who excitedly gave him a hug and grasped his right hand into a vigorous handshake. James looked dazed and bewildered as Ben patted him on the back. James turned, searching for me, and I gave him a big smile and nod. *Good,* I mouthed. Good,

good, good. Thumbs up sign. Ben looked back toward me now as well, a wide smile on his face. *Thank you,* I mouthed to Ben. He beamed and sparks flashed between us. Ben had saved James. I wanted to wrap my arms around him and kiss him in front of everyone. He was my knight in shining armor, or at the very least, my briefcase-wielding gorgeous blue-eyed knight in polished dress shoes.

Selfishly, I refused to look at Candy Cragen. I'd done my best to express what needed to be expressed. How many times, how many ways could we say we were sorry? What happened to Ernie wasn't right, but nothing could be done to bring him back, and destroying James' life over an accident wasn't right either. This moment was about us. This moment was about James, his childhood, his life. I wasn't going to walk around this town ashamed anymore.

I wasn't going to apologize anymore for who we were.

Though there was movement and chattering all around me, I became aware that the hearing wasn't over yet. The judge spoke again, something about choosing a trial date. Relief washed over me like the warm buzz from a shot of Wild Turkey.

The prosecutor said something I didn't even hear, and then Ben was on his feet. "Your Honor, given the Court's decision to try the defendant as a juvenile, we request the public, the press, be excluded from further proceedings, so we can protect the privacy of the minor."

I glanced at the news camera, swiveled away from me now and back on the judge.

"Closing the proceedings is within my discretion," Judge Fraser said. "I agree this has been a high-profile case, and we did cover some sensitive issues in the bindover hearing. I'm going to order that only those with a direct personal interest be permitted to attend further hearings. The county prosecutor's office can give news briefings afterward to the press. No more cameras in the courtroom."

"Thank you, Your Honor," said Ben.

"Now. We still need to pick a date for a hearing on the merits," muttered the judge, looking over the paperwork before her. "We can go off record in a moment, to look at tentative dates." She peered over to the prosecutor. "Prosecutor, how many witnesses do you anticipate calling? Do you think we can do this in two days, or should we set aside three?"

James whispered urgently into Ben's ear, but Ben shook his head no, shooing him off.

"Ben," James said sharply, getting louder. The prosecutor, the judge, looked over.

"James," admonished Ben fiercely. "Not now."

But James kept talking. He was getting agitated, waving his hands, arguing with Ben. I thought about his mood swings, his mixed-up senses. Oh Lord, don't let him fall apart now, not after we'd come so far.

"Mr. Atwater, please control your client," said the judge.

I heard fragments of what James was saying to Ben. "*My* case. *My* wishes. You're my lawyer."

"No James, wait, we'll talk about this after the hearing," Ben told him.

"Your Honor?" James had his hand up now, addressing Judge Fraser directly, student waiting to be called upon, like mother, like son.

The judge raised her eyebrow.

Before she could respond, James was on his feet. "Your Honor. Don't set a trial date." James didn't sound off like he did when he was ranting about numbers or bicycle repair. In fact, he sounded totally in control and confident. "I want to plead guilty. Right now, I want to plead guilty."

Exclamations erupted from the crowd.

Ben scrambled to his feet. "Your Honor, I'd like to move for the appointment of a guardian ad litem to represent my client's best interests. Since we are within the juvenile system, the Court must consider his best interests as a minor. I am bound to represent his wishes. But there is a conflict between his wishes and his best interests."

"Yes..." Judge Fraser said. She pulled off her reading glasses and twirled them. "If there's a conflict, we do need to appoint a guardian ad litem on behalf of the minor."

"Young man," she said to my son, sounding surprisingly kind. "We are going to recess now. Mr. Atwater will continue as your legal counsel. Another attorney is going to represent your best interests. I'm going to give you time to meet with and talk to both individuals, to hear your legal options and have your questions answered. I urge you to take advantage of the professional advice provided to you. We're not going to do anything further today. Court is adjourned."

* * *

I sat on the cot next to James and put my arms around his shoulders.

"The ruling is such good news, such a relief," I gushed. I gave his shoulder a squeeze. "*Thank God* that judge understands you're still a boy! You will have your life back."

After the hearing, I'd slipped out the back, not wanting yet to speak to Ben or to anyone else, really, before talking to James. The sheriff had allowed me down the hall after James had been walked back into his cell, in his leg chains.

James nodded. He also looked relieved.

"Mom," he started, "I want to tell you... I'm sorry for putting you through all this."

"Ssshhh. You don't have to say it. It was an accident. A mistake, just a mistake, that's all that it was."

He studied his hands. "More than just a mistake... a person died," he whispered. "No one ever meant for somebody to die. I'm very sorry for Mr. Cragen, for all of them. I can't be sorry enough. But I want you to know I'm sorry to you too."

My son sounded so grownup, despite the court ruling recognizing him as a child. I tried to match his gravity and maturity in my own response.

"Well, I'm sorry then too, you should know. I'm sorry you had to grow up without a father in your life. It's been a hard path for you, just like Judge Fraser said. For Will too." We paused a moment. We were veering into things the boys and I just didn't talk about. Gathering myself up, I pressed onward. "I'm sorry you overheard your dad and I arguing when you were little. That must have been very frightening for a little boy."

"Hearing, seeing," James muttered.

"I guess you saw some things too," I said.

We were quiet a moment, thinking. Choosing amnesia to wipe away painful memories had been a powerful balm, but I was beginning to understand those wounds might need sunlight upon them to really heal. Piling all that in a corner attic and throwing a blanket over it hadn't helped my boys confront what they needed to. What all three of us needed to, I supposed.

"Guess I never put together how numbers and math were a way for you to deal with all that."

"Counting," James said. "It's very orderly. Like a royal blue procession. The numbers line up and they march on. Precision. Very sharp."

"Yes, counting, counting. Funny how you're always counting, but Will didn't take to that."

James' mouth fell open, then he gave me a gentle scowl, like a teacher chastising a student who just doesn't get it. "Mom, what do you think Will is doing when he's drumming? He's keeping the beat steady, keeping the band from speeding up or slowing down. He's keeping the time. He's counting. *One*, two, three, four, *one*, two, three, four."

"Oh."

"And on the bike," James continued, "it's more counting. How many times do your feet go around, how many times does your right knee rise up in a minute when you crank the pedals? That's cadence. How many miles per hour are you going? That's speed. How long will it take to ride the distance between your starting point and your finishing point, then return? It won't be the same, because you have to factor in which direction the wind is blowing. Plus, you might be more tired on the return trip. Which cog size, gear ratio? Are you going to shift down to spin up the hills and shift up on descent, so you're always pedaling, never coasting? How many gears does the bike have? And what about your foot on the pedal? There's physics to that. They have toe clips now for bike pedals, to keep your foot locked to the pedal, so you're propelling the bike not just by pushing down but by pulling your foot up too, the whole rotation 'round. Then there's the weight of the bike. Lighter bikes are faster, of course. More rigid, absorb shock waves from the road. Racing bikes have a shorter wheelbase, their turn is much tighter. And narrower wheels and tires, of course, are more aerodynamic."

Obviously, James had given a great deal of thought to this subject. "Well, my goodness, it's easy to see why you're going to be the vale-dictorian of your class."

I remembered there was some good news to share with James. "And speaking of bicycling," I went on, "I didn't get a chance to tell you yet, but Lana picked up a used ten-speed from a garage sale for us! She brought it around just yesterday. So you two don't have to share that little Sting-Ray anymore."

"A new bike?" James jumped up and started pacing, electrified. His eyes shone, and a wide grin of excitement flashed across his face.

"Yes, something to look forward to when you get out of here," I said. "Which should be soon. Ben's a good attorney, he's going to get you a ruling of innocence, I just know it." I looked at him pointedly, motioning for him to sit at his metal chair and stop pacing. "Which is why, James, I *don't* understand you telling the judge you're ready to plead guilty."

He sat and regarded me.

"What color is the new bike?"

"It's green," I told him. "Why would you tell the judge that? Ben sure didn't want you saying that."

"Lime green, dark forest green, olive green...?" he asked.

"A very bright green, Kelly green, like a St. Patrick's Day green."

James pondered a moment, ideas flickering in his eyes. He cracked his knuckles.

"James," I snapped.

"Pleading guilty is something I want to do," he said.

"Well, I sure don't understand your decision-making on this one. You better explain yourself to me, young man."

"Mom, think about their family. Why put Mrs. Mayor and their kids through listening to a trial, listening to all the details of how we hit Mr. Cragen and he died? Everyone knows the truck hit him. Everyone knows I was driving."

"Well, thinking of their feelings and how all that is going to affect them is very kind, I do appreciate that," I said. "But you didn't do it intentionally. And what do you mean 'we' hit Mr. Cragen?"

"Oh, just me and the other kids in the car. But I did it, I was the one who couldn't stop in time," he said.

"Yes, as you keep saying," I said. The boys weren't the only ones in this family who understood numbers. True, I'm 'justa hairdresser.' But some things here just didn't add up. "Sparing them the emotions of a trial isn't going to bring him back."

"But it's something I can give them," he said, before adding, "and now that the judge has decided I'll be sentenced as a minor, the most it could be is three years."

"James, please don't. Please listen to Ben's advice."

"What does the new bike smell like?" he asked.

"Smell? Haven't noticed really any smell to it, James."

"How's Sarah Jane doing?"

I sighed, exasperated that we couldn't stay on subject. Keep it gentle, I reminded myself. Conversations with James could be challenging, but so far, he wasn't spinning off on delusions, and this had been one of our better talks in recent memory. I didn't want him to shut down and stop talking to me. My boy was growing up, I knew. Secrets were kept from him, from Will—to protect them. And now, I understood, secrets were being kept from me.

"Sarah Jane is a very nice girl, very respectful. Helps around the house. Does her homework every night. No complaints at all. In fact, we like having her stay with us. I understand things were not good at her father's home," I ventured, raising an eyebrow.

His lips tightened, and a shadow crossed his face. "No, Mom, not good for her. Not good for her there. Dark purple, dark purple, very bad." He started plunking each finger rhythmically into his thigh, counting silently to himself.

"Hon," I said gently. "It's wrong that her father was abusive. Absolutely, horribly wrong. But you can't fix everything. You don't have to take all that on yourself."

"I can do it, Mom. I'm *proud* I can do it."

"Do what?" I pleaded. "James, *what* are you doing? Why do you want to plead guilty?"

James fixed his eyes in the distance; he wasn't going to answer.

"Well," I said after a moment, "I'm hoping you'll be having a very *thorough* talk with Ben about all this, like the judge suggested." Ben will probably be able to fill me in afterward, I thought.

As if reading my thoughts, James said, "Ben explained attorney-client privilege. It goes right along with hiring an attorney; this rule that the attorney has to keep secrets of his client."

"I hired Ben," I said.

"You hired him. But I'm the client."

Well, now.

Keep it gentle.

I rose and busied myself gathering the completed school assignments folder into James' backpack, zipping it up, ready to return to the school the next morning. I ran my hands over the nylon. The backpack of the senior class valedictorian, a teenage boy locked in leg shackles by a sheriff twice his age, just to be led into the courtroom from a jail cell where he's housed right alongside adult criminals. My hands shook with anger. That damn Sheriff Robb. With my back still to James, I directed my next question toward the wall by his cot. "Did Sarah Jane ever call the cops when her father was hitting her?"

I turned to face my son. If James was taken aback that I was this direct, he didn't show it.

"She tried calling, I think her mom did too, before her mom left. No one ever did anything about it."

I pursed my lips, thinking of those fingerprint bruises on the Sheriff's wife, Shelly. Some things never changed.

"Well, it's just not right. But I hope after she gets her diploma, she's able to get herself a job, get on to better things in her life. I hope that for both of you. Actually, I heard over at Eva's that Mayor Cragen's assistant is going to be out on maternity leave and the mayor's looking to hire a new gal for typing, filing, answering the phone." James watched me, astonished. "You know, Mabel Green's daughter works there. She got married last year, expecting her baby in about six weeks," I went on. "So there's a job vacancy open."

"Sarah Jane can't work there," James said.

"Maybe not. Under the circumstances." I watched James. I felt like I was in a chess match with my own son.

"So yes," I went on, "you both need to move forward, to better things. Sarah Jane had it tough. You had it tough too, and I'm sorry there's been no car for us. Guess that's why you got into the bicycling. Guess that's why getting behind the wheel of that truck was so tempting. But some things are changing for us, James. We've started receiving child support payments from your father. There's going to be some extra money coming in, and I'm thinking furthering your education would be a very good way to spend it. College, maybe. But I don't know how we make that happen if you're stuck in kiddie prison at the state youth reformatory."

"It's up between Chillicothe and Circleville. The route of the great bicycle tour goes right past it. I'll be able to see the cyclists go by right from there, I think," James said.

"James, I don't *want* you locked up in there watching cyclists riding by," I cried. "Watching the bicycle tour that you love going by, right past you! Watching your friends going on to college without you, when all of a sudden now we've got the money to send you.

You're at the top of your class, brilliant in math, just think what you can become! I want you to fight for yourself. I want you to be strong, be brave. Why won't you fight?!"

"Mom, I *am*."

"You want to ride that bicycle tour. It's all you've talked about for the last year, James. Riding two hundred miles in two days!"

"Oh, almost forgot, I have another letter for you to mail to the Crashing Crankers Bicycle Club." He rose and pulled a sealed envelope from underneath one of his notebooks. "Next one I send, I'll make sure to put down the return address for the place in Chillicothe. Bet they might just write back."

He looked at his desk, at the bicycling magazines strewn amongst school books. Sitting here in this cell, patiently doing his assignments, writing unanswered letters to a post office box, while his dreams passed him by. Talking so infuriatingly calmly about pleading guilty, about doing three years in the youth facility. I didn't understand any of this.

"Mom," James said, softly. "Right now, what I'm doing takes more strength than riding two hundred miles in two days. There's physics to this too—it doesn't look like it from the spectator's point of view, but holding still is even harder than moving. This is the way for me to be strong and brave. I won't change my mind."

I pictured our house quivering and shaking as the train rumbled through Jackson, ferrying coal from the mines, herds of bicyclists in colorful jerseys flying up and down the hills of the Scioto River valley, young adults marching across the gymnasium stage of Jackson High in cap and gown to accept their diplomas, bulbs flashing as proud parents aimed their cameras, moving on, moving on, while James stayed still, held still, as time passed, in a cell.

He got up and gave me a hug.

"Tell Will to enjoy that green ten-speed," he added. "He should get some oil on the chain."

Chapter 28

Will

I'D BEEN TRYING to figure out why I stole all that candy. I took stuff I don't even really like that much, like stuff with caramel in it, and bubble gum flavor.

Did I want to get caught? To see how Mom would react? It never occurred to me I'd just keep getting away with it... or that somebody would lose their job.

That clerk, Bettina, saw, I'm sure of it. Why didn't she say anything?

I didn't have any answers.

Ben picked me up after school, while Mom was still cutting hair, to drive me over to the Quick Mart so we could talk to the manager. Ben said I have to fess up to everything. And apologize. Then we had to make an offer for me to pay back everything I owe. Restitution, he'd called it. He was going to try to make some deal with them where we worked out "an arrangement," in exchange for the manager not making a police report. Then, he said, after that's worked out, we got to tell Mom.

I fidgeted by the bike racks, my backpack over my shoulder. No Sting-Ray today. I'd ditched Sarah Jane so she wouldn't see me getting into Ben's car. It'd be really embarrassing for Sarah Jane to find out I was a pickpocket.

"Hey Will," Rick called out, backpack over his shoulder, pausing by the bike racks. I could tell he was curious why I was standing around.

"Hey."

Rick looked like he wanted to say something, but couldn't get the words out. "Been drumming much?" he finally said.

Ben's red Mustang swung up to the curb. "I gotta go." I felt Rick's eyes following me as I ran up to the car and tossed my books in the back seat. Maybe I wouldn't be making stupid mistakes like shoplifting potato chips and Twizzlers if I still had the guys to talk to, coming over after school for band practice. Shit. I missed my friends. Guess they're just doing what their parents made them do. But I'm pretty sure I wouldn't have stopped talking to one of them if *their* brother got into trouble. Anyway, what I had going on now was none of their business.

I was grateful Ben was helping me make this right. It was like... well, it was almost like... having a dad.

* * *

"That went well," Ben said. He held the door open for me as we exited the Quick Mart and straightened the lapels of his suit jacket. "You did good letting me do all the talking when we first went in. Then, you were respectful with the apology. And the restitution plan is fair."

"But Ben, I don't know how I'm going to earn the money to pay it off," I said. "Maybe since I'm fourteen I could get a work permit, get a summer job?"

"Maybe, Will. We'll figure it out. I might need some help around the office. I can show you how we organize documents. You could make copies, shred old files. On a part-time basis, of course."

"In your law office?" I perked up. It was interesting when Ben taught me about legal strategies, different types of evidence, questioning witnesses. Unreliable witnesses. Like the one we were on our way to see right now.

"I'm kind of surprised the manager gave us Bettina's home address," Ben said. "But it's a good opportunity for you to apologize to her directly."

Ben was right, of course, but facing Bettina had me even more nervous than facing the manager. I never meant to hurt anyone, but I had. "Will you hire Bettina back on?" I'd asked the manager after he'd accepted my apology and the restitution plan.

"No way," he'd said. "The store lost money from the missing inventory."

"But it wasn't her—it was me. I stole the stuff. She didn't do anything."

"Right, she didn't do anything, that's the problem. She didn't stop you, she didn't report the thefts, she just let you rob the place. More than once. We reviewed the placement of the mirrors and all store aisles are perfectly visible from the cash register."

I'd felt my face flush with color.

"It was completely unacceptable," the manager went on. "Bettina is untrustworthy." He'd paused a moment, hands on his hips. "So why *was* she letting you get away with it? You two know each other, or what?"

"No Mister, I don't know her. I'd never even seen her before," I'd told him. "Maybe she didn't see me after all."

He'd squinted his eyes skeptically.

"It wasn't her fault," I'd insisted.

Ben had put his hand on my shoulder and given me a little shove toward the door, with a boisterous, "thanks again, we'll be in touch soon!" to the manager. "Time to get out of there before he changes his mind," Ben mumbled under his breath once we were in the parking lot.

Back in the Mustang, Ben set the paper with Bettina's address on the dashboard, and we were on our way to Oak Hill. "You know where Boggs Road is?" Ben muttered.

"Ya, think so. I've ridden the Sting-Ray over there."

Ben glanced over, looking surprised. "Sounds like you've been riding pretty far from home. I wonder how many miles that is?"

I shrugged. James' bike didn't have an odometer. Neither did the new green bike, but with the gears and the lighter weight, it was faster and easier to ride. I'd been going further and further on my after-school rides.

"What's the longest ride you've done?" Ben asked.

"I've been out for three hours," I said, thinking. "Mom always wants me home in time for dinner and homework. Now that she's enforcing this homework hour in the evenings for Sarah Jane and me," I added, rolling my eyes.

"Three hours, that's probably at least a thirty-mile ride," Ben said. He sounded impressed. "Pretty good, Will."

He slowed as we entered little Oak Hill, a town even smaller than Jackson. On the main road was the corner gas station, the post office, and the Welsh Museum filled with photos of the Welsh mining families who settled southern Ohio. In elementary school we'd had a field trip there. They have a triple harp inside. A massive American flag flew in the breeze off the flagpole by the fire station.

Ben turned down Boggs Road, and my stomach tightened. The house numbers were on the mailboxes, and Ben pulled to the side and parked in front of 356 Boggs Road, a very small, white house with a completely bare front porch. One of the posts seemed to sag, giving the roof line an off-balance look.

Ben gave me an encouraging nod as I trudged out of the car and trailed behind him to the front door. Ben knocked. I couldn't hear any sound from within. *Maybe Bettina's not home*, I thought to myself. Maybe she'd moved and didn't live here anymore. My eyes took in the bare front porch. No rocking chair, no mat to wipe your shoes. A flicker of color caught my eye in the side yard. Some kind of sun catcher, maybe. But before I could crane my head around to get a better look, the front door opened, and there stood Bettina, the silent gas station clerk, the unreliable witness, holding the door open with a, "come on in." Almost as if she'd been expecting us.

"Afternoon Ma'am," Ben said. "Ben Atwater, attorney at law. And this here is Will Jenkins. We've come to talk to you about losing your job at the Quick Mart, if you have a moment for a conversation."

"Yes, Mr. Atwater, I understand. Will, yes, of course. Well, come on in and set down."

She ushered us into her front room, which was as full of knick knacks as the front porch was barren. She had an old pump organ kitty-cornered and adorned with little cherub angel figurines, picture frames, and ceramic flower arrangements. An assortment of colored vases in blues, pinks, violet sat atop a mirrored tray on a large bureau. Almost every inch of the walls were covered with framed cross-stitch creations, oil paintings in dark wood, antique-looking frames, and beveled mirrors. There was a wing chair and a couch that looked like something you'd see in a castle.

"Now y'all set yourselves down while I put some tea on the kettle," Bettina said over her shoulder, going down the hall to her kitchen.

"I don't drink tea," I started to say, but Ben cut me off with a sharp warning look, and I swallowed my words.

"Cup of afternoon tea would be just very nice, very nice indeed," he told Bettina.

"Uh, yes please, thank you Ma'am," I added.

She returned with a silver tray, a teapot, three cups, cream, sugar and little silver spoons. Wordlessly I noticed Bettina had set out sugar cookies, the kind with the colored sugar. Well, she must know those were my favorite since those were usually on my shoplifting list at the Quick Mart. I gulped. Sure did look like she'd been expecting me to drop by.

Ben cleared his throat and gave me a look.

I took a swallow of tea, which wasn't that bad after all.

"Ma'am..." I started.

186

"Call me Bettina, Will," she interjected.

"Yes Ma'am, Bettina, I'm here to apologize for you losing your job on account of my stealing." I looked down and my head sank. "I'm very sorry I got you fired," I said, very quietly, almost in a whisper.

I felt Bettina watching me carefully, but was too ashamed to lift my gaze to meet hers.

"All right then, Will. I accept your apology. It's okay now."

I lifted my head, confused. Nothing was okay. How could it be okay?

Shifting a bit on the couch, I looked at Bettina, astonished. "But you lost your job! Because of me. Aren't you mad at me?"

"No, Will," she said, taking a quick sip of tea. "I'm not mad at you."

"You saw me taking that stuff. You let me do it."

"I see lots of things."

Ben nodded his head, jumping in. "Right, you certainly would see things, see many things, from the vantage point of the counter and the cash register. A person stationed there, I imagine, would be able to see most of what's going on inside the store, as well as whatever may be happening outside in the parking lot. Or by the gas pumps. Or in the intersection where 93 comes into town..." Ben's words hung in the air as he waited to see if she'd take the bait.

But Bettina was looking at me, not Ben.

"Did you get caught?" she asked.

"No Ma'am."

"Sheriff Robb didn't arrest you then, hah," she chuckled, a hint of sarcasm and contempt in her voice when she mentioned the Sheriff's name.

"No Ma'am. I mean Bettina."

"Please, have a cookie," she gestured toward the tray. I obediently picked up a sugar cookie and took a bite, even though I wasn't hungry.

"Will told the Quick Mart manager what he did and apologized and worked out a restitution plan to pay the store back," Ben said.

She watched me carefully. "So then why? Why did you come forward?"

I gulped, the cookie dry in my throat. "Because you lost your job. When I found out they fired you, I told Ben. He's my brother's lawyer. I never meant for an innocent person to get blamed for something she didn't do."

Bettina nodded with satisfaction and sat back on her couch. Her eyes flickered in recognition of something larger, some deeper meaning I could not see.

"Will, innocent people get blamed every day for things they didn't do," she said. "The world can be a very unfair place." She smiled as she paused to take a small sip of tea, but it was a sad smile. "There's truth and there's lies. Malicious lies, manipulative lies. But also, harmless lies. Benevolent lies. There's not just one type of truth either, you'll come to understand, as you go through life. In fact, there are many flavors of the truth." Her words tapered off, her eyes wandering over the cluttered room, and I wasn't sure if she was still talking to us or even remembered we were in her house.

"Innocent people don't have to take the consequences, if witnesses speak up," said Ben.

"Your brother's lawyer is very smart, Will," Bettina said. "James is in good hands with Attorney Atwater."

How did Bettina know my brother is James? I wondered if James had also been stopping at the Quick Mart on the Sting-Ray. I had a strange feeling, somehow, that Bettina knew us, but shrugged it off. She'd probably just been reading about the trial in the papers.

She stood and smoothed her skirt. I glanced at Ben and understood it was our signal to leave. Had we done what we came here to do? She'd accepted my apology, told me things were okay. But still, things felt confused. Unfinished.

"How old are you, Will?" Bettina asked as she saw us to the door.

"Fourteen."

She nodded in satisfaction. "That sounds about right. Y'all have yourselves a good day now, and thank you for coming to visit with me."

On the front porch, the color from the wind-catcher flickered in the light, as the door shut behind us. Except now I had a better view into the side yard. It wasn't a wind-catcher at all. My jaw hung open, and I froze as I struggled to understand what I was seeing. Last year, in eighth grade art class, we all made garden arches, formed from twigs we braided and lashed together with burlap and then painted in bright colors. It was to be a Father's Day gift. Having no dad around, I'd given mine to Mom. But I remembered sitting a few rows behind Caroline, watching her construct her arch for her father, Mr. Cragen and painting it green, orange, blue, yellow. And here sat Caroline's garden arch, her gift to her father, not at her mother's home, but at the home of the unreliable witness.

"Will?" Ben called out.

"Coming." I joined him in the car.

We were both silent, thinking, as we headed back to Jackson.

"You know, one thing that's been bothering me about all this," Ben said after a while. "Why was Ernie Cragen over by the Quick Mart the day he got hit? Actually, many things about this whole thing bother me. But this one thing: why was Ernie over at that intersection? On foot? His office was at the insurance agency in town. That's blocks away from the Quick Mart. He wasn't filling up his gas tank. Why was he walking all the way over there, in the late afternoon?"

I swallowed and silently stared out the window. All I could think about was Caroline.

Chapter 29

James

THINGS WERE GOING JUST as we'd planned. Sarah Jane was safe. I'd be tried as a juvenile, except of course I wasn't going to be tried at all. When I pleaded guilty, there'd be no need for a trial. And in a couple of years, I'd be out.

I pictured myself a superhero with a red, white, and blue cape, soaring high with the eagles, with a force so strong that ripples of wind in my wake shattered glass and summoned waves in every lake I passed over. Almost like a supersonic boom. A symphony playing, or maybe a brass band, patriotic and bragging on every note. People might just stand and salute as I smoked by. They would gather in their front lawns and point overhead. There goes James Jenkins, protector of the weak.

I got up and started pacing the cell, counting my steps, feeling buoyant.

What else would people say about me? There goes James Jenkins, mathematical genius. Class valedictorian. Big-time bicyclist. A phenom of Jackson.

Or, would they say, there goes that crazy weirdo? He talks to himself. He sees sounds, hears colors, smells words.

I stopped walking and grabbed the side of my chair. It was chilly in the Jackson County Jail today and very still. Nobody to talk to. As usual, it was just Mr. Perkins and me, and he must be napping. Nobody else thrown in the slammer for driving drunk, for stealing, certainly not for killing someone. No wonder I was the talk of the town.

Maybe they wouldn't say any of it. Maybe people would just forget about me. Maybe Sarah Jane would forget. She'd find a new guy, not wait for me.

I turned over in my head what Mom said about going to college, about riding the bicycle tour. And we had a new bike at home, a green ten-speed. How did that even happen? Will somehow got Mom to get a new bike, when that's what I'd been wanting for years? Did she use the money she's got coming in now? Mom all of a sudden decided to take child support when we didn't need anything for all this time?

Home didn't feel orange anymore. Sarah Jane was living at my house. Was Ben living there too? Sounded like he'd been staying there, which didn't make any sense. Did the house still rumble when the train passed? It must, but the ground had shifted. Brown, it felt. Dark brown.

I sank into the desk chair and paged through my bicycling magazines. I'd sent many, many letters to the cycling club in Columbus, but they never wrote back. Sometimes I wondered if it was even real. Maybe the cycling club didn't exist anymore. I threw the magazines across the metal desk and stretched onto the cot to stare at the ceiling. Mom and Will were always getting on me for talking too much about biking, about numbers. I've tried to pay better attention to those things, to figure out if other people view things the same as me. Guess that was especially important, now that I knew my senses were all screwed up. Had I imagined the bicycle club? I wanted it so much to be real; had I made it up? I pictured an empty post office box in Columbus that no one ever checked. A bottomless cave, a dark pit leading nowhere. Where my letters just sat, unopened. Unread. Unanswered.

I was invisible, forgotten.

No, James, no, I told myself. Don't second guess this thing.

I jumped up and grabbed one of the magazines and turned to the back where it listed the name of the club, the address. My fingers ran over the letters, and I felt each one, almost like they were written in Braille, leaping out to me like sparks, each letter chiming in a different pitch like notes on the piano. Eighty-eight keys on a piano. Twenty-six letters in the alphabet. It *had* to be real.

"Come help me," I whispered. "Come help my family."

I ran my fingers over the address one more time, then tossed the magazine aside. I knew what I needed to do: fire Ben, plead guilty, and get sent to that youth facility to serve my time. Then, I just needed to hold still.

The room cooled down, back to calm, orderly gun-metal gray.

I opened my notebook and started back into my calculations.

Chapter 30

Jorie

Bags from Henry's dangled from my arms, filled with noodles, sauce, ground beef, parmesan cheese. We'd do spaghetti and meatballs tonight, I thought flatly. Walking home held no joy now, without the sounds of Will's band rocking the neighborhood. Without both of my boys at home to cook for.

I knew the day would come when they'd grow into men and leave the nest, of course. But not like this. Not at age seventeen. To just not come home one day. To be serving time, of all things. All because one moment changed everything. Crazily, I allowed a guilty moment of gratitude that my parents and Granny weren't here to see my first-born in the Jackson County Jail, but swiftly banished this thought from my head. What kind of mom was ashamed of her son, when really, there's not a thing about him to be ashamed of, not one thing at all. He had quirks to his thinking, maybe more serious than I'd thought, but weren't we all imperfect? James was wonderful, spectacular even, just the way he was. This I knew to be true, I loved him and Will more than anything. We would always keep it gentle.

The late afternoon train slowly chugged closer, roaring in my ears and filling my lungs with that familiar smell. Guess the neighbors must at least appreciate no more banging on the drums or crashing of the cymbals rattling their windows.

But when I turned onto High Street, I stopped dead. Someone had parked a strange truck in front of my house. And a new spectacle had converged on my own front yard: tents.

"What the..." I cried out, quickening my steps toward the house.

Three dark green tents were pitched in a triangle, anchored in place with rope and stakes into the ground. They were positioned so their flaps faced inward, toward the center of their camp city. There were also bicycles, two stationed on the grass with kickstands and one leaning against the garage. A bicycle pump, water bottles, zippered bags, and bungee cords laid about in the grass. *What on earth?*

"Hey! Hello?" I called toward the tents on the grass, more demand than greeting.

There was scrambling from within the tents, then the occupants emerged, two men and a woman, looking perfectly friendly and natural about whatever it was they thought they were doing.

"Oh, hi!" said one of the men cheerfully.

My mouth hung open, and before I could form my next thought, Ben's car rounded the corner and pulled into the driveway. Ben and Will got out quickly, looking as confused and curious as me.

Lana's side door slammed, and she also joined us in the driveway to see what all the commotion was.

"Y'all live here?" the man asked.

"Yes, I do live here." I didn't attempt to hide the annoyance in my voice. "I'm the *homeowner*. Your tents are in my front yard," I added, pointing out the obvious, when my declaration of superior property rights didn't seem to faze him at all. I gestured wildly toward the three tents, shaking my hands in the air.

"Yep, we pitched right here," the man agreed happily. "The space worked out just fine for the tents and our gear and our bikes."

"But, what? Who *are* you?"

"We're here on behalf of the Columbus Crashing Crankers. We're here for James. He's been writing so many letters we figured we better just come down in person and help him get trained to ride TOSRV. Are you James?" he said, looking at Ben, who raised his eyebrows and suppressed an amused chuckle.

"The Columbus Crashing Crankers?" I asked incredulously.

"We're a bicycle club," he said. "I'm Flip."

"I've never met anyone named Flip," Will said.

"Short for flippant," I muttered under my breath.

"Oh," said Flip. "That's my cycling handle. Got that when I flipped over my front handle bars. That's what happens when you only use your front brakes, you know. Broke both my wrists! But that was a couple of years ago," he added cheerfully. "And this here is Door."

The other man gave a slight bow. "Duane 'The Door' Rhodes, at your service. Call me Door."

"Is that your cycling handle? Like the truckers on the CB?" asked Will.

"Ha, ten-four good buddy!" Door laughed. "Well yah, it's my cycling handle. I got doored."

He saw our blank stares and explained, "You ride too close alongside a parallel-parked car, the driver opens the door, and—boom! I also broke a wrist in that one."

"Ummm, I see," I said. I looked to the woman, with jet-black hair, no more than maybe five feet tall, tattoos running up and down her muscled arms and legs. "And you are..."

"Fishnet," she announced.

"Fishnet? Have you broken bones too?" I asked.

She stared back, challenge in her eyes.

Flip quickly shook his head in a warning. "Don't ask."

"Right," I agreed.

Fishnet spoke. "James has been writing us about three letters a week for the past year. He's a pest; we couldn't take it anymore. We decided we had to come teach him how to ride TOSRV. To shut him up." Fishnet looked at Ben. "So here we are. Ready to ride?"

"Here you are indeed," Ben said. "But I'm not James. I'm

Benjamin Atwater, attorney at law. You can call me Ben. James is, you could say, indisposed for the time being."

"Indisposed?" asked Door. "You mean he can't ride?"

"We came all the way down here for nothing?" Fishnet demanded, as if the flawed invitation or, to be more accurate, *lack* of invitation, was somehow our fault.

"James didn't mention he was indisposed," Door pondered. "What does that mean, anyway, indisposed?"

"James is obsessed with riding TOSRV," Fishnet declared. "All those letters. We've never seen anything like it. We got a letter even two days ago. Where is he?"

I sighed. "James is my older son. He loves his Sting-Ray, loves biking, his big dream is to ride TOSRV. But I'm afraid he's not available for you to teach him how to ride TOSRV. I'm sorry he's been pestering your Crashing Bike Club with his letters. Actually, I didn't realize you'd actually *received* his letters." I thought of the hidden stash of returned letters in my drawer. How had they received them if they'd come back "Return to Sender?" Was this a different bike club than the letters in my drawer?

"Columbus Crashing Crankers is the name of the bike club," Door muttered. "Not the Crashing Bike Club."

Will stepped forward. "Teach me how to ride TOSRV. I want to ride TOSRV."

Fishnet scowled toward the Schwinn Sting-Ray on the front porch before turning her attention to Will. She looked him up and down. "You? *You* want to ride TOSRV? How old are you?"

"Fourteen."

"Too young to ride a bicycle that far," I interjected. "Much too young to ride that bicycle tour. And Will," I added more softly, "it's your brother's dream. It's not your dream."

"Mom. I can do it. I want to do it. I want to do it for James."

"I'm afraid you can't just up and ride 210 miles in two days when the event is only two weeks away, my young friend," said Flip, smiling. "Two weeks isn't enough time for a beginner to train for a ride like that."

"I can do it," Will insisted. "I'm in shape. I ride almost every single day, for hours and hours. I ride way out of town, I climb hills, ride up onto the trails."

"Will—" I started.

"Mom, please! James wanted to ride TOSRV more than anything. Just think how stoked he would be to see these guys here, real bikers! Maybe if I can do it for him, I can tell him all about it, tell him every single little detail. So he can picture it in his head. It will almost be like he's riding it himself."

I swallowed. James had spoken of the route of the bicycle tour passing right by the state youth detention facility in Chillicothe. Of wanting to watch it pass by.

"On a *Sting-Ray*?" Fishnet asked. Fishnet, Flip and Door turned together toward the front porch where the little red Sting-Ray leaned against the house. "Banana seat and chopper handlebars!"

The three of them burst out laughing, and I registered a pang of hurt pride. "Will *was* on the Sting-Ray, James too, but now they have a ten-speed. Brand new green ten-speed. Well, new to us anyway. From the second-hand store. It's really James' bike, but he's, uh, indisposed, so Will is riding it," I faltered.

Will looked from face to face of the camping bikers. "I'm serious, you guys. Three to four-hour rides after school. Ben! You said that those must be at least thirty-mile rides."

Ben nodded. "You have become quite a cyclist Will, that is a fact."

Will ran to the garage and emerged, holding his head high as he pushed the green ten-speed. Flip, Door, and Fishnet crowded closer to inspect. Will glanced nervously to their bikes, which were clearly decked out with nicer components.

Flip bent over and studied the derailleur, the cogs. "Not bad," he muttered. "We could put another cog on the front, a granny cog, so you can spin up the hills."

"Toe clips on the pedals," Door said. He picked the bike up. "Heavy. We could switch out the headset for a lighter handlebar configuration, lose some of the weight that way."

"And the seat..." Fishnet said, running her hand over what looked like a perfectly fine seat to me.

"Oh right, definitely we'll replace the seat," Door agreed.

The three of them drew closer and seemed to have some kind of conference among them. Their heads bobbed up for another synchronized appraising look over at Will, then they returned to their huddle of hushed whispers.

"Kid!" Flip called over to Will. "How long have you been going on those three to four-hour rides?"

"Almost every day. At least five days a week. For like, a month or more now!" said Will.

They hunched back into their circle. Ben, Lana, Will, and I shifted our feet, glancing at each other, waiting. Finally, they stood straight, decision made.

"'Sting-Ray' will be your biking handle." Flip declared.

"Whoop!" Will cried out. "You'll teach me so I can do the ride for James?"

"Yes," said Fishnet with an eye-roll. "We'll teach you how to ride a double-century, little Sting-Ray. Then you'll come to Columbus with us, and we'll ride the mighty Tour of the Scioto River Valley together. If you agree to our terms."

Will nodded. "Yes, I agree! What terms?"

"Strict training schedule," Fishnet said. "We're going to plan out the ride days, the distances, the routes. There'll be a few rest days built in too, so your muscles can recover. But you have to commit the time for longer rides; we've got to get you up to at least one seventy-five-mile ride, two would be better. And you have to listen to us," she went on. "Riding technique. Safety technique. If you aren't coachable, if you don't listen, you're done."

"Don't forget hydration and food," Flip said, grabbing a swig of water from his water bottle.

"Food's the best part," said Door. "We eat to ride and we ride to eat. Got to get the right nutrition to put the demand of the tour on your body," he went on. "You're going to be really hungry riding long distances so you can't just eat candy and junk food."

I saw a look pass between Will and Ben.

I was still holding my grocery bags. "Spaghetti and meatballs? With salad and garlic bread?"

"That'll work," said Flip. "Carb-loading, yep, perfect."

They all heartily agreed, and it appeared I was now cooking dinner for everyone.

"And you'll stay..." I fished, looking dubiously at the tents. "On my front lawn?"

"Yep, we'll camp out here for the next two weeks, so we can work with Will and get him ready for the ride," Flip declared. "Don't worry, we won't be any trouble, you won't even know we're here. Maybe we'll just come in to use the bathroom and take showers. And to eat, of course. But other than that, you won't even know we're here. Say, is that a drum set I see in the window?"

Lana and Ben began chuckling, Will beamed, and our new houseguests, yard guests, I supposed, resumed chatting about the modifications they planned for the green ten-speed.

Sarah Jane had come down the street and walked up to join us, backpack dangling from her shoulder as she cautiously looked over the newcomers. "The Columbus Crashing Crankers are going to teach me how to ride James' bike tour!" Will told her.

"Oh. Congratulations?" she responded.

I looked up and down the street, noting Mrs. Grenadine's curtains fluttering, taking in the oddity of the campsite and strangers in my yard. The train whistle sounded in the distance. A car rounded the corner and slowed as it cruised by the house. My insides did a somersault double-take when I recognized the Dodge Dart. Except this time, it wasn't Loretta driving: it was Garth.

Godammit, Garth! How dare he drive down my street? How dare he... *anything!* The Dart slowed, he leaned out the window, gawking.

For a second, seeing him again after all these years transported me back in time. The trepidation. Trying to read his moods, predict his actions. I should be frightened; this was the moment I'd been fearing. I should be alerting the others, none of whom seemed to even notice what was happening. But I wasn't that young girl anymore. Instead, strangely, I wasn't frightened at all. I felt... victorious. This was *my* house. There were eight people in my front yard. I set my grocery bags on the ground, crossed my arms across my chest, widened my legs into a power-stance and stared down Garth with every bit of rage in my being.

Out of the corner of my eye, I became aware Flip, Door, and Fishnet had abruptly abandoned their conversation and pivoted to join forces with me and silently stare down Garth and the rusty Dodge Dart. For a moment, it almost seemed like we were suspended in time. Will, Ben, Lana, and Sarah Jane had frozen. The ground rumbled underneath High Street as the afternoon train approached. The rumbling and shaking grew, the bicycles trembled and glowed with heat and seemed to levitate a few inches from the driveway. I heard the pedals and wheels of the Sting-Ray and the ten-speed start whirling and spinning all on their own, with otherworldly fury. The three Crashing Crankers bore into Garth with a piercing death glare that was almost palpable.

The rumbling from deep in the earth ran up my legs, not locomotive, not earthquake, but something much more powerful. There were eight of us here, in my front yard, but I felt my parents and Granny were here as well. And many more. My Welsh ancestors. I had a strange sense James was here too.

In a second, it was over.

Garth ducked his head back inside the car, cowered behind the wheel, gunned the gas pedal and moved along. My eyes followed the Dodge Dart as it slunk away, and I could swear as it disappeared around the corner that Garth became weaker, clumsier, more irrelevant, while I grew stronger, smarter, more confident. I wasn't really sure what had just happened. But almost by osmosis, the audacity, the excitement, the athleticism these cyclists and my two sons had summoned by even imagining the epic bicycle adventure had bolstered me as well. And with Lana, Ben, Sarah Jane, all of them here, I felt surrounded by family, in a way I'd not felt since—well, not in a very long time. I wasn't the sole base holding up our triangle anymore. I knew enough geometry to understand that a larger base, with more surface area, can support more weight. It didn't make any sense, but somehow, I knew the battle was won.

Garth wouldn't be back.

The others, now unfrozen, oblivious, continued their cheerful chatter about the bicycle tour and spaghetti. Will was engrossed in the conversation and completely unaware his biological father had just passed no more than fifty feet away.

The bicycles were back where they belonged, on the ground, their pedals stilled. The cyclists from Columbus had produced a toolbox from their truck and encircled the ten-speed. "You'll have more than ten speeds after we get that extra cog on the front," Door told Will. I watched them and struggled to comprehend. Was I imagining things?

"I'll give you a hand getting these groceries inside, Jorie," said Lana, picking up a bag.

I blinked. "Yah, sure... thanks." With a last glance at Door, Flip, and Fishnet and a final check of the empty street, I picked up the other bag and followed her into the kitchen. We set the groceries on the counter, and Lana started unpacking as I pulled out pots and pans to get water boiling for a big pot of spaghetti.

"You got a crowd to cook for now," she said.

"What next?" I said, shaking my head, grateful for the calm of kitchen work. There was no need with Lana to bother with any pretense over Will doing this bike thing. I was shocked, yes, and some might think me too permissive, but somehow letting Will do this, honoring his brother, felt exactly right. No need to mention the Garth sighting, either. That mess had been swept into the dustpan and chucked in the garbage. A lovely, freeing space in my heart opened up, almost like I was floating on a wave of peacefulness and hope. I wandered into the front room and paused by the window, watching Will, watching the strange cyclists, watching Ben. Ben chatted animatedly with the bikers, casually putting his hand on Will's shoulder and giving my son a reassuring pat on the back. I saw how Will looked to Ben, how Will lit up in recognition of Ben cheering on this new endeavor.

Lana came up behind me. She followed my gaze toward Ben. "Jorie. What are you going to do about that handsome, nice fellow who's been sleeping on your couch?"

I watched Ben's lips move, the silhouette of his stance and allowed myself to enjoy the buzz of attraction.

"And he seems to have a great relationship with Will, too," she added.

"He's too young for me," I said. "He should find himself a nice young single gal, get married, start a family. Plus, he represents my son. Probably not even ethical for an attorney to carry on with his client's mother. Though I suspect he's not going to be James' attorney for much longer."

We stood together, watching Ben talking to Will. "You've got a lot to offer, Jorie. He'd be lucky to have ya."

"It's not like I've got a very good track record in the romance department," I reminded her.

She waved her hand dismissively.

"You sold yourself short by saying yes to Garth. Don't sell yourself short again by saying no to Ben."

Chapter 31

Will

School today was torture, each minute dragging, dragging, fingers drumming on my desk, counting out the seconds until I was finally freed for my very first training ride with the club. The Crankers told Mom I'd have to skip school for a few days of intensive TOSRV training and amazingly, she agreed. But today I was to go to school while they worked on my bike. They had lots of bike parts in their truck, tools, everything. They'd even produced a helmet they said I had to wear, though it looked like some kind of stupid white Martian bowl hat. *Not* cool.

"Sting-Ray," Door called out when I approached the house. "Check out your amped-up machine, my friend."

"Cool!" I ran up the driveway and dropped my backpack to the ground, skidding to my knees in front of the green ten-speed.

"New cassette," Door said, pointing to the shiny, clean new sprockets on the rear hub. "And new chain. You've got to keep your chain cleaned and lubed; bike will ride better that way." He wiped grease from his hands with a rag and continued pointing out the modifications. "We put on different pedals and gave you toe clips.

We'll show you how to put your foot in for mount and dismount. You can always flip the pedals over and let the clip fall upside down when you first push off, till you get situated, then slip your feet into the clips. There's a new granny gear on the front cog, so you can spin up hills," he said, staying in the vicinity of the pedals before moving up the seat post. He patted the narrow black space-age looking seat, with red script lettering announcing the brand. "New seat. Firmer, more aerodynamic. Changed out the headset," he went on, pointing to the handlebars. "Also lighter." He moved on to the wheels. "These are lighter wheels, and we gave you new tires that are a bit narrower for road riding. And new brake pads; the ones on there were pretty worn, which isn't safe, especially if you're going to find yourself braking in rainy conditions."

Flip stood near, hands on hips, watching. "TOSRV goes on, rain or shine," he said. "Unless there's thunder and lightning. You don't want to be out on a bike and get struck by lightning."

I must have looked taken aback as I gulped, because he quickly added, "That doesn't happen very often. Don't worry, kid."

"Water bottle cages, place to carry a pump under that top bar. Padding on the handlebars. Front headlight and flashing rear light." Door nodded and stepped back, admiring his work. "What do you think, kid?"

"I don't even know what to say," I stammered. The bike, cool as it was before, was unrecognizable. It was magnificent. I wished more than anything that James was here—if he could see this, he'd probably blow a gasket. But how were we going to pay for it? Mom and Lana had pulled together extra money for the garage sale bike. I'd no clue how they'd done it. Maybe Mom was taking extra customers at the salon, 'cause we've never had extra money for *anything*. I'd even seen her looking at a brochure about some correspondence course for some kind of technical looking training program, but she'd stashed away the brochure before I could get a closer look. I might be a dumb kid, but I knew there's no way my family could afford new wheels, new seat... all these parts.

"Umm, did you talk to Mom about the cost of the parts?" I asked.

Flip and Door glanced at each other with some unspoken understanding. "Cost is covered, Sting-Ray, no worries. All you gotta do is ride."

Fishnet emerged from one of the tents to join us. "Are you ready to ride?" she demanded.

"Sure," I insisted, but truth was, I was a little scared of her and more than a little scared to ride the ten-speed with all the changes. Maybe I was getting in over my head. I tentatively stepped toward the bike and lifted it a few inches, awestruck at how light it had become. "Wow."

"It's going to handle differently than what you've been used to," said Door, as if reading my thoughts. "Once you get out on it, you'll see how it feels. Don't worry, you'll get used to it. We'll talk you through it."

"You still sure you want to do this, kid?" Fishnet looked at me, her eyes running over my arms and legs. I resisted the impulse to flex.

Can I do the ride? I wondered. James is three years older, but he believed he could do it. Mom always told us, we're fifty percent genetically identical. I ran my hand over the new seat, thinking of James sitting in his prison cell right now, no sun on his face, no wind in his hair, no rush of power and freedom when his legs start pumping the pedals. I'd never understood it before, when he was so into the Sting-Ray. But now, I got it. I only had one brother in the whole world, exactly one person out of more than four billion people I could call my brother. Mom'd been telling us that all my life. And this was the only thing I could think of to do for him.

"I'm ready," I told Fishnet. "Ready to ride. Let's go."

To prove my point, I swung my leg over the seat and then wobbled and struggled to keep the bike from toppling over.

"Whoa," Fishnet directed. "You are *not* ready. First of all, what are you wearing?"

"Jeans," I offered, stupidly.

"You don't bike a double-century in jeans. If you want to be a serious rider, you're going to dress like a serious rider."

"What do I wear?"

She sighed. "Get off the bike. But before you swing your leg over that bar, hold the brakes. I want you to hold on to the handlebar and squeeze the brakes with your hands every time you mount and dismount. Immobilize the bike, so you don't fall over," she instructed. "And we have to adjust the seat for your height too, so your knee is only slightly bent when your leg is all the way extended on the pedal. You've been riding this thing with the seat way too low," she muttered, shaking her head.

I swallowed and did as I was told. Once off the bike, I pressed down the kickstand and waited, embarrassed, as Fishnet critically looked over my outfit. "I could go put on a pair of gym shorts," I offered.

"Naw, we've got some biking shorts in the truck that'll probably fit you," Flip called out as he opened the back door and rummaged through some bags before producing a pair of black lycra shorts he held up to show me.

"Man, those are tight, I'm going to look ridiculous in those, you guys! Can't I just wear my jeans? Or my gym shorts?"

"No, you cannot," Fishnet said sternly. "Not for the kind of riding you're going to do. Or that you *say* you're going to do."

Flip turned the shorts inside out. "These are made for riding, Sting-Ray. Chamois liner, padding. Trust me, your butt will thank you after you've been in the saddle a few hours. And you'll need a jersey or a shirt with some bright colors, so you're visible in traffic."

Between this get-up and the geek-helmet, I was going to look like some kind of clown. I'd never seen anyone riding around Jackson looking so ridiculous. But it was pretty clear they were expecting me to do exactly what I was told. I didn't want to blow it, so I grabbed the clothes and changed in my bedroom, while they took turns changing in the bathroom. Soon I saw there would be four of us parading down the streets in black lycra, brash jerseys, and geek-helmets. Jackson

County'd never seen anything like this, I was pretty sure. I hoped no one from school saw me.

Once outfitted, helmet on, water bottle filled, Flip produced a pair of riding gloves from the truck. I didn't think anyone had ever given me so many things in one day, even on my birthday or Christmas.

"The shoes," Fishnet said to them, looking at my feet.

"They'll have to do for now," said Door. "Let's get him out riding, get started. See what we got to work with here. Tuck your shoelaces into the side of your shoes, kid, so they don't get caught in the chain."

They each retrieved their bikes and helmeted up, looking very official and surprisingly un-clown like, cool even. I'd never felt so nervous about a bike ride. For sure, I wouldn't be able to keep up with them.

"Okay," said Fishnet. "Listen up, Sting-Ray. We're going to take a relaxed pace, no more than twelve, thirteen, fourteen miles an hour. We're going to take one of these country roads out of town, try to avoid heavier traffic. Obviously there's no biking culture here, so you're going to have cars pass, and you're going to stay to the right and ride in a straight line. Make sure you signal when you turn right and left, you're going to check over your shoulder before you turn left, you're going to stop at red lights."

"Bikes stop at red lights?" I said, but she ignored me and went on.

"You're going to keep an eye on that rearview mirror."

I closed one eye and tried to squint through my sunglasses at the small oval mirror attached to my helmet, angling it to show what was behind me.

"Door is going to lead, then me, then you, then Flip is going to bring up the back," she said. "You pay attention and don't lap the wheel of the rider in front of you. Otherwise you can bring the whole line down. When we stop, we call out that we're braking so the rider behind you has a warning. When a rider passes another rider, they call out 'on your left.' Do you understand?"

"Yes," I said. I'd never given riding this much thought.

207

"We're going to ride forty miles today," Fishnet said.

"I know a good route," I told them.

Everyone nodded.

"And one more thing, kid," said Fishnet. "Don't stare at my butt when you're behind me."

I gulped, and we were off.

Chapter 32

Jorie

I'd been thinking about synesthesia, and wondering if I might actually have it too. Sometimes when waking from a deep sleep, there was an image in my head. I knew it wasn't real, but I could linger over it and explore it before giving way to opening my eyes. Some days it was a clear, sand beach, with ocean horizon and sky so impossibly blue it almost hurt. Or it might be a silvery icy crevice between rock formations covered in snow, crystallized icicles hanging like chandeliers. Places I'd never been in my life, and yet there they were, somewhere in my sub-consciousness. I see them clear as day. And my boys. Without seeing or hearing, each one had a distinct feeling to me, a smell, almost a presence. I wasn't musical, but there was a note I heard in my head, a different note that went with each one of them. James' pitch was a bit higher and Will's pitch a bit lower. I was pretty sure I could find each of them in complete darkness, just by listening, just by feeling.

Even with our triangle splintering off into different directions, I must always be able to find them. And they must be able to find me.

Today, after work, I'd walked past the car dealership and paused a few minutes for a daydreaming detour through the lot. Mileage was scrawled on the front windshields. I'd peeked in through the driver's side at the interiors and imagined myself at the wheel—driving to work in winter weather, driving to and from the grocery store in the rain, picking the boys up and dropping them off wherever they needed to be. Some of these used cars were almost in reach, price-wise. A car would be a practical thing to spend the child support money on, for sure. Lord knows, the Jenkins family could sure use a car.

A salesman spotted me, straightened his tie and started walking over, but I shook my head no, waved and turned to leave. He wouldn't be making a sale today—not from this customer.

Yes, a car would be a very practical thing to buy. Buying a car would be the expected thing to do, a next logical progression in the acquisition of family transportation options, and it would make nothing but sense. But I had another thought for the rest of the money. After many fitful nights, lying awake and despairing over James in a jail cell, torturing over the best way to use the extra money, I'd settled upon a more long-term investment.

"Hello, hello, Mrs. Jenkins, please come in," Miss Ritchie beckoned me to enter her math classroom at Jackson High. School had let out for the day so the halls were empty of hormonal teenagers. She'd readily agreed when I'd phoned earlier to request a quick chat, after I'd called the attendance secretary to call Will off for the day.

Now *that* phone call had been fun.

"Jackson High School, how may I direct your call?"

"Good morning, it's Mrs. Jenkins. Will won't be in school today. Well, James too, of course."

"Oh, okay Mrs. Jenkins. Will feeling under the weather this morning?"

"No, in fact, Will's very healthy these days."

"He going in for a checkup with the dentist or the doctor or something?"

"No, nothing like that, no medical appointments today."

"Oh, okay... so, the reason I should mark down for the excused absence..."

"Will is training today for a major athletic event."

"A major athletic—"

"Will is training to ride the Tour of the Scioto River Valley."

"Umm, you mean that thing they keep talking about on TV, with the thousands of bicyclists—"

"Yes, that's the very one."

"—the one where they ride two-hundred miles in two days? *Will Jenkins* is doing that?!?"

"Will Jenkins is doing that."

"Well, my stars! But Mrs. Jenkins, what reason should I put down for the excused absence, ya know, the student handbook lists very specific pre-approved reasons for an excused absence, I'm not sure how that fits—"

"I'll pick up his assignments when I stop over after school to pick up James' assignments."

"Oh, but—"

"Thank you! Bye now!"

Now I settled into one of the wooden chairs with the flip-over school desk writing surface, feeling very comfortable in the math classroom decorated with posters of algebraic equations, columns comparing fraction to percent to decimal, and three-dimensional shapes with geometric formulas for area, volume.

"Your boys are absolutely gifted in math." Miss Ritchie beamed as she came to join me. "Both of them. I'm so glad you've come in to chat.

I beamed back. Here was a teacher who cared, who really taught, who wanted my children to succeed.

"And James, keeping up so well, even under the circumstances, going to be valedictorian of the senior class even..." she went on. "You must be so proud, I mean, well, even under the unfortunate circumstances."

"Yes, and thank you from the bottom of my heart for everything you've done for Will and James. I want to talk about James, actually," I began. "I value your opinion." I pulled out the brochure I'd sent away for about a correspondence course. "I suspect college may be out of the question, so just in case, I want him to have something to do, something to look forward to, something to keep his mind active so he can keep learning. Do you mind looking this over, and telling me if you think this would be a good idea for James?"

She put on her reading glasses, opened the brochure and together we leaned over to study the description of the correspondence program, "a very technical cutting-edge program," the brochure boasted, that employed zeros and ones, and something very new, "a language based upon math, a language for computer programming," something about as far-flung from the job prospects in Jackson County as a trip to Mars. It was called Fortran.

Miss Ritchie was silent for a moment as perused the brochure, looking very thoughtful.

"Do you think this course is a good investment for James?"

Finally, she looked up and pulled off her reading glasses.

"Yes," she replied. "Absolutely. Yes."

* * *

Walking home, Ben's Mustang swung by. He pulled over and leaned across the seat to roll down the window. "Does the prettiest hairdresser in the county want a ride?" he said with a wink.

I gave an exaggerated grimace. "Really. Is that the best you've got?"

"Well, what've *you* got?" he said.

"Does the handsome lawyer in the red muscle car want to go grab an ice cream?" I responded.

"Mrs. Jenkins, are you asking me on a date?"

I rolled my eyes and pointed toward the Shake Shoppe. "Attorney Atwater, I'm asking if you want an ice cream. And I'm thinking I might start going by Ms., not Mrs., you know—like the women's libbers."

He laughed and parked the car. "Well, well, well. *Ms.* Jenkins. *Ms.* Marjorie Jenkins. I like the sound of that. And I'll remind you to call me Ben," he said, walking up to join me.

"Ben, Benjamin, Mr. Atwater, Attorney Atwater, Attorney-at-law, my son's legal counsel," I pondered. "Defender of the accused juvenile delinquent."

We ordered cones, raspberry chocolate chip for me, vanilla and chocolate double-scoop for him. The day was warm enough for us to sit at the outdoor tables with umbrellas in front of the store. We pulled paper napkins from the dispenser and shooed away the bees.

"The accused cannot be dissuaded from pleading guilty," he said, after we'd sat in comfortable silence for a few moments, working on our dripping cones.

I regarded him evenly, trying to read what remained unspoken behind those blue eyes. "I don't understand. Everything went so well getting the judge to agree to try him as a juvenile. You're a good attorney. He could contest it, make the prosecutor prove the case," I said. "Why does he want to hand it all over?"

Ben didn't reply.

"You know why," I said. A statement, not a question.

"Jorie. I'm bound by attorney-client privilege."

"Well, you said you think he's going to fire you as his attorney. What about after that happens? I want to know why my son is making such a bad decision. I'm trying to understand this. And I need to understand why you can't tell me."

"The privilege continues even beyond termination of the attorney-client relationship. I can't talk to you about whatever James may or may not have shared with me."

I shook my head, frustrated. "Well, doesn't the prosecutor have to dismiss charges if new evidence comes up? Couldn't you take a look into how it was investigated, the witness statements from the McKowan brothers, the injuries, the mechanics of the accident?'

"I'll say it again, you really did miss your calling, Jorie. You shoulda gone to law school instead of beauty school. Yes, the prosecutor has to turn over exculpatory evidence. Yes, I have reviewed the details of the accident investigation, the witness statements, everything you just mentioned. And, you should know, I put in a formal request to Sheriff Robb to reopen the investigation."

"You did? What did he say?"

"He said no," Ben said, leaning back in his seat and wiping the last of the ice cream from his fingers. "In his view, a confession is a confession. And the other person who said no and very unequivocally instructed me to stop looking into the details, was James. Your son. My client."

"Who is only seventeen years old!" I threw up my hands. Drips of ice cream flew off the cone into my hair.

"That's right," said Ben evenly, watching my eyes. He leaned over with a napkin to dab away the ice cream. "James is only seventeen years old. He's very aware that he's only seventeen years old and very aware that the legal ramifications of sentencing are very different for a person who is seventeen years old as opposed to a person who is eighteen years old."

"Well, I don't understand it," I said. "He doesn't know what he doesn't know about the world, he's quirky with numbers, with counting, he's got his senses all mixed up, he's... he's... he's just a *teenager*. What can a teenager do, anyhow?"

"They can do plenty," said Ben. "Look what this teenager coming down the street is doing."

We turned to gawk as Door, Fishnet, Will, and Flip came flying down Main Street, decked out in bright colors and black biking shorts, bicycles flashing in the sunlight, pedals humming. They were talking to each other as they rode, yelling actually. Cars braked as everyone stopped to watch. The man working in the Shake Shoppe leaned on his elbows out the serving window and craned his neck to get a better look.

For a second, it seemed like it was only my boy riding. I blinked hard and the moment passed, the other three riders springing back into view.

Will gave an exuberant grin when he spotted Ben and me outside the Shake Shoppe. "Hi Mom!" he screamed as their peloton screamed past, and in an instant, they were gone.

Ben laughed. "Never a dull moment in Jackson."

"That's probably the most excitement this town has seen all year," I said. "Usually there's nothing but dull moments. I miss the dull moments. They were much more predictable." I thought about those strange few seconds with the Crankers when Garth had driven past the house. "Do you think I'm being too permissive letting Will go to Columbus with that crew? I mean, we don't really know them."

"Jorie," Ben took my hand. "As for Will, they seem okay, but I can have my paralegal run the backgrounds of the Crashing Crankers if it will ease your mind. And as for James, I'm sorry. You have to trust I'm doing all I can, from the perspective that I have to represent my client and his wishes. And I do expect he's going to discharge my services in the very near future."

The whole thing seemed to have momentum as unstoppable as Door, Fishnet, Will, and Flip rolling down Grove Hill. But Ben had not removed his hand from mine, and the firmness of his touch radiated hope, comfort, and just a hint of possibilities yet unseen.

"There are a few things left to try," Ben said. "I'm going to talk to him about pleading *nolo contendere*. No contest," he clarified, seeing my puzzled expression. "I think it's better for him to plead no contest to vehicular manslaughter rather than just admitting, if the judge will allow it. It still gets him to the sentencing stage of things, which is where he's so focused on getting to. And then, there's the allocution."

"Allocution?"

"Yes, he's going to have the right to make a statement before the judge imposes sentencing. He'll get to speak. To offer more information, tell his side of what happened, apologize, whatever he wants to say. If he makes a sincere apology, it might affect his sentencing."

Well now, won't that be an enlightening speech, I thought. The drama and entertainment the Jenkins boys provided this town never ceased.

"Thank you for getting those news cameras out of that courtroom," I told Ben.

Chapter 33

James

"THREE MORE DAYS. Three more days until I can plead guilty and get sentenced as a juvenile."

Sarah Jane was here for her after school visit. "The hearing is Monday?" she asked, twirling her mood ring around her finger and not meeting my eyes.

"Mmm hmmm..." I felt so good about this. I'd fire Ben, represent myself, get Judge Fraser to do exactly what I planned for her to do. They all thought they're in control, but really it was me, my hands controlling all the strings of the marionette. I pictured a puppet with a little yellow hat, strings tied around his limbs, limp without a brain in his head, no muscles, no nerves. The puppeteer controlled everything. He could make the puppet walk, leap, dance. He controlled the puppets even if he was only a teenager and the marionettes were all grownup lawyers, judges, sheriffs. This all smelled like grapefruit. I was so clever I couldn't even stand myself.

"What if something goes wrong?" Sarah Jane said.

"What could go wrong? You heard what Sheriff Robb said when he testified: a confession's a confession. Couldn't be more clear."

"James. What if someone investigates more?"

"No one's gonna do that, don't worry." Maybe Ben had started doing it, I thought, remembering him bringing up how the injuries didn't match the mechanics of the accident. I kind of respected him for figuring that out, seemed almost mathematical of him. But he'd be shut down as soon as I fired him, and thanks to attorney-client privilege, he couldn't say anything. The puppeteer was also a ventriloquist. Marionettes don't get to decide what to say.

"The McKowans have stuck to the story, right?" I asked her.

Sarah Jane nodded. "Ya, they did. They stuck to their witness statement." She ran her hands through her dark hair. "Guess they saw enough of me running down from the trailer when things got rough with Pa. They always let me use the truck when I needed to escape, didn't bother me with questions. They just knew how things was."

I ran my hand down her arm. "You look good. More relaxed. Have I ever seen your arm without any bruises on it?" I held her hand to my lips and gave a tender kiss.

"I don't feel relaxed," she said.

"Are you going to graduate?"

"I suppose. Appears I am."

"Hey!" I wrapped my arms around her and rocked her happily. "Hey, hey, hey. Look at you. High school graduate! You can do anything." Sarah Jane was a beautiful, creamy, delicate cornflower blue. Tinges of sunny yellow too, like a field of wildflowers. The most beautiful colors in the universe.

I thought back to the day Sarah Jane and I first got together. It was back in January, one of the best days ever, even though she'd been sad that day too. I'd seen her crouching on the floor behind the stairwell at school, back up against the wall. She was in the dark, behind some stacked-up folded tables. Everyone else was passing by, carrying books, on their way to their next class before the bell rang. No one else bothered to look down through the cracks in the stairs.

But I'm always listening to what my eyes, my ears, my nose are telling me. Her eyes popped in the dark like the raccoon who stalked our garbage cans in the alley. I'd ducked behind the stairs, then swiftly slid onto the floor next to her. "Hey," I'd said. She'd turned away, not wanting me to see she was crying.

"What's wrong?" I had asked.

"You don't want to know," she'd said.

"Yes, I do," I'd said, totally serious.

"You don't want to hear my problems," she'd whispered.

"Yes, I do," I'd whispered back.

Then she'd looked at me, *really* looked at me, like she was noticing me for the first time, like no girl had ever looked at me before and the world opened up like a black & white television changing to color, every color imaginable, and I knew I was passing over a dividing line in my life, where everything from that point forward would be defined: before Sarah Jane, after Sarah Jane. And it was all worth it. Everything we were doing was worth it.

She pulled away. "I don't feel right about this."

"You can get a job and never go back to that trailer," I said.

"I don't know what I even want to do or who would hire me. And how can I do anything when you're locked up, taking the rap for me? I'm the one who drove without a license, I'm the one who was going too fast, couldn't stop— "

"Shh!" I plastered my hand over her mouth. The room went crimson red, and that fishy smell filled the air. My stomach clenched. I jerked my head toward the hallway. Leroy Perkins was in his usual cell, and who knew where Sheriff Robb was lurking?

"Keep your voice down," I whispered. "Don't talk like that. We did the right thing, I'll be out no later than my twenty-first birthday, and you're safe. No one saw anything, no one is gonna say anything..."

Sarah Jane's mood ring had turned a murky, muddy, gray.

"But James," she whispered into my ear. "I need to tell you something. The crash, the accident, Mr. Cragen lying in the road. When we switched places..." she paused a moment.

"What," I said.

"I think the clerk from that gas station saw us switch places."

Chapter 34

Jorie

WASHING THE DISHES FROM SUPPER, my thoughts swirled in worry over my children. James' sentencing hearing was in only two days, and in just a week, Will would leave for Columbus and the big bicycle ride. Everything was happening too fast. I wanted to hold them, just wrap them in my arms and stop time, while the world spun around us.

The warm water and the suds of the dish soap soothed my cracked hands. I studied them as I worked, skin aging too quickly, hands that saw too much water and shampoo from cleansing away built-up conditioner, dandruff and sloughed off skin cells from the good women of Jackson. I scrubbed their scalps, stripped down all the oils, then conditioned back up for softness, freshness. Renewal. Seeing them relax under the heat of the blow dryer, then smile in wonder when I turned their chair and offered the mirror so they could see the back and inspect the finished result. Seeing how they walked out a bit more confident, spring in their step, head held a little higher.

That, at least, I knew how to do. There was some sense of accomplishment. But for my boys, these wrinkled hands were powerless.

Ben came up behind me at the kitchen sink and wrapped his arms around my waist, resting his head on my shoulder. Reflexively, I tensed, but forced myself to let it go, gingerly exploring the feeling of being encircled by strong but gentle arms, strange and new, and yet at the same time familiar. I wasn't sure if I was more surprised by this swift and sure display of affection or how normal and right it felt. But he should find someone his own age, have his own kids. I'm 'justa hairdresser,' no comparison to his law school education. He was handsome, and I was just some hick woman, divorced to boot. *But, but, but.*

I forced my head to shut the buts off.

I turned, encircled his arms with mine, and our lips found one another.

Ben's lips were warm, soft, everything I wanted.

Abruptly, he pulled away, a little red, and gave a small nod over my shoulder. I turned to see Sarah Jane standing behind us in the kitchen door. I hadn't heard her come in.

"I'm so sorry, excuse me," she muttered, backing out of the kitchen.

"No, no, wait," I said, straightening my blouse and setting the dishrag on the counter. "It's okay, Sarah Jane, don't go. Is there something you need?"

She looked from me to Ben. "There was just a question I wanted to ask."

"Of course, anything. Ask me anything."

"I was just wondering, Mrs. Jenkins, what you think of Mayor Cragen?"

"Well, I'm not really sure what you mean, dear." I tried to read Sarah Jane's face. "I can tell you I think of her often, I feel bad for her, as a wife who lost her husband, as a mother raising kids on her own..."

"What do you think of her as a mayor?" Sarah Jane pressed. "As a leader. Do you trust her? Do you think she's the type of person who does the right thing in her job?"

"Why, yes. Yes, I do think that. Why do you ask?"

She turned and retreated to James' room, closing the door.

Ben and I pivoted back to each other, puzzled over Sarah Jane.

Our moment had been broken, and now I was as flustered as a schoolgirl. I wanted to tell him I hadn't meant the kiss, that it was a mistake, that I needed to focus on my children, and figure out how to help them as well as this troubled, strange girl who'd come to live with us. Would she tell James she saw Ben and I kissing? And what if Will had been the one to walk in on us? James and Will had never seen me dating or even having a man to the house. Did I have any right to that kind of life, especially with everything going on now?

Ben seemed to sense that all the "buts" had returned and were screaming through my brain.

"It's okay, Jorie, don't say anything. No pressure." He put his hand on my cheek for a moment before withdrawing. "I have some depositions to review." He winked and wandered to the other room.

I leaned against the sink and touched my hand to my lips.

Chapter 35

Will

TODAY, the Crankers and I planned to ride seventy-five miles, and I didn't even have to go to school. I thought that the rides had gone well so far. I wasn't sure if I was measuring up, but they seemed to approve of my biking.

Flip pulled his bike up next to me once we were on a less busy road, out of town. "Sting-Ray, let me explain some things about the tour. The ride mostly follows Route 104. After leaving Columbus, we're going to have food stops in Circleville, Chillicothe, and Waverly. There's a food/rest stop every twenty-five miles. Get off your bike, eat, and take a rest, a longer break at the lunch stop. Eat before you're hungry and drink before you're thirsty. Keep hitting your water bottle while you're riding, actually you're going to make sure you're well-hydrated by drinking plenty of water from now on out."

Flip had waited until we were about seven miles into our ride to start talking. Having that quiet time helped. I always felt nervous at the start of these rides, unsure of my legs, worried about keeping up. The thought of today's seventy-five miles loomed in my mind—it would be my longest ride ever. I listened to Flip carefully, keeping my eyes on the road.

"Usually takes about six to eight miles into a ride to get settled, get the blood flowing," Flip said, apparently reading my mind. "Don't worry if you feel rickety at the start. Keep going. Adrenaline's going to kick in about seven miles into your ride, you'll settle down and start feeling real good."

"You're going to be mostly flat coming out of Columbus, and then the rolling hills start," he went on. "Don't stand on the hills, shift down and spin up. Let the roll coming down the last hill get you half-way up the next."

"Okay," I said, huffing for breath. "Got it."

"You'll figure about ten miles per hour, real time," said Flip. "You're going to ride faster than that, but if you figure in rest and food stops, it's probably going to end up averaging to ten miles an hour. So you're going to think about ten hours from leave time until crossing the line into Portsmouth. That's a long day, a long time in the saddle, which can be fatiguing. So, at the breaks, you're going to walk around a little, stretch."

"Ten hours..." I repeated.

"Now it might not take that long, or it might even take longer. But mentally," Flip said, "prepare yourself for ten hours."

"Which means you gotta pace yourself, Sting-Ray!" called Door, over his shoulder. He wavered, blinking out of my vision. I wiped sweat onto my shoulder, Door coming back into view. "Don't go all gang-busters from the start and burn yourself down. Ride for endurance, not speed."

I shifted down to show off that I knew to spin up the crest of the peak of Sour Mash Run. More sweat ran into my eyes, and I thought about putting a sweatband under my helmet. We all quit talking for a moment as we worked up the hill, and then, down the other side, I shifted up, coasted a moment before power pedaling, faster and faster. We flew together, like a flock of birds in formation. "Twenty-two miles an hour," I heard Door mutter, looking at his fancy odometer.

They shifted, then Door dropped back to place number four and Fishnet took the lead. She slowed to more of a touring pace. As usual, I felt them scrutinizing my positioning. If I veered too close to the bike in front of me, I got yelled at. If I started braking without warning the biker behind me, I got yelled at. Draft line was what it's called.

"You stay in formation with us on TOSRV, Sting-Ray," Fishnet said. "There'll be long draft lines going by, but don't jump onto one of those. Too many inexperienced riders. One guy doesn't pay attention for a second, the whole line can go down."

"I've seen it happen," Door chipped in, his voice cheerful. "One person crashes into the next and they all go down, like dominoes."

I nodded. "Okay, got it." I figured these guys knew everything there was to know about crashing. They sure seemed to like talking about crashing, anyway.

"And when a big line passes, you stay to the right, ride in a straight line," said Fishnet. "If we're the ones doing the passing, let 'em know 'on your left.' Though you won't be leading our line, of course."

I'd never imagined there was so much to know about bicycle riding. The point of the draft line is to block the wind. The leader plows into the headwind and the followers draft. After a while, the leader drops to the back, and the next rider takes a turn at the front. By yourself, you'd tire pretty quickly, fighting the wind the whole way. By taking turns, the collective team is faster and conserves energy.

There was something to be said for learning how to ride together, as a group. Besides getting the benefit of drafting, it was fun having other people to talk to. Much different than my solo after-school rides where I got lost in my own thoughts and then ended up making bad decisions, like shoplifting candy bars.

About two hours into the ride, Fishnet called out she was stopping, and we braked carefully, together, the line coming to a halt. She pointed to a grassy spot out of the sun, under a shade tree. Everyone dismounted. We pulled out the snacks: apples, power bars, peanut butter sandwiches, sunflower seeds, raisins. Gatorade, too. The guys kicked up their kickstands while Fishnet leaned her bike against the tree. She saw me watching. "Kickstands aren't sexy," she declared. "Unnecessary weight too."

I looked down, considering my own kickstand. I couldn't think of any reply.

"Today might average out to about six to eight hours," Door commented. "That's a pretty full day on a bike."

"It's further than I've ever gone," I told them, settling on the ground with my food.

"So what about James?" asked Door. "Did your brother ever ride that far?"

"I'm not sure," I admitted, glancing around at their faces. "James was off on the Sting-Ray all the time, and he was always talking about biking and TOSRV, but honestly, I can't tell you the longest ride James ever did."

"You two weren't riding together?"

"Naw. Biking was James' thing. Drumming was my thing. Plus we only had one bike," I reminded them.

The whole thing was so weird, I thought. James stopped biking; I stopped drumming. I started biking. The things James wanted the most in the world—a ten-speed, to ride TOSRV—were my life now. I had to live out my brother's dream for him, 'cause he could not. I didn't even know what my dreams were anymore.

"He wrote a lot about average speed and distance in his letters," Flip said, laying on the ground with his bandana pulled over his eyes to keep the light out. "Didn't sound like he had an odometer; he was looking at maps and routes and figuring out his distance that way."

"Ya, James would've done that," I agreed, remembering him spreading maps across his desk in his bedroom, sometimes using a compass or ruler to calculate between different points.

227

"His letters were very *colorful*," Fishnet said, biting into an apple. "We couldn't resist coming down here to meet James Jenkins in person, after all those crazy letters. Don't worry, kid, we like crazy," she hastened to add. "We just didn't know he was in the big house, the slammer, the pokey... guess he's got a lot of time on his hands for letter writing... and here we are now, riding with his fourteen-year-old brother."

"Huh?" I swallowed my peanut butter sandwich, freezing. "The big house?"

"It's okay, we know your bro is in jail, Sting-Ray," said Door. "We picked up the local paper in town, read all about the trial."

"Oh." I looked down and twirled some grass between my fingers.

"Don't worry, kid, it's cool. Everyone's got someone in their family, you know."

"My cousin got busted for underage drinking and possession of a gram of pot last year," said Flip.

"It was just an accident," I said, stiffening. "James just had an *accident*; he didn't mean to hit Mr. Cragen." I dug my shoe into the earth, rubbing a pointless hole into the soil. "The only criminal in our family is me. I'm a thief."

Fishnet looked fascinated. "So we're riding today with a thief, little Sting-Ray. You didn't tell us that. Bet there's an interesting story there."

They all looked at me, waiting. I should have kept my mouth shut, but at this point, I might as well own up to it. "I did some shoplifting from the Quick Mart, that one we passed when we headed out of town. On my after-school rides. I was stopping there and pocketing a bunch of candy and chips and junk, and the lady who worked there saw me but never said anything. And then she got fired. But she still didn't say anything."

"Whoa, that's weird," Door said. "Why was she protecting you?"

"I don't have a clue. But I apologized to the management and to her, and now I'm paying the store back this summer. Gotta work off my debt." They looked at me with something almost like admiration, or at the very least, keen interest. I felt a little less like a kid. "Restitution," I decided to inform them, "is what it's called."

"You'd never met the lady before?" Door asked.

"Nope, never."

"That is a mystery, then," Door said. "So you're paying back the store, but that's really not paying back the lady who got fired, is it? Though I do respect your loyalty to your brother, my friend."

"Well, he's the only brother I've got, jail or no jail. We're fifty percent genetically identical and there's four billion or more people in the world, and he's the only one I can call my brother," I said, and they all burst out laughing, though I really didn't see where I'd said anything at all funny.

* * *

The rest of the ride went great. I felt strong, no trouble keeping up, and riding my bike seventy-five miles made me feel way cool. Nobody at my high school had ever done anything like this, for sure.

As we headed down Schoolhouse Road, my thoughts turned to Caroline. Soon we'd be out for the summer. Every day in the hallway I was blowing my chance to talk to her, and unless we ran into each other over the summer, I'd lose my chance till August. That garden arch sitting in the side yard over at Bettina's house really bothered me. Did Caroline have any idea her art project was on display over in Oak Hill?

We closed in toward the end of the ride, but it was still midafternoon.

"Hey! Guys," I called out. "Do you mind if I stop over at a friend's house before heading home?"

Door broke pace from the front of the draft line and dropped back to ride across the pack, so we could all talk. Flip sat up from leaning over his handlebars and relaxed, shaking out his arms and hands and rolling his neck. "Sure, Sting-Ray, you got your miles in, you did good today."

"It's still early," Door said, looking at the others. "We could stop by that bar in the bowling alley for a cold one."

"That sounds really good," Fishnet chimed in. "And ten-cent wings."

They seemed pretty happy with this plan, so while the three Crankers rode on toward town for their beers, I split off on my own down the east end of Boggs Road, which led into Oak Hill, toward Bettina's house.

I slowed the bike as I approached the lopsided white clapboard house. Just as before, there was nothing at all on the front porch, but now the colorful burlap garden arch was gone from the side yard. I pulled up and dismounted, stiff from the long ride. It felt good to take off the helmet. I wiped sweat from my face with the back of my arm. Really needed to get that headband before TOSRV.

I glanced up and down the street. Quiet, no neighbors out. The curtain moved in Bettina's window, and a moment later she opened the door, before I could even knock.

"Will. How nice to see you again. Did you ride your bicycle over here?"

"Yes Ma'am, I mean Bettina. I rode my bicycle seventy-five miles today."

She looked surprised. "You look hot—better come in for a cold drink and some cookies."

I couldn't argue with that. I followed her into the hall, and she gestured toward the front sitting room. "Sit down and rest. Seventy-five miles on a bicycle! You're doing something we don't see other people around here doing, riding a bike like that."

"I'm training to ride the Tour of the Scioto River Valley. It's next weekend. It's a famous bicycling event called a double-century, where you ride one hundred miles on Saturday from Columbus to Portsmouth and then one hundred miles on Sunday from Portsmouth back up to Columbus. Over three thousand people are going to be riding."

"Really?" She stood with her hands on her hips. "I think they were talking about that on the news. And how did you get the idea to try this?"

"Well, it was my brother's idea, James. He's the one who always wanted to ride it. They call it TOSRV for short."

"Ahh, James. Yes. I see. Would you like iced tea or lemonade, Will?"

"Lemonade, please. And Ma'am, I mean Bettina, do you mind if I use your bathroom, please?"

"Of course, down the hall," she pointed. She headed into the kitchen while I found the bathroom, decorated with interesting small paintings of animals dressed in regal clothing: a cat in a crisp white sailor outfit, a weasel holding a pocket watch, dressed as a train conductor, a fox wearing a beret, swinging a golf club. Before finishing up I washed my hands and face with soap, splashing the stinging sweat out of my eyes with cold water. My legs were kind of rubbery now, shaky almost. Maybe riding seventy-five miles wasn't so easy after all. I straightened from the sink, kind of light-headed. The fox in the painting smirked at me.

Leaving the bathroom, my attention was drawn to a bedroom to the right, and I paused in the hallway to sneak a glance inside. Through the open door was a black wrought-iron bed and an old-fashioned nightstand. On the nightstand sat a picture frame with a smiling photo—of Mr. Cragen. Caroline's father. I gasped for breath. The whole lop-sided house swam in my vision. I staggered and the hallway wall came up next to my face.

"Will." Bettina appeared from behind and steadied me, holding my arms and guiding me to the front room couch.

"You sit, now. And drink some lemonade and get some food into you. It's okay to lie down too, if you need to. I think you almost lost your balance, there."

"Uhhh, sorry." The house stopped wobbling and steadied itself. The lemonade was cold, and I crunched the ice cubes. My vision settled down.

"That's it," Bettina said. "When you put that kind of demand on your body, you've got to fuel it back up. Drink some more. I imagine you'll be one of the youngest people in that group doing that big bicycle ride." She paused a moment, watching me, then rose to turn on the window fan before returning to the big wing chair. "So, why *are* you doing it?"

I bit into a cookie. "For James. It's his dream, but he can't do it right now."

"You were always close, you and James," she said. "When you were little."

I froze, the glass of lemonade in my hands. "You knew us when we were little?"

"Hon, your mama and papa and you two boys used to live here in Oak Hill. When y'all were very little. Lived in a little house just down the road a bit. Your mama pushed you up and down the street in a stroller, James too, when he was a baby. I guess you were too young to remember any of that," she added, seeing my astonished face.

I used to live in Oak Hill? I couldn't remember living anywhere except our house on High Street. I scrunched my forehead, concentrating. The raised voices, counting under the covers with James until the shouting and thumps stopped. Which bed were we hiding in? Which bedroom? My hazy memories didn't line up with the layout of the house we lived in now. But Mom never mentioned us living somewhere else, just stuff about Dad keeping the car when they got divorced. Funny, it never even occurred to me, but of course someone must've had to move, either he moved out, or we moved out...

"You knew my father?"

"Knew of him, I suppose," said Bettina. "Garth Jenkins. Can't say I ever had a conversation with the man, but people hear things, you know. I did used to talk to your mama sometimes."

"I haven't seen him in years. I don't even remember what he looks like," I said. My eyes wandered toward the hall, thinking of Caroline and the photo of her father on Bettina's nightstand. "But," I went on boldly, making a decision. "I don't think he was a good guy. I think

James and I hid when we were little because we were scared." I waited to see her reaction to this announcement, to confirm if I was correct.

"You should probably talk to your mother about all that."

"Well, she never talks about him. At all. I didn't even know we used to live over here in Oak Hill. Why do you think she doesn't tell me anything about my dad?"

"Will," said Bettina, "your mom is a very strong lady and a very good mother, from what I remember. She would do anything to protect you and James. Sometimes staying quiet about things is a way to protect people. And your big brother, James, I think he would do anything to protect you, too. And now here you are, growing up, chasing your brother's dream, honoring him—you're trying right now to protect him too. That's why you're planning on riding that bicycle two hundred miles, isn't it?"

My eyes wandered again toward the bedroom. I set my lemonade on the tray she had perched on the ottoman and nodded my head toward the side of the house. "You took the garden arch down. Out of your side yard. The one that Caroline made in school for her dad."

Bettina watched me evenly.

"And you have a picture of Mr. Cragen in your house," I said.

"What do you want to know, Will?" she sighed. "We were in love. Is that what you're asking me?"

"But he was married," I cried, wincing at the fourteen-year-old whine in my voice.

To my horror, she started crying. Too embarrassed to watch her cry, I kept my eyes on the plate of cookies, not looking up until Bettina pulled a Kleenex from a box on the side table. She wiped her face before speaking. "Yes, he was. Married to the mayor of Jackson. The father of two children, including your friend Caroline. Which is why I broke things off the day he was struck by that truck. I knew it wasn't right, couldn't go on. The way things were, it wasn't fair to his wife or the kids, not fair to me either. So I broke it off. Ernie was upset when he left the store and maybe that's why he wasn't paying attention crossing the road." She let out a sob and gulped for air. "I think about it every day, running all that through my head."

I stared, my mouth hanging open.

"So yes, I took down that garden arch 'cause what if one of his kids came by here, saw it, recognized it? The family's suffered enough."

"And you let me get away with robbing your store, getting you fired..." I muttered, almost to myself, trying to get my head around all of this.

"You, your brother, your mom—you've suffered enough. Your brother's girlfriend, with the long dark hair—she's suffered enough. The Cragen family has suffered enough. People make decisions to protect the ones they love. And others shouldn't interfere in those decisions.

"Will," she went on. "When you do something really hard—something like riding your bicycle two hundred miles in two days, for instance—you need a reason to fall back on when things get harder than you imagined. What if it's really hot, like today, and you get a little light-headed again? What if the hills are too much and your legs give out? What if your body just can't do such a long ride? You need your own private mental inspiration, a reason that's private just to you. That's what will keep you going. That's why I asked why you're riding TOSRV. And you don't even need to tell me your reason. But you need to figure it out, and have it ready in your own head."

"Doesn't Mrs. Cragen have a right to know the truth? And Caroline?" I said.

She ignored this, sticking with the TOSRV motivation speech. "I think protecting and honoring your brother is a wonderful reason to ride. Doing something for someone else will give you more strength than just doing something for yourself."

"I think you must have seen the car crash when he got killed," I said, feeling we were in two different conversations. "When my brother was driving the McKowan's truck... James was with his girlfriend you mentioned with the long dark hair, Sarah Jane's her name..."

"Are you going to tell your friend Caroline that the garden arch she made for her father was here in my yard, that you saw his photo on my nightstand?" she asked, cocking her head to the side.

"No," I answered, right away. "It would only hurt her."

Bettina nodded. "Then we understand each other."

I finished my cookie and lemonade.

"Are you feeling better?"

"Yes Ma'am, Bettina, my legs don't feel like jelly anymore. Thank you for letting me cool off here and for the lemonade and cookies and... information." I stood to get ready to leave. "Do you mind showing me which house my family used to live in?"

She walked with me to the front porch and pointed. "If you go three houses down to that alley, take the alley to the next block over, it's that brown house on Maple Street. Sure you're okay to ride your bike home?"

"Yes, I'm good now."

"I'll be watching you on the TV," she called after me as I rode away. "All those cyclists in the crowd when they show TOSRV on the news. I'll look for you, Will! I'll be thinking of you."

I gingerly set off on the ten-speed, spinning in low gear on my wobbly legs as I slowly navigated to the alley, careful on the gravel. I followed her instructions around to Maple Street and pulled to a stop in front of a brown house. It was even smaller than our house, kind of a sad, cardboard shoebox of a house. I pulled a drink from my water bottle as I perched on the bike, looking. The house sat stubbornly still, telling no tales.

The sun beat on my helmet. Time to ride home.

Chapter 36

James

Court day. I wore my khakis, same white button-down shirt that Mom washed and pressed for me each time. Same tie. My dress shoes were double-tied, all the scuffs rubbed out. They shone like money. Ben sat next to me, for now at least, but he probably knew I was going to fire him 'cause he seemed unusually quiet, kind of sad almost. Instead of taking notes or flipping through his file, he looked down at his hands, like he was thinking deep, deep thoughts about them.

On the other side of Ben sat the guardian ad litem. Judge Fraser appointed him to represent my best interests, since I was being tried as a juvenile. The man probably meant well, but I'd refused to speak a word to him.

I turned to scan the courtroom. Things were different than before. No reporters, no television cameras. Mrs. Cragen was here as usual, but today her children were with her. Caroline went to Jackson High; she was in Will's grade, and her younger brother, Fred, must be in sixth or seventh grade. The kids stared at me. For a second, I remembered Mr. Cragen's eyes in that flash in time when he flew up and was suspended in air, flying almost, before he smashed into the windshield. His eyes had spoken sadness in that split second, and his children's eyes told the same story today.

Sarah Jane slipped into the back row. She didn't look very happy either, in fact, her eyes were puffy and red like she'd been crying. I hated seeing her like this, the whole point of this was to never see her looking like that again. Plus, it was annoying that she kept staring at the back of Mayor Cragen's head instead of looking at me.

I didn't see Mom anywhere.

Off balance, I shivered. Big, black, dreary waves roared up, ready to sweep all of us into the abyss. It was a cold wind blowing in this courtroom.

"Where's Mom?" I whispered to Ben.

"Your Mom decided she's not coming to court today, James," Ben said. "She's not in agreement with your decision not to contest the charges, I'm sure you know. She felt it was just too much to watch you plead. Too emotional." He watched for my reaction and I frowned, silent, trying to process Mom not being here. Mom should be proud of me for being strong, for being a protector. I wished she understood. I ached to feel the rumble of the train going by.

"All rise," called the bailiff.

Judge Fraser entered in her black robes, and it was the sound of a heavy, heavy symphony, heavy on a deep, dark bass line, maybe even like a funeral march.

I shook myself. *Stop it, James.* This was no time to fall apart. I tried to conjure up what kind of music went with the strong, centered nucleus, packed with strength. Maybe Led Zeppelin. I thought about my stereo at home, the records in my bedroom, the floorboards rumbling.

"Good morning, everyone," Judge Fraser said as she settled like a queen on her throne. "We're here today on Case Number JUV 77-03-212, in the matter of James Jenkins, a minor, for an adjudicatory hearing on the charges of vehicular manslaughter. In the courtroom we have the prosecutor, guardian ad litem, and the juvenile defendant, with counsel. Before we go forward, are there any preliminary matters we need to address?"

Ben looked to the side and gave me a knowing, but defeated, look, which was my cue.

I raised my hand and spoke. "Your Honor, Judge Fraser, excuse me—but I wish to fire my attorney and represent myself today."

She frowned. No one seemed happy with me today.

"Have you discussed this with Attorney Atwater? With your guardian ad litem? With your mother?" She stopped and scanned the courtroom, saw Mom wasn't here today, before her eyes traveled back to me, full of irritation and accusation.

"I've given great thought to my decision and stand by it," I said, trying to keep the quiver out of my voice. Why was everyone trying to pressure me out of my own decision?

"Attorney Atwater?" said the Judge.

Ben quietly coughed as he rose to stand. "I've attempted discussion with James multiple times on this subject, Judge, and he is quite fixated on his decision to proceed without counsel. I've advised him regarding options and possible consequences, as to both the delinquency he's charged with and the sentencing possibilities. Cognitively, at least, I believe he understands."

"And Guardian ad Litem—have you spoken to James Jenkins?"

"I've tried, Your Honor," said the man. "James won't speak to me. Except to tell me I remind him of a porcupine."

There was a burst of laughter from behind me which sounded like Caroline's little brother Fred, before the mayor hushed him sharply. Okay, I felt kind of bad about that. The guardian ad litem had a thick hairy beard, and well, porcupine had popped into my head. And the way he walked; it seemed like a waddle. I hoped he wasn't taking it too personally. But now I saw that Judge Fraser *really* didn't look too happy with me.

"I see," she said. "So young man, I previously advised you to take the advice of counsel and the guardian I appointed for you, but you are not heeding that advice, and I understand you wish to represent yourself. Are you making that decision voluntarily?"

"Yes Ma'am," I answered.

"Knowingly?" she went on.

"Yes Ma'am."

"No one pressured you into this decision?"

"No Ma'am."

She let loose a very loud, dramatic sigh. "All right then. We will proceed. Attorney Atwater, you are excused."

Ben closed his briefcase and moved from the defense table back to where the spectators sat. The guardian ad litem gave me a dirty look. Well, I was on my own now.

"Prosecutor?" Judge Fraser nodded to the other table.

"The State is ready to proceed, Your Honor," said Prosecutor Dean.

My time to speak again. My hand went up. "Your Honor, Ma'am, Judge Fraser? I wish to plead."

"You wish to plead guilty to the delinquency charges, James?"

I spoke carefully, remembering what Ben had said. "I wish to plead no contest."

I thought of math, how endless different equations can be applied to reach the same number. The way you go doesn't matter, 'cause you end up with the exact same result. Show your work, the teachers always told us, show us how you reached that result. But today, I *wouldn't* show my work. All that mattered now was getting to that number.

The judge flipped through her paperwork for a moment, almost as if she hadn't heard me or understood what I was trying to do. Couldn't we speed things up here? I just wanted her to send me to the state youth facility and let me serve out my time.

"No contest?" she finally said.

"Yes Ma'am, yes Judge," I said.

"Very well. So again, I will ask you. Are you making this decision knowingly?"

"Yes."

"Voluntarily?"

"Definitely."

"No one pressured you into this decision or promised you anything in exchange for your plea?"

"No Ma'am."

"You understand that by pleading no contest you accept a finding of guilt for what you are accused of, and that you will be sentenced on that delinquency."

"Yes, I understand."

"Prosecutor, are you satisfied?" Judge Fraser asked.

"Judge, the State accepts the no contest plea."

Judge Fraser nodded and made a note in her file. "Very well, James, I'm accepting your plea of no contest to the charge of vehicular manslaughter, a felony, and before we move on to sentencing, we will have allocution. Are you prepared to allocute?"

Huh? I had no idea what this word meant. Maybe I was thinking about something else when Ben tried to explain it to me? Allocute, allocute, wait a minute... was it like *electrocute*? Ben never mentioned the electric chair. Was I getting the death penalty? Did kids get the death penalty? I smelled the sizzle of burning flesh, heard the snap and pop of volts of electricity coursing through my body like something out of Frankenstein. This was bad, very bad, very red, smelled like fish. Where, oh where, was Mom?

I swallowed hard, my throat dry, wishing I could have a glass of water. My tie was too tight, like a noose around my neck. Judge Fraser was a hanging judge, for sure. The courtroom was quiet, but I felt the weight of all their stares, those kids especially, Fred and Caroline. Their eyes shot bullets into the bullseye on my back.

It was lonely here at the table without Ben. I glanced back toward him, wishing he could throw me a life raft.

"I'm going to explain allocution to you, James." I tried to focus on what the judge was saying. "You've already given your plea of no contest, so I am going to go ahead and adjudicate you delinquent as to the felony offense of vehicular manslaughter. But before we move on to sentencing, the Court wants you to make a statement and explain what happened. Explain how the accident happened that led to Mr. Ernie Cragen's untimely and tragic death. Do you understand?"

"You want me to tell everyone what happened?" I said.

"You may proceed when you're ready," Judge Fraser directed.

"Didn't you hear the part before about me confessing to Sheriff Robb?"

"In *your* words, James," the Judge said. "I want to hear what happened in your words."

I swallowed again. My tongue was in the way, no good place to stash it out of the way. How ridiculous was this pink tongue flailing around in my mouth, hovering in there like a slimy eel?

They were all waiting. I have a secret I'll never tell. True. But I must speak now, get through this.

"I was driving," I started, figuring it was always good to keep reminding them that *I* was driving. I took a breath and went on. "We were heading into town, I wasn't paying attention like I should've, just didn't see Mr. Cragen in that crosswalk until it was too late, and I just couldn't stop in time. I'm very, very sorry it happened."

"Back up, James," said Judge Fraser. "You were in the truck with a young lady in the front seat and the two McKowan brothers in the backseat, I believe. Where were you going?"

"Just into town. No place in particular."

She stared into me a few moments, pitcher on the mound, waiting to see if I'd add to this answer before pelting her next question skillfully into the strike zone, right into the catcher's mitt.

"And how well do you know the McKowan family? I don't believe I've seen any of them at any of these hearings for you. Why were you driving their truck?"

"Umm, guess I just know them 'cause they live down the hill from Sarah Jane's place. They let me try out the truck so I could see what it was like to drive a truck."

"With no driver's license?" Judge Fraser sounded angry. "Was this the first time, or had they allowed you to drive their vehicle on other occasions as well?"

The McKowans had never minded when Sarah Jane needed to borrow their truck to escape her Pa. They'd stuck with the story when Sheriff Robb came upon the accident scene. Ben had mentioned they were on the Prosecutor's witness list to be subpoenaed, which gave me yet another reason to avoid a trial. The last thing I wanted was to get any of them into trouble. Probably better to make it sound like a one-time thing. "This was the first time. It was really stupid of me, and again, I'm very, very sorry."

The Judge ignored my attempts to cut to the end of the story.

"So let me understand this, James. You're telling me this was your very first joy-ride in their truck without a license? You weren't going anywhere in particular. You came around the bend from Route 93 at a very high rate of speed, right into a residential and business neighborhood with a crosswalk and a speed limit of 25 miles per hour." She stopped and looked at me, waiting. "Didn't you see the speed limit sign?"

"Probably, I mean, I'm not sure," I said, fumbling like a football player dropping the pass.

"Do you mind telling me *why*? I really need to hear why you were driving so fast, so recklessly."

Again, my tongue was a barrier to breathing, to talking, to swallowing.

"No particular reason, Ma'am. It was very stupid of me. The worst mistake of my life."

"Well, were you distracted? Showing off?" she said.

"Oh, yes, maybe distracted with everyone talking and stuff, the radio on."

"I see," said Judge Fraser, gazing at me unflinchingly. "And will you tell me, please, which gear you were in?"

I shuffled my feet under the chair as my mind scrambled in the dark. Which *gear*? "Drive," I answered. My voice sounded out of tune, an unnatural pitch.

"No, no, the Court understands the vehicle was in drive and not reverse, James. I asked you which gear you were in. In the manual transmission truck. When you popped the clutch, which gear were you in?"

I tried to picture Sarah Jane at the wheel and remember what she was doing. Where was the clutch? It's a foot pedal, I was pretty sure. Where was the gear shift? Was it a lever by the steering wheel? Or that stick coming up from the floorboard between the front seats? It was an H pattern, I thought, but just wasn't sure. How many gears were there? All I could think of were the gears on the Sting-Ray. I gear up to ride faster, so the number in the truck must also go up at a higher speed, but I just wasn't sure. I hated not being able to produce a number. Damnit, I was almost eighteen but didn't know things other kids knew. These questions were making me angry; I just wanted to get sentenced. I saw Judge Fraser watching me struggle and decided the best thing to do was make for the side exit. Which for me, surely, was to play the dumb kid.

"I don't remember. Your Honor," I added, trying to sound as respectful as possible.

"You don't remember?"

"No Ma'am. I don't remember."

"I see." She made a few notes in her file.

I longed to sit somewhere quiet and get lost in some long division. For this to be over with.

After a few minutes, Judge Fraser spoke again. "I'm going to commit you to a two-year sentence with the Ohio Department of Youth Services, James, which takes into account some credit for time served. You will stay there until near your twentieth birthday. Going no place in particular, for no particular reason, at an unconscionable high rate of speed, distracted, other details you can't bother remembering... directly caused the death of an innocent man. You're going to have plenty of time to think about the enormity of that. Before we go on, are there any questions you have for me, and is there anything else you wish to say as part of your allocution?" Her eyes wandered to the Cragen family.

I wanted to ask if we were clear now that I wasn't being sent to the electric chair, if the place would be the facility in Chillicothe, the one right along the TOSRV route, if I'd be able to see the bicyclists going by, if Sarah Jane could visit me there, if I could take that correspondence computer programming course Mom told me about, if the cell would be gray, what it would sound like, smell like, if maybe the Judge might let me out for a few hours so I could make my valedictorian speech at graduation, assuming the school let me, which was doubtful. But none of that was important right now.

I cleared my throat and turned to Fred and Caroline. Mayor Cragen was watching. Ben, Sarah Jane were watching. But I spoke only to the kids. "Hey, Caroline and Fred." I started softly, trying to go slowly and choose the right words.

"Living without your dad is really, really hard. It hurts. Like a wound that leaves a big hole in the middle of your gut. Scar tissue starts to grow around it, but it'll always be there. You're going to miss him different ways on different days. Some days you're going to miss him all day long, and some days, way in the future, you're going to have trouble remembering him. Or you're going to realize you've gone a few hours or maybe a whole day without thinking about him. That will hurt too. And it's forever. I wish I could change that. I wish I could bring back his life. The two of you will learn to be strong for your mom and for each other. There are over four billion people in the world, four-and-a-half I think, but out of all those people, you only have one sister, one brother. Watch out for each other."

They stared, speechless. The courtroom was stone silent.

"I'm ready now, Judge Fraser, to start serving my sentence. Thank you very much."

The show was over; I stood up and took my bow.

From the back row, Sarah Jane started sobbing.

Chapter 37

Will

Two DAYS until the big one! The plan was to go to school today, do one more training ride after school with the Crankers (fifty miles, they'd decided), then have a rest day on Friday. I wouldn't be in school on Friday. We'd load the bikes, all the gear, into the Crankers' truck in the morning. We'd check into a hotel in downtown Columbus—my first time staying in a hotel. I wondered if there'd be a swimming pool. Color TV too, I bet. Fishnet, Door, and Flip said on Friday evening we go to the big COSI science building downtown to register and check in. We'd each get a number to safety pin to our jerseys.

I'd never been away from home for three days, three nights, except for a week at boy scout camp the summer between fifth and sixth grade. Sitting in math class, my mind kept turning over the same number: Two Hundred and Ten. Two Hundred and Ten miles. *I was going to ride a bicycle Two Hundred and Ten miles. In two days.*

I sat a little taller in my seat. Ms. Ritchie droned on about the quadratic equation. I looked at my classmates; none of them had a clue what I was doing this weekend or what it would take to do it. None of them had ever ridden fifty miles after school on their bikes, I was sure. None of them seemed to understand the quadratic equation either.

My gaze fell on Caroline. She was making notes, anxiously trying to listen to Miss Ritchie. She seemed worried.

She must have sensed me watching since suddenly she lifted her head my way and met my eye. My stomach somersaulted, but instead of ducking as usual I kept eye contact. For the first time, she looked away first.

I thought for a moment, then waited until Miss Ritchie's back was turned to write on the chalkboard before quietly ripping out half a page of notebook paper. I paused, hunching to keep other prying eyes from reading my note:

Caroline,

Hey, I can help you with this math stuff in fourth period study hall next week. If you want.

I'd be happy to help.

Will

I crinkled the paper into a ball and tossed the wadded-up note onto Caroline's desk, once Miss Ritchie had turned her back again. Caroline unfolded the note, smoothed out the wrinkles, and read. She looked over again and gave a small nod.

My face erupted into a wide grin, which I buried quickly back into my notebook when I caught Rick's eye and saw him watching. Maybe understanding math better than every other kid in this room was not such a bad thing after all.

Chapter 38

Jorie

WHAT KIND of mother was I? A bad mother? A good mother? What assortment of troubles and secrets did other families wrestle with behind closed doors?

After finishing up at the salon, I made my customary stop at Henry's before walking home and fixing up meatloaf, baked beans, and mashed potatoes for supper. These days we'd added the leaf to extend the kitchen table so everyone fit: Will, Ben, Sarah Jane, Flip, Door, Fishnet, me. Sometimes Lana. I'd never seen anyone eat the way these bicycle club people eat. Every morsel disappeared and yet my pantry still felt full, my shopping money not depleted. Something wasn't adding up; but I couldn't figure out that math.

Will was bright-eyed, glowing from the sweat of his late afternoon ride, the last training ride before the big event. My son had changed so much just over the past few weeks. Something about him was stronger, more confident, even despite the childish shoplifting thing. If I could turn our lives back to what it was even three months ago, how would I have reacted to *that*? I'd be appalled, of course. I didn't raise my children to lie and steal. That's not us. But with one son in lockup for the next two years, we were grading on a curve for what was considered "normal."

But it made sense, in an odd way. Will was upset about the accident and his brother's arrest and acted out by stealing. I'd be lying if I pretended it didn't bother me that Will went to Ben first, over me, his own mother. Ben helped me talk through my shock when they told me about it, including consideration for the fact Will had come forward to take responsibility. Maybe a father figure could fill some gaps after all. If Ben had been in my life sooner, would James have been in that truck? Would Ernie Cragen still be alive?

Bad mother? Good mother?

James had at least perked up so much when I'd finally told him that Will planned to ride TOSRV. There was no jealousy or self-pity. In fact, he'd been ecstatic.

"Spectacular, spectacular," he'd gushed, pacing back and forth excitedly in his cell. "It's purple, it's fireworks, it's a ten-minute drum solo, it's Orange Crush, it's a chocolate sundae with pineapple and strawberries and chocolate sauce and whipped cream..."

"And the Columbus Crashing Crankers showed up!" he went on, beaming. "I just knew they would show up, someday. All my letters... finally!"

Apparently, I was the only one in the family upset by any of this.

I made a mental note to find a time to talk to Sarah Jane. She seemed quieter and more withdrawn each day. I saw how things weighed on her; she was probably worried about visiting James once he transferred to Chillicothe.

But tonight, my focus was on Will.

After supper I ran his Epsom salt bath. This had started as a joke with us—"Mom, that's for old people!"—until he tried soaking in it after one of those long bike rides and discovered how good it was on his sore muscles.

Will took a good soak and once he was in his pajamas, I settled on his plaid bedspread, surrounded by posters tacked on the walls, mostly bands and drummers. Keith Moon stared down at us with beady eyes and playful defiance, drum sticks mid-twirl. "How're you holding up?" I asked. "Sounds like today's ride went well?"

"Ya, it did." Will distractedly tossed his tennis shoes into the corner. He'd been quiet at dinner.

"Are you scared?" I asked.

"A little. Nervous, I guess, about keeping up with everyone and riding that far."

I regarded Will in his Scooby-Doo pajamas, voice in transition and stubble-free early teenage face. "They're all older than you." I gestured toward the front yard. "Most of the people doing that ride are older than you."

He glanced at me sideways. "Will James be staying in jail?"

I swallowed. "They're moving James tomorrow from the Jackson County jailhouse to that youth correctional facility by Chillicothe. He'll stay there for about two years," I finished, my voice a whisper.

We looked at each other. Without a car, visiting James was going to again require reliance upon our friends for transportation. My daily visits wouldn't be possible. And somehow, a visit must be figured out for Will, who hadn't been permitted to visit in the county jail and hadn't seen or talked to his brother for weeks.

"So, while I'm on my way up to Columbus tomorrow, James will be on his way to Chillicothe," Will said slowly, finally voicing the polar divergence in my sons' paths tearing my heart out.

"He knows you're riding TOSRV. The route goes past the correctional facility. He's so excited."

"Do you think he'll be able to see me pass?" Will asked. "I really hope he can see us."

"I'm not sure, hon, I don't know how close the road is, or what they'll be able to see from in there. But if there's any way to see it, we can guarantee your brother will find a way to do it." I put my arm around his shoulder. "You know, you don't have to do this. No one will think any different about you if you decide not to."

"Quit trying to talk me out of it," he bristled, brushing my hand from his shoulder.

"Sorry," I pulled back.

"Mom, I'm trying not to get psyched out. Don't you believe in me? Don't you trust I can do it?"

"I trust you," I said, but stopped to think. The things we didn't talk about, the holes in our stories, lies of omission... I'd always thought I was protecting my sons. But the missing pieces of information were there all the time. They were the missing integers, leaving our equations incomplete. We tiptoed around the huge holes, not even realizing they defined the very path we walked. And now my boys were growing up, but I'd denied them the tools they needed to navigate their own decisions. I decided it was time to trust my son with the truth.

"Will, I want to tell you some things about our past. About your father," I went on. Will's eyes flickered and widened. "The reason we split up, all those years ago... well, things weren't good. In fact, they were more than 'not good.' Things were violent. *He* was violent. Towards me. But you and James were there, you saw it, you heard it. It's why I left. It's why the three of us live on our own."

"The brown house," said Will. "We lived in a little brown house."

"Why yes, I'm surprised you can remember that, you were so little."

Will paused a moment, looking at his hands. "In Oak Hill. The cardboard brown house. Does my dad still live there?"

"No," I answered evenly. "We recently learned he lives in MacArthur, and he's taken some renewed interest in you, your brother and I. He's paying child support now. He's wandered into town to see what we're up to. You need to know that. You need to be careful if he approaches you."

"I wouldn't even know what he looks like," Will scoffed.

I tucked my hair behind my ears, got up and returned a moment later with a photo retrieved from a box buried deep in the back of my closet. "Here." I handed it to Will. "This was taken more than ten years ago, of course, but you get the general idea."

Will took the photo, and I watched his face as he studied it wordlessly.

"He looks like me and James," Will whispered.

It was probably reprehensible not showing my children a picture of their father, but I'd tried so hard to erase the past. Too hard. The floorboards started gently rumbling as the train from Portsmouth approached. "Yes, I suppose y'all both look like your father, but the resemblance stops there. You and James are nothing like Garth Jenkins."

"Sarah Jane told me that psychologist, Dr. Davis, interviewed him to get ready to testify at the trial. She said Dr. Davis talked about how he would hit you." Will's lip quivered as he fought back tears.

"He's not a good man. It's the unfortunate truth, I'm sorry." My own eyes filled with tears, and I felt shame, inadequacy. How I'd failed these wonderful boys. Other children in town had fathers, good fathers, but I had chosen poorly, and now poor Will had to hear these awful stories about our past.

"Sarah Jane's pa hit her too," he said. "I heard it, when I was riding the Sting-Ray on the trail past their trailer. She was really scared. Why does that stuff happen? Isn't it against the law?"

I sighed and looked at my hands. "It is against the law, you're right, but sometimes grownups don't handle things the way they should. Sometimes things just get complicated for lots of different reasons. It's hard to explain."

"Well, it must've been my fault," Will declared, raising his chin. For a second, I saw the man he'd become. "My fault that all that happened. My fault and James' fault too, that he hit you, that you had to leave, that you guys split up. We weren't good enough. If we'd been better kids, it wouldn't have happened."

My mouth hung open, my brain scrambled to process what I was hearing. "Will! Why would you ever say such a thing? That's not true at all. *None* of it was your fault, or your brother's fault."

Will watched me, his face a puzzle as he struggled to believe what I was telling him.

"Will," I pleaded. "It's very important you understand. It was not your fault our marriage ended. It wasn't your fault, it wasn't James' fault, and... it wasn't my fault either. None of us are responsible for his behavior. Only he is responsible for his behavior." I was astonished at the words coming out of my own mouth. Did I even believe them? Was absolution possible for myself as well as the boys? For deep down, I'd blamed myself just as Will had. Emotions played tricky games, muddying our thinking. But logic was our salvation. Logic—it was like math, like nature. It was truth, pure, unequivocal truth.

"Every person in this world is responsible for their own behavior. What your dad did, he chose to do. I could offer up theories on why he got violent, excuses, but in the end, he owns it. Now, I made the choice to leave, to live a different life. Where we could be peaceful and safe. I deprived you of your own story, of knowing your father, and I'm sorry for that, but I'm not sorry for keeping you safe. And I own that."

"Mom," Will said. "You don't have anything to be sorry for. You saved us. You protected us."

"So now, repeat after me," I instructed my son. "It's not my fault. Come on, say it."

"It's not my fault," Will repeated, unconvincingly.

"Say it again," I told him.

"It's not my fault, Mom."

"Again."

Will held up the photo and addressed his father's picture: "It's not my fault, Dad."

"Okay," I nodded. "Do you believe it?"

"Maybe," Will allowed, which I suppose was honest. At least it was a start.

"Do you remember any of it?" I asked, realizing this was the question I'd been most afraid to voice.

"I think so. I have a memory of hiding under the covers with James and us counting. Don't know if that happened more than once or I'm just remembering one time. But I remember feeling scared. The numbers, the counting, helped."

I shook my head, cursing all of it. "Well, I wish things could've been different. That you didn't have to grow up without a father, with just about the only divorced woman in Jackson for a mother."

"But you're the *best* mother in Jackson. Hey—this weekend is Mother's Day! Oh," he exclaimed, running his hand over his shaggy hair, "I'm going to be off on this bike thing on Mother's Day."

"Don't you worry about any of that." I waved my arm dismissively. "Made up greeting card holiday... what you're doing is so much more important. I'm so proud I could burst. That's my Mother's Day present. No one in this town has ever done what you're going to be doing, least as far as I've ever heard. You ride like the wind. Y'all hear me? *Ride like the wind.*"

I stood and wandered to his bedroom window. Door, Fishnet, and Flip sat around a small campfire by their tents. "And stay together with the Crankers, okay? Don't get separated from them." I turned to look at Will, but when I turned back to look out the window, the yard was empty. I blinked, then they were all there again.

"You okay, Mom?"

"Huh? Oh, yes, I'm fine." The flames flickered from the campfire and the cyclists chatted and sipped from their cups as the train rumbled by. I squinted and blinked a few more times to check, and the scene remained unchanged. I rejoined Will on the side of the bed. "There's just one thing you have to promise me."

"What?" he said.

"After this bike tour is over. You go on riding as much as you want if you like it and it makes you happy. But I want you to promise me you'll pick up those drum sticks. Have the boys over. Your friends. Your band."

He thought for a moment. "Maybe I'll do both."

Chapter 39

Will

Woohoo! Go-To-Columbus Day was here! My duffel bag was packed: geeky helmet, the black padded biking shorts, my Jackson High gym shirt. And, of course, the new bike. The Crankers helped load the ten-speed onto their truck, and we were pretty packed down with four people, four bicycles and all our gear. I never dreamed of doing a road trip like this. My grandad mined coal, my mom's divorced, the train tracks ran fifty feet from my house, we didn't have a car, and my brother was in jail, but *I* was going to bike two hundred miles!

Mom, James, Ben, *everyone* was going to be so proud.

Everyone back home would know my name.

I wouldn't just be James Jenkins' little brother anymore.

But I sure wished my big brother was here to see all this.

Chapter 40

James

Gᴜʟᴘ! Go-To-Chillicothe Day was here! I was terrified. Really never thought out how it would feel being moved from my familiar, quiet, cool, gray cell. Sure, it was boring, but I commanded the predictability in here just as sure as I commanded my bike down Grove Hill, avoiding every memorized pothole and crack, a very precise equation. Now, I would be thrown into chaos. Too many voices and smells and colors would suffocate me. I would drown.

"Okay, James," Sheriff Robb said, as he unlocked the door and swung it open. "You're going to come sit in the office for a minute to sign some paperwork so I can process you out of the county jail."

He sounded bored, not caring what happened to me next.

"Uhh, sure, okay." I followed him down the hall, swinging my arms oddly while still shuffling in the leg chain. It felt strange to not be handcuffed this time, like when he walked me to the courtroom. I tried to give a brave, grownup man-to-man nod to Leroy Perkins as we passed his usual cell. *Bye now, take care, hope you can quit drinking*, I wanted to tell him, but he just scowled in my direction.

"Damn strange boy," he muttered.

The Sheriff led me to a metal desk and pointed to a folding chair. I sat and watched as he shuffled through his paperwork.

"So, are you gonna drive me to the place, Mr. Sheriff Robb?"

He chewed his gum. The spearmint smell was antiseptic, didn't smell good at all, but somehow it got my stomach to rumbling.

"Naw," Sheriff Robb said. "Department of Youth Service is sending a van. They'll take custody of you and will transport you to the youth facility."

"Will we stop for lunch on the way?" I hated how childlike I sounded. "And do you have any recommendations how I should pack my clothes, my books? My toothbrush? What's the address of the place? Will I be able to send letters from there? Do they give you stamps? Does the post office pick up mail there? How am I going to get my homework every day? Do they have a shower? Not like the one in gym class, I hope, everyone sharing the same big shower? I'd rather have my own shower, you know…" I let my voice trail off as he stopped writing and stared at me coldly.

Something in his stare jolted back memories of my dad hitting my mom. I recoiled. I closed my eyes a second, remembering the feel of the flashcards in my hands as a kid, memorizing the multiplication table. Breathe James, I told myself. I pictured numbers.

"Well now, aren't you full of questions today, James?" the Sheriff said. "Guess you'll have to learn to talk to other people to get your questions answered instead of talking to yourself all the time. Like you used to do riding around on that little bicycle." He seemed to chuckle at some joke that only he got. "You can practice your socialization skills with your roommate."

Roommate? I wasn't going to be in a cell by myself?

This was not good. Not. Good. At. All.

I couldn't have a stranger in my space. It'd be too loud. Too bright. They wouldn't understand my counting. I needed to pace and count my steps. I needed quiet for my long division, my calculus.

And I didn't want to practice my "socialization skills," whatever that meant.

It struck me that there was no one, not one person, not even Sarah Jane, possible for me to live with like that, in such close proximity, to talk to like that, every single day.

Except my brother.

Chapter 41

Will

I SHARED the back seat with Door. Fishnet drove and Flip rode shotgun up front. Everyone had their water bottles on hand so we could pre-hydrate for tomorrow. Flip had the radio turned up loud, and my hands reflexively drummed along to Aerosmith.

"Blowing out of town, yeah baby, back north to civilization," Flip laughed.

"TOSRV, here we come," yelled Door.

"So stoked to ride it again," Fishnet chimed in, banging on the steering wheel like a drum as she crept up past the speed limit.

We flew up and down the hills. Butterflies took a little flip in my stomach; I wasn't used to riding in a car, let alone this fast. The familiar landmarks of my long bike rides flashed by too fast to process. The billboard for the Chevy auto dealership. Stuckey's Diner. Apple orchards. The Baptist church. The bridge over Salt Lick Creek. Each mile I worked so hard for when I pedaled up this way, sweat stinging my eyes, breathing in deep and studying every detail along the way. It felt like a violation to pass it all at fifty miles an hour. As each mile took us further and further away from the hills, away from Jackson County, the more nervous I became. Columbus was in the middle of the state. Portsmouth was on the Ohio River. What was I thinking, that I could ride a bicycle across half the state?

"Hey, where are we going for our carb-loading tonight?" asked Flip.

The Crankers started excitedly discussing restaurants in Columbus I'd never heard of. Mom, James, and I never went out to eat. Wouldn't be in the budget, Mom would say. Then she would give us a little math lesson about the cost of this or that at Henry's, what's on sale, how she would plan what she was going to cook and make a list for shopping. Mom's so smart. She worked out the percentages and stretched every penny. With a spurt of horror, I realized that we were only a half hour from home, but I was homesick.

What would James say? I wondered, embarrassed for my small-town high school freshman cluelessness.

I looked out the window, watching the other cars go by.

James was on his way to Chillicothe sometime today. I wished more than anything he could see all these bikes loaded on this black truck, could see our new green ten-speed. He used to go on and on about the great bicycle tour. James knew every detail about TOSRV. Why hadn't I listened to him more carefully?

Maybe we'd see each other going by, here on this road.

I pressed my forehead to the window and focused on looking for my brother in every vehicle we passed.

Chapter 42

Jorie

"Phone call for you, Jorie!" Beverly called from up front.

I set down my scissors and wiped my hands on a hand towel. "Excuse me for just a moment, will you please, Barb?" Barb nodded, and I swiveled her slightly toward the mirror before stepping to the front desk to take the phone Beverly was holding for me.

"Hello, this is Jorie Jenkins."

"Good afternoon Jorie, it's Candy Cragen calling."

My stomach lurched. Was she calling to gloat about James starting to serve his sentence today? Clutching the side of the counter, I fought away any quiver to my voice. "Good afternoon, Mayor. What can I do for you?"

"I'm sorry to bother you at work, Jorie. There's something important I need to discuss with you."

"Something important?"

"It's about James, about Ernie, about Sarah Jane," she said. "If you have any time, I'd sure appreciate if you could stop by my office."

I looked at the clock and glanced toward my waiting customer. "Yes, of course. I can be there after I finish my one o'clock hair appointment."

"That will be fine, thank you, Jorie. I'll see you then."

Chapter 43

James

A BIG WHITE van with three rows and cages on the windows was my ride.

Three other boys were also on their way to Chillicothe. Two were already in the van when I got in, and we stopped at the Washington Courthouse to pick up the third on the way. Two men in blue uniforms with armpit stains sat in the front, one of them drove. They talked to each other, but a glass divider made it impossible to hear anything. In the back, we looked each other over out of the corner of our eyes. No one spoke.

Mom had come and Sheriff Robb allowed her to talk to me for a few minutes in the jail office.

Neither of us wanted him listening to us, watching us, so not much was said, but seeing Mom grounded me like an outlet plugged into a very solid circuit. When it was time for her to leave, she gave me a long, long hug. It was orange, warm, the rumble of the train, the clanking of the dishes in the hutch, the smell of chicken and biscuits, the crisp white of my notebook before my number two pencil started filling it with equations, the sparkling garnet of the rose bushes by our front porch and the red of my Schwinn Sting-Ray chopper bicycle. I had closed my eyes and focused, willing myself to memorize the moment.

Sarah Jane hadn't come to see me off. I was trying not to think about this.

The leg shackles hung heavy on my ankles.

I stared out the window and started to silently count.

Chapter 44

Jorie

"She wants to talk to me; I'm heading over there after my one o'clock." Ben was my first phone call after I hung up the phone with Candy Cragen. "What do you figure this is all about?"

"I don't know," said Ben. "No idea. Trial is done, sentencing has been handed out. What did she say?"

"Just that it's important. And that it has to do with her husband, James, and Sarah Jane."

Ben let loose a low whistle. "I'll meet you over there, Jorie."

A wave of relief and gratitude washed over me. I didn't have to do this by myself.

"Ben—" I stammered, grasping for the right words. He'd reflexively been my first call, not just for legal advice, but because, in my heart of hearts, I needed to hear his voice and wanted him by my side. So much hung between us, left unsaid after that kiss, and I felt him waiting and listening through the phone. But now wasn't the time. All I could manage was a simple "thank you," before setting the phone back in the cradle.

Chapter 45

Will

Everywhere I turned, there were people on bikes, riding bikes, pushing bikes, loading bikes off cars. Cars with bicycle racks on roofs, racks across trunks, license plates from all over. Ten-speed bikes, twelve-speed bikes, twenty-one-speed bikes, touring bikes, racing bikes, recumbent bikes, handlebars taped in every sort of color. Jerseys showing off logos and hometowns of different cycling clubs. Helmets, water bottles, pumps. Men, women, a few kids, a few really elderly, yet athletic-looking people. Mostly men, though. Some were already in their black lycra shorts, muscular thighs, carrying their bikes on their shoulders with the cross bar hoisted up there like backpacks. They paused to look over each other's bikes, talking in excited conversations about cog size and gear ratios. They picked up each other's bikes and exclaimed over which was lighter. People called out greetings as they recognized riders befriended on past TOSRVs. Someone teetered over the crowd balancing on a unicycle, just like a parade or the circus. I gawked; I'd never seen so many people gathered in one place for cycling.

They all gathered in front of the check-in, at the COSI building in downtown Columbus, a museum with many floors and all sorts of exhibits about science and engineering. A huge cloth banner hung across the main foyer, "Welcome Riders to the 1978 Tour of the Scioto River Valley."

We stood in line at the registration table and, when it was my turn, I shifted back and forth on my feet as I presented the registration form we had filled out at home, complete with Mom's signature giving me permission to ride.

"Welcome to the mighty TOSRV," the woman at the table smiled at me. She accepted my paperwork and after looking it over for a moment, found my name on a roster and put a check in the column to show I was checked in. "Here's your packet." She handed me a plastic bag. "There's a map in there, some emergency numbers, information about first aid and the locations of the food stations. Safety pins to pin your number to the back of your jersey."

I pulled out a brightly embroidered patch and my rider number tag. I saw I would be rider number two thousand, four hundred and three.

"You must be one of our younger riders. We get a few younger than you, but not many. Some of the younger kids ride in trailers their parents hitch to the back of their bikes."

"I'm riding my own bike," I said, trying to stand up taller.

"Great," she said. "You're going to have an awesome time. Any questions?"

"What time should my group take off in the morning?"

"Your group?"

"Ya, my friends. Right over there." I gestured over toward Door, Fishnet, and Flip.

She leaned to peer around me. "I don't see them... but, well you, your group," she nodded, "are free to take off at any time, but there's an organized slow roll out of the city that kicks off at 7:00 AM. They blockade off the roads from traffic to get the cyclists out of the downtown area. Also, it's best to get on the road early for a century ride. It'll be quite a crowd near the start, but you'll see it disperse pretty soon as folks get going their different speeds."

I nodded. "Okay, thank you." I paused a moment, wanting to ask more questions. James should be here, not me. This was a mistake, trying to be my brother. This was his world. I shook my shaggy hair out drummer-style (the drummer is always the coolest person in the band, after all), trying to show I knew what I was doing.

"Good luck," she told me, before beckoning to the next person in line to come forward.

Chapter 46

Jorie

"JORIE, THANK YOU FOR COMING." Mayor Cragen greeted me warmly, no hint of awkwardness between us at all. She gestured toward a couch and chairs grouped tastefully into a conversation area by the window of her office.

Instead of remaining at her desk, she joined me on the couch, like we were equals, which of course couldn't be further from the truth.

"I hope you don't mind, but I asked Ben, Mr. Atwater, that is, to meet us here as well," I said, perching on the edge of the couch, clutching my purse in my lap. On cue, Ben appeared in the doorway, his forehead scrunched into a question mark as he looked from me to Mayor Cragen.

"Yes, of course, please come in Mr. Atwater, join us. Would anyone like an iced tea? Or a cup of coffee?"

Ben quickly appraised and slipped into his smooth lawyerly manners, honed from years of experience putting clients at ease. "I won't say no to a cup of coffee, thank you kindly, Madam Mayor. And please, call me Ben."

He eased into the chair nearest my end of the couch and shot a tiny wink my way.

"Very good," the mayor responded, rising and making her way over to a side table where a pot of coffee, sugar, creamer, and napkins were arranged on a large silver platter. She poured coffee into a Styrofoam cup. "My gal, who handles all my office help, is out on maternity leave, so I'm relegated to handling my own coffee making these days. Trying to locate the right file in these cabinets, get letters typed up, answer the phones..." she waved her hand toward the vacant receptionist's desk and shook her head helplessly.

"Can't imagine," Ben said. "I'd be lost without Lori handling my dictation, keeping my schedule organized, pulling files."

I looked at Ben, snazzy in his suit and tie, those always-polished shoes, his leather briefcase resting casually against the upholstered chair. He had a whole-page ad in the phone book, I reminded myself. Mayor Cragen was elegant in her own cream-colored suit, pearl necklace, those four-inch heels, and the too many bracelets. Her office was a suite, really an executive suite, since executive is exactly what she was. Framed diplomas hung on the walls, a large ficus plant was bushy and full in a rattan planter, and the oriental rug under our feet was thick, deep in jewel tones. This was Jackson royalty. Ben and Mayor Cragen were professionals. They had people to make their coffee, keep their schedules, answer their phones. A woman like Candy would be a much better match for Ben. They would make such a handsome power couple.

"Jorie? Coffee?" Mayor Cragen asked. "And please, both of y'all, call me Candy."

I was 'justa hairdresser,' walking to work in my jeans or corduroys. I swept up hair from the floor and my back ached by the end of the day from leaning over the shampoo sink. My thoughts weren't important enough for anyone to take dictation. No one made my coffee. No one organized my schedule.

Ben lightly brushed my hand to prompt me to respond. I tried to center myself. "No, no coffee, thank you."

Why was I here?

Before, I'd longed to sit and have a cup of coffee with Candy and just talk, woman to woman. But it seemed that moment had passed. I'd tried to apologize, best I could, but apparently it wasn't enough. Today my child, in leg shackles, was transported to what amounts to prison. I wasn't in the mood for a social call.

I sighed deeply and dove in. "Candy, please let me offer again, I'm so, so sorry for your loss. Ernie was a good man, a good father. He didn't deserve to have his life cut short, and you and the kids don't deserve any of this. I just can't imagine the pain your family is going through. We are deeply, deeply sorry it happened. If there was anything I could do to change things, I wish—"

"Jorie," said Mayor Cragen.

I closed my eyes. How much suffering must be endured? How long must we make payments on a debt that could never be repaid? I was angry, but I'd no right to be angry, to ever be angry. Especially with her. She was the victim.

Still, I must speak for my son. I clenched my purse and forged on. "What you heard about us in court, how James gets his sense of smell mixed up with his sense of sound, the colors, the counting and the math, the Sting-Ray, the way he goes on and just rambles," I paused to gulp for breath. "It's not the whole picture. It doesn't even begin to *touch* who he is deep down in his heart. What I wish you could understand, what everyone could understand, is how kind he is. How *selfless*. How *gentle*. James, my James, is—" my voice caught in my throat, emotions rising.

"Jorie," she said again. "Stop. Please listen. James didn't hit Ernie."

I opened my eyes.

"The kids switched places. Sarah Jane Billings came to talk to me yesterday and told me everything."

"What?" I whispered.

"Sarah Jane was the one driving the truck. Not James."

I gasped. And in one instant, just like that, my entire world swiftly righted itself, and the nightmare that started with James' phone call from jail two months ago mercifully, finally, ended. "But..." I started. "I don't understand."

Ben jumped in. "Sarah Jane is eighteen, James is seventeen. James knew if he was tried as a minor, he would serve less time than if she was tried as an adult."

"That's right," said Mayor Cragen. "That's what Sarah Jane told me. It was James' idea. He pulled her over into the passenger seat right after the crash, then when the sheriff and the emergency vehicles came upon the scene, he ran out there and told everyone he couldn't stop in time."

My brain struggled to process what I'd already known to be true, pieces of the puzzle sliding into place, solved just like a math problem. "He wanted to protect her," I said quietly, almost to myself. Because, of course, he did. He'd seen how things were for Sarah Jane getting hit by her pa, just like he'd seen those things played out in his own family.

"Sarah Jane was quite upset when she came here yesterday," Mayor Cragen went on. "Apparently, James has been insisting they stick to their story, but the guilt was eating her up."

I rested my eyes on the leaves of the ficus plant and felt peace wash over me. *James didn't do it.* He wouldn't have to carry the burden of taking another life, even unintentionally. He wouldn't be haunted by regret, wouldn't have that stain on his soul, wouldn't have that darkness following him the rest of his days. But Sarah Jane...

"I wonder what made her come forward now," Ben said.

"Maybe his transfer to the youth correctional facility made the reality of it all sink in," said Candy.

I rubbed my forehead. "What happens now?" I said. "To James? To Sarah Jane?"

"Well, we need to discuss all of this," said Candy. "Are you sure you won't take a coffee, Jorie?"

"Well, yes please, maybe I will after all." I accepted a cup and the warm drink worked its magic, restoring me down to my very soul. I sipped and allowed the feeling to radiate. For the first time in months, I relaxed.

Candy settled into the pillows backing her couch and started slowly, thinking out loud as she spoke, "Even though James was already sentenced, my initial thought was that with this new information, the sheriff must reopen the investigation, and the prosecutor surely must dismiss the case against James." Candy's brow furrowed in concentration.

My heart quickened. James would be getting out. James would be coming home!

"And Sarah Jane?" I pressed, meeting Ben's eyes as we shared a worried glance, pondering Sarah Jane's fate. If it was all true that James switched places with her to prevent her from being tried as an adult, she must be up against serious consequences. Ben met my eyes and the gravity of his gaze confirmed my worries.

Of course, there were laws, there were consequences. But she was really just a kid, too.

"So like I said, my first thought was that the charges against James would be dropped, there would be a reopened investigation and charges brought against Sarah Jane," said Mayor Cragen. "But after speaking with Sarah Jane further, I've had some different thoughts. About her, about how some matters in this county are handled. So, I started a new plan into motion, and some of that is going to happen today, this afternoon. I'm going to get Sheriff Robb on the phone here in a minute and call him down here, but I wanted to talk to you first."

"She's dealing with so much, only eighteen, no family to help her out," I said. I looked at Candy. "You know, Sarah Jane left her home because her father was abusive. She's been staying with us."

"I do know," Mayor Cragen said.

I sat up straight, surprised.

"She told me about it. Like I said, she was quite upset when she came to me yesterday. We had a long talk. I've struggled with wanting answers, wanting to make some sense of this whole thing. It was very important for me to know why they were speeding around that corner, why they couldn't..." She paused a moment, trying to control her emotions, tears welling in her eyes. "What I learned," she went on, "is that Sarah Jane, your son, and the McKowan boys jumped in that truck and gunned it out of there because she was fleeing her father. He'd just beaten her. She was upset, she was hurt, she was crying... and she was behind the wheel."

There's so much I wanted to ask. James hadn't had his bike with him that day, all I could guess was he must have ridden the school bus home with Sarah Jane after school. Had James been there when Mr. Billings beat his daughter? Had James gotten in the middle of it some-how? Or had he been over at the McKowan's when Sarah Jane fled down the trail to their house?

"She was desperate to escape. She told me she was terrified. I believed her," Candy said.

I nodded and sipped my coffee. "I believe her too. The night she appeared at our door, she also arrived in the McKowan's truck. She said they leave the key in it for her in case she needs to run. She had injuries that night too, from her pa. A busted lip, bruises on her face, her arms."

"And the day Ernie was killed, the medical records showed she had injuries consistent with physical abuse, not just from the car crash," Ben said. "Linear marks on her back, as if someone used a belt on her."

I shivered and winced to think of a man using such violence upon his own child. I didn't understand why the doctors who saw her after the accident wouldn't have done anything. I didn't understand why the teachers who must have noticed marks and bruises on her at school wouldn't have done anything.

"But no driver's license," Ben pointed out, sadness in his voice. "It's absolutely understandable why she was fleeing. But there's a pattern here of repeated driving without a license."

"A pattern..." Mayor Cragen mused. "I'm wondering if there's a pattern of her calling for help and getting no response."

"Help from the police? From the sheriff?" I said, pulse quickening, thinking back to my conversation with James. "James and I talked about how her father is abusive, and I asked James if she ever called the police. He told me that she had, but they didn't do anything about it."

Candy Cragen crossed her legs and seemed to choose her words carefully. "I don't want to put you on the spot, Jorie, but I'd like to learn more about calling for help, about nothing happening. Sarah Jane indicated that you might know something about that as well. Do you think that happens, is it common?" She sipped her coffee. "I'm here to listen. I want to understand."

"I know it happens," I told her and Ben. "First of all, lots of women don't even dare ask for help. They don't say anything to anyone. They'd never make a call to law enforcement or say a word, even to their own family or friends." I considered my own situation, all those years with Garth and Loretta, going through it now. And we were grown women; Sarah Jane was just a kid, without her mother in the same household to try to protect her.

"Then," I continued. "When something snaps, and you decide you've just had enough, you can't take it anymore, something has to change and you're desperate, you pick up the phone and you *do* make that call."

Candy watched me, and I saw she knew I was speaking from personal experience.

"You call law enforcement," she prompted. "Then what happens next?"

"Dispatch asks some questions: 'well honey, what were y'all fighting over, how long y'all been married, he provides for you and your children, right? He didn't cut the skin now, did he, so you're not bleeding, right, no broken bones? Y'know all married couples have their moments, honey, bet if you go on and stay with your mother or a girlfriend a few days it'll all blow over, and he'll come around with a big bouquet and y'all gonna make up just fine.'"

"Dispatch doesn't even send the call to the line for a cruiser to head over?" Candy asked, her eyes narrowing.

"You tell Dispatch how scared you are, that you're hurt, that you think he just might kill you, that you've got babies needing protection." I squeezed my fists into an angry ball. "You plead. *Please send a deputy over.* Dispatcher finally agrees. You wait, thirty minutes, forty-five minutes, an hour, an hour and a half. Cruiser finally pulls into the driveway. After you made that phone call, you've locked yourself and the babies in the bathroom; you've been waiting in there all this time. Trying to keep them quiet with some counting games. Counting on fingers and toes. Running the water in the tub to try to drown out the sound of him breaking things in the next room. Listening to try to figure out if he's still in the house."

Ben had set his coffee on the side table and was bent forward in his chair listening, elbows on his knees, head buried in his hands.

Of course, Ben and Candy had heard the testimony about the violence in my past, but it was still hard to say the words aloud. My heart pounded, and I raised my chin. Dammit, Garth wasn't going to rule my life anymore, and I was going to tell this story. I went on. "Finally, you hear car doors opening. You open the bathroom window so you can hear them talk in the driveway. Friendly talk. A little bit of 'now, ya can't beat on your wife, Garth, go walk it off or head over to the bowling alley for a cold one. We're all good now, right?'"

"The sheriff wouldn't even talk to you?" the mayor asked.

"Sometimes yes, sometimes no. Didn't seem my side of the story was all that important. Mostly it was a light little lecture for us both to calm down and separate a while till things blew over."

"Did they fill out a written report, ever file any charges on your husband?" Mayor Cragen asked.

"No, Ma'am."

Ben reached for my hand and squeezed. He lifted his head, and I saw that his cheeks were damp. "My God," he said. "Jorie."

He wiped his eyes with his other hand. "Now, of course, that was some years ago," Ben said to Candy. "But in our research for the trial, we located Jorie's husband so he could meet with the psychologist, and we did learn that he's had domestic violence charges in the next

275

county over, against his current wife. So maybe that county handles things differently than Jackson County, or maybe things have gotten a little better over these past years for victims."

"But they *aren't* better here," I said, "if Sarah Jane had the same problem with nothing coming of her asking for help. Wonder if her pa ever got charged with anything?"

"Yes, I've been wondering all of that as well." Mayor Cragen swung her legs toward her desk and stood. "I wanted to talk to you first. But I've got a plan."

I regarded Candy, reappraising my harsh opinions about her. Maybe we were lucky to have her as our mayor, looking out for us. She seemed to genuinely get it. She seemed to care.

"And I appreciate you sharing those painful memories, Jorie," she added, as she stepped over to her desk.

"I know why Sarah Jane came forward and finally spoke up," I told her and Ben. "It's because she feels safe enough now to tell her story. That's what gave her the strength, the strength to protect James like he tried to protect her."

"You and Sarah Jane are both strong and brave women. Now watch." Candy picked up the phone. "Jackson County Dispatch? Hi Missy, it's Mayor Cragen calling. Will you do me a favor, hon? I need you to walk over to me the tapes y'all store of phone calls to the sheriff's office. That's right, I need those recordings. And will you please make copies for me of the call logs from the last two years?" I watched her listening to questions from over the phone, before responding, reassuring. "Yes, that's right. No, don't worry about that, Sheriff Robb's my next call right after I hang up with you, so it'll be approved, certainly. Yes, I sure do know it'll take a little while to make those copies. It's very important, hon, you bring them right down directly to me as soon as you've got it all together, okay? Today, yes, yes, today. In fact," she looked over to Ben and winked. "I'm going to send over a very reliable attorney, Mr. Ben Atwater is his name, he'll help you compile it all and carry it over here. Yes, hon.

That's right. You go on and get started with that copying, and Mr. Atwater is on his way over to help out."

"Now..." she muttered to herself, before picking up the phone again. This time, her voice was lower, more authoritative. "Sheriff Robb? Candy Cragen. Will you walk over to my office? Yes, right now. It's important."

She hung up and nodded. "We're going to get to the bottom of this. And part of why I called you here is I suspected that you just might get some satisfaction out of watching it all unfold."

Chapter 47

James

THE JAIL for kids in Chillicothe was more than one building. There were cottages where we slept, a dining hall, classrooms for the boys still in school, and meeting rooms for group counseling. A visitation area had couches and scattered tables and chairs by a big window for when families came to visit. I kept my back turned to that building since I was pretty sure no one would be coming to visit me. A big outdoor area had basketball hoops, tether ball. Rows of vegetable gardens where the boys could take turns working. There was even an auto shop where we could learn how to work on cars, which sounded kind of interesting.

We, the inmates I supposed we were called, all wore the same orange jumpsuits. The guards wore blue button-down shirts with badges.

Everything was red brick, and each brick lined up neatly, practically begging me to count them. I gave a lot of thought to the bricks; were they exactly the same? Or were they like clouds or snowflakes, each one a little bit different, a special and unique brick? They smelled like earth to me, new and old at the same time.

Glaring spotlights, brighter than any streetlamp I'd seen, lit up the whole thing at night and shone into our rooms. A high barbed fence encircled the whole thing.

The feel was too much laundry starch, swirling lights, barking sounds, heavy boots on hard floors, crying at night, crossing off days on the calendar, rules hovering overhead like a heavy blanket, a fake roof camouflaged to look like the sky, but if you tried to fly above it with your superpower cape, you'd smack your head right into it.

Cause you were locked down.

The orange of the jumpsuits was *nothing* like the feel of orange from home. It wasn't warm; it was cold, very cold, and so sharp you could cut your finger on it.

I was scared. Alone. *Hold still*, I told myself. Strength. I squeezed my fists together hard. I had to hold still until my time here passed, for Sarah Jane. For Sarah Jane to be safe.

Zeroes and ones. Turning over in my head how completely empty zero was, absolute zero. It's one hundred percent complete nothing, no shape to it, defined by everything it's not, rather than anything it is. And then, it swoops and grows, touching and becoming each point all along the way, until it reaches one, completes every-thing, one hundred percent full, with no room for anything else.

Panic started erupting at odd points. Panic I could not swallow down, but strangely, what seemed to help was air drumming and counting. Just like Will. Listening to his drum solos or hearing his band practicing had been kind of cool. When I was on the Sting-Ray I could hear them from three blocks away, unless the train was going by. Why didn't I ever tell Will? Drumming and counting, so orga-nized, so solid. And everyone knew it's much better to be on solid ground, not drowning in quicksand. I practiced drumming different beats on the tables, or on my thighs, rocking back and forth some-times, thinking about our house rumbling and shaking.

For now, I was just trying to learn the buildings, the bricks, the courtyard, the tables, the chairs, the lights.

For now, I was trying to figure out the rhythm of breathing in a place like this.

For now, I pretended the other people weren't here. I wasn't ready to deal with them yet.

Chapter 48

Jorie

SHERIFF ROBB KNOCKED ONCE, then pulled the door open to Mayor Cragen's office, without waiting for her to tell him to come in, which seemed kind of rude.

"Mrs. Mayor?" he stuck his head in and then blustered into the room. He stopped short, unable to disguise his surprise to see Ben and I drinking coffee with the mayor like old friends playing gin rummy.

"Afternoon, everyone," Sheriff Robb nodded. "James got off just fine on his way to Chillicothe this morning, Jorie," he added, down-right magnanimous, as if he cared a hoot about my son's welfare.

Ben stood and brushed past the sheriff as he made toward the door. "Excuse me folks, I've got an errand to run. Thank you for the coffee, Madam Mayor."

Sheriff Robb's eyes narrowed as he watched Ben leave, then he sat, crossed his arms, barely hiding his impatience that he'd been summoned here. This man doesn't like women, I realized. Especially women in positions of power. Any deference shown to the Mayor was simply pretend, and it was taking a lot of effort on his part to keep up the pretense.

"What's this all about, Mrs. Mayor?"

"*Ms.* Mayor, Sheriff. It's *Ms.* Mayor," Candy corrected him.

A little smile crept over my face, and I silently savored the feel of the word, stretching it out and testing the shape of it, the buzz at the end. *Mizzzz.* Just like those magazines I saw at the drugstore, all those feminists on television, Gloria Steinem.

"Oh, yes Ma'am, *Ms.* Mayor," the sheriff said. He turned to me, curiously. "Jorie? Odd to see you here chatting with Ms. Mayor. Is this about your son's case?"

"This is about my husband's death," Candy said. "The investigation, more specifically, the *holes* in your shoddy investigation. You charged the wrong person."

A shadow crossed Sheriff Robb's face. "Hey now. A confession's a confession. You don't get more direct evidence than a confession."

"It was a false confession," said Candy Cragen. "James Jenkins wasn't driving that truck. He took the rap for his girlfriend 'cause he knew he'd get a lighter sentence tried as a juvenile than she would as an adult."

"Sarah Jane Billings? Sarah Jane Billings was driving the truck? And how is it that we know this?" he sneered.

"James doesn't know how to drive, let alone a stick shift truck," I said. "I told you that right from the start, that he doesn't know how to drive. The McKowans left their keys in the truck so Sarah Jane could get away from home when she was in danger."

"Sarah Jane came to me and told me exactly what happened, in great detail," said Mayor Cragen. "Her father beat her that day. She ran for help, she and James and the neighbor kids jumped in that truck. She was upset and drove too fast. She hit Ernie. She killed Ernie."

"Her injuries, documented at the hospital, were consistent with belt marks on her back. And consistent with an impact of the steering wheel to her front," I informed him, channeling my inner hairdresser-wannabe-lawyer moment, feeling more powerful even as I sensed Sheriff Robb's anger growing, being schooled by two women ganging up on him. "It's why James insisted on pleading out to the charges, why he fired his lawyer," I said.

"And why he struggled at his sentencing hearing," Candy said. "He couldn't really tell the judge the way it happened because he was making it up."

Sheriff Robb scratched his chin, thoughtful. "Is that so? Well, well. Sarah Jane Billings. How 'bout that. Guess that's about what one would expect from a country kid, trailer trash." He nodded to us. "Thank you for the information, ladies. I'll turn her up and arrest her right away. We'll reopen the investigation, based on these new developments."

"You'll do no such thing," said Mayor Cragen.

"Excuse me?"

"You aren't arresting that girl. And you don't need to go turn her up anywhere. She's staying with the Jenkins, and come Monday morning, she'll be here. Starting her new job as my receptionist."

My mouth hung open.

"You're hiring the person who hit Ernie?" Sheriff Robb sputtered. "What in tarnation! She's got to be prosecuted, brought to justice. I've got an oath, ya know! Protect and serve."

"Is that so?" Candy cocked her head. "Very interesting. I'll agree with you there, about the obligation to serve the public. To *protect* the public. To see to it justice is served."

"Yes ma'am, Mrs. Mayor, I mean Ms. Mayor. I've got a job to do."

"And so do I, Sheriff. Which is why after it came to my attention that the girl repeatedly called your office for help but nothing was done to protect her from an abusive father, I was certainly obligated to look into things further. I'm sure you understand."

"Not sure I'm following you," he growled.

"Sarah Jane tried calling the police when her pa was beating her," I raised my voice, unable to suppress my anger any longer. "Just the way I used to call for help back when I was with Garth. And nothing was ever done!"

Sheriff Robb shifted in his chair. "That's just a pack of

unfounded allegations. Were any reports made? I don't believe you're going to find that a report was made."

Mayor Cragen rolled her eyes. "Exactly, thank you for making our point. We'll be taking a look at the reports, or lack of reports, of course, but more importantly, we're going to be looking at the call logs. And matching them up to whether any report was written up, whether any investigation was even started."

"Call logs! Call logs can't tell you anything!"

"Oh, did I just say call logs? Well yes, of course, the call logs, but the tapes too. We'll be listening to the recordings of the calls and transcribing what those callers were telling Dispatch, word for word. Not just calls from Sarah Jane, but all the calls, from everyone, with a special focus on calls reporting domestic abuse." She leaned forward and spoke emphatically. "It'll all be part of a comprehensive review of Jackson County's systemic failure to respond to and prosecute domestic violence in our community. And I do believe, Sheriff Robb, that failure rests squarely upon your shoulders."

The sheriff's mouth tightened into a furious frown, and he glared at Mayor Cragen.

The door opened, and Ben, with Missy from Dispatch entered, their arms filled with boxes of files and tapes. "Oh good." Candy Cragen jumped up and directed them to a side table, where they started piling the boxes.

"What? You can't do this! By what authority are you confiscating records and property of the County Sheriff's Office?" Sheriff Robb demanded, scrambling to his feet. "With all due respect, this isn't an investigation you have any jurisdiction to make, Mrs. Mayor. You've got no authority over my office. I'm an elected official in this county! I don't answer to you."

"Oh, I suppose that's right, Mr. Sheriff!" Candy cried out, a giant smile she couldn't keep contained lighting up her face. "Did I say *me*? Well, it's not just me, of course, and I'll remind you that it's Ms. Mayor, not Mrs. Mayor."

Ben and I exchanged a quick, victorious smirk.

But Candy wasn't finished. "I took the liberty of contacting the Ohio Attorney General's Office, after Sarah Jane told me about her calls for help with no response. Why, here's the subpoena right here. Hold on, now." She stepped over to her desk, pulling open the top drawer. "Here it is! Let's see, we have a subpoena from the Attorney General for the files and recordings, so isn't that convenient that we already gathered all that up? We certainly wouldn't have wanted anything to turn up missing. Oh, look, there's something else here too. It's a court order, directing you to tender your badge and step down, while the investigation is pending. Administrative leave, it says. Would you like to see?"

Sheriff Robb's face turned beet red as he looked from face to face. "What is this? Let me see those damn papers!"

"Go ahead and put your badge and gun on the table," the Mayor directed. "I've already alerted Deputy Benson that he'll be stepping in, in the interim."

Ben walked over to the mayor, she handed the papers to him and he strode across the room and handed them to Sheriff Robb.

"Sheriff," said Ben. "I do believe you've been served."

Chapter 49

Jorie

Once relieved of his badge and gun, Sheriff Robb stormed out of Mayor Cragen's office.

"Ben," said Mayor Cragen, pivoting toward him. "I had Deputy Benson take Sarah Jane's statement after she came to speak to me. And I put a call in to Prosecutor Dean late this morning to instruct him I don't want to press any charges against Sarah Jane. Mr. Dean's working on putting together a motion to vacate the charges against James and get an order for his release. It would be wonderful if we could get that done as soon as possible."

"Well then, let me step right down the block to the Prosecutor's office, and see if I can assist walking that order through to Judge Fraser for her immediate signature," Ben responded, not missing a beat. He checked his watch. "Still time to get that order filed before Court closes for the afternoon." He tipped his fingers to his forehead with a gentlemanly salute before heading out. "Duty calls, ladies."

My brain reeled from the swift turn of events.

"How'd you like the look on Jason Robb's face?" Candy said to me, once we were alone.

I regarded the badge and gun on Mayor Cragen's table. I knew justice had been served, but couldn't take glee in it, not yet anyway. "You know he roughs up his own wife," I whispered. "I see bruises on Shelly when I cut her hair."

"Jorie, I know it," Candy said. "We've all known it, haven't we? For years? None of us did a thing about it, and that's going to end. No more keeping secrets like that."

She sighed and reached once more for the phone. "Sheriff Benson? Candy Cragen here again. Will you please send a cruiser around to Jason Robb's house for a welfare check, to make sure Shelly is okay? Send a car right now. And make sure they separate her from him and speak to her privately."

"Anyway," she went on, nodding with some satisfaction after she set the phone down. "Now your boy gets to come home to you."

"I just can't believe it," I said. "Feels like we're waking up from a bad dream. But," I hastened to add, remembering her loss, "How are you getting along? I know you're missing Ernie."

She looked down, tapping her stiletto-heeled foot for a moment on the rug. "I miss him, but... you know he had someone else," she murmured, looking up at me. "Had himself a girlfriend. She stays over in Oak Hill. She works at that gas station. They thought I didn't know. Probably the whole town knows."

"Oh, Candy." I blinked hard, truly shocked. How little we ever know of people's true inner lives. Candy and Ernie were always considered a golden couple, the couple who had everything. "I'm so sorry. I didn't know." I thought for a moment. "And if it's any consolation, hairdressers know everything, so if I didn't know, the whole town probably doesn't know."

"I like to tell myself he was over there that day to break things off with her," said Candy. "Maybe he was, maybe he wasn't. But a little make-believe rewriting of history helps me get through the hard days."

"Is that why you're hiring Sarah Jane to work for you? Why you don't want her charged?"

"No... I think with that, it's just realizing destroying more lives in this town isn't going to fix anything. I needed to understand why, and finally, I feel I have some answers. I decided to forgive Sarah Jane. She's had plenty of suffering in her young life. Deciding to help her, to protect her, feels right. It brings me some comfort, and... it's the right thing to do for Caroline and for Fred. Though I'd never want them to hear about their father and that woman," she quickly added.

"No, of course not," I assured her.

"And making peace with your family, making things right so your boy James can come home... well, just look what your boy Will did, rescuing my mother. He probably saved her life. I've got my mother to be grateful for, I've got my children to be grateful for... even if I can't figure out how to mourn a cheating husband. I don't think anyone's written a playbook for that game."

I felt comfortable enough to give her a hug as I rose to leave. So many unanswerable questions; why torture ourselves chasing the truth if only to beget more hurt by knowing it? "He loved you," I said. "I'm sure of it."

Candy nodded, stoic even as sorrow passed across her face. "In the beginning, I think maybe he did."

I gave her hand a final squeeze. I wanted to tell her to be strong, but platitudes weren't necessary. This woman was the definition of strength and a dynamo of can-do power. She'd set up the whole county-wide investigation with the attorney general after learning of Sarah Jane's calls for help, even before I'd confirmed it to her from my own experiences. Her children, our town, the people of this town, were all lucky to have her at the helm.

She gathered herself enough to offer a tiny smile as she walked me to the door. "You know Jorie, I think your Will and my Caroline have a crush on each other."

"Lord, our families are traveling down the same road of fate." I shook my head. "Let's just hope everyone stays out of trouble."

"And speaking of roads, you must be awfully proud of Will riding that big bicycle ride across half the state. He's sure brave to attempt something like that."

"Thank goodness he's not by himself, or I'd be worried sick," I told her. "Some of James' pen pals from a bicycle club are looking out for him. I asked Ben to check out their backgrounds, but they seem on the up and up. You must not have driven down High Street lately, 'cause you'd see their tents right in front of the house."

She cocked her head and twirled one of her bracelets.

"So I've had those bicycle people camping out in my front yard and Ben camping out on my living room couch. Ben is staying for protection, in case my ex tries anything." I blushed, feeling perhaps I'd shared too much.

"Well," she said. "Most lawyers wouldn't do so much to help a client. Seems to me that he really cares about you." She put her hand on my arm. "And you deserve it."

I paused at the door. "Thank you so much for everything, Ms. Mayor. Happy Mother's Day," I added.

Chapter 50

Will

"Wake up Will, time to get ready." Flip gave my shoulder a shake.

I groggily put together that it was morning, very early morning. The big day was finally here. We packed up quickly and helped ourselves to a breakfast set up in the hotel lobby: pancakes, maple syrup, sausage links, muffins, bananas. My favorite part was the little individual butters with peel-off lids like in the school cafeteria.

We filled our water bottles in the bathroom sink of the hotel before checking out, then loaded our duffel bags onto a big truck, tossing them onto a large growing pile of luggage from other riders. A driver would transport the gear to Portsmouth where we'd pick our bags up tonight, after we'd finished our one-hundred-mile ride.

Door had the bike pump in the parking lot by the truck. We took turns checking our tire pressure, using the pump. The Crashers looked over their own bikes, my bike too, checking components, oiling chains, tightening whatever needed tightening with a multi-tool. The Kelly green of the ten-speed shone, and I pressed on the tires, double checking the pressure.

The air was chilly this early in the morning, and the grass sparkled with dew. I zipped up my light windbreaker that I'd be able to roll up and slip into my saddle bag later, when it warmed up, but for now my bare legs had goosebumps.

Around us, other riders made the same preparations, and then small groups quietly embarked on their slow roll over to the starting point. Soon, we were on our own bikes, and I kept my eyes on potholes and traffic lights as we rode through downtown in the morning fog. A rider from another group pulled alongside. "Just shout out if you need anything," he told me. "You're a really brave kid riding TOSRV all by yourself."

"Huh?" I turned toward him, but he'd pulled forward to rejoin his own group.

As we approached the start point, throngs and throngs of bikers gathered. We dismounted and pushed our bikes to a spot in the crowd where we waited for start time.

I looked around. Three thousand five hundred riders were here, one of the biggest rides in the country, to cycle over two hundred miles in two days.

The quivering of my knees was more my own nerves than the morning chill.

Fishnet looked at me. "Easy, Sting-Ray. We wouldn't have brought you along if we didn't know you could do it."

I gaped, surprised, unable to find my voice. It was probably the nicest thing she'd ever said to me.

"Will, remember the six-to-seven-mile thing," said Flip. "You might start stiff until you warm up and all those endorphins kick in. First six to seven miles, just concentrate on staying with our group. Ride in a straight line, don't lock your pedals up in the spokes of someone next to you, don't lap the wheel of the biker in front of you and don't jump on the back of anyone else's draft line. TOSRV isn't a race, but some people here act like it is. There'll be some turns and some traffic lights until we're out of downtown Columbus, then the road is going to open up straight and flat, at least at the beginning. The group is going to start spreading out at that point, so you won't be so packed in with the other riders. So keep your head down and all you need to think about right now is the next six to seven miles, okay? Then we'll talk again."

I was so grateful to be here with the Crankers. I scanned the crowd for the man who'd said I was riding TOSRV by myself, but didn't see him.

"Okay, got it." I swung my leg over the top bar as they announced over a loudspeaker we were three minutes away from push off.

Resting my elbows on the handlebars, I thought how scared James must be, waking up this morning in that place in Chillicothe, knowing he has to live away from us for two years, locked up. James had to be brave. And now I had to be brave too. For my brother.

With my free leg, I twirled my pedals into position, slid one foot into the toe clip and pulled the strap snug.

I was ready.

Chapter 51

James

Rules and schedules didn't bother me one bit. They were the beams and the wooden frame holding a house sound, counteracting gravity. They withstood heat, cold, wind, and storms. I didn't mind getting yelled at. I didn't mind buzzers and whistles.

Interestingly, they were big on marching here. After breakfast in the dining hall, we lined up outside, two long lines, three people across. Then we marched. In unison. Almost like a military thing. Three rows up, I saw the back of the head of my new roommate, Damon, his hair midnight as charcoal. In for stealing a car, he'd told me last night. At first, he'd seemed like he wanted to fight, laughed at my math books, even kicked one on the floor and then it was yellow-bellied fear, curling myself into a ball, shrinking.

"What are you in for anyway, ya damn math-freak?" he finally demanded.

"Hit and killed a man," I replied.

"Oh. Okay, man." And with that, he'd recoiled, backed down, shrunk, which gave me space to inflate back up to my normal size, and I realized *he* was scared of *me*. Which felt like the tuba in the Monty Python music.

We discovered we're the same age. Damon's family lived hours away, and just like us, they had no car and no way to come down here to visit him. His girlfriend couldn't make it down for visits either. So, we had that in common. He told me how no white people lived in his neighborhood, but he rode the bus over an hour each way to go to a school on the other side of Cleveland, so they could be integrated. I told him how no black kids went to my school or even lived in Jackson, so we weren't integrated at all. I told him about the country kids who rode the bus in for school but were looked down on by the townies.

He'd then gone on to tell me all about how to hotwire a car, and I'd told him all about the great bicycle tour that was happening this weekend, and how we were right at the fifty-mile halfway point on the route.

"You can see that road from the exercise yard," he'd told me.

And as we marched that morning, which smelled like apples, I thought about how much better it'd be if my brother's drums kept the time to our marching. In the distance I saw the road, which must be State Route 104, running north to south, from Columbus right into Portsmouth, in a beautiful straight line, just like calculus from zero all the way to one. There would be bicyclists flying down this road today. My brother would be riding down this road today. On a new green bike. And I smiled.

For the first time in a long time, I smiled.

Chapter 52

Will

"On your left!"

Over and over, I heard the call as packs of cyclists whizzed by. Their speed didn't bother me. The four of us were locked into a solid, easy pace. True to promise, my jitters faded away after settling into the ride and getting through the first several miles. We'd already passed the first food stop, which meant we were over twenty-five miles into the ride. My legs felt good today, and I felt confident on the ten-speed. One fourth done, I told myself proudly before remembering that meant three-fourths still lay ahead. This seemed to loom too large, psyching me out. Best to put the numbers out of my mind for now.

The flat wide road started to rise and fall as we entered rolling hills, roller-coastering up and down, gears clicking efficiently as we shifted down and then back up again. I worked on the climbs, then coasted and let the breeze wash over my face on the descents. These measly little slopes had nothing over my Appalachian foothills and trail-climbing back home.

Fishnet pulled up next to me and Door and Flip rode abreast in the lead. Our line of four was now a moving square. "Eighteen miles to Chillicothe, kid," said Fishnet.

Door looked over his shoulder. "Which means lunch in a little over an hour." He gave a cheerful thumbs up sign.

"Cool," I cried out, but my thoughts weren't on lunch.

I was doing it, I was riding. It was pure joy—like flying. Flying my bicycle one hundred miles across half of Ohio. Never in my wildest dreams had I ever imagined being able to do something like this.

James was eighteen miles away. We continued to work up and down the hills.

Silently, in my head and in my heart, I started to count.

Chapter 53

Jorie

TRAFFIC WAS AT A STANDSTILL. I strained my neck and tried to see around the car in front.

"Traffic jam on a Saturday?" Ben puzzled. "Roads must be closed off on account of the bicycle tour coming through town."

I glanced at my watch, fidgeted. We were just about to Chillicothe. From up ahead we heard horns honking, but nothing moved.

"Folks need to learn how to be patient," Lana said. She sat in the backseat next to Sarah Jane. "We must be pretty close to the turnoff to James. Gonna get our boy!"

Sarah Jane sat on the edge of the backseat, twisting in all directions to look around. She'd sat on the side of the tub and brushed her hair one hundred strokes this morning, and now it shined inky black. On the way home, Sarah Jane would scoot over into the middle seat—to make a spot for James.

I clutched the release papers Ben had secured from Judge Fraser late yesterday afternoon.

"You can see the turnoff up on the right," said Ben, pointing.

I rolled down my window and stuck my head out for a better look. "We've been about five hundred yards from that turnoff for twenty minutes now," I said. Lines of restaurants and stores were visible in the distance along the main drag through Chillicothe, and in the other direction, far away, I saw lines of bicyclists on the road parallel to us. From this far away they appeared as little blots of slowly moving color, and try as I might, I couldn't make out any details or faces. My Will was over there, I thought, heart quickening. I turned back to my right and looked back across the field, past the turnoff. I estimated the fence to the youth facility was about a mile in that direction. My James was over that way, I thought.

Will was riding toward James. Their paths were going to converge. I'd be damned if I was going to sit and wait, stuck in this car.

I opened the door and got out.

"What are you doing?" Ben called.

I stood a moment, hanging onto the car door.

"I'll meet you there. I'm going to walk."

"Jorie!" Ben called. "Hold on, wait! It's important! I didn't want to do this now. But there's something you have to see. It's quite extraordinary and umm, disturbing. Brace yourself." He pulled a paper from his pocket and handed it through the open window to me.

I unfolded the paper and started scanning a photocopy of a newspaper article from The Columbus Dispatch about a terrible crash, a drunk driver who had hit and killed a group of bicyclists riding on a country road. The date of the article was last summer. Three bicyclists, killed.

"What does this have to do with—" I started.

"My paralegal did a little research on the bike club, as you had asked, and she found it," Ben said, as he jumped out of the car. "I never imagined she would find—"

I stared in shock at the photographs of Flip, Door, and Fishnet.

Lana had also jumped out of the back seat and gasped as she read over my shoulder.

"They're dead?!" she screamed. "But we can *see* them! Is this some kind of joke? We've heard them talk, we've seen them drive, they've eaten your food. Haven't we all seen them? How on earth is this real?"

"I've seen them," Ben said, running his hand through his hair. "I don't know what any of it means, but I've seen those three people in that newspaper article, just as real as life."

"Yep, they've eaten with us," Sarah Jane piped in from the backseat.

I stared at the article, stunned.

"Is Will safe? How can he be with people who don't exist?" screamed Lana. "Where are my cigarettes?" She leaned into the backseat to dig in her purse.

My mind raced, searching for an equation, a number, a solution. There were four and a half billion people in the world, people in the world because they were living. But that was just a snapshot. Billions more lived in the past and maybe they were also still here, somehow. We just couldn't detect them with our five senses.

I thought back to the levitating bicycles when Garth had driven past the house.

There were no numbers for this. Or, maybe, we just hadn't figured out the equations yet.

Inexplicably, I felt a sense of calm. I had no doubt Will was safe.

"James summoned them," I said. "They exist. He wrote them letters, and they came. We needed them. Will needed them. I can't explain it. But I know, somehow, I know it's okay."

I slammed the door shut, ducked across traffic and hopped into a barren cornfield, rows hoed and lined up ready for planting. In the distance loomed the tall chain fence of the youth facility. The sun was warm on my face and a light wind blew my hair. The release papers were in my hand. There was nothing in the world I wanted more right now than to see my boys.

I lifted my face toward the sky and ran.

Chapter 54

Will

PEDALS POUNDING, blood rushed through my legs, my veins, my brain, oxygen flowing to each cell, as rhythmically as the roll of my snare drum. Numbers flashed before my eyes. The sun glinted on the helmets of the riders around me.

Up ahead was the fence, the gate.

"Hey," Door cried, startled as I broke formation. "Kid! Sting-Ray!"

I checked over my shoulder and pulled to the right, off the road, squeezing the brakes to a stop as I rolled up to the fence.

"Where are you—what are you—oh, okay!" Door yelled. "His brother's in there," I heard him telling the others.

"Sting-Ray, Sting-Ray. Okay, Sting-Ray," said Flip, understanding. "Braking," Fishnet called out to the rear, and the Crankers stopped pedaling, slowing to a stop behind me. I sensed them hanging back, giving me space.

I hopped off the ten-speed, pushed the kickstand hard and ran up to grab the wire of the fence. I blinked hard and tried to focus beyond the holes in the wire fence, past the guard tower, below the massive spotlights.

More than anything, I wanted to see my brother, and I realized, my mother too. I wanted to tell them I wasn't scared anymore. I knew I could finish this ride. Before, I'd just hoped that I could do it. But now I knew. And the feeling was better than anything I'd known in my life.

In an exercise yard in the distance, standing around on black asphalt by the basketball hoops were lots of boys, maybe hundreds of boys, all in orange jumpsuits. They tossed balls, or huddled in small groups. I searched, looking from person to person, trying to recognize James' frame, his face. I'd never find him. There were so many. A flash of blue and fluttering white in the field beyond the far fence, on the other side of the exercise yard, caught my eye. As it came closer, I realized it was a person running toward the fence. I blinked again.

Mom?

Chapter 55

James

THIRTY MILES, at least. Thirty miles from Jackson, from High Street, from our railroad tracks, from our house that rumbled and shook. But no matter. I felt the shaking now. I could feel it all the way from here. Vibrations rumbled up my legs, my spine, between my shoulder blades, and it was the beat of Will's bass drum, the dishes clanging in Granny's hutch, the creak of the floorboards, the chandelier swaying like a symphony. It was warm, it was orange. It was the smell of home.

"Hey man, your bicycle tour is going by out there, over on 104," said Damon, pointing. "Think your brother might be going by? Hey man, where ya going?"

I ran to the picnic table closest to the fence by the road and hopped onto the table to better see. Streams of cyclists came down the road, packs of them, long lines, white helmets, flashing wheels. Hundreds and hundreds of them. I'd never find him. Where was he in the pack? Had he made it this far yet?

What I wished more than anything I could tell my brother, my mom too, was a surprising revelation, I think I've made a friend. After all that fear over having a roommate, dealing with the other boys in here. Somehow, talking to Damon was easy. I'd never just made a friend like that before, somehow different than what I had with Sarah Jane. And the easiness of it had made me better somehow. Natural. Normal.

I closed my eyes a moment and billions of numbers converged, shrinking in a single magnificent stroke to one, to two, to three. Me, in an orange jumpsuit. My brother, on a green bicycle. My mother, running through a field, carrying something white.

When I opened my eyes, I saw only two people. Will was to my right, the rider stopped at the fence, a green ten-speed bike parked behind him. Mom was to my left, at the other fence, a white paper in her hand.

An imaginary line appeared connecting the distance between us, making a triangle, a perfect, beautiful, isosceles triangle.

"Hey!" I hollered and started jumping up and down, waving my arms.

"Hey! Hey!"

Chapter 56

Jorie

I RAN AS hard and fast as my legs and lungs allowed, stopped finally by the high wire fence. Both my boys popped into my vision instantaneously, but I wasn't worried, knowing I could hear their notes, their pitch, feel their presence. Knowing I could find each of them even in utter darkness.

James jumped up and down on a picnic table, grinning wildly.

Will held the green bicycle over his head with both hands, pumping it victoriously toward the sky like a trophy.

"Hey!" they shrieked. James waved his arms over his head.

"Hey!" I cried, waving the white release papers in the air.

We jumped up and down, waving and dancing. "Hey! Hey! Hey!"

"Mom!"

"Will!"

"James!"

Throngs of cyclists paraded down the road behind Will, hundreds, maybe thousands. Other kids in the same orange jumpsuit as James stood back, their basketball games paused, gawking as James yelled and did jumping jacks on the picnic table. Ben had finally made it to the parking lot of the state youth facility. He, Lana, and Sarah Jane were getting out of the car, turning to watch us. On some level of subconsciousness, it came to me that maybe I was a little bit in love with Ben. I knew now that I wanted Ben in my life. And what I wished for more than anything was to tell James and Will that while our family may be changing, might be growing, nothing, ever, would change my love for them. And someday when I'm long gone, they'd still have that one person in the whole world, fifty percent genetically identical, that one person each can call their brother. I focused my attention back to my sons. Everything else faded into the periphery.

"Hey!" We jumped and shrieked. I laughed as tears streamed down my face.

We were as magnificent, as complete, as precise and pure and true as a mathematical equation. And yet, we were more than that. Something else was here... something that could never be quantified. It could not be measured. It could not be seen, heard, smelt, or tasted. But it was real. It breathed life into us. Love.

Keep it gentle, boys.

Keep it gentle.

The End.

Book Club Questions

Here are some questions for you and your book club to enjoy!

1. Play armchair psychiatrist: Do you suspect James might have been diagnosed with other conditions besides Synesthesia? Do you think he needs mental health treatment? What types of treatment may or may not have been available in a rural area in the 1970s?

2. Why did Will want to push himself and train to ride the bicycle tour? Did you learn anything from the story about long distance cycling?

3. How does Jorie struggle with her feelings for Ben and why is she so cautious about entering into a new romantic relationship? How does Jorie view the class, age and educational gaps between herself and Ben?

4. What is your impression of Mayor Candy Cragen? Was she a likeable character?

5. At what point in the story did you begin to suspect all was not as it seemed with the crash that killed Ernie Cragen?

6. Discuss the bicycle club. How does their role in the story illustrate themes of perceiving our world through our five senses and the

exactness of mathematics and equations versus Synesthesia and the supernatural?

7. Discuss bravery and the various ways the characters took it upon themselves to protect other people, either through action, sacrifice, secrets or telling the truth.

8. Do you think James and Sarah Jane will end up staying together as a couple?

9. Play armchair attorney: How was James treated by the legal system? What was your reaction to a minor being held in an adult jail, put in leg shackles or handcuffs, and the factors determining whether he would be tried as a juvenile or bound over and tried as an adult?

10. How do you picture the small rural southern Ohio town of Jackson? What would it have been like to live there in the 1970s?

About the Author

Catherine Pomeroy (pronouns: She/Her/Hers) is a writer and child welfare attorney who lives with her husband in Chagrin Falls, Ohio. They are a blended family with four adult children. Catherine is an avid cyclist who completed the Tour of the Scioto River Valley (TOSRV), a two-hundred-mile two-day bicycle tour, in 1981 when she was sixteen years old. Music, love of family and adventure inspire her writing.

For more on Catherine, please visit her website: catherinepomeroy.com

Also by Catherine Pomeroy: *The Gulch Jumpers*

Made in the USA
Monee, IL
19 July 2022